"Look, I've tried to cooperate, but I'm getting tired of it all. What right do you have to keep after me? I haven't done anything except go after a story. I've told you everything relevant to Granger's death, and the rest is my business."

"Okay, Astrid," Detective Riley said blandly.

"May I go now?"

"Just one more thing. What would you say if I told you we had a witness to your quarrel with Granger? Someone who heard the whole thing?"

"Heard?" she said quickly. Her hand gripped the gold chain at her neck. "I don't think I'd believe you."

"Really? Two people shouting at each other on a balcony on a hot night? And one of them saying something about finding ways to silence the other? You don't think anybody heard that? Didn't you say those words to Granger?"

"I may have. I don't remember exactly. What difference does it make? I've told you how he died."

"Supposing we have a witness with a different version?"

"I think you're bluffing. If you have a witness, why don't you charge me with murder?"

"We'll see," was all Riley said, and the gold chain suddenly snapped in Astrid Cain's fingers.

THE WATCHER

KAY NOLTE SMITH

ace books
A Division of Charter Communications Inc.
A GROSSET & DUNLAP COMPANY
51 Madison Avenue
New York, New York 10010

THE WATCHER

An ACE Book, by arrangement with Coward, McCann & Geoghegan

First Ace Printing: February 1981

Published simultaneously in Canada

2 4 6 8 0 9 7 5 3 1
Manufactured in the United States of America

To Phillip

I

IMAGE

Chapter One

"Death is the great equalizer," Martin Granger often said, smiling as if to acknowledge that the thought was, after all, bromidic. Then he would lean forward, the smile fading but his gray-green eyes glowing like beacons above the promontory of his nose; and he would add, "It is our duty to see that all people are made as equal in life as we all shall be in death."

Nearly always, whether he was speaking to students, colleagues, or politicians, his audiences were stirred. They exhibited a thoughtfulness that was often tinged with guilt.

But on the hot June night when Martin Granger met his own death, there was an audience of only two people, and neither of them felt guilty.

At ten o'clock Granger was home, in his brownstone just off Riverside Drive, working in his study on the third floor, slumping in a soft leather chair and frequently allowing his glance to wander to the balcony. By angling his head slightly, he could see a slice of sky; he watched a jet streak north, its red and green stars flashing, then sighed and turned back to his papers.

As director of the Institute for the Study of Cultural and

Ethical Values, which occuped the entire building next door, he was obliged to review and authorize the new budget. But figures did not interest him. Only people did: people in all their maddening diversity of needs and problems and talents. He had dedicated his life to them, and also the work of the Institute. The dedication had been rewarding.

When he had taken over the Institute twelve years earlier, it had occupied only one floor of the building and had been as unknown as most of the other Institutes for Something or Other that filled three columns in the Manhattan phone book and offered their dry catalogues of research studies to the business and professional communities. Singlehandedly, he had changed that. His goal had been nothing less than for the Institute to examine late-twentieth-century man in relation to his society. And to attain that goal, he had been able to conceive of projects that both attracted and served a wide range of interests: Chemists and biologists studied the physical effects of living in various social conditions, while sociologists and psychologists concerned themselves with their subjects' emotional lives.

"Why, yes, we're a think tank," he told one of the first reporters to take an interest; and he had posed laughingly beside an Institute bulletin board with a poster reading, "Think or Thwim." Soon all the more sophisticated publications knew what the Institute was and could refer to it simply by its acronym, ISCEV, confident that their readers understood. Within a few years, ISCEV was high on the lists of many corporate and government benefactors at funding time.

But the money was simply a necessary evil, Granger thought, initialing a section of the budget. The real satisfaction lay in the minds he had been able to enlist in the cause of social equality, in the idealism he had been able to recognize and to channel.

He tossed the budget onto the desk and stood up, stretching thin, ropy arms toward the ceiling. He wore jeans, a T-shirt, and loafers; each item had been custom-made, the T-shirt of cotton as fine as silk and the shoes of butter-soft kid. He wore several copper chains and a peace medallion; his thick graying hair hung an inch and a half below his earlobes. He looked like a medieval monk dressed as a twentieth-century teenager.

It was a joke among the staff of presidential contender Hart Collins that if their man won—as he showed good signs of doing—Martin Granger would attend the Inaugural in top hat and jeans. When he flew down to the Collins horse farm in Kentucky to feed the staff ideas for speeches, they found his informality charming, and they sometimes stayed up very late with him, discussing his books, *Rethinking the Social Order* and *Inalienable Wrongs?*

Granger lowered his arms and wandered out to the balcony. Two floors below, on his flagstone terrace, the wicker lanterns were lit, casting swaying patterns on the greenery and glinting on the sharp metal projections of the abstract sculptures that were placed around the edges of the terrace. He looked up and watched a light blink on in an apartment directly across the court. From inside his study the intercom buzzed, signaling the front door. Eagerly he went back in and pressed the communicator switch behind his desk.

"Yes? Oh, it's you. Surely I didn't say I'd be finished with the budget tonight? Because I'm not." A female voice spoke for a moment, and then he said, "Well, of course you can talk to me. If the day comes when I have no time for my staff, then my staff should have no time for me. Come up to the study."

At street level, a woman came into the entry hall and got into the small elevator. When she opened the door to the study, Granger lay on the couch, one leg up, his fingers cradling a bony knee. "How mysterious and urgent of you," he said. "But I'm quite alone. Lauren is out for the night, as usual, so no one will bother us."

The woman closed the door behind her, took a long, careful breath, and began to speak. At first Granger smiled tolerantly; then the smile, like his clasped fingers, began to whiten. He sat up. "So the demure little creature is not what she seems? You've been lying to me?"

"'Creature,'" the woman shot back. "That's the way you think of people, isn't it?"

When Granger stood, his tall body unfolded jerkily. "What kind of woman are you, to come spying on me behind David's back?"

Their voices began to rise. Attracted by the sound, someone moved into a position more advantageous for listening and watching.

Granger began to pace the room in long zigzag strides. Sometimes they carried him out to the balcony, as if he wished to put the woman and her words behind him, but always they pulled him back. "By the time I'm finished with you," he shouted, "there won't be a paper in the country that will hire you!"

The woman became as angry as he but, in contrast, grew more rigid. She spoke of ways to silence him. Their voices rose higher, both skidding perilously along the boundaries of control; finally one slipped over and became gloating and righteous. Then, as the wicker lanterns swayed in the garden below, the watcher heard a grunting sound from Martin Granger, who staggered at the edge of the balcony.

He teetered for a frozen moment and then went over the short, narrow railing. There was a dull, wet sound, followed by a ripe, melonlike thud. Martin Granger's body hung head down like a grotesque ornament on one of the metal sculptures, speared just above the waist by a jagged spike, his head resting on the flagstones at an impossible angle.

On the balcony the woman with whom he had been arguing stood looking down, motionless except for her hair, which stirred as if the wind itself were shivering at what had happened.

She stood there for some time. Then she went back into the study and stood at Granger's desk. At length she picked up the phone and dialed. "Police?" she said. "I want to report an accident."

From another vantage point, the watcher looked again at the terrace garden, at the thing that was now as still as the sculpture from which it hung. No voices, or blinds, had been raised in alarm. In windows on all sides of the court, air conditioners hummed impassively, like ranks of unblinking robots to whom life and death were, as Martin Granger had said they should be, equal matters.

Chapter Two

Lauren Granger extended a perfectly manicured hand toward her breakfast tray. The brioches were warm, the coffee steamed; she nodded at the maid who had brought them.

The girl hesitated. "Mrs. Granger, they called from the Institute while you were sleeping. They wanted to know what to do with the doctor's things. His personal things in the office. They wondered if you would like to go through them."

Lauren gathered the long, curly mass of her hair into one hand and swung it over her left shoulder. "I think you had better tell them I couldn't do that. It's only been ten days, after all. Ask them to find storage space somewhere over there. As a matter of fact, they can store the things from here, too, from his study. Ask them to send someone over to go through them and pack them. Maybe his secretary."

The maid's eyes widened. "His secretary? But isn't she . . . I mean, is she still there?"

"Oh yes, that's right. Then have them send somebody else. The sooner the better."

As the door closed behind the maid, Lauren broke off a piece of pastry, stretched her long legs over the covers, and leaned back against the quilted headboard.

Her bedroom, on the second floor of the Granger brownstone, was suffused with a soft, peach light—peach because it absorbed that color from the bed, the walls, and the thick carpet and cast it back in conscious flattery. Her skin, evenly tanned to the same dark honey color as her hair, had the taut smoothness that sun and grooming offer as a defense against the approach of forty; her feet, as neatly manicured as her hands, were soft, with perfectly shaped toes. She looked down and wondered, as she often had, what her life would have been if she had had a different kind of body—perhaps a short, lumpy one, or perhaps a nun's, unused and always hidden. Or if she had never left the safe harbor of her life in Minneapolis to try for something more. Or had never gone to that party after the concert and met Martin. . . .

From hidden speakers in the room came barely audible music, from a classical station, which played throughout the house most of the day. She frowned, aware of it for a moment, and then reached for the current issue of a news magazine, leafing through it to see if there was a story on Martin. There was; she read it slowly, sipping her coffee. "Whether or not people agreed with his theories," it concluded, "no one argued with his egalitarian goals. This country has always given them lip service—and often more than that, of course—but Granger found new words and raised new questions. One memorial to that achievement has been planned already: A few days after the tragic accident, trustees of the Institute that Granger headed voted to rename it in his honor."

The Martin Granger Institute, Lauren thought; was he now in the heaven—or hell—in which he had not believed, smiling at his reward? Or would he consider it too showy? There was no way to tell what would please him. There never had been. In the beginning, he'd made her feel she was a worthy partner for the rising Harvard scholar—"a coupling of Beauty and the Beast," as he used to say. Then, all too soon, he'd become the sharp, brooding man who would tell her to look as spectacular as possible when they went to a ceremonial affair and, when they were alone, would say, "I don't know how people can take me seriously when you parade yourself as one of the seven physical wonders of the world."

Her rising anger was directed only partly at herself. What did anyone know—what could anyone know—of being told since childhood that "Monday's child is fair of face" and what more could she want or expect out of life? But how was she to be satisfied with that, when she could see the kind of respect and admiration granted others? "That's charming," Martin had said, when she first confessed it to him. "A girl who could simply coast along on her looks but who has real ambitions—that's positively charming."

The pastel phone on her bedside table purred. She hesitated, half hoping it would be Karl and half despising herself for that hope. "Hello?" she said, her voice as silky as the sheets.

"Mrs. Granger, this is Jake Waldo."

She shifted quickly into the bland politeness she used for Martin's friends. "Why, Mr. Waldo. I hope I didn't forget to thank you for coming to Martin's funeral and for the lovely flowers?"

"No, of course not. I was honored to be one of the hundreds who paid tribute to him."

"And I was honored to have you there."

"That's kind of you." The voice hesitated, and Lauren summoned her memories of the man. Martin had introduced her at a recent banquet: the banker who looked like a country squire in some old British movie and whose hard fingers had taken her own in a firm, dry handshake. "Of course I was just a lay admirer of Martin's," Waldo said. "I'm a businessman, not a philosopher."

"A lot of businessmen admired him, I guess," she said, stifling a yawn.

"I like to think so. Of course, the family intellectual is my son. Did Martin tell you that? That Jake Waldo, Junior, was one of his junior assistants?"

"Oh . . . young Jake," she temporized, making a wry face at the thought of Martin's telling her anything about the Institute. "So your boy won't be continuing the family tradition?"

"I don't want him to. Politics has had enough Waldos."

"Really? I thought I once heard Martin say New York politics without a Jake Waldo would be like Boston without a Kennedy."

Waldo paused. "I'll get to the point, Mrs. Granger. You know that I'm heading the New York State effort for Hart Collins. We think he has a real chance, that the country may be ready to come out of its conservative backslide. Your husband's intellectual support was a great help to us and, frankly, so was his presence at certain parties and fund-raising affairs. But he's gone. It occurred to me to wonder if you would want to carry on for him, in his stead." Lauren sat up very straight against the quilted headboard. "Of course," Waldo went on, "Martin never said whether you took an active interest in his work and in issues like the campaign."

"I'll bet," she said, before she could stop herself.

"If you're interested," he went on smoothly, "we could make good use of the prestige of Martin Granger's widow. Mrs. Granger? Are you still there?"

"Yes," she said. "I am. And yes, I'd be glad to discuss all this with you. Maybe we could have lunch? This afternoon would be just fine for me."

Waldo laughed. "Are you decisive, Mrs. Granger? Or just impulsive? Either way, I look forward."

When they had arranged where to meet, Lauren put down the phone, her long fingers staying on the receiver as if her mind were too busy to order their removal. Minutes later the phone rang again. She started and snatched her hand away. Then she answered.

"Oh, Karl," she said. She listened. "No, I don't think so. As a matter of fact, I've decided it's over." She raised an eyebrow. "If you want to put it that way, fine. Maybe that's what I was doing, slumming. But now I'm through."

She swung out of bed and pulled on a creamy silk robe. Singing a wordless little song to herself, she slipped through the open French doors and went out on her balcony, her glance sliding mechanically over the terrace and its sculptures and the buildings across the court, until her violet eyes came to rest in space.

Detective Paul Damon stood to one side of a door with peeling paint and knocked with his gun. "Police!" he called. "Open up!" Behind him, in the hall of the welfare hotel, he sensed rather than heard the breathing of his partner, Hugh Riley.

The two of them waited a moment. Damon called again, then rattled the doorknob, which to his surprise turned in his hand. He kicked the door back against the wall and saw two things with one sweep of his eyes: a crumpled form on the bed and the length of a switchblade knife, held by a wiry young man who crouched in front of the room's one window.

"All right, drop it," Damon said, advancing slowly on one side while Riley moved in on the other.

"I'll drop it in your gut, that's where," said the man. His voice rose, and he began to swear at them, abuse and spittle showering the room's fetid air.

"Put it down," said Riley, edging closer. "You're done

carving for the day. Come on, come on, put it down, scumbag."

The man turned angrily to Riley, and in that instant Damon grabbed his wrist. As the pressure increased, the knife wavered and then clattered to the floor.

"Nice shooting," panted Riley, as they worked to cuff the slippery figure. "And welcome back from vacation."

Finally they were able to look at what remained of the female body on the bed. It was both colorless and vivid, with the pallor of the advanced drug addict and the dried red lips of many stab wounds.

"Jesus," said Riley, the flush of his exertions fading from his round face. "I never get used to that."

"I have," said Damon.

Six hours later the prisoner was booked and delivered to Centre Street, the victim's body had gone to the morgue, and Damon and Riley were walking up the stairs to the squad-room on the second floor of the stationhouse.

"Hey, Counselor, you're back," said one of the other men on the squad, looking up from a typewriter. "How do you spell consensus?"

"One c, three s's. And don't call me Counselor."

"Right," said the man vaguely. He picked up a battered dictionary and tossed it aside. "Now you're back from vacation, we can lock up Webster again."

"Jesus," said Riley, sinking into a chair by a desk near a window, "you haven't even had a chance to get home yet, have you?"

"No. I flew back this morning and came on duty right from the airport." Damon took his worn suede jacket, hung it on the back of the desk chair, and put his gun in the drawer. Muscles swelled along the back of his dark shirt.

"So tell me about it," Riley said. "You survived two weeks

in the Berkshires with Mother Nature?"

"She's reasonable, once you get to know her."

"Never. I hear you can hardly find a deli up there."

"Ten miles to a general store."

Riley shook his head in mock disbelief. "So what did you do with yourself, all alone up there? Wasn't it kind of boring?"

"A lot less than that stakeout last month. I read, and looked at the lake and listened to music. And if things got dull, I went for a walk."

Riley tried to visualize it but failed. "Well, they're not dull around here. The Vasquez case went to trial. Did you read about it?"

"No. I was on vacation from newspapers too."

"They threw out the landlady's testimony on some technicality I never heard of—you might know what it was. So the bastard got off. Can you believe it?"

"Oh, yes."

"And why not? They all get off. That scumbag we just took in, I bet he doesn't do more than two years."

Damon leaned back, rested his jaw on tented fingers, and watched Riley rise and move in angry circles, running a hand through his tightly curled, wheat-colored hair, denouncing the legal system. "Hugh," he cut in finally, "police work stops with the arrest. Isn't it enough that we do a good job when we collar them? We're not responsible for what happens in the courts."

"When they throw the guys back on the streets, then we're responsible, right?"

"We're just here to enforce the law. Let others do the interpreting of it. Let them be the ones who twist it and play games with it."

"You know something weird? You've got a worse opinion

of the courts than I do, and you're the one with the law degree."

"Which I've never used and would rather forget."

Riley flung himself back in the chair. "Ah, hell, I'm not in the mood to have this discussion again. You always come up with the same arguments."

Damon smiled. "And you don't?"

"Riley," someone shouted from across the room, "didn't you catch that Granger case—the accident on Riverside?"

"Yeah."

"Then some woman on the line wants to talk to you."

Riley walked over to pick up a phone. Damon sighed and stretched his hands along the battered top of the desk, flexing his blunt, strong fingers. After a moment he pulled a typewriter toward him and began to do his reports on the day's work. He disliked paperwork as much as any man on the squad, but his face did not show it.

It was a square face, with a wide mouth bracketed by two lines that could grow as deep as cuts, and a strong blade of a nose. As he worked, a shock of his straight, blue-black hair angled down to the eyes, so dark they nearly seemed to match it.

He was in his eighth year on the force. Two years earlier he had been made a detective and had served tours of duty on Vice and Narcotics before being assigned to Homicide. Of the twenty-six men on the district squad, his arrest record was currently the fourth highest, and Riley's was third.

Riley walked back to him, pulling at a pale, wiry eyebrow and frowning at the notes he'd just scribbled. "Anonymous call," he said. "About a strange one that happened while you were gone. Martin Granger—he's the guy who heads that big Institute and gets his picture in the paper with Hart Collins? He fell off a balcony at his house and landed on a piece of sculpture that got him right in the gut. Like some Japanese falling on a big sword. His secretary was there and saw it, and she called us, but he was DOA. We talked to the neighbors and got nothing. His wife was out for the night, and the cook lives in, but she was so sound asleep it almost took a cannon to wake her up. And a derrick to get her out—fattest woman I ever saw. Anyhow, forensic didn't come up with anything, so it was all pretty cut and dried. But it just didn't smell right to me."

"Why not?"

"Well, for one thing, the secretary wasn't just a secretary. She gives her name as Astrid Cain, but a couple days later she's got another story and some more names. She says she's really a Mrs. Astrid Chapin, and on top of that, she's a reporter who writes under the name Anne Cain, working at the Institute undercover in order to do a story. And the reason she didn't say so right away was because it, quote, didn't seem relevant. Close quote. So I checked with her editor at the *Blade,* and he— Hey, what's the matter?"

Damon was staring at his hands; he flexed them sharply. "Nothing. Go on."

"So her story checked out with the *Blade.* But at this Institute, nobody knew she was a reporter. She says Granger knew about it, but he's dead, isn't he?"

"What difference would it make?"

"I don't know, I don't know. I just didn't like it. She was kind of a snotty broad, too. But there was nothing else to do, so we filed it as an accident. And now I just got this call."

"From whom?"

"Some woman. Says she's been too scared to call till now, and she won't give her name. She claims she had her windows open that night and heard Granger and the secretary quarreling. Around ten-thirty, just before he died. She's positive Granger called the other party his secretary. And the quarrel was violent, she says. Lots of shouting." He checked the notes he carried. "According to her, Granger called the secretary a liar and said he'd expose her. The secretary was shouting things about finding a way to shut him up. Then the damn woman on the phone says she can't talk anymore and hangs up." Riley tapped the paper as if he could jar more information from it. "Maybe she made it all up. Maybe she heard it on the next-door TV. Or maybe she's telling the truth and this Astrid Cain got so mad at Granger that she helped him off the balcony. What do you think?"

"I think you don't pronounce her name right. It's Ah-strid. With an 'Ah' sound."

Riley stared. "You know her?"

"If it's an Astrid Cain who works for a newspaper, yes. I met her. A long time ago. She was an actress then."

"And maybe she still is—with a Little Miss Innocent act." Riley began to march around the desk, fingers combing his hair. "If this is anything, it could be really something, you know what I mean? And if you knew this Cain woman, that could be a big help." He stopped short. "How well did you know her, anyway? Is she the kind who could push a guy off a balcony?"

Damon hesitated. "I think she is the last person in the world I would have expected to commit murder."

"Yeah?"

"Of course I haven't seen her for eight years."

"Hey, you mean she was a real actress? Not the kind that Vice hauls in?"

"A real one. I think the word is . . . struggling."

"But when you and I go after them, the struggle is over, right? I'll talk to the lieutenant as soon as he gets back. OK with you?"

Damon turned to look out the small window, where a screen of mesh turned the light to gray. "Whatever he says."

"Hey, I'm glad you're back."

"Thanks, Hugh. I've got paperwork to do right now."

But it was some time before he turned to do it.

At five-thirty he was standing in the subway, headed downtown to his apartment, the suitcase that had been in his locker all day wedged between his legs. The train was choked with people; the bodies of strangers were jammed intimately against his own.

He made himself relax. After all, he thought, what better relationship could one have to the human race?—intimate and impersonal, all at once. The secret was to be unmoved, to be the still eye of the human hurricane around one. Not to be like Riley, for instance: keyed up and cast down a dozen times a day by a victim, a trial, a woman, a party, a new departmental regulation, a new case. . . . The two of them would work out their strategy on the Granger business the next morning. He had known from the start that he would be assigned, if only because it was assumed that he of all the men on the squad would feel most comfortable with the milieu in question. He had done nothing to indicate otherwise; when he joined the force, he had done so on the private condition that he would do whatever was asked of him, without seeking to question or change it.

Besides, he thought, it was just another case, no different in principle from that of the dead whore. He would look for evidence that Astrid had killed a man. If there was none, fine. If there was, he would help turn her over to the courts—and to the law that she had begged him not to give up. That would be poetic justice, he thought. The kind that would make her smile. Unless she was guilty.

For a moment he could see that smile, as clearly as if he were coming down the steps of the law school building to where she waited for him, her smile growing as he came closer, as if his movements controlled it.

He turned his head sharply, meeting the blank, unprotesting gaze of the body wedged next to his. He told himself to think of the reports Riley had given him to read.

In them Astrid stated that she had begun working for Granger six months before, on a leave of absence from the *Blade,* with a view to a series of articles. And Riley was right, to the extent that it seemed too long a time and too elaborate an undertaking just for some articles. But to kill the man? That wasn't possible, he thought as the train lurched to a stop.

Even if it was possible, it wouldn't matter.

His apartment was near the river, a loft he had furnished and decorated, in a block of warehouses and offices. The elevator was tiny and primordial; as it groaned to a stop, he thankfully put down his suitcase and undid the complicated set of locks.

"Paul, Paul, Paul, Paul!" The voice crescendoed from the other end of the apartment, and a small figure in white shirt and slacks hurled itself at him while the voice went rushing on. "I knew you'd be back today, so I came over right after my lesson to clean up the place and wait for you. I just had to see you. Did you have a good time? Did you work hard today? Are you tired? Are you hungry?"

"I can't tell you unless I can breathe." He disengaged the girl and swung her down to land on her feet. She was twenty but looked less, with a thin little cat-shaped face the color of tea, in which gleamed small, very white teeth and dark, gold-flecked eyes.

"You didn't think I would be here? You mind that I came? If you want me to go, you just say it and pfft, no more me. Or is it no more I?"

"Marie," he laughed—he couldn't help it; she often made him laugh—"can we go a little more slowly, please?"

She pulled away from him to sit cross-legged on the floor. "All right, I'll stay here and say nothing. I'll improve my mind while you unpack, and then I have a lovely present for you."

He raised his eyebrows at her and headed for the bedroom. She watched him go as if she wished her eyes could hold him back.

Five years earlier, when Damon was a patrolman in the South Bronx, he had pulled Marie Lazare from the floor of a rotting basement and from the sweaty grasp of the first of six animals who were lined up above her. She had tasted the rancid cloth they stuffed in her mouth and the fear that rose to meet it; she had heard one of them say, unzipping and showing himself to her, "This is from the Barracudas, baby." She knew what price she was going to pay for the contempt she had shown the gang that claimed to own the streets. But as she prayed for sudden paralysis, so she would not feel what happened to her flesh, the gargoyle face above her own had disappeared, and in its place she had seen Paul Damon's.

He had taken her to the stationhouse to give her statement and then delivered her to her weeping mother. She had not seen him again, but his face had stayed in her mind like a talisman of strength, warding off the grubby reality of her life.

When she was nineteen, she had seen him by chance on the street and had followed him home. He had listened quietly to the story of the life she was building, working as a cosmetics clerk and taking voice lessons with every dollar she could save. "And now," she had said, "I see you again, and I know I want to be with you. I could be a good woman for you. I'll come sometimes, but only when you like, and I can make you supper, and you can tell me about the brave things you did all day. We can listen to these records you have, and then we can go to bed. I don't think I will be very good at first, because I have not wanted anyone to touch me since that night, but I know it will be all right with you."

He had looked at her helplessly. "No. It's out of the question."

"Why? Because I am too young for you?"

"That, too. I'm nearly twice your age. But that's not all."

Both hands had flown to her cheeks. "I never thought. You have a woman already."

"No."

"Then why? Am I too thin? Too stupid? You don't like Haitian girls?"

"No," he said sharply. "Don't talk that way. You're fine, just fine. It's not possible, that's all. I'm not a man who likes emotional baggage in his life."

She had sighed. "You see, I am too stupid. You will have to explain that to me. Do you mean that you don't want to be involved with a woman? But that is no problem. I am the only one who gets involved. You don't have to do anything at all."

He had burst out laughing. When she came a week later, he had let her in again, and again and again, and finally he had accepted her visits as a part of his life. On the night he finally took her to bed, he had said afterward, "You're lying there thinking that this changes things, that I need you now. But I don't. I'll take whatever you offer, as long as you want to offer it, and I'll enjoy the taking. But that's all. How can you settle for so little as that?"

"When you've had nothing, a little can be a lot."

As long as he doesn't know it's everything, she had thought.

She watched him now as he came back into the living room, dressed in tan cords and shirt. He stretched out on the couch and sighed with pleasure, looking around the large room. He had paneled three of the walls in dark wood; books and records filled the other. There were straw scatter rugs on the dark floor, and the furniture was sparse but carefully chosen for the beauty of its wood. "You're staring at me," he finally said. "Is there a reason?"

She smiled. "No." Then she jumped up. "Stay right there. Don't move." He heard her running to the kitchen. It was quiet for some moments, and he closed his eyes and let one arm slowly fall to the floor.

There were sudden sharp noises and scuffles, and a ball of white fur hurtled at him, landing on his stomach and furiously flicking its tail across his thighs. Marie stood above him, laughing.

Damon's eyes opened, but he did not move. "Take this dog."

"Paul, he's yours. I said I had a present for you, a welcome-home present, and he—"

"Take this dog." The words were chipped out of ice.

She grabbed frantically for the animal and sank with it into a chair as Damon rose.

"Get that animal out of here. Don't you think if I wanted a dog, I'd have gotten one? Get rid of it."

"But . . . he has nowhere to go. I found him."

Inexplicably, that seemed to make him even angrier. "A dog is the last thing I want in this world, so get that straight. And a stray. . . . I never asked for a present. Get it out of here. Get it out!"

She was gripping the puppy so tightly that it began to whimper.

"All right," he said, his voice more normal, "put it down. I won't hurt it. I won't hurt either of you."

She complied, her eyes never leaving his face. The puppy ran in small circles for a moment, then flopped on the rug and stared up at them.

"I never saw you mad before. Never."

"And you won't again. I'm sorry. There's no excuse for it."

"Is there an explanation, then?"

He squared his shoulders. "It was a stupid overreaction, because of something that happened years ago and doesn't matter anymore."

She saw the anger in his eyes, as sharp as lightning and as quickly gone. The deep lines that framed his mouth seemed to relax by an effort of will. It's himself he's angry with, she thought suddenly. The dog rolled over at her feet and put up its paws. He would not look at it, she noticed.

"Come on," he said shortly. "We'll go out to eat. Put the dog in the kitchen, and tomorrow you'll take him to a shelter."

She realized he was not to be argued with.

They walked up to a Spanish restaurant in the Village. During dinner he kept her talking steadily, asking about her boss and her fellow workers, whom she could mimic expertly, about the music she was studying, about the tiny studio apartment she had just rented.

"I tell you everything," she said, "but you tell me nothing."

"That's the mark of a good detective."

Back in the apartment, when the puppy ran to meet them, she scooped it up. "I don't care what you say. I won't take him to a shelter. I'll take him home with me. Maybe he won't like living in a place the size of a shoebox, but he will like it better than being put to sleep forever." To her annoyance, she began to cry.

"All right," he said gently, "I've changed my mind. The dog can stay. For a while, anyway. It seems this is the year for strays to show up on my doorstep. No, don't say anything. Just get the dog settled in. Fix whatever it needs."

For half an hour she puttered, arranging bowls and papers

and food, laughing at the puppy and playing with him till he finally curled up in exhaustion. Then she came to sit on the floor in front of Damon. She rested her chin on his knee and looked at his eyes; they were very dark and far away.

"Paul? Can't you tell me what it was?"

"I've told you; it doesn't matter anymore."

"Of course it does. Something that hurt you so much?"

"No. What matters is that I hurt you. I'm sorry."

"That's all right. I'm tough."

"Are you?"

"Yes. But not tonight. Tonight I want to stay with you." She tried to keep her voice light. "I want to make up to you for what happened years ago."

"That doesn't concern you."

"But you do."

"I don't know why," he said. He pulled her up to lie beside him; he touched her small breasts beneath the white shirt and laid the span of one hand across her hipbones.

When she looked up at him, his eyes were so close it almost hurt to see them. Yet they were not looking at her, she felt, and she moved up defiantly to take his mouth. It seemed to her that she was urging him back from some distant place, and even when his body was fully, unmistakably, in the present, taking urgent possession of hers, she knew that she had claimed him for only those brief moments.

She woke in the middle of the night, aware that he was moving in his sleep, and raised herself on one elbow to look at him. The pale moonlight turned the bars on the window into bars of shadow across his face; he seemed to be fighting against them, turning his head from side to side and muttering. She leaned over but could catch only one sound. She repeated it softly—"Astrid"—but it made no sense to her.

She watched him till he ceased moving and the bars lay still across his face.

Chapter Three

"I'm not stupid," said Lauren Granger sharply. "You spent an hour upstairs in the doctor's study last week. Now you're back for 'routine questions.' Obviously you don't think his death was an accident." Wearing an ivory pantsuit, she was sitting on the huge mushroom-colored suede couch in front of the flagstone fireplace in her living room. The terrace garden was visible through the wall of glass behind her. "You're not considering suicide?"

"Would that surprise you?" Riley asked.

"It would shock the hell out of me."

"Why?"

"Because Dr. Granger was not the suicidal type."

"How would you describe him, then?"

After a pause she said, "Satisfied. Very satisfied with his work." She extended one foot, arching it, and looked at the two detectives blandly.

"We're not thinking of suicide," Riley said.

"That's a relief. But what, then? Because the secretary was here when it— Oh. You think the secretary killed him?"

Damon waited for a reaction; she merely looked thoughtful. "What can you tell us about her?" he asked.

"Not much, really. She came over here sometimes to work

with him. I suppose I saw her ten times or so, just in passing. I didn't learn till afterwards that she was a reporter."

"Did your husband ever indicate that he knew?"

"Never."

"Did you ever have a chance to observe their working relationship?"

"No. She'd go straight up to his study. I think she did stay through dinner one night, but I was on my way out."

"So you had no real impression of her?"

Lauren shrugged. "A secretary? I'm afraid not. Oh, she was attractive enough, if you like the earthy type."

Damon looked evenly into the violet eyes. "Did your husband like it?"

She gave a creamy laugh. "He wasn't having an affair with her, if that's what you're getting at."

"Excuse me, but could you be sure of that?"

"Yes. Oh, yes."

"Well, thank you, Mrs. Granger. Now we'd like to talk to your cook."

"Of course." She rose from the couch, smoothing her jacket. A glossy woman, Damon thought. Beauty in acrylic. "You'll have to excuse things," she said. "I'm having the place redecorated." She waved at boxes piled in one corner of the room. "That's Dr. Granger's collection of Aztec and Indian masks." She touched a switch, cutting off the music that had been playing throughout the house.

"He must have been a nut for that kind of music, too," Riley said.

"Yes," she said shortly. "We both were." She took them along a hall and opened a door opposite the dining room. "Jones, these policemen want to talk to you."

At a round table in the center of a large kitchen, flanked by gleaming equipment of every kind, sat a woman whom Riley's original reports had described as a forty-year-old white female.

But Damon's impression was not of sex or age or of any attribute other than flesh. She was a pyramid of soft rolls and pillows, supporting a head that was tiny in contrast. She was drinking coffee and eating cake.

Lauren sat next to her. "The floor is yours, gentlemen."

"There's no need for you to stay, Mrs. Granger," Damon said.

"It's my kitchen. And my cook."

Riley began. "Miss Jones, you told me that you went to bed around nine on the night Dr. Granger died, in your room behind the kitchen here. Why are you so sure it was nine o'clock?"

"I always go then. Unless there are people to dinner."

"So when Astrid Cain came to see the doctor that night, you didn't hear the doorbell ring?"

"No."

"Did you hear them talking later on? Did they wake you up?"

"You did, afterwards."

"Sorry about that." Riley grinned, but there was no response. "How many times have you seen Miss Cain?"

The woman didn't answer; she was eating again.

"Did she ever come in here to talk to you? You know, just to shoot the breeze?" No answer. "Were you ever upstairs in the study when she was working for Dr. Granger?"

"She doesn't go upstairs," Lauren said. "She doesn't go anywhere."

"Yeah. Well, Miss Jones, do you know anything at all about Astrid Cain?"

"She liked the Chicken Kiev."

"The what?"

Lauren cut in again. "No doubt that's what Jones made the night Cain stayed to dinner. Is that right?"

The woman nodded, a slow undulating of chins.

"How do you know she liked it? Did you talk to her that night?" No answer. "Did Dr. Granger ever talk to you about her?" No answer. Riley began to pull at his left eyebrow.

"Stop eating," said Lauren sharply. "Try to answer these men. The doctor would have wanted it."

"Miss Jones," said Damon, sitting in a chair opposite her, "that looks to me like kugelhof."

For the first time the raisin eyes looked up. "Yes."

"You made it, I suppose?"

"Yes."

"My father used to make it once in a while. He's quite a cook, but all he has time for now is doughnuts and muffins. He has a shop." She looked at him unblinkingly. "Did Astrid Cain tell you she liked your dinner?"

"Yes."

"What did she say?"

"That when she first put her fork in, butter squirted out, the way it should with Chicken Kiev."

"I know a famous restaurant where it doesn't. Did she tell you while you were serving dinner?"

"Yes."

"And when was this?"

"In the winter. Early February."

"Was it just the two of them?"

"Yes."

"You must have overheard some of their conversation. What was it about?"

"I don't know. She was asking about Michelangelo."

"Asking what?"

"I don't remember."

"Did you have the impression that Miss Cain and the doctor got along well with each other?"

The woman appeared to be studying him. "If you like kugelhof, take a piece."

"Thanks, I will." It was the lightest he had ever tasted. "You are something of an artist, Miss Jones."

She wiped her flat lips. "I don't remember anything about Astrid Cain. I don't know anything about her." She raised the coffee cup to her mouth, like a big period to the conversation.

"How long has she been with you?" Damon asked Lauren as she took them back to the front door.

"Forever. About twelve years, I'd say." She stopped, one hand on the doorknob, the other posed between her breasts. "I don't like having the police around. But if there's a possibility Martin was murdered, you'll do what's necessary."

"That's right," Riley said. "Ma'am."

She turned to Damon. "I want to be kept informed about what's happening. So don't by any chance decide you don't want to tell me, because I have friends who can put pressure on you. Keep that in mind." She smiled; it was dazzling.

"Man, I'd like to see that cook as the anonymous caller," Riley said, as he drove them back to the stationhouse.

"Can you?"

"I don't know. The voice isn't right, but it isn't wrong, either. The way she talks, one grunt at a time; that's way off. But it fits that she could have been scared to call, with the Ice Lady for a boss. What do you think?"

"I think you haven't got anybody better."

Riley sighed. Over the past week they had taken what time they could to recanvass the apartments overlooking the Granger courtyard and to talk to the few people next door at the Institute who had been working in some of the rear offices and labs. "Don't forget that gabby grandma who lives opposite. She admitted she looks out her windows all the time."

"But that night she didn't look until he was already dead."

"Yeah. So she says." Riley drove gloomily for another

block. "OK, how about this? The Ice Lady made the call herself. She wanted her old man dead, so she hired Cain to do the job for her. Then Cain starts wanting more money, so she decided to turn her in anonymously."

Damon looked away. An image had come into his mind, of Astrid in their old apartment, reading in the sagging armchair, where the light from the cone lamp made a dark red haze of her hair, looking up and saying, "Damon, do you think that people ever change? Really change, I mean, in the fundamental things?" He shoved the image away and answered Riley. "If Lauren and Cain were in it together, then Lauren would know that Cain could implicate her. It doesn't hold up."

"All right, all right. But you know what I think? I think you don't want to believe she did it."

"You're wrong. It doesn't matter to me, one way or the other."

"Was the story assigned to her," Riley asked, "or did she come to you with the idea?"

Hal Ruby leaned back in his swivel chair and stared at them across the clutter of the desk in his office at the *Blade* building.

"Tell me why you want to know, and I might answer."

And you might not, Damon thought. Ruby's face was a tired, slightly puffy mask of civility that could crack in a moment, he'd bet.

Riley tried again. "We have reason to believe that she did not tell us the full story about her conversation with Dr. Granger the night he died."

"Is there some reason she should? She was a reporter on a story, and I'm not going to have her harassed by the police because of it."

Riley was growing flushed, and in one of the unexpected

outbursts that made Damon enjoy working with him, he said, "I read that *Blade* editorial, the one that said the police depend too much on muscle and guns. Maybe this is one reason—people like you who won't even answer routine questions."

Ruby's laugh called awkward attention to the skin beneath his jaw and eyes. "Beautiful! An open admission that brawn is a substitute for brain."

"Don't put words in my mouth."

"You'd rather have your foot?"

Damon cut in. "We're not here to search your newsroom without a warrant. We just want answers to some simple questions. I'd hate to have to send a memo to all Homicide divisions, telling them you wouldn't cooperate. Your crime reporters could find themselves filing a lot of no stories."

"Oh, I don't think you'd do that," Ruby said mildy.

"No. Any more than you'd refuse to tell us whether or not the story was her idea."

Ruby tapped a pencil against his cheek. "Yes, it was. I'll give you that much. She wanted to do something on Granger and the Institute from the inside. His name was starting to crop up in some campaign stories, so I OK'd it."

"Was that kind of story in her line?"

"Not really. She usually did features and profiles in the arts."

"She said you got her the job with Granger. How were you able to do that?"

"She said she knew his secretary was leaving, so I asked John Flood at Columbia to recommend her. I told him I knew a bright woman named Astrid Cain—that's the name Anne wanted to use—who had good secretarial skills and wanted to work at ISCEV. Flood called Granger, Granger liked her, and that was that."

Riley leaned forward. "So there was no way Granger could have known she was a reporter?"

"Of course not. That would defeat the whole purpose."

"You gave her a leave of absence to do the story," Damon said. "Wasn't that an unusual arrangement?"

"Maybe. But I liked the way she begged for it. Like a nun in heat."

You bastard, Damon thought.

Riley cut in with the bluff they had planned. "She said she had some other reason to work for Granger, something personal. Did you know about that?"

"Yes, but she wouldn't say what it was. Something to do with her husband—that was my guess. She was a clam about her private life."

Riley's expression didn't change, but Damon knew he was grinning inside. "Did you ever meet him?" Riley went on. "Dr. David Chapin?"

"No."

"Did she ever talk about him?"

"I just said she was a clam. Do you know what a clam is? Something that doesn't open up."

"What kind of story did she file on Granger?" Damon asked quickly. Ruby sailed his pencil onto a stack of papers. "You haven't run a piece by her on Granger; we've checked. Why? Hasn't she filed it yet?" Ruby retrieved the pencil. "I see. She filed it, but you didn't run it. Why? Well, let's see, for the *Blade* not to run it, that would mean either that it was badly written—which I doubt, if you thought she was good enough to let her try it—or else it was too anti-Granger. Which was it?" He waited. "Of course, there's a third possibility. Maybe the article was written too well."

Ruby's pencil slammed on the desk. "All right, you supercilious bastard, this discussion is over! As of this second. I'm not opening my mouth again."

"Oh, I get it," Riley said. "A clam."

* * *

"No, I never heard her quarreling with the director. Not that he would have put up with it if she had. I always thought she was a model secretary."

The man was the eleventh staff member to be questioned by Damon, in one of the two conference rooms made available to him and Riley by the acting director of the Institute. And the eleventh to give the same answer to the question.

"She seemed sympathetic to the Institute goals, Dr. Corderman?"

"Oh, yes. And particularly interested in Field Studies, I thought. Of course, I may be prejudiced, since that's my department. We send people out to work with various culturally deprived groups, to study their attitudes and adaptive mechanisms, and of course to help them if we can. She came around a number of times, asking about our programs and our personnel, even people who worked here in the past. And she seemed very interested in young Jake Waldo, one of our newer people. I saw her eating lunch with him in the park several times. Of course, what I took for sympathetic interest could just have been her reporter's nose, couldn't it?"

"That's possible." A certainty, he thought. From what he had been reading of and by Martin Granger, there was no way Astrid could be sympathetic. "Well, I think that's all, Dr. Corderman. Thanks."

When the man had gone, he finished his notes, then pushed the notebook aside. His reflection looked back from the polished wood of the conference table, the nose and mouth sharply defined but the eyes merely two dim holes. Like Justice, he thought, blind to all considerations but the facts. And was a person's character a fact?

"We've got it, Damon, bingo and jackpot!" Riley's voice burst ahead of him into the room. "I just got it from the personnel director: Dr. David Chapin is a fellow of this

Institute, on leave of absence since two months before Cain came to work. It's right there in the files—her address is the same as his. And people here didn't even know she knew him. What do you make of that, my friend?"

"I make it that your guess about a personal motive was a good one. But we still don't know what it means."

Riley stared at him. "Why are you talking like a DA? I didn't say we had enough yet, not even to go ask Cain some questions. But look how much we have got." He plumped down into one of the chrome and velour chairs and ticked off points on his fingers. "She was on the scene when he died. She had the means, the way that balcony is set up. She lied about Granger's knowing she was a reporter—I backed that up with everybody today, didn't you?" Damon nodded. "She came here for something besides a story, something to do with her husband, and she kept it a secret. She was nosing around here, asking questions about guys who used to work here—I got that from three or four people today, and I bet you did too." Damon nodded again. "By the way, she got the address from personnel of at least one old employee, a Harry Pine. Now, add all that up and don't tell me things aren't looking nice and suspicious."

"I don't tell you that. I just say it could add up in a lot of different ways."

"Yeah, I know that. But I keep remembering what you said about her—that she used to be a very determined lady."

The puppy skittered under the table, grabbed the plastic bone, and trotted back to the couch, wagging its tail beseechingly.

"Hasn't anybody told you that life isn't just a bowl of bones?" Damon patted the silky white head and gently disengaged the object from the animal's teeth. "OK, one more time. Go get it, Sancho!"

After two weeks I guess it's here to stay, he thought. Marie hadn't begged him to keep it permanently, although he could tell she had had to exercise self-control. They had talked about the dog only once, really, when he had told her to give it some kind of name.

"It should be something brave, to inspire him," she had said. "Maybe some wonderful hero from a book." Something must have shown on his face, for she had said quickly, "No, no, maybe not."

"Go ahead," he had told her.

"Well, I was thinking of Don Quixote, because I heard he was a knight and fought very bravely."

"Against windmills?"

"But he was an idealist, they said."

"And also a madman, did they tell you that? I find it interesting that Cervantes tied those two qualities together."

She hadn't liked that idea, so they'd settled on Sancho Panza—Sancho for short—because, as she put it, "A good, loyal friend who goes with you everywhere; that's just right for him."

I should call her, he thought, but he did not move.

When the phone rang, he went to it with a twinge of guilt, but the voice was not hers.

"Hello, Dad," he said. "How are you? I'm sorry I haven't been up in a while, but things have been pretty busy."

"That's all right." The old man always sounded weary and hearty at the same time. "There's nothing new with me, anyway. If sugar and coffee don't come down, I'll have to raise my prices, but that's nothing new. Listen, Paul, I've been trying to get you since yesterday. Your Aunt Loretta died."

"Oh. Well, Dad, I'm sorry. I really am."

"No, no, it's a blessing for her."

"Yes, I suppose." He saw the wasted, papery face of the aunt with whom he'd spent his boyhood and adolescence in a small New Jersey town, after his mother died.

"She talked about you right at the last. She was praying for you."

"Was she?"

"Now, don't sound like that, Paul. I know she could drive anybody crazy with her religion, but she had a good heart."

"Somehow that's not what I remember her for."

"She took you two boys in, didn't she? And she did something nice at the end. That's really why I called. She left you five thousand dollars."

Damon didn't answer; he thought of the times when that sum would have given him back his days and nights, would have taken him from the cabdriving, the luncheonette, and God knows how many other jobs and let him go to law school years before he was finally able. "Well, that was very nice of her," he said. "I'm sure I'll find a use for it."

There was a question he had to ask, even though he knew the answer in the pit of his stomach. "And what about Sam?"

"Paul, I argued with her, I didn't care how sick she was, but all she talked was forgiveness and love."

"Sam gets five thousand, too?"

"Yes."

"Well, that was also very nice of her. But maybe she didn't realize how little heroin you can buy for five thousand. At Sam's rate that might last a whole month."

"He has to give it to you, Paul. I'm going to tell him that. He's your brother. He owes you more than five thousand."

"Six was the actual figure, Dad." He permitted himself a short laugh. "When you see him, tell him not to shoot it up all at once."

"He owes it to you, that was the bargain—"

"I don't want to talk about it, Dad. I don't care about it anymore; I've told you that a dozen times. Let's talk about something else."

When they were saying good-bye, he heard himself ask, "Dad, do you remember Astrid?"

"Of course I do. From the first time she came into the store and tried the doughnut flavors and got me to tell her about what you did for Sam." There was a careful pause. "Why do you ask?"

"You liked her, didn't you?"

"More than that," said the old man gently. "Have you seen her again?"

"She's the suspect in a possible homicide. I'm on the case."

"Oh, my God," sighed the old man. "I don't think I understand anybody anymore."

And perhaps I never did, thought Damon as he hung up. Not Aunt Loretta, who talked only of love but must have hated deeply; certainly not Sam, who must have had destruction buried in him all along, like tiny seeds at the heart of a melon; and perhaps not even Astrid.

He stood up and began to pace the room, unaware that Sancho trotted beside him in the expectation of some new game. There had been two calls that afternoon, drawing the net a little tighter, and tomorrow they were going to question her, to see if she would give them, as Riley put it, "a little rope to start hanging her with."

He had made one of the calls himself, to the home of the Harry Pine whose address she had gotten from the Institute: Although Pine had died five years before, she had gone to see his mother anyway and had asked a lot of questions.

The other call had been incoming and had been routed to Riley: A Professor Llewellyn Jones from Columbia had decided there was something he should report. Anne Cain had just called him, he said, asking him not to tell the police that she had been to see him two months earlier, when she'd tried to get a strong negative statement about Granger for an article she was doing. At that time she had said she was talking to other public figures, like Senator Roscoe Harding, who had also expressed some disagreement with Granger and his theories.

"But why would she call Jones?" Damon had asked. "To ask him not to tell us? That's like waving a red flag. It doesn't make sense."

"She's probably talked to Ruby and heard we're sniffing around, and she's running scared," Riley had countered. "When they get scared, they get stupid; you know that. And stupid is beautiful for us."

But it wasn't like her to run scared, Damon thought; the call was out of character. Then he shrugged at what that phrase implied—that character was something immutable, like the stars. Like Sam's.

He stopped so abruptly that Sancho yelped, skidding on the straw rug. He went back to the phone.

"Riley? Damon. About Mrs. Pine—I've been thinking I might get more from her if I went to Philly and talked to her in person. And I could make a swing to Washington and see this Senator Harding, too. I'd like to set it up first thing in the morning and go. If the lieutenant objects, I'll do it on my own." He laughed shortly. "I got some unexpected money tonight, so I might as well use it in a good cause." He listened for some moments, squaring his shoulders. "I know, Hugh, but it's occurred to me that it might be better if I don't go the first time you talk to her. Take Parsons with you. If I come in on the next go-around, there might be more shock value in her seeing me again." He told himself that was the only reason.

"Come on, Sancho," he said lightly when he had hung up. "You want a game of windmills before we go to bed?"

The jet climbed out of Dulles airport at nine-thirty. Damon closed his eyes and felt the day slide back and away from him.

But soon the plane leveled off, and the aisles came to life. He unbuckled the seatbelt and stretched his legs as far as the seat ahead would allow. After ten minutes he made himself take out his notebook and consider the record of the day.

The notes on Harry Pine's mother, who had said: "Miss Cain seemed to want to find something that would reflect negatively on Dr. Granger. And even when I told her everything and showed her Harry's letters, I'm sure she wasn't convinced. I thought that was odd, seeing as she was doing work for them. That's what she said, you know, that she was doing a follow-up study on former Institute personnel and there was some mixup in the records, so she hadn't known Harry was dead."

And the notes on Senator Roscoe Harding, who had said: "It didn't take much to see what that little redhead was up to—she wanted me to take a good swipe at Martin Granger. I'm on record against his godlessness, of course. I said that years ago, when his first book came out and the bleeding hearts were making a fuss over it. But I have to give the devil his due—Granger had some very decent ideas about equality for all Americans and why we haven't got it yet, and I won't be made to say he didn't. She wanted me to, all right, but I guess I can handle a reporter after all these years, especially a lady reporter."

Damon smiled wryly. If Astrid had been intimidated by someone like Roscoe Harding, then she truly had changed.

He stared at his notebook, looking past it into the distance—where she was standing as she had been the first time he saw her: on the platform at a rally.

She had been helping a friend to protest the university's decision not to renew a young instructor's contract on affirmative action grounds; he was a white Anglo-Saxon, and a minority group member was needed in that department. "The only thing that should matter is merit," she had said. "You can't make up for discrimination in the past by discriminating now in the other direction."

"Shut up, you Wasp bitch," a heckler had called. "You want to keep the world just for Wasps."

"You ain't even going to this school," another had called. "So what the hell business is it of yours?"

"Injustice is everybody's business," she had shouted, her body taut in a rust-colored sweater and skirt, her cinnamon hair whipping in the breeze. But the catcalls had risen, a chorus of "Lady Wasp, Lady Wasp, fly away home."

He had stood up, propelled by the kind of emotion to which he still was prey in those days, his words coming out like knives. "Shut up, all of you. Let her talk. She's paying you the compliment of assuming you have minds, so don't destroy the illusion. Shut up and listen like human beings." The heckling had subsided, more from surprise than anything else, he supposed; and when he was leaving the rally, she had come after him, rushing, as she so often seemed to be, all energy and earth tones, like a crisp, windy day in early fall. "Who are you?" she had said. "I want to thank you. But why did you say it was an illusion?"

They had gone somewhere, some bar near the campus, and talked till closing time.

Astrid the fighter, he thought, staring past his seatmate at the black circle that was the night sky. She had had such a painfully innocent belief that the fight was worth the candle, that nothing else mattered, not even defeat.

He sat very still. Astrid the fighter, who hated giving up, who would do whatever she thought was right. . . . Wouldn't that include *anything?* She was out to get Granger; that was now unmistakably clear. Couldn't she convince herself that he was evil and that if a chance arose, it would be right to kill him?

Could the idealist have become a madwoman? He put away his notes and leaned back in the seat.

Chapter Four

Hal Ruby stared at the closing door of his office, little lines of irritation working their way around his eyes.

He had tried unsuccessfully to reach Anne Cain for days, and now she had burst in unannounced, to sink into the big chair opposite and confess, "Hal, I'm in trouble with the police." And when he told her that he knew, since some of New York's finest had been to see him last week, she had looked as if she expected the chair to close in on her from behind.

Finally he had gotten the story from her: how two detectives had come to her apartment the day before, questioning her over and over about what had happened with Granger the night he died, insinuating that she hated him, and asking about her husband. "Hal . . . I should have told you this, I guess, and I'm sorry. . . . He's on a leave of absence, but he works for ISCEV. And the police will find out, if they haven't already. Maybe I should have told them yesterday. Hal, they think I killed Granger—I know it. What am I going to do?"

At first he had been so angry that he hadn't realized how her hazel eyes were darting or how far her chin had fallen from its usual cocksure lift. "Did you kill him?" he had asked abruptly. "Hal!" she had wailed, putting her head into those lovely, elegant hands.

And then she had begged him to tell the police that the *Blade* had wanted and initiated the Granger story. He hadn't told her it was too late for that.

He rubbed the spot on his temples where his headaches usually launched themselves. The Granger story was in his files, and that's where it would stay, he thought. A piece that called into question the motives, the methods, and nearly everything else about a major adviser to the presidential candidate the *Blade* had since endorsed—that was his private property, underscore private. And now, ironically, she was as anxious as he to keep it so.

He leaned back. In the room was still a faint touch of her perfume, which usually made him think of woodsmoke and velvet but was now going straight to his temples. There was no way around it, he thought; the publisher would have to know that there was trouble. He reached for the phone.

Damon and Riley came out of the lieutenant's office and moved silently to a desk. A summer storm was hurling waves of rain at the windows, and the ceiling lights shone like dirty moons.

"He's been getting pressure from downtown," Riley said, folding a paper airplane out of a departmental notice he'd fished from a wastebasket.

"Looks that way."

"Suddenly he wants to know why we don't have more results. Jesus, we've got Cain to admit she didn't tell Granger who she was till the night he died. She admits they were quarreling, but she won't say what it was about. And when I give her every opportunity to come clean about her husband's job, she doesn't. Maybe I should have come down on her harder, thrown the husband thing right at her. And bluffed it out about a witness, too."

"You have to play it the way you see it."

"Yeah." Riley sailed the paper plane at the window and missed.

"Hugh," Damon said suddenly, "did you always want to be on the force?"

"Sure. Well, since I was about eight, I guess."

"Would you ever give it up?"

"Quit, you mean? Do something else?"

He looked so bewildered that Damon laughed. "Never mind. Let's get back to work."

"Right. Let's find the missing husband. I'll see if his parents know anything new this week, which they won't. You going to keep on with that list of his friends?"

"I guess so. But first I think I'll look through the whole file again. See if we missed anything."

"Suit yourself." Riley moved to another desk.

Damon took out the file that contained reports on everything they had done so far and went back to the original interrogations: of Astrid, the cook, Lauren Granger. There was nothing that he hadn't already considered a dozen times. He took out the forensic report; for a moment there was a light prickling across the back of his neck, the kind that sometimes presaged a useful hunch. But the longer he looked, the more normal his neck began to feel.

After half an hour with the file, he put it away, reached for a list of names, and picked up the phone. He spoke to a young woman who said she was sure her husband hadn't seen David Chapin for at least two months, not since the night he and Astrid had gone to the theater with them, when David had been so quiet and Astrid had disliked the play so much, but then of course she had been an actress once, did Detective Damon know that?

He hung up, hesitated, and dialed a number that was not on the list. After a long wait she came to the phone.

"Paul!" There was such delight in her voice that he closed his eyes for a moment. "How are you? How is Sancho?"

"Fine. But I think he'd like to see you tonight. Would that be possible?"

There was a pause, then a whispered "Oh, yes."

It was impossible to hear what the senator was saying, apart from what she took to be something about "a great man" and to pertain to Martin, but Lauren nodded gravely while sipping her champagne punch.

Even in the crowded hotel ballroom, where an orchestra interspersed every third number with the Collins campaign song, "You Gotta Have Hart," and where all of Washington who wanted to have him was parading that desire, Lauren managed to stand out. She was wearing black—a long-sleeved, high-necked dress that had made her look as chaste as grief when Hart Collins introduced her from the dais; but when she mingled afterward, people behind her were conscious only of a long triangle of honey-colored flesh beneath the swept-up hair, for the dress had no back and sloped to a deep V four inches below her waist. More than once she had turned to face a pair of hungry eyes, as she had just done with the senator, and it had given her intense pleasure to watch the eyes perform the visual equivalent of a stammer and turn respectful. She felt, she realized suddenly, like the effect she had planned to create from the dais: serene and pure.

She disengaged herself from the senator's verbal grasp and slowly moved closer to the dance floor, where Collins was waltzing with his wife, Honeybud. Honeybud, she thought, would have trouble adjusting to life as the First Lady, since all she really cared about was raising horses; but Collins, they said, had the blend of ruthlessness and compassion that had often characterized successful presidents. Besides, his silver hair and matching voice and his Southern-aristocrat manners added a special meaning to his campaign speeches—particularly the one on "The New Equality."

That, Lauren thought, had been the greatest pleasure of all: to hear him say that the way to make the country's social programs really work was to create the right psychological climate, to offset Nature's discrimination by assuring that the disadvantaged would not feel their lack of natural gifts as a lack—and to accept the nods and grave smiles that were directed to her. Not to Martin, but to her.

She thought of his constant reminders that she really was incapable of understanding his work: "However, not to worry, my dear. No one expects wisdom from an ornament."

"But I gave up my own career in order to help you," she would remind him.

"Now, Lauren," he would say gently, "do you really think it could be called a career?"

That would drive her, sometimes, to ask why on earth he had married her. Because he had grown so indifferent to her so quickly, after that first year, when he proved to be so awkward and unsatisfying a lover that she hadn't known whether to laugh or to cry, and had sometimes done both. She had accepted the way he was; it was only another proof that his concerns were all of the mind and not of the body. At least, she thought, she had shown him—over and over, with more men than she could remember—that there was one place in the world where she was the expert, not he. But then why had he wanted her, if not for her skill in that one place? He would not answer that question, though, except to sigh heavily; and after a while she had stopped asking.

There had to be an afterlife, she thought; Martin had to be somewhere watching her, witnessing her revenge, seeing how easy it had been for her. So easy that it shouldn't have needed

Jake Waldo to start her in the right direction, to let her discover that she knew enough of the buzz words to hold her own in a conversation about Martin's theories. And now it was she who received the tributes paid to them, she who finally was recognized as somebody, not just *a* body.

She smiled and waved at Collins and Honeybud, who waltzed over. "Lauren," he said, "the evening won't be complete until I dance with you," and he swirled her onto the dance floor, flashbulbs popping and people clearing away because they danced so beautifully. And then she let Collins coax her to the bandstand to take the mike and sing a chorus of "You Gotta Have Hart," with everyone cheering and applauding when she finished, and telling her what a beautiful, really professional voice she had.

It was four o'clock before she finally got to her room, the evening wrapped around her like a cloak she did not want to take off. She did undress and get into bed, but sleep was impossible, so she took out the papers they had all picked up in the lobby and began to leaf through them, barely seeing the words.

It was in Rose Custer's column in the New York *Sentinel* that Martin's name seemed to reach up and grab her: Custer had just learned that his death was still being investigated by the police, with murder as a possibility, and as a suspect, *Blade* journalist Anne Cain—who had posed as his secretary for months and had come up with quite a story on him, revealed now for the first time. Among her charges were that a number of ISCEV people seemed to have been ruined after working with Granger; that the ISCEV atmosphere was one of a dictatorship, maintained by subtle but deadly means; and that, in general, the egalitarianism which Granger preached had dubious results in practice.

The pleasant sense of the evening fell away from Lauren as if it truly had been a cloak; in its place so many feelings closed around her that she took only the most easily identifiable of them, anger, which she directed toward her watch, because the hour was still too early for using the phone.

Jake Waldo read the story at seven-thirty, taking it in slowly, as he did his raw egg and wheat germ. With some effort, he kept his usually florid and amiable face from changing, but his large mouth settled more firmly around his prominent teeth. He put the *Sentinel* down and looked across the breakfast table at his son, who was staring out the window at a barge crawling up the East River far below. "Read this," he said.

Young Jake took it. His father watched for some play of emotion on the thin face, but when he saw something flicker in the large gray eyes, he could not decipher it. The boy finished and looked up, his features arranged into polite attentiveness. "Well?" Waldo said.

"Well what, sir?"

"What do you think? You know this Anne Cain, I suppose?"

"Yes. But we called her Astrid. She seemed very nice. I talked to her a couple of times."

"What about?"

"Oh, how I worked with the kids at the juvenile home, whether I liked it, what I did in my spare time. Things like that."

Waldo hesitated. "You don't see her as a possible murderess, then?"

The boy smiled faintly. "How does one tell?"

"What about these things she's supposed to have said about Granger?"

"You mean, do I think she's right?"

"Don't be foolish. Remember, I knew Granger. I mean, why would she say them?"

"I don't know. Why does anybody say anything?"

What was happening to the boy? Waldo wondered. What was draining him, making him into this pale, obedient creature who never laughed anymore? "Jake," he said suddenly, "I'm very proud of you. You know that, don't you?"

There was a pause. "Yes, I do, sir."

"Well, good. Look, this business in the paper; it could have an effect on the Collins campaign. So naturally I'm concerned. If you have any thoughts about it, I'd like to know them. All right?"

"Sure. But I have to go now. They've got a new art class ready for me at eight-thirty."

"Can you really teach those hoodlums anything?"

"How does one tell?" This time the boy did not smile. "Well, good-bye, sir."

Waldo sighed and drained his health drink. At least, he thought, the boy was doing something worthwhile instead of learning how dirty life could be in the business of politics. And banking.

The phone beside the breakfast table rang. "Jake Waldo speaking. Ah, Lauren, good morning. No, it's not so good, you're right." He listened for some moments. "No, let me do that. I'll find out what's happening with the police and the DA's office. You just concentrate on reassuring people down there." He paused. "There isn't anything to Cain's story, is there? Because if there is, I want to know right now." He listened, nodding. "Good. I knew there couldn't be."

Rose Custer sat in her usual booth at the bar on 40th Street, a favorite newspaper hangout. Many of her colleagues stopped by to exchange quips and gossip and to wonder, as they often did, how she had come by her latest scoop. As usual, she was not saying. Behind the dark glasses she always wore was one of the shrewdest minds in the business, and below them one of the most closed mouths.

She lit one cigarette from the butt of another, waved away a young City Hall reporter who was approaching like a shark, and smiled to herself. They would never know, she thought, that this one had fallen into her lap; let them think it was the Custer genius at work. Which in one sense it had been: Cain had been sitting right here in a back booth, looking like a crying jag waiting to happen, but it had taken a good eye to know it. And considerable skill to say the right things to keep the spigot open. Too bad, she thought, that she couldn't have cited Cain herself as the source of the story, but that would have been going too far. After all, Cain had made her swear that everything was off the record, just one colleague unloading on another.

She felt a tiny twinge from the conscience she thought of as a vestigial organ, and she snapped her fingers for more Dubonnet. The twinge went away. There was, after all, that night last summer when Cain had refused to come up to the apartment for a nice private dinner and whatever it might lead to, tightening her luscious little mouth as if she'd caught a bad smell. Maybe Cain thought she had forgotten, but she hadn't. Be nice to Rose Custer, she thought, if you want Rose Custer to be nice to you.

Still, there was no hope now of getting anything more on the story from Cain. She took a long draw on her cigarette and leaned back to mull over the problem, behind the double screen of glasses and smoke.

They were using the lieutenant's office. Damon walked past the closed door again, making at least his tenth trip up and down the hall. He was wearing cords and a light, shortsleeved shirt; the heat was so thick that the ceiling fans merely stirred it, but now he felt as if there were a chill in the place, and he wished he had a sweater.

The decision to ask her to come in for more questioning was as much the result of pressure from outside and above as of the need to confront her again. Since the Custer column had appeared three days earlier—for which Custer had of course refused to divulge her source—reporters had materialized like mosquitoes after a rain; the lieutenant was getting queries and demands from downtown, extra men had been assigned to the case, and the DA's office had asked to be briefed on developments to date. "My, my," Riley had grinned, "we seem to be raising Cain, don't we?"

He passed the door to the office again; she had been inside for twenty minutes now. Riley had laid out the basic plan for the questioning, and he had simply agreed: "I'll go in tough, go over the so-called accident again, and start on the Custer piece. Then suddenly she finds herself talking to you, and when she feels she's got a friendly ear, you bring up the husband. Then we wind up with our witness pitch. And we hope like hell."

The door opened suddenly. "OK, you take it for a while," Riley said. "She admits the Custer story is true, that she wanted to expose Granger as a bad guy. But it was all for purely professional reasons, in quotes. She's pretty uptight, so go in there and remind her that you're Mr. Nice Guy."

She was sitting facing the desk, so that Damon came in behind her. He walked over to the desk and looked down at her.

When she saw him, her eyes were all that moved; they grew slowly wider, as if she were trying to pull back to a perspective of distance.

"My usual opening is to say that I'm Detective Paul Damon and I'd like to ask some questions."

"You," she said faintly.

"Yes."

"But that—that isn't possible."

"It's happened."

She raised her hands as if in slow motion and then clasped them tightly. She wore a plain gold wedding band, Damon saw; and a flat necklace, also gold, was visible in the open neck of her beige shirt. Her hair was a bit shorter now, curving along her cheek and jaw like two smoky red half-moons, and there were clouds of shadows under her eyes. He put his hands on the back of the desk chair.

"Where is the other man who came with Riley last week? Detective Parsons?"

"He's here. But I'm Riley's regular partner. I've been investigating Granger's death for the past month."

She turned to look at the door, picked up her bag and put it back on the floor, smoothed her skirt under her legs. "So you didn't stay a patrolman. Should I congratulate you?"

"If you like." The wood of the chair pressed against his fingers. He took them away. "More to the point, I should congratulate you. I see you're doing well in the newspaper business, and you're married now."

"Why won't they believe me?" she asked abruptly. "I've told them over and over how he died, but they don't believe me."

"Hugh Riley is a suspicious man." He sat down, took some notes from his pocket, and laid them on the desk. "And to be fair, you have not explained a number of things about your relationship with Granger. If you would, maybe I could help."

"You," she said again, softly.

When he realized he had been looking at her without speaking, he said, "What was Granger's reaction when you finally told him you were a reporter?"

She turned away. "Rage. He was very good at rage."

"Wouldn't you have expected him to be angry?"

"Yes, of course."

"Why did you tell him that particular night?"

"Because . . . May I smoke?" When he nodded, she pulled a cigarette from her purse and inhaled deeply as she lit it. "Because it was time for him to know. My work—my story—was finished."

"What made you angry that night?"

"I didn't like him, and I'd had to spend six months as his dutiful secretary. It was a pleasure to finally let out what I thought of him."

"Is that what started the quarreling?" She didn't answer. "Did you tell him you had written an exposé of him?"

"I've admitted we had a fight, but I don't think I have to tell you or anyone else what it was about."

She looked at him defiantly, her face slightly flushed. For the next ten minutes he tried to get her to explain the quarrel, but she would not. "Just write down that I hated him," she said finally. "Isn't that what you want to hear?"

"I want to hear the truth."

"You have. I did hate him."

"Why?"

She looked away; the light struck her face so that he could see tiny beads on her upper lip. "I had reasons."

"You must know you're not helping yourself at all. If you had some private grudge that has no bearing, why don't you tell us so we can clear it out of the way?" She didn't answer. "Have you consulted a lawyer?"

"Why? I'm innocent."

"You can't possibly be that naive."

She turned back to him. "Perhaps I'm learning not to be."

"When you were working at Granger's one night last winter, you stayed to dinner. The subject of Michelangelo came up. Why?"

She looked startled. "It was a . . . theoretical discussion, about Granger's views of the genius."

"Which are?"

"You must know them. That the genius owes something to the nongeniuses of the world."

He waited for a few moments. "You told Detective Riley that your husband used to be with Westchester University."

"Yes. He lectured and did research in neurophysiology."

"Where does he work now?"

Her chin lifted. "He doesn't need to work. Surely you've learned that he's the only son of Chapin Pharmaceuticals."

"You didn't answer the question."

"Didn't I?" She reached into her bag for a tissue. Her mouth, the upper lip sloping down in a finely drawn, delicate line, trembled while she took a deep breath. "You know, don't you? You know that he was with the Institute."

"Why didn't you tell us?" She began to fold the tissue down into smaller and smaller squares. "When did you tell Granger that you were David Chapin's wife?"

"That same night."

"Why not before?"

"For the same reason I couldn't tell him I was a reporter. How could I get the job? And the story?"

"Was it because of your husband that you hated Granger?"

"Partly."

"Could you explain that?"

"Yes. But I won't."

"You must know how bad such a refusal looks."

"I can't help that." She locked her arms across her chest.

"Are you cold?"

"A little."

"When is the last time you heard from your husband?"

She hesitated. "The night Granger died."

"Why isn't he with you, to help you through all this?"

"I . . . don't know."

"Did he know that you hated Granger?"

"Yes."

"Did he know of the story you were planning?"

"No."

"But he knew you were working for Granger?"

"Yes. I wouldn't do it without his knowing."

"Would you say your marriage is a happy one?"

"Yes. Why do you ask about my private life?"

"Because I think it bears on what happened the night Granger died." He paused. "Did you kill him?"

"No. Do you think I did? That I could have?" She leaned forward, her eyes no longer hazel but almost green. "Do you really think I could kill a man? Do you, Damon?"

Damn her, he thought. Damn her for looking and sounding the same.

"You don't think so. I can see it in your eyes."

"Then why won't you explain your actions? Why won't you give me something to go on, so I can stop this investigation? Why won't you tell me what I need to know in order to help you?"

But for ten minutes more she refused, saying, "I don't know" and "I can't tell you," lighting cigarettes and then stubbing them out half-smoked, shifting on the seat of the hard, high-backed chair. Finally, abruptly, he went out, leaving her alone for a while and then returning with Riley, who took the chair behind the desk.

As soon as she saw Riley, she jumped up. "Look, I talked to you when you came to my apartment. I came down here when you requested it. I've tried to cooperate, but I'm getting tired of it all. What right do you have to keep after me? I haven't done anything except go after a story. I've told you everything relevant to Granger's death, and the rest is my business."

"OK, Astrid," Riley said blandly.

"I don't remember asking you to call me that."

"We like to be friendly. Besides, Anne Astrid Cain Chapin is quite a handful of a name. And you don't want everybody to know all of it, do you? You like to parcel it out, so people can't tell whether you're a reporter or a secretary or the wife of an Institute fellow, or what."

"May I go now?"

"Sure. Oh, wait, just one more thing. What would you say if I told you we had a witness to your quarrel with Granger? Someone who heard the whole thing?"

"Heard?" she said quickly. Her hand gripped the gold chain at her neck. "I don't think I'd believe you."

"Really? Two people shouting at each other on a balcony on a hot night? And one of them saying something about finding ways to silence the other? You don't think anybody heard that?"

She turned to Damon; despite himself, he felt his hands clench.

Riley went on. "You didn't say those words to Granger?"

"I may have. I don't remember exactly. What difference does it make? I've told you how he died."

"Supposing we have a witness with a different version?"

"I think you're bluffing. If you have a witness, why don't you charge me with murder?"

"Is that what a witness would have seen?"

The gold chain suddenly slipped from around her neck and dangled from her hand in two pieces. She reached down for her purse and shoved them inside. "You said I could go."

"Sure. But let us know if you plan to leave the city or change your address."

For several moments after she left, Damon stared at the door, still seeing the thin shoulders held forcibly straight and the long fingers fastened whitely on her purse.

"She did it, goddammit, I know she did!"

In his mind he heard denials of Riley's words, and he tried to ignore all of them, Riley's words and his own.

But he stayed very late that night, taking out the file on the case, going back again and again to the beginning and working his way through.

She reached her apartment in Gracie Terrace and put her key in the lock shortly after eight. The slight effort of turning the metal seemed to take the last energy she had, and after she had stepped inside and called, "David?" and heard, as usual, nothing but silence, she leaned back against the door for a long time.

A crowd of reporters had been waiting for her outside the stationhouse, to question her with the strange mixture of tolerance and contempt the press reserved for one of its own in trouble. She had fenced as well as she could, refusing explicit comment on what had happened upstairs but leaving room for them to reach some conclusions, threading her way through the mental minefield of what could and couldn't be admitted.

She forced herself to move, through the foyer and the living room, past the study, where David's chair yawned, to the bedroom. She sank on the edge of the bed, kicked off her shoes, turned on the phone answering device, and listened, stretching her toes in the thick blue carpet, to requests to call two reporters she had never heard of and also Hal Ruby. Would he fire her, she wondered, or would he find it more politic to let her hang herself?

She reset the phone device to "On" and turned on the radio. After a moment she identified the music: Schubert. The "Death and the Maiden" quartet. If she were not so tired, she thought, she would find that ironic. Or ominous.

She reached into the nightstand drawer to take out a letter. It was postmarked the day after Granger's death, from somewhere in the city. She read it over for the hundredth time:

> Dear A, I've heard on TV that he's dead. You must know what I feel. I can only hope that you didn't do what you went there for. Forgive me for letting you come home to an empty place and for making you wonder where I am. I've decided to go away for a while, to be with nobody but myself—where or how long, I don't know. But I have to. Take care, water the ferns, and don't worry about me. XXX David

The words gave her no more assurance than they ever had; they simply stared back at her, as blankly as David himself could sometimes do. She put the letter down and curled up on the bed, burying her face in the spread.

As if it had been waiting for this moment, the thought of Damon leaped at her. She shivered, as cold again as she had been when she saw him—his face a careful mask, his eyes like caves where things were hidden. Should she believe what had flickered in them—or accept the mask of his face?

The first time she had seen him, she thought, when she had run to thank him for defending her against the hecklers, she had had the impression that his face was scarred in some way; but when they had gone to a bar near the campus to talk and she could study him in the dim light, she had seen that his face was not scarred, only carefully guarded. It was almost ugly, she had thought: the nose too large, the dark hair too straight; but she had liked to watch it, as he listened to her talk about the theater.

She did not know why she had thought he would care to hear, but she had. She had told him a great deal, even about reading a book on Sarah Bernhardt when she was a child, of being fascinated by an actress who was flamboyantly larger than life, both on stage and off, and whose private motto was *"Quand même"*—"In spite of everything." She had told him about discovering, in college, that the grandeur and excitement and romanticism of Bernhardt and her time were regarded by her teachers and classmates as melodramatic and shallow; and that since coming to New York to seek a career in acting, she had become even more certain that she was a spiritually displaced person, with her heart in Bernhardt's century while the rest of her existed in a theatrical time that revered plays about people trapped in ashcans.

"But you keep on?" he had asked. *"Quand même?"*

Then she had made him talk about himself; he told her he was finishing his second year of law school and began to describe the classes and the varying skills of the faculty and to explain the career options that were open to him.

"You talk about it rather impersonally," she had said. "Is that because it means so little to you—or so much?"

Later, months later, he had said to her, "You ask questions as if people's emotions could just be opened for inspection like parcels." But that night his answer had been merely, "I admire what the law stands for. And right now the law says it's closing time. Let's go."

As they walked up the street, he asked her why she had come to the rally. "You must know it's a lost cause. We can argue that letting a white instructor go in order to meet minority hiring guidelines is racial discrimination, but the administration has the federal government behind it. That teacher won't be reinstated."

"Say that I did it for my own sake, then, so I'd know I had tried."

"But if you know you can't win, what do you achieve?"

"Then why did you stand up to defend me?"

She had seen the reason in his eyes for a moment, but he

merely said, "It's very late. Let me put you in a cab."

For two weeks she had not seen or heard from him; finally she had gone to the luncheonette he had casually mentioned to her, in a semidecayed block on Broadway in the Nineties.

The grizzled man who was alone behind the counter had the same face as Damon, but his was less guarded. "A friend of Paul's?" he said eagerly, and within ten minutes he was telling her about Damon—about sending him and his brother to live with their aunt in New Jersey after his wife had been killed in a holdup of the liquor store they used to own, and about Damon's anger when the two killers were out on parole three years later.

He had pressed her to try an eclair and a cinnamon bun, at least—"I switched to this after my wife was killed. Who would think to rob a doughnut and muffin shop? Besides, I love to bake"—and for a moment some quality in him had reminded her of her own father, in the good years, before he retired. Then he told her how, when the boys came back to the city to live, they had agreed to finance each other's educations. "They were very close, my boys. A wonderful thing, for them and for me."

"Are they still close?" she had asked, unprepared for the heavy sigh that answered her.

"No, they're not," the old man said finally. "To tell you the truth, because you're a friend of Paul's, they don't speak anymore. Not since Sam was in college. I don't blame Paul, you understand, not a bit. He worked so hard to put Sam through school, and then Sam, before he even finished . . . Well, don't they say it's the really smart ones who can go the furthest off the track? And Sam was brilliant, you know. A really fine, brilliant boy."

"What the hell are you doing, Dad?" an angry voice had said, and she had turned to see Damon standing behind her.

He had barely listened to his father's reply, telling her they were leaving, guiding her out the door and heading up Broadway, gripping her wrists as if he were using handcuffs. "Why were you quizzing my father?"

"I wanted to know about you."

"Why?"

She did not answer. "Where are we going?"

"To satisfy your curiosity."

He lived in a brownstone near Columbia, in a fourth-floor walkup. As soon as the door was opened, a large white mongrel dog flung itself at them. "Hey, Cyrano, hey, take it easy, boy," he said.

The room was sparsely furnished except for books. On the wall above his desk were tacked some snapshots of the dog and a reprint of the Constitution.

"Well?" he said. "Let's hear your instant analysis of the owner, based on his possessions."

She did not answer. The dog padded over to her and stood on its hind legs, pawing at her thighs. She noticed that it walked unevenly and that one leg was short. "Is he named Cyrano because of the play?"

Damon called the dog to him and knelt to scratch its muzzle. "Would it matter?"

"Yes, it would. If you were one of those people who think *Cyrano de Bergerac* is just a lot of romantic nonsense . . ."

"Then what?"

"I don't think you are."

He looked away from her, smoothing his hands along the dog's back. "He lives up to his name more than most people could. For one thing, he's not a whiner. I found him in an alley, where some bastard had beaten him two thirds of the way to death and then left him to face it alone. But you weren't even howling, were you, boy?—just dragging yourself along, looking for a place to lick your wounds and come back to life again." He paused and looked up at her. "But you didn't come here to discuss Cyrano, did you? Or to discuss anything at all."

"Not if you don't want to."

"Oh, but it's a question of what *you* want. Would you like to see the rest of the place? I have a bedroom furnished in early thrift shop. Isn't that what you want—to see the bedroom?"

"If you like."

He stood up, took her hand, and pulled her to a room where the twilight threw a pale wash of blue on the white brick walls.

She had stood by the bed while he stayed at the dresser, staring at her, running one hand along the edge of the wood. She knew he was goading her, daring her to say something to soften the deliberate crudeness of his action.

The light in the room had begun to go, draining away his expression, leaving only the shadowy monolith of his body, from which she caught a faint scent of lemon and sandalwood. She thought she would rather die than move or say a word. Finally he said, tauntingly, "Tell me what it was that you wanted," and against her will she had had to whisper, "You."

She had felt his hands pushing back through her hair till it hurt and his mouth opening on hers. When they were on the bed and he was poised above her, she dug her hands into the thatch of his hair and pulled his lips away from her flesh. "If I left now, this moment, would you come after me?"

"No," he had said, shaking his head free. "But you're not leaving." His lips had touched her breast, then his teeth had sunk deep, pinning her beneath him.

She sat up sharply on the edge of the bed she shared with David.

How hard Damon had struggled, she thought, not to accept the bondage of flesh that existed between them. "Why can't I stay away from you?" he had said, almost angrily, many times, before he'd finally given in and she had moved into the apartment.

Could one ever break that bondage? she wondered. Was the memory still in him, buried? And if so, how deeply?

There could be no more sessions like this afternoon's, she thought, when she had hardly known what answers she was giving him. It was only by grace of her years on the stage that she had kept from saying something that would give her away.

She shivered slightly. Damon, she thought, would have to be used.

Chapter Five

Dr. Harvey Baxter of Westchester University took a seat on a bench, with the self-consciousness of one who was about to betray a conviction. He had decided it was only right to do so in person, not on the phone; he looked about the stationhouse with curiosity.

Mentally he had always pictured police premises as something drawn by Hieronymus Bosch, places where the wretched were abused by the ignorant, and it was disconcerting to find them so colorless and himself sitting down as if he were waiting for nothing more than a driver's test. The men who moved in and out were rather ordinary, a little earnest-looking, perhaps, and tending to overweight, but that was all. Finally someone appeared who seemed more suitable—a tall, square-shouldered man whose face could have come from a darker, cruder time—and Baxter was oddly satisfied when the man introduced himself as Detective Paul Damon, to whom he had spoken on the phone.

They went upstairs, to a corner desk in a busy room. "All this business in the paper," Baxter said. "There's no question of its being true? Astrid really did dislike Granger?"

"If you saw yesterday's papers, you know she made that clear to the press."

"Yes, of course. Well, there is something I didn't tell you when you called me last week. Something that might be a motive for . . . well, a motive. David is very wealthy, I suppose you know that?"

"Yes."

"How wealthy, he's never said. He never had much use for money. But he told me that now he had found one. He was going to give most of his money, his shares in Chapin Pharmaceuticals, to Martin Granger."

He waited, half expecting some reverberation in the room now that he had actually given this information to the police, but nothing happened. The detective's expression did not even change, although the two lines around his mouth grew deeper.

"When did Dr. Chapin tell you that?"

"Well, that's the odd thing. The day that Martin Granger was . . . the day he died."

"Had Dr. Chapin told his wife, do you know?"

"He said he was going to tell her that very night."

The detective moved abruptly, but it was only to reach into a drawer for another pencil.

Now that it was out, Baxter found, it was easy to answer questions, to say that for some months David had seemed to be going through a strange time, and that although the marriage seemed to be a good one, David had given the impression—nothing very explicit—that things had been less happy in the past year.

Finally the detective was finished. "We're very grateful to you, Dr. Baxter. What made you change your mind and come forward with this information?"

"Well, of course, I admired Martin Granger. If there's any chance that she . . . that he didn't die by accident, then something has to be done." He shifted in his chair, deciding not to tell the man that what had changed his mind was the phone call from Astrid, the seemingly casual call in which she had asked him not to tell anyone what he knew about the money.

"So, what is this new development?" said Lieutenant Klugman, looking up from a stack of papers.

"A motive," Riley said. "Good old-fashioned money, what else?" He filled in Klugman, concluding with the confirmation they had just received from the treasurer at the Martin Granger Institute. The grin he had been suppressing took over his face.

Klugman smiled back. "Nice work, you two. This is going to make the DA's office happy."

"They want to shut her up, don't they?" Damon said.

"What do you think? There's Hart Collins, head of the DA's own party, out telling America to vote for him because he can make welfare programs work better by applying Granger's ideas—and there's Astrid Cain, shooting off her mouth to the press that Granger is definitely not one of the good guys. So all the money boys in the party, from Jake Waldo on down, want the DA to shut her up. But he can't do it without a decent case."

"And we're going to give it to them," Riley said. He put his arm around Damon's shoulders as they left Klugman's office. "Hey, you want to go for a beer?"

"No thanks, Hugh. I think I'll stick around for a while."

"Don't tell me you're going to go through that damn file again."

"I might."

"What the hell for?"

"Oh . . . call it a desire for overwork." Or, he thought, a feeling he had not been able to ignore since he had seen her again: a feeling there had to be something to show she might be innocent.

Sancho was sleeping on an old blanket under the chair, making little contented sounds. Damon sat by the window, looking out at the dark shapes of warehouses and the lights of the New Jersey skyline beyond the river, like vertical fireworks. On the windowsill a beer was starting to lose its foam.

He had been home for only ten minutes; the evening had suddenly filled with the murder of another junkie whore, like the one who had been killed the day he came back from vacation.

Whores, he thought, sipping the beer, were the most romanticized creatures on earth. Maybe in the nineteenth century, when the "heart of gold" myth had started in fiction, there had been an excuse: So many doors were still closed to women, even sensitive, intelligent women, that selling their bodies could have been a legitimate necessity. Not that today's whores were all stupid—some of those he'd hauled in regularly when he was with Vice had a ready wit as sharp as claws—but most of them had nothing in their hearts except a bitter mixture of loathing and insecurity, in which one could no longer tell the cause from the effect and for which the usual antidote was drugs.

Dealing with them was the one aspect of police work to which he had not become fully inured, even after all these years. After a while any cop gave up wondering about the deepest reasons human beings did what they did; but he had never quite accepted that there were women who could make the choice to become whores. Stupid, he thought, but there it was.

He sighed, admitting that he was giving himself a disquisition on the world's oldest profession so he would not have to think about the other things that could be done for money. Like murder.

If only, he thought, he had been able to reach Granger's personal physician. The idea had come to him after lunch, out of the blue, when he was working on something else: Suddenly all his past brooding over the file had jelled into the realization that nobody had checked with Granger's own doctor. Suppose there were something in the man's medical history to account for what had happened, to show that she hadn't . . . But he had been unable to reach the doctor, and then the murdered whore had intervened. Maybe tomorrow . . .

Sancho gave a sleepy little snort. Damon smiled wryly. That's right, boy, he thought; it's never smart to get your hopes up too high.

Out of nowhere, just as his idea had come this afternoon, he saw himself sitting in an eighth-grade classroom, hands moist and hope rising at the thought of giving the oral report and sharing one of his Books with his fellow students. He had always thought of them, he realized, as if they were spelled with a capital B. His Books.

He had begun to find them after he and Sam were sent to live with their Aunt Loretta—after their mother died, in a way so senseless, and so cruelly unavenged, that he had not been able to put its memory to rest, even in those peaceful new surroundings. At first Loretta had been concerned, her voice sugared in sympathy; but gradually it had acquired the vinegar of disapproval. The phrase that seemed to be always on her lips was "a normal boy"; he heard daily of this desirable creature, who apparently was moved only by church, school, and sports, in that order, and then only to states of cheerful obedience. He had accepted that he was not such a boy; he had felt that he did not particularly want to be. The things that seemed to be evidence of his difference were better experienced alone, he discovered, whether it was something as heavy and painful as what he felt about his mother's death or something as dizzyingly pleasurable as the state that certain kinds of books induced in him.

They were, usually, works of history and biography. The story of Christ's sacrifice, which Loretta urged on him, moved him hardly at all; what did was a story like that of the Curies, whose perseverance had finally reduced eight tons of pitchblende to one gram of radium salts. He had haunted the local library, looking for more such stories: of the building of the Panama Canal, of Pasteur's battle against anthrax, of Lewis and Clark's expeditions—of anything that told of a stubborn belief, held in defiance of Nature's odds or other men's views, which was finally brought into actuality.

For the book report in the eighth grade, he decided to tell the story of Walter Reed and his men, of how they had tried everything in order to isolate the cause of yellow fever, suffering in the tropical heat and the primitive conditions—some of them even dying—until finally they'd established that the deadly carrier was the Anopheles mosquito. As he told the story, he could hear his own voice rising in excitement. But when he finished, there was no particular response, just the same restless inattention with which his classmates greeted so many things. He had wanted to cry; instead he told himself that it would be foolish to discuss his Books with anyone again.

Except, of course, with Sam, because Sam felt things that were different, yet somehow the same. His passion was chemistry, and Damon, uninterested in the actual experiments Sam was plotting, could look at him and know that the gleeful intensity of his expression came from something deeper than chemistry, something the two of them shared.

But Sam let others see it.

He and Damon set up a primitive lab in an abandoned

icehouse, scrounging all over town for equipment, laughing over the excuses they made up to wheedle money out of Loretta. When the lab had been in secret operation for a month, the owner of the icehouse died; his widow unlocked the door a week later and exploded with rage.

She charged to her good friend Loretta that her husband would never have given permission for the building's use, as Sam claimed; and Loretta agreed, sending all the lab equipment off to the town dump, suspending the boys' allowances, and ordering them to Bible study class twice a week.

If only, Damon had thought, Sam would not beg and cry so hard for the lab, the nakedness of his feeling making his voice almost unrecognizable. He told Sam, "You've got to be like the Invisible Man," in the book they had just read. "Don't let them know anything about you. Don't let them see what you want, or they'll find some reason you shouldn't have it."

Sam would not listen. He had had a streak of recklessness in him even then. He told everyone, including one of his teachers, Roy Vance, the newcomer who taught algebra. And Vance, to Damon's surprise, called Loretta to request a meeting of all parties concerned. She agreed—but only, Damon had thought, because she was certain she was right.

They all met in the algebra room after school. Vance got Loretta and the widow to agree that the crux of the matter was whether or not Sam could have been *given* the key and the permission to use it, as he said. Then Vance asked question after question, in a polite, dry voice, writing down the answers on the blackboard under headings like "Proven," "Possible," and "Not Known." After half an hour he laid down the chalk and said quietly, "We've established that the key was kept in different places, including on the owner's person, and that his widow cannot say whether or not he was carrying the key at the time Sam alleges it was given to him. So, there is a reasonable doubt that Sam is lying. And since in justice a person is innocent until and unless we can *prove* him guilty, shall we agree that Sam is innocent?"

Damon saw the two women swallow their anger, like two indigestible apples, and consent. And that was the miracle to him—not the restitution of his and Sam's allowances nor the tight-lipped forgiveness that was a substitute for apology, but the fact that the anger had had to bend before Vance's calm elucidation of the facts.

Two days later he told Sam he knew what career he wanted. He had felt, he remembered, as if Vance were a lifesaving drug. After school, over milk and cookies, he would sit in Vance's tiny apartment, drinking in a new world: listening to Beethoven or Brahms or to Vance's reading from Shakespeare, Hugo, and Rostand; looking through Vance's library; or discussing the ways in which he should go about preparing to become a lawyer.

When he was fourteen, he was called into the principal's office and asked a series of careful questions about his relationship with Vance. He knew what was at stake without being told, and he struggled to be calm and logical so that he could make the officials understand the truth: "We listen to music and talk about things. We're just friends. All we do is talk." But the importance of it kept rising in his stomach and clogging in his throat, and to his fury, he wound up crying that he loved Vance and would kill anyone who hurt him. Two weeks later Vance was dismissed and left town, to a tidal wave of whispers that he was homosexual.

For weeks Damon choked on the knowledge that his losing control, showing how much he cared, had probably helped to destroy his friend. Even learning that Loretta had been behind Vance's dismissal did not help; he had a searing, shouting fight with her that had no result except to underscore the futility of showing what one felt.

Much later, when he was driving a cab in New York to help put Sam through school, Damon had picked up two men one night, and in the sagging face and dead eyes of the one who was clearly the prostitute of the pair, he had recognized Roy Vance.

"Did you identify yourself to him?" Astrid had asked when he told her about it, and he had tried to explain why he couldn't.

"I didn't want to embarrass him, you see. No, that's not fair; there was more to it than that. Here was this piece of human wreckage, but he had been different once. I had learned about justice from him, and then I couldn't use any of it to help him. I was so goddamn helpless. . . ." He had felt himself starting to cry, for the first time since he was fourteen. Cyrano had begun to whimper, and that, ludicrously, had only intensified the crying; but Astrid had helped, just by holding him, just by existing.

Later that night he found he was able, for the first time, to talk to her about what the law meant to him. "Vance read me something from Aristotle once, and it was as if everything I'd been trying to explain and understand was in that one line."

"What was it?"

"'The law is reason free from passion.' From all of the feelings that can make people weak or vicious or just plain dumb. It's above all that, something bigger than those who have created it. They can weep or whine or try to kick their way out, but the law is . . . impervious. To everything but the idea that men should have honor and should deal fairly with one another."

"You're saying it's better than life," she said slowly.

"Yes."

"And I say the theater is larger than life, or should be. Are we both saying, then, that there's something wrong with life?"

"I don't think so. Only with the way so many people live it."

"Maybe they don't have something in them that lets them

feel the way you do about the law, and I about the theater. Some capacity is missing."

"Or else we've got something that isn't normal."

"Or else it's just a difference, nothing more. There are two kinds of beings within the human race, and whichever kind one is, that's it. And you and I are of the same kind."

Maybe then we were, Damon thought. But now? The law student and the actress, who had become a cop and a . . . a what?

He finished the beer and stood up. Tomorrow, he thought, he would try Granger's doctor the very first thing. He checked his watch: after midnight. He decided to shower and go to bed.

Sancho came awake with a growl and trotted out from under the chair, ears cocked. It was a sign, Damon knew, that the ancient elevator was groaning its way up. In a moment he heard it, too, stopping opposite the door.

She had not called to say she was coming, he thought; in fact he had not talked to her for a week. He realized he did not want to answer the knock. You bastard, he thought, and went to the door. "Marie?"

There was a pause. "No."

He had no awareness of undoing the locks or opening the door, only of seeing her there, her face looking drawn in the hall light. "You," he said finally.

She gave a pale half-smile. "I have to talk to you, Damon. May I come in?"

Everything he knew told him to refuse. "All right," he said.

When he turned from rebolting the door, she was standing in the middle of the room with Sancho circling around her. "I didn't think you'd ever get another dog," she said.

"Someone gave him to me."

"Ah."

She bent over to scratch the dog's ears, and suddenly he was seeing her with Cyrano, sitting on the floor to brush the dog's coat, wearing his navy robe and listening to his halting explanation of how things had seemed different for him, more peaceful, since she had moved into the apartment—how the day by day occurrences at law school seemed to have lost their power of control over his mood. "I'll tell you what I think, Damon," she had said. "I think what you are is happy." She had reached up to touch his face. "Do you know that you look a little incredulous, and also a little embarrassed?"

That was the difference between them, he had thought: She was happy as openly and trustingly as an animal, which could not question its feelings but took them as an axiom, almost as a right.

"You think I'm naive and innocent, don't you?" she had said. "That I'm like Cyrano, only I should know better?"

It was one of the first times he had heard his own thoughts coming from her lips. "I suppose I do."

She had bent over the dog and whispered, "Tell him he's a twentieth-century cynic, and we sentence him to six months of dog biscuits."

Cyrano had stood up and begun to bark at him; Astrid had folded over with laughter; and he had joined in, wrapping an arm around each of them until the three of them sprawled on the floor in a tangle of limbs and laughter.

"What breed is he?" she asked, and he saw that she was not laughing and that it was Sancho she was asking about.

"New York streets."

She stood up and looked around the room, at the wall of books and records, the gleaming woods of the table and floor. "Don't you keep the Constitution on the wall anymore?"

"No."

"Who is Marie?"

"She's . . . the friend who gave me the dog. What is it you want, Astrid?"

"Give me a minute, Damon, please." She untied a sweater

from her shoulders and laid it on a chair. She wore a gauzy blouse and skirt of a pale, smoky blue. Everything about her seemed muted and soft, except for her voice, which had ragged edges. "How is your father?"

"Fine."

"And Sam is still. . . ?"

"The same. No, actually he's worse."

"When I worked for the upstate newspaper chain, before I went with the *Blade,* I did a story on a place that has a good record with addicts."

"Sam is beyond anyone's power to reach him."

She moved across the room, her walk both aimless and strained. "I suppose you see a lot of people like him in your job."

"Yes."

"That must be hard."

"I don't think about it."

"Ah. I should have known that, shouldn't I? Tell me, do you like being a detective?"

"Yes. It means I ask the questions. What do you want, Astrid?"

"I want . . . something to drink. May I?"

"What would you like?"

"Chablis, please. You see, I haven't changed."

"Oh?" He picked up Sancho and took him to the kitchen, closing the door.

"Aren't you having anything?" she asked when he came back with a glass for her.

"I never drink on duty."

"Damon, please. Don't. Can't you talk to me as if we were still . . . friends?"

"All right."

"Thank you." She took a swallow of the wine. She was close

enough for him to catch her scent, and he moved away. "You said you would try to help me."

"I think what would help you most would be to tell the truth."

She laughed, rolling the wineglass between her palms, and perched on the edge of the rosewood table. "The truth could never hurt, then?" He did not answer. "What if the truth is something that could make a bad situation worse?"

"It should come out, no matter what."

"Really? I can remember a certain incident whose truth you wished had never come out."

"What was that?" he asked, genuinely puzzled.

"Why, your high school teacher. What was his name—Roy Vance—the one who inspired you to become a lawyer and then was run out of town. Don't you remember telling me about it?"

She was not a mind-reader, he told himself. She had simply known him well. A long time ago. "Why do you bring that up?" he asked.

"I don't know." She laughed again. "Probably because I'm nervous. I came to talk to you, and you stand there like a statue of Justice with your eyes blindfolded. And yes, I remember that story, too—what Justice is blindfolded to is people's feelings, all their craziness, so that none of it can stand in the way of truth. Isn't that the way Vance explained it to you?"

"What are you suggesting?" he asked. "That I should not be concerned about the truth of Granger's death?"

"No." She was moving her wineglass in circles on the table, not looking up. "I'm suggesting you should also be concerned about me."

He tried to see past the wings of hair that shadowed her face. "What does that mean?"

"Are you going to let them keep after me this way? Or are you going to stop them?"

"I'm doing what I can." He hesitated, then said, "Do you know whether Granger took any kind of medication?"

She looked up. "No, I don't. Why?"

"I wondered if he had any kind of medical problems. Anything that would— Never mind."

"You mean something that would have a bearing on the way he died?"

"I said never mind."

"But I have to know! Are you looking for something that could help me? Are you trying to get me off?"

"We're conducting an investigation. If there's anything that would support your account of the way he died, we'll find it."

"'We'?" she said sharply. "Or just you?"

He didn't answer.

"You're the one who'd like to clear me, aren't you?"

He still said nothing.

She finished her wine and put the glass down slowly, as if more than the wine were finished. Then she stood up, with an oddly bright smile. "I came to see if you were open to the possibility of calling off the investigation. And it seems you are."

"Don't put words in my mouth."

"But you could do it, couldn't you? Couldn't you?"

"Maybe."

"You could say that on the basis of how well you knew me, I couldn't possibly have killed anyone."

"No," he said.

She came around the table to stand in front of him. "And you did know me well," she said softly. "Very well. If you helped me, I could . . ." She leaned up, hands at her sides, and moved her lips from one corner of his mouth to the other.

He stepped back. "I don't want to misunderstand this. Are you offering to pay me if I help you?"

She closed her eyes. "Yes."

"That would be corruption of a police officer."

"How could it be if I'm innocent?"

He squared his shoulders. "Please leave. Now."

She did not move, except to open her eyes. "Do you want me to swear to you that I didn't kill Martin Granger? That's easy. I'll take an oath." She reached for his right hand and brought it up to hold it on the soft cloth over her left breast. "I do solemnly swear," she said, holding his hand with both her own, "that I did not kill Martin Granger. Do you feel better now?"

He thought that he would despise himself if he did not take his hand away; slowly his fingers slid over and down the slope of her breast. She shivered. "I want you to go," he said.

"No, you don't," she whispered. "You never did."

He could not look at her face, at her eyes. He followed the line of flesh that narrowed from her throat to disappear in the smoky blue cloth, and he clenched his hands, now at his sides, to ward off the remembered sensation of her skin, to paralyze the nerves that once had been encoded with the sight and scent and touch of her and were now responding again, blindly.

It was they, not he, who reached to push the blouse from her shoulders, who saw her hands lift to help and then to slip away everything else, so that finally, at last, her long, slender body came fully into his vision. One of his hands moved to her hip, his thumb running along the slant of the bone as if he were using his mouth.

"Oh, God," she said. "I can't . . . Damon . . ."

"You're not leaving," he said, remembering that he had used those words to her the very first time; then everything seemed to be as it always had been, and he pulled her against him to blot out that thought, and all others; to let himself, for once, surrender completely to feeling with no thought of the consequences; to rediscover every narcotic angle and curve of her body and every sure touch of her hands and mouth, growing more insistent; to know that the blood beating in his veins was sounding just as violently in hers, and in the same rhythm; and, when his body was inside hers, controlling the sounds that came from both their throats, to let himself feel nothing but the sweet torment of muscles and, finally, the long wave of its release.

After a long while he put out one hand to touch her again, just to feel that she was there, and would be there in the morning, smiling, telling him to get up or he would be late for Con Law and he wouldn't want to miss the lecture. . . .

His hand touched a bare floor. He opened his eyes. The scratching pressure beneath him was the straw rug. A light was shining to the left of his eyes, and there were some soft sounds he could not identify. He lifted his arm and looked at his watch, with the strange sensation that he was checking the year, not the hour. He saw the separate hairs on his wrist and the thin line of an old knife wound, earned in his patrolman days.

He sat up. The soft sounds had been the whispering of her clothes; she was smoothing the blouse into her skirt and slipping on her shoes. She looked up and saw that he was watching her. Her shoulders rose and then fell in an abortive movement, as if the air were pinning her back. "Damon, this wasn't—"

"Don't say anything."

She picked up her purse. At the door she fumbled with the locks and then paused without turning around.

"I said don't."

She nodded. Then she was gone.

He was suddenly cold, not from his nakedness but from the

knowledge of what he had been feeling while she was with him, and of the terrible ease with which it had all returned.

He got to his feet, took his clothes, and went down the hall to the shower. But the plumbing in the building was old, and he could not get the spray as strong as he wanted—strong enough to deaden.

He had built such a careful edifice of his life, he thought, using the police force in a way that was probably not the best motive for an officer; but he had given good service for what he had taken. Until she came back into his life and made cracks in the structure. And then tore it down completely.

He looked down at his body, which had behaved as if the last eight years had never taken place. He grabbed the coarse sponge as if it were a scourge and began to rub at his skin.

Why did she do this to me? he thought. Why did she come to stir up the past? Maybe, he thought, she was simply getting panicked and desperate, as Riley contended. Maybe she had come for his help, not really thinking it out, and then when they were together, alone, she had been unable to hide what she felt. . . .

Jesus! he thought, lifting his face as if to drown in the spray; do you still believe in Santa Claus, too? Think like a cop, he told himself. Remember she's the suspect in a homicide.

Why had she come? When there was no need, when he had already been trying to do the very thing she wanted—to get her off. But of course she didn't know that.

Still, he thought, she had known what she was doing—had wanted to manipulate him into something. But what? Then he called himself a fool, for she had said what it was, so clearly there couldn't be a misunderstanding. The Astrid of years ago wouldn't have done it, but this was the Astrid of now, of tonight, who was willing to use anything, who counted on her ability to reduce him to a state of helplessness. . . .

Goddamn her, he thought. But she wouldn't have another chance. Never again would he be made to feel helpless. Never. He swore it.

She had sworn something, too, he thought, had lifted his hand to her breast and had made him . . .

There was, he thought, a word for those who sold themselves. A word that might have referred to something excusable in the nineteenth century. But this was the twentieth.

"Okay, lady, this is it," said the taxi driver. "Gracie Terrace. Isn't this what you wanted?"

The woman lifted her head and stared as if he had just announced their arrival on the moon. "Oh," she said. "Yes, it is."

Now there, thought the driver, who was studying to become an actor, there was a quality that some of the girls in his class ought to be able to see. For Lady Macbeth, in the sleepwalking scene. Or maybe Ophelia, after Hamlet rejected her.

The woman handed him a ten-dollar bill and walked away. "Hey, don't you want any change?" he called, but she didn't even look back.

Lady Macbeth was it, he thought. Wishing for all the perfumes of Arabia.

Chapter Six

Lieutenant Klugman spoke sharply. "When did you get this, Damon?"

"Just this afternoon."

"All right, give us the whole picture."

Damon looked around the lieutenant's office, where they were gathered—he, Riley, Klugman, and Assistant District Attorney Ben Lowell. The call had come in an hour ago, from Granger's personal physician, in answer to the message he had left the day before.

He took out his notebook. "Granger had a condition called cardiac arrhythmia, a kind of mechanical malfunction of the heart that causes an irregular heartbeat."

"Wait a minute," Klugman said. "There wasn't anything on the autopsy report about a cardiac condition."

"What he had is something that normally doesn't show up. It doesn't leave any physical traces of itself, you might say. But the person who has it is subject to spells of momentary weakness and can even come near to fainting."

"So? Make a connection."

"Cain's version of what happened that night is that Granger gave a kind of grunt, slumped over the railing, and then fell.

We didn't buy it because there was no explanation for that kind of behavior. But this could provide an explanation. If he was under stress—and she admits they were having a violent argument—then he might have suffered one of the spells of weakness that are characteristic of cardiac arrhythmia."

Riley swore gloomily.

"How the hell did Forensic miss that?" Klugman said.

"I don't know."

"They weren't looking for an out for her," Riley said. "He was."

Damon turned on him, his voice level. "Listen, Hugh, I'm not any happier about this than you are. Just get that straight, OK? But she's not out. This condition doesn't leave any traces of itself, so there's no proof at all that he had an attack that night. She's not out."

"Maybe not," said Ben Lowell. "But a defense attorney could certainly make good use of that condition to establish a reasonable doubt."

Klugman sighed. "Well, Ben, what do you think, then?" The three of them looked at Lowell, whose eyes had been circling their faces like a pair of high-strung, intelligent watchdogs.

In his two years with the district attorney's office, Ben Lowell had prosecuted fifty-one felony cases and won forty-six of them. He did not plan to stay much longer than another year—his thirty-first birthday was his target date for going into private practice—and the Granger business could provide him with the kind of send-off he wanted. That is, if they really had a case.

Not that he was the only one who wanted it, he thought, adjusting the knot of his tie with a snap of his wrist. The big man, Mr. District Attorney himself, had been wearing that pinched but righteous look that meant pressure was being put on him and he was pretending it had no effect.

Lowell's fingers began to drum on the fair-sized pile of press clippings he had brought with him. Representing every paper but the *Blade*—and virtual silence from that quarter was interesting, he thought—they ranged from breathless tabloid announcements that Cain had admitted to spying on Granger and actively disliking him, to speculations about how and when Hart Collins might react, to the most recent word from Rose Custer: a column citing an anonymous former employee of the Institute to the effect that Granger had been impossible to work for. And there was the article on the "Comments" page of the stately morning paper, in which the acting director of the Martin Granger Institute, ostensibly writing about nothing except the Institute's programs, had neatly managed to defend the dead man's reputation without acknowledging that it had been challenged.

The three detectives were still looking at him. "There is a great deal at stake here," he said finally. "Collins is very close in the polls. Some people think that what we do here could make a difference."

"We know what's at stake," Riley said. "Granger had a lot of powerful friends. But did he have one deadly red-haired enemy?"

"Certainly she was an enemy," Lowell said. "We can establish that with half a dozen witnesses, if not more. And we can show a strong personal motive for getting Granger out of the way and doing it that night. But we don't even have to prove motive, you know. And that's all we've got. I don't see one shred of physical evidence that she did in fact cause his fall from the balcony."

Riley leaned forward eagerly. "It was absolutely physically possible for her to come up from behind and send him over."

"Yes. And the defense can show that his falling was equally possible. More so, with this cardiac condition."

"If you bring the arrhythmia out first, in the ME's

testimony," Damon said, "you can take the sting out of it."

"I know that," Lowell snapped. "Suppose you stick to investigating and leave the trial strategy to me."

Lieutenant Klugman cut in. "Hugh, anything more on that anonymous caller?"

"No, dammit. We've been back to the cook again—I still think she's a possibility, but I don't know if she's got all her marbles—and to that old lady across the court. Nothing. But I think we're going to hear from her again. I really feel it."

Lowell raised a thick, dark eyebrow. "I can't put your feelings on the stand."

Riley sighed and fell back in his chair. The four men were silent. Lowell's fingers began to drum once more on the pile of press clippings.

I might be in Lowell's place, Damon thought, studying him dispassionately. If I had stayed in the law, I might be the one with the power to decide whether to take her to trial.

Lowell's glance darted to him for a moment and then moved on. What had drawn Lowell to the practice of law? Damon wondered; was he one of the pragmatists or the idealists? When he himself had been in school, most of his fellow students had seemed to fit into one or the other of those categories: the pragmatists, who paid lip service to the Magna Carta and the Constitution but whose sights were really fixed on the huge salaries they hoped to earn in corporate law, and the idealists, who planned to join some government agency that offered free legal services to the poor. The former he had usually disliked; the latter had made him uneasy. Their sincerity, which he did not doubt, had seemed focused more on the poor than on the law.

But one could not in fairness expect too much from the students when one considered their professors. In one way or another, most of them taught the law not as a system of principles but as a set of arbitrary rules that could be used either cleverly or stupidly—as if the courts merely provided a setting for games of oneupsmanship. Which, of course, they often did.

Astrid had argued with him: "It can't be as bad as you say. You may be describing the rule, but surely there are exceptions?"

That was in the days when one could still believe her. And for a while it had seemed that she was right, because of the day he had walked into a new course on Constitutional Law and seen Judge Garrick Evans at the lectern. Evans's imposing, white-haired figure had looked like Moses the Lawgiver on the stained-glass window of Loretta's church, and Damon had been prepared to mistrust the resemblance. But then Evans began his lecture by reading, without any preface, the Preamble to the Constitution, his deep voice making the sonorous phrases sound new-minted—"We, the people of the United States . . . to establish justice . . . provide for the common defense . . . secure the blessings of liberty . . . do ordain and establish this Constitution . . ." When he had finished, he gazed at his audience for a long time. "Ladies and gentlemen," he said finally, "you are undertaking the practice of law. I have just read you your oath of office. The law will demand more of you than your knowledge and your time; it will demand your honor. Try never to forget that."

Your honor, thought Damon, staring into space, past the pile of press clippings in Lowell's hands; "Your Honor" was the title granted to a judge. What could be granted to a judge—or a woman—who betrayed the very word?

Lowell was speaking again, crisply. "In my view, the circumstantial case against Cain is good, but not decisive. I take it you've shown me everything you have?"

"Yes," said Riley. "That's everything. Isn't it, Damon?"

The other three turned to him. He could simply say nothing, he thought. He could leave it as it was. Something private. And ugly.

"Damon?"

"No, it isn't everything," he said, knowing it was the sound of his voice that made Riley look at him strangely. "There is one thing more. Astrid Cain has made an attempt to bribe an officer on the case."

"What?" Riley was out of his chair.

Damon rose, too, but slowly, almost formally. "I was acquainted with the suspect in the past, as you know. Last night she came to my apartment and made an attempt to trade on that acquaintance."

"Trade?" asked Lowell sharply. "In what way?"

"By offering to sleep with me if I called off the investigation."

Riley spoke first. "Well, well, well," he said softly and began to grin into space.

"Jesus," said Klugman, "that wasn't very bright of her."

Lowell, for the first time during the meeting, was sitting perfectly still. "No, not bright," he said finally. "But useful. Yes, I think that is quite useful."

"Mrs. Chapin, how nice to see you again. It's been a good long time. You are alone?"

"Yes, Fritz, I am." Astrid let the proprietor lead her back to the small corner table of the restaurant and fuss over her as he whisked away one of the table settings. "And what can I give you tonight? Some of the sauerbraten that Dr. Chapin was so fond of?"

She wondered if he was fishing for information about David or merely trying to be helpful; either way, it didn't seem to matter. "I put myself in your hands, Fritz. Whatever you think." She told herself that no matter what he brought, she would eat it. An hour ago she had realized she hadn't had anything for two days but cups of coffee and some fruit and hadn't spoken to anyone since the taxi driver who brought her back from . . . from Damon's. Suddenly it had hit her—not the hunger but the silence—and she had leaped up to dress and almost run down the street to one of the neighborhood restaurants, certain that the presence of something other than her own thoughts would somehow change those thoughts.

But it did not. As she took one of the crusty salt sticks from the basket on the table, the questions leaped back into her mind: What was happening at the stationhouse? Would Damon do what she wanted? Had she been able to reach him?

She snapped the stick in half and put it down untasted. Eight years ago, she thought, in the most crucial decision of his life, she had not been able to reach him. The private, unassailable part of him, whose existence she had always recognized but which had never threatened her, had turned from a shadow that could be brushed away into a barrier she could not cross.

At first the shadow had seemed so insubstantial: hardly more than an awareness that her own struggles and disillusionments in the theater weighed too heavily on him, that he could not understand her capacity to shake them off. "How can they ask *you* to be in such garbage?" he would ask when she was offered a role in some experimental play being done off-Broadway; and she would say that it had to be expected, since so much of the theater was focused on the absurd and the depraved, and what did it matter, since she had no intention of taking the role?

She had still been struggling then to convince herself that she could make a career of playing in summer stock and going anywhere in the country, if she could get the job, for revivals of classics she liked. But Damon could not accept it. For their first summer, when she was doing stock in New England, he came up for all of the plays and was appalled to see her as the ingenue in seven Broadway sex comedies that were, he said, identical and mindless. "It's like watching someone who could play Mozart do nothing but Muzak. It's not right that you should have to do it, not right!"

Ironically, as she began to feel her own dissatisfactions with the theater more keenly, he was growing visibly more excited about his future in the law.

The reason was Judge Garrick Evans—as she learned two months after Damon had walked into Evans's class. "I couldn't believe him at first," Damon told her. "But the man is living up to the way he sounded that first day. My God, he knows so much! And he can make things so brilliantly clear!" What Damon had not put into words—but what she could hear in his tone—was that the existence of the professors he could not admire and the students he could not understand was being made to seem irrelevant by the existence of Garrick Evans. And when Damon was given the job of clerking for Evans while he studied for his bar exams, she thought that the look on his face, the mixture of incredulity and embarrassment that she knew meant he was happy, had never been so strong. She had told him he shouldn't stake so much on one man, but he hadn't seemed to hear.

It had taken her a while to realize that the look was fading. She was preoccupied with her own realization—that she actively disliked much of the work she had done, or could foresee doing, in the theater. Only gradually did she become aware that Damon had ceased talking about his work for Evans. "Something's wrong, isn't it?" she had asked; and he had answered, too casually, "No, nothing at all. Just some clay feet I don't want to make too much of."

When something went unmistakably wrong, he did not tell her at first. But one night, when she was watching him as he sat on the couch, petting Cyrano but looking inward, she said, "Whatever it is, it's going to tear you in half if you don't talk about it." And finally he had, telling her about the night when Evans had left the office without some important papers and he had decided to take them to Evans's apartment and leave them with the doorman, if necessary.

"It was such a nice night that I took Cyrano and walked down. The judge was home by the time I got there. He said he was alone. We talked for a couple of minutes, and Cyrano wandered off to explore. Then I heard him barking, and somebody hollering. I ran to see, and in the kitchen a man was standing by the counter. He said, 'Jesus, I didn't expect no damn dog. I don't like dogs.'" Damon's hand, still moving over Cyrano's back, dug in with greater pressure, and the dog closed his eyes contentedly. "Evans said the man was there to discuss the catering for a party, and I forgot all about it. That is, I tried to. But I couldn't shake the feeling that I'd seen the man somewhere. And about a month later, I woke up in the middle of the night, and suddenly I knew. But I couldn't believe it. So I checked—I called one of the cops who'd been in a class of mine. He took me to the detectives who were working on a case against a big narcotics dealer. And there it was in their files--a picture of the 'caterer.' Except his name was Riva, and he was a known associate of the dealer's—the dealer whose case had just been thrown out of court on a technicality. By Garrick Evans."

He told her that he had waited a week before confronting Evans—and that Evans had denied it and tried to make a joke of it.

"Don't you have to take this to the special prosecutor?" she said.

"What good would that do?"

"He's supposed to clean up corruption in the courts and the police force, isn't he?"

"Sure. And how many of his indictments have resulted in convictions? Besides, it would just be Evans's word against mine. And you can be damn sure he'd be able to produce a 'caterer' who'd swear he was the man in the kitchen."

"But, Damon, you have to try. You have to fight it, no matter what."

"Quand même?"

"Yes. Yes."

"And what if there's some perfectly innocent explanation?"

"Why didn't Evans give it to you, then?"

They had argued about it half the night. But finally, after he said, "Evans can't be corrupt, I just won't believe it," he had stopped abruptly. "I hate people who don't want to learn the truth. All right. I'll go."

The attorney on the special prosecutor's staff had been jubilant; it was the first time they had anything more than suspicions about Garrick Evans to go to work on.

For the next few days, Damon had behaved like a man who walks calmly away from a car in which he has crashed, a man in limbo between the action and the realization of its meaning. She finally coaxed him out to dinner, at a place they could not afford. The food and wine had made his eyes darker, but no less distant.

When they got home and unlocked the apartment door and switched on the lights, there was a small red lake in the center of the floor.

It was she who first saw the white shape under the table, but it was Damon who said, "Cyrano?", as if he were commanding reality to obey.

The dog's head was thrown back, and where the throat had been there was a second, grinning mouth, from which the lake was forming. The white fur that Damon had groomed so carefully was spattered red, as if the dog had tried to shake free of that second mouth. The brown eyes were open, no longer trusting, frozen in pain.

Damon knelt to touch one of the limp white ears. He stayed that way while she sank into a chair and stared at the two of them, praying that he would get up, would move, would do anything to show that he was unlike Cyrano, that he was alive.

Then she saw the note pinned to the back of the couch. Cut from newsprint, it read: "The dog died because he was nosy. Learn from the dog."

She held it out to Damon; his eyes focused on it, and then she saw him come back to life, and wished he hadn't: A jolt of rage gripped him with the violence of an electric current and ran all the way through his body before it finally receded, leaving him to stare at his shaking hands.

Her own hands clenched, and she felt a surge of nausea; she heard a voice say, "Mrs. Chapin, is anything wrong?", and she looked up into the concerned face of the owner of the German restaurant.

"No, Fritz, thank you. I'm fine."

"But the food—you don't touch anything."

She saw that he was right. What was making her ill, she told herself, was the heavy, spicy smell of the food in front of her, not the memory of what had happened eight years—or two nights—ago. She mumbled some apologies, paid, and walked back up the street to her building.

When she unlocked the apartment door, she hesitated to turn on the lights because she might see a lake of blood on the floor and Damon kneeling beside it.

She turned on the lights; the room was empty. Automatically she called out, "David?" and listened to the silence. She sat heavily in an armchair. She had wept bitterly for the death of a dog, she thought, but she would never shed a tear for Martin Granger's. Yet each had changed her life. And Damon's, too. Would he blame her for Granger's death, as he had for Cyrano's?

Later that night he had wrapped the body in old blankets and gone to Evans's apartment. When he came back, his anger had a new element. "I told him I wanted him to see my letter of resignation, and then I pulled back the blanket. He gagged, had to run to the bathroom. Then he told me he had

had nothing to do with it. He begged me to believe him. And the worst part is that I do. I don't think he knew what they were up to. I think that until tonight he had convinced himself he was taking payoffs from civilized human beings—may he rot for it."

Then he had turned on her. "I let you talk me into it!" he shouted, mimicking her: "'Damon, you have to try, you have to fight.' Well, I did what you wanted. I went to the special prosecutor. If I hadn't, Cyrano would still be alive. What kind of advice have you got for me now? Get another dog and get him killed, too?" Then he had seen that she was crying. "I'm sorry, Christ, I'm sorry," he said, reaching for her. "You're just as vulnerable as he was, and just as brave." But there was as much anger as comfort in the way he held her.

In the months that followed it had seemed to her that only two things had reality for him: the pain of Cyrano's death, which did not diminish but remained a flickering redness in the depths of his eyes, and his need of her; she felt that her body was the one place where he could forget. When she tried to get him to talk about what he was feeling, he refused. He would say only, "I'll be all right when they convict Evans."

He had gone back to driving a taxi, although there were jobs with law firms he could have had almost for the asking. "I'll decide what to do when Evans is convicted," he said.

"But you will keep on studying for the bar exam?"

He had shrugged. "I guess so."

He passed the exam, was approved by the character committee, and was sworn in as a member of the New York bar. Two weeks later he learned that the special prosecutor's office was dropping the attempt to indict Garrick Evans. Their only witness other than Damon had changed his mind about testifying, and they had decided they couldn't risk a case that was too weak.

She had known she could not push him or argue with him

then. When someone is fighting with pain, she had thought, all you can do is watch. And wait.

One night she knew that the fight was over—knew as soon as he came home, by the sudden, tight calm of his face.

She was reading in bed; he sat at the foot and told her that that afternoon he had taken the entrance exam for the New York Police Department.

"Why would you want to do that?" she said carefully.

"Because I've decided I'm not going to practice law."

Within the space of that moment she had been jolted back in time, to the sight of her father's face and the sound of his weary voice saying, "I'm sorry, *kära barn,* but I just don't want to go on anymore." But it was Damon's voice, and Damon's face; and she answered him carefully. "Could you tell me why?"

"I'll try. You see, I've been asking myself how it would be if my future were like the last nine months."

She made herself go slowly and cautiously. "I know this has been a terrible time for you. But why do you think it's a pattern for the rest of your life?"

"Because that would seem to be logically consistent, given the way the world is. And I don't think I want a future like that. I want to get something out of life besides a feeling of . . . of futility. And helplessness. Astrid, I'm turning thirty, and I don't want to live the rest of my life that way."

"I don't understand," she said faintly.

"No? You should. Aren't you thinking of leaving the theater?"

"But not for that reason! Because it isn't giving me what I want! I want the sense of being consumed by what I do."

"That sounds nice. Maybe it would be, in another life. But in this one, there's too much danger of winding up like a moth with a flame."

She forgot caution and slowness. "But you're only talking

about one man—one rotten judge! You can't give up for that. It's crazy!"

"Is it? You know as well as I do that there are plenty of Evanses in this world and that one of them could be on the bench in any case I tried. And if he was, what could I do about him? Yet I'd despise myself if I didn't try. So I would try, and then . . . what would it get me?"

"The satisfaction of knowing you had done what you could!"

"Sorry, I can't see that as a shining reward. I'd have been much better off, you know, if I hadn't cared that Evans was crooked. Then nobody would have been hurt. Suppose it was you whose throat I had found cut?"

"I'd still say you should have done it!"

"Then you'd be a fool. A dead one. And I'd have to kill Evans with my bare hands. Which would make me a moth—headed straight for the candle. No, Astrid, it's much better if I do something that hasn't got any flames."

"And how do you think you're going to live without the very thing that makes you feel alive?"

"I'm going to work in a place where they train you to develop emotional calluses. Isn't that a nice way to put it? I've been spending time with a couple of cops I met in law school, and they said that's what they were told when their class of rookies was sworn in. And that's just what I want, a job where I can be in control, not at the mercy of—"

"Now I understand," she had cut in. "It's not just Evans. It's Sam, and Roy Vance, and all the other people in your life whom you ever let yourself love. You're going to let them have that kind of power over you? Let them set the course of the rest of your life?"

"I'm the one who's setting it."

"You won't be living! If you give up fighting and caring, if you stand aside and do nothing but watch, you'll be just like my father—dead years before you die."

He did not answer, and she had turned away, helpless. But the next day she told him she would fight him all the way. "Go ahead," he said.

She told him it was contemptible to abandon the ideal of justice. He said, "I'm not. I'm just going where they don't play games with it, where the issues are nice and primitive—good guys versus bad guys—and everybody knows which side he's on."

She clipped newspaper stories about cases he had been interested in and tried to make him talk about them. He said, "Don't waste your time. You can't get to me that way anymore."

She said he was giving up only in order to avoid pain and called him a coward. He said, "Why are you so goddamned anxious for me to get hurt?"

The more bitterly they quarreled, the more violent was the lovemaking that followed, as if their bodies were fighting to form a bridge across the widening distance between them.

One morning, in the dawn light, she awoke to find him looking at her, his eyes rising from the marks his teeth had left on her thighs and breasts, to her mouth, and then to her eyes. For the first time he said to her, "I love you."

She took his hand and kissed each finger. Then she asked, "The same way you love the law?"

On the day he was accepted as a probationary police officer, she told him she could not stay with him any longer if he joined the force. "I feel as if you're using me, as if you only want to escape from things and I'm the means of escape."

He said nothing for a frightening length of time. Then, "You'll have to do as you like."

"I can't stay and watch you commit suicide."

"I know that's the way you see it."

"It is."

He had watched while she packed a small suitcase. Formally they made arrangements for her to pick up the rest of her things the next day, when he would be out.

At the door she said, "This was the last way I could think of to reach you. I thought that if you wouldn't let me go, then you wouldn't give up . . . other things. I prayed you would stop me. But it didn't work."

"No."

She had searched his face for some sign—of anything—but found none, and suddenly she had wanted to force some show of life from him. "Now you can add me to the list of things that hurt you because you loved them."

"Yes," he had said, still impassive. "But you're the last."

And I may be hurting him again, she thought, huddled in the armchair, staring unseeingly across her living room.

Then she shook her head violently. What had happened two nights ago could not be allowed to matter now; none of it, neither the violence of his response—nor her own, which had been such a betrayal of David that she still could not face it. Nothing about Damon could matter now, except whether or not he had believed her.

When she heard a knock, she was puzzled; no one had rung up from downstairs, and the building security was excellent. She went to the door and looked through the peephole. She saw Damon, and even before she saw that Riley was with him, she knew he had believed her. She unlocked the door.

"Mrs. Chapin," Riley said. "I think you probably can guess why we're here. We're here to arrest you for the murder of Martin Granger."

She had planned exactly what to say when and if this moment came, but her mind could recapture none of it, and all that came out was "Yes."

The two men stepped inside. Riley took a card from his pocket. "I'm going to advise you of your rights." He began to read. "You are advised that you have the right to remain silent. You don't have to say anything unless you choose to do so. Anything you say can be used against you in a court of law. You're entitled to have an attorney present in any questioning, now or in the future. If you don't have an attorney, the court will appoint one for you. Do you want a lawyer?"

"I . . . yes, I do. May I call him and tell him to meet me?"

"Go ahead."

Her feet carried her to the bedroom. Her hand reached for the phone.

Why don't you congratulate yourself? she thought. Everything worked out as you planned. You made them believe you're guilty. Even Damon. You got them to arrest you for murder.

Why don't you congratulate yourself?

II

BLINDFOLD

Chapter Seven

A veil of smoke drifted across the table toward Ben Lowell. He brushed at it; it merely swirled into a new shape and hung there. His eyes were smarting, but since he never did anything that could later be construed as putting unwarranted pressure on a suspect, he had let the Cain woman keep on smoking. She had been perfectly willing to talk while they waited for her lawyer, but this was her fifth cigarette in the hour they'd been at it. The cigarettes, he thought, and a kind of tight glitter in the eyes were the only signs that she might not be as composed as she sounded.

He adjusted the knot of his tie, which was still snug under his white collar, and looked around the stale cubbyhole, located off the squad room. "Let's clear the air in here," he said. "In more ways than one."

Her expression did not change, but she put out the cigarette.

Lowell glanced at the two detectives near the door. Damon stood with his arms folded. Riley, who was hunched forward on a metal chair, got up, opened the door, and moved it back and forth several times, until a brief sensation of fresher air reached Lowell and he nodded. He checked the tape recorder to see that it was still running properly.

"All right, Mrs. Chapin," he said, faintly stressing the name, "since you're willing, let's go back over some things again." She looked at him calmly, her face illuminated by the lamp that had been arranged to shed a soft but direct light on her.

"Did you know your way around the Granger house pretty well?"

"I'd been there a number of times, to work."

"Always in the study?"

"If you want to know whether I was familiar with the terrace and the location of the sculptures, yes, I was. In fact, the week before, we'd worked out there one whole afternoon, since the weather was so nice."

"Why don't you stop trying to second-guess me and just answer the questions?"

"Because you've asked most of them three times."

"I hope we're not boring you," Lowell said softly, but she did not react. "What did you and Martin Granger quarrel about?"

"I've told you that's something I'll answer when my lawyer comes."

And Sanford Marsh, thought Lowell, would tell her not to answer any more questions, unless he were one lawyer in a million. "How many shares in Chapin Pharmaceuticals does your husband own?"

"I'm not sure."

"That's odd. For six months you were able to convince Martin Granger and everybody else of your efficiency as a secretary, but you don't even know how much your own husband is worth?"

"I know that he and his parents shared a controlling interest in the stock, but David was not one to keep a running count of his assets. Of course I knew he was wealthy."

"Why do you speak of your husband in the past tense?"

That was the wedge, Lowell thought; each time, the mention of the husband made a pulse appear in the base of her throat. As if she knew it, she put up a hand to close around the collar of her brown shirtwaist dress. "It's just a figure of speech," she said.

He cocked his head to one side. "If you were in my position, what would you make of the fact that the suspect's husband hasn't shown up since the night that the man he worked for died?"

"I suppose I would find it . . . odd."

Without pausing, Lowell said, "Why did you hate Granger?"

"I don't remember telling you that I did."

"No? What about that, Paul?"

Damon uncrossed his arms. "Last week when you were here, you said you hated Martin Granger."

She's not too fond of Paul Damon either, Lowell thought, noting the way she sat forward abruptly without turning around. He had not confronted her with her attempt to bribe Damon—that would be held for future use—but it was interesting that she had avoided looking at him all night.

He took her for the third time through her story of the so-called accident. At the end she leaned forward and said, "That's how it happened, that's what I've told you from the beginning, and that's all I'm saying until Sanford Marsh gets here. Then I'll tell you everything, and you'll know it's the truth."

"It's interesting the way you keep repeating your story of how he died. Word for word. Like a record."

She sat back and reached for another cigarette.

Lowell stood up and motioned for the two detectives to leave the room with him. "Let her sit for a while," he said when they were in the squad room. "I'm out of ideas for the moment."

Riley combed his hair with his fingers. "You know, the other times we talked to her, she was uptight, but tonight it's different. And she sure was playing it cool with the crowd downstairs."

"What do you mean?"

"There was a batch of reporters waiting when we got here. Don't ask me how they knew we were bringing her in—sometimes I think they know these things before we do. Anyway, she didn't duck the flashbulbs at all, and she said, 'They're arresting me for killing Martin Granger, but before much longer you'll all know that I didn't do it.'"

"Either she's confident," Lowell said, "or she's a hell of an actress."

"She was an actress," Damon said. "Don't forget that."

"I don't forget anything. By the way, you look like hell tonight. A lot worse than she does."

"It's hot in here, that's all."

Lowell shrugged. "I want to call my wife. We'll go back in five minutes."

He made his way to an empty desk and phone. The squad room was fairly quiet, with only two other men in it, talking to an old woman who kept repeating, "I never once remember him taking the stuff, I never even seen him do it once."

They all had wretched memories, Lowell thought, and wretched grammar. And wretched lives. Anybody who believed that growing up poor in New York City didn't increase your chances of taking up crime was either blind or flying on the right wing. There had been many weeks when everybody he took to court was below the poverty line; those weeks only strengthened his resolve that when he was in private practice, the well-heeled clients would pay for a monthly quota of those who couldn't afford to pay. He smiled, dialing his home number; if this were a few years from now, he might be the lawyer that Astrid Cain was waiting for.

And she'd be one of those who could finance the monthly quota.

He was telling his wife that he had no idea what time he would be home when a tall, slender man came into the room. It was Sanford Marsh, he knew; there was a look of money, of growing up with it and old with it. And a lot of it, Lowell thought, had come from being one of the good legal shepherds to the Chapin family. He cut off the conversation with his wife and went across the room. "Ben Lowell, district attorney's office," he said, holding out his hand.

"How do you do." The older man was a head taller than he, and that head was patrician, with large, even features and hair the color of pewter. "I believe you are holding my client, Astrid Chapin. Perhaps you'll be good enough to tell me the charge and your reasons for it."

Lowell took him to a desk and for ten minutes presented the facts that were adding up to Murder Two. Marsh made numerous notes in a fine, slanted writing. Lowell had mastered the art of reading upside down, because of its usefulness in court, but Marsh seemed to be using a private shorthand.

Finally he said, "I'd like to see Mrs. Chapin now, if you please."

"She's told us repeatedly that when you got here, she would answer all questions. I intend to hold her to that."

"Well," said Marsh in a gentle voice, "I'll have to see what she means, won't I?"

He was with her only a short time. When he came out of the cubbyhole room and said, "Mrs. Chapin is ready to make a statement now," his voice no longer sounded so gentle.

After they were all assembled and Lowell had switched on the recorder again and made his identifying comments, Astrid turned to Marsh. "A month ago I took a sealed package to my lawyer and asked him to hold it till I requested that he deliver it to me. He did not, and does not, know what it contains. Tonight I asked him to bring it. Sandy?"

Marsh, the lines around his mouth gathered into knots, took a small manila envelope from his briefcase. "The writing on the tape that seals this," he said, "states that it was received on July 27 and is to be held for Astrid Chapin."

Riley and Damon had pulled up chairs. Riley craned forward as Marsh placed the package in the center of the table.

"Inside is a tape cassette," Astrid said. "It was made on the portable recorder that I use in my work, for interviews. When I went to see Martin Granger on the night he died, I recorded our conversation. All of it, including his death, is on that tape. When you listen, you'll hear that he died just as I've always told you he did, that I did not kill him."

Lowell's first thought, when his mind geared up to the level of words again, was, You grandstanding bitch! His second was a moment of pity for the stricken look on Marsh's face. Then he noticed the other looks: Riley's eyes frozen open, as if he had forgotten how to close them, Damon's narrowed, and Cain's still glittering, with what now looked to him like triumph.

He closed his hand over the envelope and pulled it toward him. "Just supposing this is what you say it is, and that has yet to be established, why didn't you turn it over to the police weeks ago?"

"Astrid—" Marsh began, but she cut in.

"There are things on that tape that put me in a bad light, that I didn't want to come out. I thought you would believe me without it, but obviously I have no choice now."

"Did Granger know you were recording the alleged conversation?"

She hesitated for a moment. "No. I thought that if I—"

This time it was Marsh who cut in. "Gentlemen, I demand the right to speak to my client again privately."

I'll just bet you do, Lowell thought. He stood up. "Be my guest. I've got some listening to do."

He took the envelope, bounced it on his palm, switched off and picked up the recorder on the table, and signaled Riley and Damon to follow him out of the room.

She turned to Marsh. The civility of his manner, she thought, would be maintained at all costs, like the press of his beautifully tailored suits, but his pale blue eyes were fixed on her like probes.

"Now, Astrid," he said quietly, "I think you had better start explaining."

"Sandy, I'm sorry. I suppose it looks as if I were just using you, not telling you in advance, but I—"

"Perhaps it looks that way because that's the way it is."

"No. Please don't say that. I wanted them to see that this was all my doing, that it wasn't some ploy you had set up for me. Besides, I kept hoping I wouldn't have to use the tape."

He folded his hands on the table and studied them; they were deeply veined, with long fingers. "I have always supposed that an attorney's job was to advise his clients, not merely to deliver their packages. You have put me in an awkward position. Mr. Lowell now perceives that my client has not trusted me. And, what is more important, I've had no chance to decide whether it was wise to turn over the tape at this time and in this manner. You have given away a critical piece of evidence without your lawyer's advice. Or even his knowledge."

It was, she thought, like being slapped by a velvet fist. "I'm sorry, Sandy. I just didn't think."

"From now on, you must. And you must tell me everything."

"Of course. But once they hear the tape, they'll release me."

"How can you be so sure of that?"

"You'll know it yourself as soon as you listen."

He reached into the briefcase. "I hope I'm right in assuming that this other envelope contains my copy."

"Yes. I gave them the original."

Marsh sighed. "And you asked me to bring a recorder with me so I could listen, too?"

"Yes."

"I see that you planned every detail. Did you also plan my reaction? No, ignore that question. There is no point in recriminations now. But I do need to know why you made this tape."

"I had some questions for Granger, and I wanted a record of the answers."

"So you could print them?"

"No. That wasn't the reason. It was . . . I made it for David."

"David?" His pewter eyebrows lifted.

"So he could hear . . . whatever Granger said."

"And has he heard it?"

"No."

"Ah. Because you haven't seen David since the night the tape was made."

"That's right."

"Tell me; if he had heard this tape, would he still have disappeared?"

Whatever had to be kept from Marsh, she thought, it would never do to forget that he was a perceptive man. "I don't think so," she said. "Sandy, please just listen to the tape. You'll understand when you've heard it."

"All right."

She heard the clicks of the equipment as Marsh put in the tape, then a pause, then Granger's distant voice saying, "How mysterious and urgent of you. But I'm quite alone. Lauren is out for the night, as usual, so no one will bother us."

She closed her eyes. *Quand même,* she thought. In spite of everything, she had done it, and now it was finally over. As soon as they released her, she would have duplicates made of the transcript of the tape, which was locked in a safe deposit box, and then she would hold a press conference, so that everyone would finally know the truth. David would surely hear about it, wherever he was; and then he would be saved—David and all of Granger's other victims.

She wished suddenly that her father could be here, too, to see how she had fought this monstrous thing, this cancer of the spirit. Once, she thought, her father had explained to her the challenge and the problem in treating cancer; she must have been about eleven then. One day, he had told her, maybe not until the next century, it would be conquered, just as tuberculosis and smallpox had been in their times.

He had always talked to her of medicine as a crusade, and she had thought of his surgeon's gown and instruments as the green uniform and shining weapons of a heroic figure. Until the day he gave up, at fifty-three, and retired from the practice of medicine, for no reason he could give to her, or to himself. "I can't explain it, *älskling min.* I just don't want to do it anymore. Perhaps I am just tired."

But it wasn't tiredness, for he had tried many other things—cruises, fishing trips, various kinds of volunteer work. Nothing seemed to alter the weariness that became his habitual state, as if he had no more inner resources with which to face the business of living. She had thought of him sometimes as a ship that was sinking, inch by slow inch, with only one violent shudder—the heart attack that killed him when he was barely sixty.

The heart attack one could understand; but before it occurred, what was the thing that had drained the life from him? She had never known; not then, not now. There seemed only two possible explanations: Either he had made some terrible error in his work, which had wiped out his confidence and motivation, or else the love he felt for his work had simply deserted him. The first was too painful to accept. The second was unintelligible.

Did everything go back to him? she thought. Was one forever bound by one's childhood, which laid the blueprint for everything one would ever love or care about or do?

Or was the world so full of people who retreated from the things they once loved that it was simply in the law of averages for her to meet two others—and to cry to each of them, "You'll be just like my father!"

Before the image of Damon could come into her mind, she ordered it out. Think of your husband, she thought. Because for David's behavior there was an explanation, an outside cause that one could fight. And, in defeating it, one could turn David back into a man who had once known how to smile. . . .

She had been Anne Cain for two years—taking her first name, which she had never used, in order to signal her new career—when the Tri-County newspaper chain sent her to interview a young scientist at Westchester University. At first he had been distant and uncommunicative, his manner at variance with the casual blond good looks that had made her think of a tennis pro. But at some point during the interview he must have decided she was capable of understanding him, and he had begun to speak more rapidly and intensely, spilling out the words as if he could not control their speed, explaining the great unsolved problem in his field: to determine how the central nervous system stores its information.

"For instance, you had to *learn* to walk. The knowledge wasn't wired into your system at birth, the way it is with animals. You had to acquire it. But how did you do it? Somehow your nervous system was modified, changed, so that it would forever after contain the information about how to walk. But how did those changes actually take place? What literally happens, physically, to modify the interactions between neurons? We don't know, you see. We don't know *how* we automatize our knowledge, how we store it. But the man or woman who finds out is going to win a Nobel Prize, you can be sure of that."

"And you've made a step toward that knowledge?"

"Yes, but a very small one. I work with the octopus—because it has an anatomically simple system, and it can be trained to discriminate between things, between circles and triangles, for instance. I've managed to find that, as a result of that training, a certain synapse is modified—that there is a permanent change in its biochemistry. Which still leaves hundreds of unanswered questions. Like whether this mechanism applies to higher forms of life. So you can tell your readers that I spend my time with octopi and the biochemistry of one synapse. Very far removed from the problems of the real world."

"Apparently that's not what the American Science Foundation thinks. May I see whatever it is they gave you?"

He had rummaged in his desk and found the scroll that signified his recent election to that august body; and when she took it and said, "I think what you're doing is wonderful," that was when the smile had appeared, as delighted as a child's, transforming his face.

The day after her article on him appeared, he sent her a note: "You understood what I said about my work. Now I think I'd like you to get to know me, too. May we have dinner soon?" In one corner he had sketched an octopus, holding out a flower in each of its arms.

She had seen him smile often in the weeks that followed, as he took her to operas, concerts, plays, and restaurants so exclusive that she had never heard of some of them. He would laugh openly at her pleasure, yet he was oddly defensive about his ability to provide it. Sometimes, when they were going home, he would stop the car and jump out to press some bills into the hands of a beggar or a drunk. "Charity is good for the soul," he would say lightly.

She learned that all the Chapins believed it; his mother, a large, handsome woman, worked tirelessly and expertly for a dozen different charities, and his father, who had just retired from the board of Chapin Pharmaceuticals, was already heading the drive for a new local hospital.

"I want you to meet my sister," he said one day, although he had never before mentioned that he had one. They drove to what looked like a secluded private estate but wasn't, and there an ungainly woman in her late thirties was brought out and flung herself at him. "Davey, Davey," she cried, "did you bring me a surprise?" He had; and Rosalie Chapin cooed with delight as she unwrapped the doll and began combing its hair with clumsy strokes. When they left, David said, his voice shaking, "Why should I have everything and Rosalie nothing? If I believed in a God, I'd hate him for that kind of cruelty." It was hours before he smiled again. And when he did, he said, "Maybe there is a God, after all. Someone had to send you to me—I couldn't have deserved it on my own."

He seemed delighted by her, almost as if she were a species he had never encountered before and was now studying intently. He commented on things she had long taken for granted in herself—from the way she approached her work, to the relaxed absorption with which she listened to music, to something as small as her automatic awareness of people's voice and vocabulary patterns; he seemed to notice, and appreciate, everything about her. "I like the way you write about people," he would say, "as if their problems and achievements are a kind of drama." Or, "Do you know that you listen to the Verdi *Requiem* with your whole body?"

It was impossible not to respond to someone who seemed so completely aware of her. She began to love him for the very fact that he could make her feel some response; no man since Damon had done that, and she had begun to fear she was turning into the thing she most feared: a person deadened inside. Perhaps, she had thought, one's first love affair was, by its nature, more searing than anything that could follow; perhaps one had to pass through such a thing before one could come out on the other side and learn to love more quietly, more sanely. And be able to enjoy a man's person, and his body, without feeling that some part of oneself was locked in his keeping.

They were married before hundreds of guests on the lawn of the Chapin estate. Rosalie was there, at David's insistence, wearing pink and lurching after him whenever he moved. For the picture of the whole family, Rosalie sat on David's right, clutching his hand, and David himself was smiling, for once as if he wanted the whole world to see.

The smile, she thought, had begun to disappear after he accepted the fellowship at ISCEV. He took it because he would be able to concentrate fully on research without the distraction of teaching, and for several months he was happier than ever—happy for her, too, because she had just been offered the job with the *Blade.* But gradually he grew preoccupied and silent. One day, unable to reach him at the Institute, she learned from his mother that he was with Rosalie and that he had been increasing the frequency of his visits. When she asked him why, he said, "I never could accept it, about Rosalie and me. But Martin has made me understand that we're both victims of Nature's discrimination. And somehow that makes it easier to see her." He began to go even more often, saying little about the visits or about anything else.

They had been married a year and a half when he told her

that he was taking a leave of absence from the Institute, with Granger's blessing. He could give no real explanation, except to say that he felt "paralyzed" and needed time to re-evaluate his work, to see whether he really wanted to go on with it.

This time, she had thought, it would not be as it had been with her father—and Damon. This time she would not be helpless, unable to understand or to act. Because this time there seemed to be one clear cause: Martin Granger.

She had read his books and articles, aware of her relative ignorance in the fields of sociology and philosophy. As far as she could understand his turgid prose, Granger seemed to be arguing that there were discrepancies of wealth and ability among men, which were caused by "Natural discrimination" and which society must balance out. It was, she had thought, a standard line of political and social theory, except that Nature was accorded the fundamental role in most social injustices. It had made her impatient, as philosophy always had in college; philosophers were so out of touch with reality, issuing abstract pronouncements that no one could take seriously and that were more a way of dramatizing problems than of really solving them.

She had decided that Granger's influence over David could not come solely from his writings. But what was the source, then? As David grew more and more distant, sometimes sitting in his study for days, locked in a silent inner struggle, she had begun to think of him as the victim of some kind of brainwashing. Like the young people who abandoned their lives and the parents who loved them to join the service of some religious leader. Or the robed, chanting figures one often saw on Fifth Avenue, their eyes as glassy as their shaved heads.

But if that was the kind of thing Granger was doing, why had he picked David? And was David the only one? She realized that she would have to learn more. And as David receded further from her reach, diminishing, as he did so, her ability to respond to him, she had felt as if she must fight not only for him but also for herself. For her very capacity to love.

She had told David about her plan quite openly: "I'm going to take a leave of absence, too. I have to understand what's happening to you, so I want to get to know Martin Granger without his knowing who I am. Tomorrow I'm going to be interviewed for a job as his secretary, and if I get it, you can't ever tell him who I am. But you can stop me right now, if you want. All you have to do is say you don't want me to do it."

He had looked at her with a strange eagerness, the first she had seen in him for weeks. Then weariness had seemed to fall over him like a curtain, and he simply said, "Do whatever you like."

She had not said anything to him about what she was observing at the Institute: Granger's personality, which was an odd combination of the autocratic and the generous; or the quality of moral fervor that surrounded him like an aura, reminding her again of a religious cult leader, except that he was so patently not religious; or the fact that he spent a good deal of time with certain people, all of whom seemed to be like David: not only talented but vulnerable, in some way she could not yet define.

She hadn't talked about any of it to David because much of the time he was unreachable. Sometimes he would go away for days—to see Rosalie, she was sure; and when he came back, his face would look so tortured that she would cry out and try to hold him and comfort him. Sometimes he would let her; sometimes he would shout at her and tell her to leave him alone. He talked to Granger, she knew, on the phone, late at night. The next day, if she tried to ask about the conversation, he would say that she was not entitled to know because she was spying on Granger. "Shall I quit?" she would ask; and the fact that he did not tell her to was what gave her hope.

When she had seen him for the last time, his face was so

drawn that it seemed never to have known how to smile: He had told her he was thinking of giving up neurophysiology and would be turning over his stock shares to Martin Granger. She had fought with him, telling him her suspicions, screaming what the man was trying to do to him. . . .

"I think that's the most vicious thing I've ever heard," said a voice; it was her own, on the tape recording. Marsh was frowning as he listened.

"I find I don't particularly care what you think." That was Granger, his voice tightly controlled after the earlier outburst. "This conversation is finished. And so are you."

"My God, you're a monster. I wish that you could be . . . I wish that I . . ." The sentence faded away, unfinished, and there was a pause. Nine seconds. She had timed it often.

Then a sound: Granger, grunting.

Another pause. Seven seconds.

Then her voice: "I don't think that you deserve to—" The words cutting off, then her cry: "Dr. Granger! What's the matter?"

Another pause. Five seconds.

Then her voice, moving away: "Oh God, oh my God, my God."

A very long pause—nearly three minutes.

Then the sound of a phone being dialed.

She looked at Marsh.

"That's it, Sandy. This is where I called the police. And about a minute later, I must have remembered the tape, because I shut it off."

Marsh listened until the final sound. Then he turned off his own machine and placed the tips of his fingers together, studying them. Finally he said, "I was never an admirer of Martin Granger's."

"I didn't think you would be. Sandy, you do hear it, don't you? The relationship of the voices there at the end—mine close to the mike and his farther away? He was on the balcony, and I was standing right by the desk, and my purse, which I left slightly open, with the recorder in it, was on the desk. You can hear that I didn't move, that I didn't go over to push him. In fact, during those pauses I was looking away, trying to think what else I could say to him. As soon as I looked back and saw him slumping over the railing, I called out."

"Yes, you did."

"Do you know that it was two days before I even thought to listen to the tape? I was . . . very upset."

"Yes, you must have been." Marsh unlaced his fingers. "You know, there are some very fine lawyers who have had more criminal trial experience than I."

"What difference does that make? It's just a question now of my giving them a detailed statement before they let me go."

"Yes, you'll certainly have to do that." He took a yellow pad from his briefcase and uncapped a large, old-fashioned ink pen. Then he laid it down. "I thought at your wedding that you were a very high-spirited young woman. Now I'll amend that to 'headstrong.' And hope I don't have to add 'foolhardy.'"

"Jeeesus Christ," said Hugh Riley.

The three of them stared at the recorder as the sounds finished and the tape rolled on silently. Finally Lowell shut it off.

"I suppose that really was Granger?" Riley asked.

"How do I know? I never heard the man's voice."

"But to talk that way . . . I mean, Jesus, he sounds like he was foaming at the mouth."

"Yes." Uncharacteristically, Lowell ran both hands through his hair.

"You know something?" Riley said. "I can see why she

hated him. He does *not* sound like one of the good guys."

"Keep that opinion to yourself," Lowell snapped. "You're not to discuss this tape with anyone. Or even to mention its existence. Is that clear?"

"Yeah. Sure."

"Damon?"

"It's clear." Damon rubbed his eyes; he had stared without moving at the tape for the whole twenty minutes of its run.

"I wouldn't care," said Lowell, "to see his widow's face if this gets out and turns into a Top Ten record. Not to mention some other faces, like Hart Collins's. The election is only two months away."

Riley got up and began to pace the small area in the lieutenant's office, where they had gone to listen. "I guess it has to be Granger, all right. Cain wouldn't dare fake it."

"If she got some old crony from the theater to help her fake that kind of dialogue, I'll add libel to all her other troubles." Lowell brought a fist down quietly but firmly on the desk. "Maybe it's not that kind of fake, but it could be a splice job. Or anything. We'll get the experts to check it out every which way. It's just too damn convenient that she has this thing to whip out of her lawyer's briefcase."

"But what if it is for real?" Riley asked.

"Then Martin Granger really did talk that way about . . . people. Of course," Lowell added thoughtfully, "she provoked the hell out of him."

"I don't mean that," Riley said. "I mean, does it really show she couldn't have pushed him?"

Lowell began to rewind the tape. "It certainly shows that she wanted to. After all, he threatened to ruin her. No wonder she wasn't keen on handing this over—I never heard a motive laid out more clearly. Provided the whole thing isn't a fake, of course." He frowned. "And if it is, why give herself that kind of dialogue? Why keep threatening to kill the man? Unless she's clever enough to inculpate herself to make it more convincing. And I'll just bet she is that clever."

"Hey!" Riley swung around. "What she said there toward the end—that business where she swears she'll find some way to shut him up—that's just what our anonymous caller said she heard, practically the exact words."

"Then why in hell can't you find her?"

"Do you want us to keep looking? I mean, is Cain off the hook or not?"

"If we release her," Lowell said, speaking slowly for once, "she'll give this tape to the press." He looked down at it as if it had turned into a snake.

"So what do we do?" Riley persisted. "Damon, what do you say?"

Damon's eyes were burning, and the muscles around them jumped. An image of Astrid seemed to be caught in his vision, pushed in and out by the twitching muscles. It was clear now, he thought, why she hated Granger. For what the man had said was not only unspeakably ugly, but it pertained to something she could not be objective about—people's giving up their careers. "Objectively," he said, "I think the tape seems to corroborate her story of the death. But that's only on a first hearing."

Lowell nodded. "And don't foget how careful she was to press that story on us." He had found the passage he wanted to play back: the dialogue and pauses at the end. The three of them listened once again, then two more times.

Damon pressed his fingers over his eyes, where the image of her was still flickering and smiling, as if it still had confidence in its power to reach him. "Hugh," he said abruptly, "there was a carpet in Granger's study, wasn't there?"

"Yeah. A pretty thick one. Brown, I think."

Lowell cocked his head to one side. "A carpet. Now, isn't that interesting. Because all the tape tells us is that there were some long pauses before and after Granger gave that grunt. It doesn't tell us what Astrid Cain might have been doing during those pauses. Doing silently, I mean, so that a tape wouldn't pick it up."

"Oh boy," Riley said.

Both of them looked at Damon. He took his hands from his eyes. "Yes," he said. "She could do anything."

Chapter Eight

The lights in the cell went off at eleven, but a pale frosted rectangle in the ceiling stayed on all night, to keep her always visible through a panel in the door and to ward off the blessed unconsciousness of sleep.

The thing to do was to lie quietly and try not to think or feel anything. To forget the dreadful, plastic cheeriness of this place, with its bright colors and its mocking simulation of freedom, which allowed one to go to the gym or the library or the beauty parlor or the shower or the dayroom. To forget those two times each day when everyone had to be locked in her cell for the count. To forget the plastic bubble at the end of the corridor, from which the officer surveyed everything and controlled the cell doors from a panel of switches, closing them not with a clang but with a grinding electric whir that seemed even more final.

Above all, to push one's memories back to a distance.

They had to be held at the wrong end of a telescope, till they were as meaningless as a play about a doll: a tiny, unreal doll who had had metal cuffs snapped on her wrists and a plate of numbers hung around her neck so she could be photographed . . . who had sat in a paneled courtroom watching

Sanford Marsh struggle with a judge who declined to release her on bail . . . who had been put, five days ago, into a rattling van that went forever till it crossed the bridge to Rikers Island . . . and who was led eventually to this five-by-eight cubicle, where the intercom in the ceiling played a rock radio station constantly, from five-thirty in the morning till lights out, like a dentist's drill of alien sound from which there was no escape. . . .

Five days, she thought, turning on the bed that was as narrow and hard as the cell door, staring at the rectangle of false moonlight in the ceiling. Only five days in this place, and how many ahead of her? "Detained, awaiting trial." For murder. She had screamed at Marsh, at Lowell, at Damon, who was no longer there, screamed and demanded to know why the tape hadn't led to her release, why they refused to believe it . . . and Marsh had kept telling her that it was a two-edged sword, that he was doing all he could, under the circumstances. . . .

She closed her eyes, willing the thoughts to go away. Think of nothing, she told herself; and then she thought of a game that might make it happen: if she imagined her apartment and everything in it and then, one by one, mentally blanked out the objects—the fern in the kitchen, the orange cup she always had her coffee in, the living room chairs, in which one could sit so blissfully and be alone, the stacks of beloved records, Bach through Wagner, the books, the typewriter, everything—until there was nothing left but a void, a deep, black hole into which she could disappear and leave all thought and feeling behind. . . .

Finally she did fall asleep, one arm over her eyes. At two A.M. she woke, as suddenly as if someone had shouted her name. No one had—only her mind, which had flooded with the knowledge that her plan had boomeranged and was now lodged against her throat.

She began to shake, the violence coming from deep in her bones. She got up and began to move, lurching against the desk and chair and metal closet that filled the room and left her only a narrow path. She tried to hold her arms across her stomach, but they would not stay; her body was on fire with inner motion. She stretched its length against the brick wall, only to be thrust down into an animal crouch, then up and along the narrow path again, to return and meet the intractable wall once more. When a limb had been frozen, she thought dimly, it came back to life with pounding, burning insistence; and what had been frozen in her was fear, which was now claiming its right to exist and was her master.

After what could have been minutes or hours but was measured in struggle, not in time, she was able to crawl back to the bed again, a fist wedged into her mouth to hold back the sounds. At length the pain of her teeth sunk into her hand became greater than the fear, and she took her hand away. The motion in her body diminished slowly, to the occasional hiccup of a shiver; and when the cell light came on at five, she was quiet once again.

Sanford Marsh went up the walk to the Women's House, observing his feeling of revulsion and reprimanding himself for its cause.

Despite thirty-five years as an attorney, he had never become inured to the fact that prisons were a necessary part of the legal system. The law was such a noble entity, representing man's willingness to abide by a rational code; yet the law was tied to the ugliness of incarceration. As if a saint were coupled with a prostitute. He knew that this was a foolish notion, that prisons were required to implement the goals of the law, but he never could shake the feeling. It reminded him too forcibly that men were capable of animal instincts as well as high ideals.

Pushing the thought out of his mind, he was led to a tiny room labeled "Lawyer Visits," which had space for a table and two chairs and nothing else.

His client was pale, which only accentuated her hair and eyes and the coral slope of her mouth. She looked, he thought, like one of the roses in his solarium: a Tropicana, all flame colors. How could she survive in a place like this? But of course, he reminded himself, roses also had thorns. "My dear, how are you?" he said.

"I don't see any point in discussing that."

"The books got here all right?"

"Yes. Thanks very much, Sandy. It's a sacrilege to read Hugo and Rostand with my sophomore-year French, but with the dictionary, I manage. And it's something I've always meant to do."

"Then I'm glad I could find the books for you."

She leaned across the table. "Is there any news of David?"

"No, I'm afraid not. Even though his father has hired two more private detectives to look for him. But he must have told you that himself. He said he came to see you last week."

"Yes, he did. I wish he wouldn't come again."

"Why on earth not?"

"Sorry. I shouldn't have said that. But everything seems a little close to the surface these days. Louis is very polite, but I'm sure he blames me for David's disappearance. Not that he's wrong, I suppose. Maybe he even thinks I did kill Granger."

"You do him an injustice when you say that."

"I hope so." She sat back. "Why didn't you let me know you were coming?"

He hesitated. "I wanted to surprise you with some good news. The trial date is set. We're on Judge Cox's calendar for the first week in December." She said nothing. "That's only two months. Ben Lowell seems as anxious to go to trial as we are."

"What's the date today?"

"October ninth."

"Two months." Her hands were on the table; suddenly her fingers laced together. "I'll be out of here in two months?"

He put his hand over hers. "Astrid, I'm doing everything for you that I know, but the outcome of a trial is never certain. You mustn't let yourself think that it is."

"I know. I'm not to count on anything. Even that the jury will believe what they hear on the tape." She stopped. "What's wrong?" she said, and he knew what his face must be showing.

"I have something to tell you, to discuss with you, about the tape."

"What?"

"Ben Lowell and I have agreed that it should not be introduced in evidence."

She pulled her hands away. "I suppose I should have expected this."

"Of course I wouldn't make any deal with Lowell until I had your consent. You do realize that?"

She nodded slowly.

He thought of the carefully guarded conversations in which Lowell had broached the idea: "It's undeniable, Marsh, that your client makes a number of inculpatory statements on that tape . . ." "You know, Marsh, I can interpret those crucial segments at the end in exactly the opposite way . . ." "Do you really think, Marsh, that the public should hear what Granger says on the tape? He was obviously speaking in anger, and I sure as hell wouldn't stand by everything I said when I was angry, would you?"

It wasn't, Marsh thought, that it wouldn't be the right

decision. It was just that there were too many outside considerations, from the fact that he would not mind doing what he could to help defeat Hart Collins—a kind of personal manipulation of the law that would have violated everything he believed in and therefore had to be scrupulously avoided—to the fact of Louis Chapin, who did have to be considered because he was paying the bill for his services: "Is there anything you can do, Sandy, to keep from attacking Granger too badly in court? Anything that's consistent with her defense, of course . . ."

"But the truth is on that tape," she was saying.

"I know that, and you know that. But you also know what Lowell contends—that during those pauses at the end, you came up behind Granger and pushed him over. And unfortunately, he's right. I mean, he could argue that very convincingly." He waited for a response, but there was none. "My dear," he went on, "you do realize that the tape is equivocal, don't you?"

Her smile was brief and did not reach her eyes.

"I've wondered," he said carefully, "why you didn't realize it before. Why it never occurred to you that those pauses at the end were open to another interpretation."

She sighed. "Don't think I haven't asked myself that question. I guess the answer is . . . that I was there. If you go through something and a tape is recording it, then it seems self-evident that there can't be anything on the tape but the truth. Because you were there. You *know* what happened. And it just doesn't occur to you that other people will hear anything in it but the truth."

"I see. I suppose that could account for it."

"Or there's another possibility. That I'm just a person who fails to visualize all the consequences when she takes an action." Her eyes closed for a moment, as if some inner pain had reached up to touch them.

"Let's return to the issue," Marsh said firmly. "In plain language, I believe the tape could do you as much harm as good in court, maybe more, and I don't want to run the risk."

"But if Lowell could use the tape against me, then why would he agree to keep it out?"

"Because he also knows it's equivocal. But there is a *quid pro quo,* of course. Lowell is not anxious to have Granger's admissions on the tape made public. Any more than I want a jury to hear the way you raved and threatened to kill him."

She began to laugh, a mocking sound that seemed as alien from her as a bitter scent would be from a rose.

"My dear, what is it?"

"Nothing," she said, stopping the laugh. "Nothing."

Everything, she was thinking. The tape, which was supposed to do so much, save so many people. Including herself. The tape, which she had guarded so carefully . . .

She had waited for David to come back, to give it to him. Three weeks had gone by, with no word from him. But with eulogies to Granger all over the press, and clear indication that Hart Collins was campaigning on the dead man's shoulders, using his ideas without knowing the things that were on the tape. She had begun to wonder what means she had to reach David—and everybody else.

Hal Ruby had been her first thought. She had gone to him, ignoring his dictum that she was not to discuss Martin Granger again, telling him, without saying what it was, that she had evidence of the strongest kind to back up the thesis of the article he had rejected. He had been firm in his refusal to consider reopening the subject.

Four nights later, when she came back from a fruitless trip to Lilac Hill, in the hope that Rosalie might have heard something from David, she found that she had been robbed, her apartment in disarray, the television and her typewriter gone, as if the theft had been a normal one. Except that the contents of her desk were gone, too, including all that had pertained to Martin Granger—all her notes and her copies of the article she had given Ruby. Everything but the tape, which she had put in her safe deposit box at the bank.

Her first thought, after the shock had subsided, was that at least there had been no Cyrano to suffer. And that had brought home the realization that she was up against some fairly powerful forces. Even if she called Hal to confront him directly, he would deny any connection with what had happened. And perhaps he had none; perhaps he had inadvertently passed on information about her to someone. No matter which, she would be even further from her goal.

She had decided, for the moment, simply to call the police and report the theft; and, as she was reaching for the phone, the idea had come: Why couldn't the police become her protectors? She had put the phone down. If the police were investigating her, if they suspected her of killing Granger, that would nullify the others, whoever they were. And ultimately she would be in a position to use the tape in a very powerful way, a way that would help so many people. . . .

"Astrid," Marsh was saying, "are you all right?"

"Yes. I suppose you could call it that." She studied his face. "Sandy, do you honestly think it's best not to use the tape?"

"I do."

She sighed. "But the truth about Granger will still come out in court?"

"As it explains your actions, certainly it will."

"Sandy, you have to promise me that people will hear about the souvenir collection."

"You force me to remind you that I am in charge of your defense and that when you try to run things yourself, the consequences are unfortunate. Don't forget that it was you who turned the tape over to the police without my prior knowledge. You deprived me of that option, and now I must insist on keeping others open. I frankly haven't settled on my full strategy yet. I suggest that you either leave it to me or engage another attorney."

"The above described person," Damon typed, "a widow whose apartment overlooks courtyard and back windows of Granger brownstone, did not observe anything at time and place of occurrence. At approximately 2300 on 6/23, she did observe body impaled on terrace."

He paused for a moment, then finished. "Statements are essentially unchanged from those given in interviews on 6/24, 7/27, and 8/20."

He pulled the sheet from his typewriter to read it over before signing. There was nothing in the report, he thought, to indicate the way the woman's eyes had glittered in the prune of her face, as if they fed on neighbors' secrets; or the way her disappointment at not having witnessed a murder had kept escaping, like the gray hairs from the knot on top of her head; or her insistence on repeating that Granger's body had looked "like a doll stuck on a spindle." All of that was stripped away by the bare, stilted language of police reports, which reduced everything to "time and place of occurrence," "perpetrator," and "incarcerated, pending trial." And that was just as it should be, for facts were all that mattered in police work.

Incarcerated, pending trial. On Rikers Island. In a cell. In hell. He shook his head sharply. Facts were all that mattered. And the fact was that she was guilty. He would find the proof. It was out there somewhere, had to be out there. Had to be.

But not with the widow. If she had been the anonymous caller, he thought, she would have declared herself long ago, unable to hold it in. He signed the report, his last of the day, added it to the others, and turned to the window. Some dead leaves were sailing aimlessly in the airshaft. The wind pasted one on the window and then snatched it away.

"Hey, Damon," someone hollered behind him, "call for you. On two."

He picked up a phone. "This is Detective Damon."

"This is cosmetics salesperson Lazare."

"Marie," he said quickly, "how are you?"

"I am fine. Working hard, singing hard. Very busy. And I guess you are, too?"

"I'm afraid so." He paused, feeling the heavy awareness of the many days since he had talked to her. But there was no time now, for anything except . . . "I'm on a case that's been taking up most of my days and nights."

"Ah. You are brave and wonderful, solving everything?"

"How many times do I have to tell you that I'm not one of your storybook detectives?"

"I'm sorry, Paul."

"So am I. Listen, Marie, I've got to go out now and question a potential witness. I'll call you soon. This weekend. OK?"

"Yes, of course. I'm sorry if I bothered you, Paul."

"You don't bother me!"

"That's good," she said lightly. "At least I think it is. Well, good-bye, Paul."

He hung up slowly. She deserved some explanation, he thought. But how could he explain it? And what was there to explain, anyway? He had a job to do. And he would keep on with it, even if his day was officially over. One more effort might make the difference.

He pulled on his suede jacket and left the stationhouse. Heading downtown, he angled toward the West Eighties and Riverside Drive, his eyes automatically scanning the streets for anything or anybody that looked "wrong." It was good to be back in control, he thought, after behaving for half the summer like a helpless fool.

The maid who answered the door of the brownstone recognized him right away. "I'll tell Mrs. Granger you're here."

"Thanks, but I didn't come to see her. I'd like to talk to the cook again."

"Jones? I guess it's all right. This way, please."

The woman was seated at the round table in the kitchen, boning and skinning chicken breasts. Her fingers were swollen with fat, but they worked dexterously. From the short sleeves of her green dress the doughy wings of her arms swayed in a corresponding motion.

"Hello again, Helen," he said. "I hope you don't mind my calling you Helen."

"I don't care."

"I thought you might give me another cup of your wonderful coffee."

"If you like."

When she started the awkward process of rising, he said, "I can get it myself." He went to the counter and poured a cup. There was music in the room, as there had been in the hall. "I like that. The Waldstein sonata, I think." She looked at him blankly. "Beethoven. The composer?"

She slipped a knife into a chicken breast and pulled off the skin in one piece. "This is for galantine. She's having people to dinner. Do you ever make galantine?"

"No. How do you do it?"

She told him, in detail; as she talked, the vast pudding of her face seemed to stir with some animation. He was counting on that. If she really was mentally defective, as he had begun to suspect, at least she could function in one area.

After asking a few questions about the galantine, he said cautiously, "Helen, I'd like to talk a little more about the night Dr. Granger died." Her face wobbled into stillness again. "I think you know something you haven't told us. Isn't that so?" She didn't answer, but she put down her knife. "I don't blame you for that. No one likes to get involved with the police. But this is very important. Now, I know you said you were asleep when the officers knocked on your door that night, but just tell me this. If you hadn't been sleeping—and this is only hypothetical—you *could* have gone from your room down the hall to the living room, couldn't you?"

"Yes."

"And if you were in the living room, you could have stepped over to stand by the terrace doors, couldn't you?"

"Yes."

"Were they open or closed?"

"Open."

She had never said this much; he did not dare to distract her by moving a muscle. "Did you open the doors?"

"Yes."

"When?"

"Before I went to bed."

"All right, leave that for the moment. Now, *if* you got up and went to stand by those open doors, you could have heard voices from the study upstairs, couldn't you?"

"I suppose so."

"And if you looked up, you could have seen the balcony?"

"I suppose so."

"Helen, were you there?"

Her face was an impassive surface on which he could find no hold, no sign of tension or evasion or anything else. "You saw it, didn't you? You saw Astrid Cain come up behind the doctor and push him over. Didn't you, Helen? You saw her kill him. Didn't you? I know you did."

She pulled back a little, and he realized his voice had risen. "You can't know that," she said.

"You're right, of course. But I do know that Astrid Cain killed the doctor, and that's why you have to tell me what *you* know."

"I was asleep." She picked up the knife again.

"My, you are eager," said Lauren Granger's voice behind him. "I'll have to see that Ben Lowell hears about your industry." She touched a switch that turned off the music, and came to the table. She was wearing a honey-colored silk robe that matched her hair, which was pulled back with a scarf as violet as her eyes.

He had kept his eyes on the cook's; they had seemed to retreat when Lauren came in, but what had they retreated from?

Lauren pulled the sash of the robe tighter and let her fingers play along the hanging tassels. "Jones, I wish to God you had seen that crazy bitch do what she did. But since you didn't, let's concentrate on tonight's menu. There'll be eight of us now. Jake Waldo just phoned to say that he's bringing the mayor and his wife. And we'll start at nine instead of eight-thirty."

Damon stood, knowing nothing more could be done now. "Thanks for the coffee, Helen. And, Mrs. Granger, I hope you have a successful dinner party."

"You can count on it." Lauren smiled. "With Collins doing well in the polls and the Cain creature put away, what else do we need?"

"Nothing you can't buy easily, I'm sure."

Lauren stifled the retort that came into her mind and watched him go down the hallway.

After all, she thought, he was going to be an important prosecution witness. She had wheedled the story out of Ben Lowell, who looked like a cat with cream on its whiskers every time the man's name came up. It would be gratifying, she thought, to watch the red-haired bitch's face when the detective told the court how she had tried to bribe him. And to watch the jury. The average juror, Ben had assured her, would not look kindly on married ladies who offered to sleep with other men. She laughed, aware that she had become righteous very quickly.

Jones was looking at her hesitantly.

"Yes, what is it?" she said.

"The maid told me. You might be moving to Washington."

"Oh, that's all very tentative. It depends on what happens on November third. The election—surely you know there's a presidential election?"

"But if you go . . ." Around her tiny eyes, the woman's flesh gathered in anxiety.

"Then you'd go with me, of course. I wouldn't throw you into the ranks of the unemployed. I know you'd be quite helpless."

"Yes," said Jones, relaxing.

How, wondered Lauren, could the woman be fool enough to not realize that anyone else would grab her services in a minute?

But with what Jones knew, she thought, there was no chance she would ever let her go.

"Hello, Anne," Rose Custer said. "Or I guess we call you Astrid now, the way the police do."

"Yes. Astrid Cain Chapin. Number 63591."

Across one of the thirty-two tables in the visitors' area, Rose was studying her. Or at least she seemed to be. Her eyes, as usual, were masked by huge dark glasses above the hawklike nose and chin.

"You don't look as bad as you might," Rose said. "But I'm not crazy about your dress designer."

Astrid looked down at the shapeless jumpsuit she was wearing and pushed away the memory of the strip and search that took place before one put it on and after each visit was over. "I wear my own clothes the rest of the time, but this is our special for visitors."

"Lucky me," Rose said.

"Did you have any trouble getting in here?"

"Nothing much worse than going through airport security. Anyway, how could I resist after your letter? An exclusive interview with Granger's killer—that's worth a little trouble."

"His alleged killer. Remember that, or there won't be any interview."

The bark that Rose gave was apparently a laugh. "You look like such a creampuff that I keep thinking there's nothing inside but cream. I shouldn't forget the way you interviewed America's new genius playwright and showed him up as a prize jerk."

"That wasn't very hard. Or very much fun."

"No? You don't like to make them squirm?"

"I prefer the kind that doesn't need to squirm. Like the man who founded the Center for Classical Drama. I liked doing the piece on him."

"Tell me something. What the hell made you leave the theater for the newspaper business, anyway?"

"The truth? I thought that if I were a reporter, maybe I could learn some of the reasons the theater was in the state it was. Why everything I loved about the nineteenth century was either despised or forgotten by the twentieth."

"I thought colleges weren't supposed to give people diplomas until they were cured of being romantics."

"I had some professors who tried very hard."

"So what did you learn when you quit the stage for the typewriter?"

"That I really love writing. And something I should have realized before: that the theater is an effect, not a cause. The stage reflects deeper things, the basic attitudes and ideas that people accept. Or think they should accept. And when I realized that, I got more and more interested in looking at some of those attitudes and ideas. In psychology and the social sciences, for instance."

"And that's how you ran into Granger?"

"Not exactly. It was more that he ran into me. Or over me."

Rose grunted. "All right, let's get a few things up front before we start. Like why I'm the one you want to talk to. After all, the last time I saw you, that night in the bar, you told me your story in confidence, but I printed it anyway. Why do I get an encore?"

Astrid felt the pleasurable tensing of her mind; it was good to be functioning once more, facing challenges. "At first I was furious with you, of course. But then you did some digging on your own and ran that story on the former Institute man who was so disenchanted. I liked that; you were willing to consider that I was telling the truth."

Rose shrugged. "It made a good story, that's all. But what about the *Blade?* Why aren't you giving this to them?"

"Why should I give Hal Ruby anything? He acts as if I don't exist. Besides, I happen to think you are very good."

"How true." Rose pushed up the glasses to rest on her hair. The hawk became a rabbit, for her eyes were small and close-set, with pale lashes.

"Keep your hands on the table."

"What?"

"Hands have to stay on the table, remember?"

"That's right. Jesus." The glasses came back down. "All

right, I'll tell you why I printed the story you gave me that night. A, it was too good to pass up, and B, I was ticked off because you'd made it so plain you weren't smitten by my charms."

Astrid thought that was just the reaction she had counted on at the time; but from now on, everything would be on the level. "I'm sorry, Rose. I'm just not—well, I'm sorry."

"It's OK." The hawk grinned maliciously. "But I bet I wouldn't have any trouble if I were in this place."

"No, you wouldn't. But you don't want to be."

Rose was silent for a moment. From the tables near them came the murmurs of other visits; an old black man was saying, "I pray God for you," repeating it over and over to a sullen young girl. "All right, Astrid," Rose said. "Confession time is over, so let's call the score even and get on with my exclusive. It'd better be worth the trip. What's it all about?"

"Something I learned about Martin Granger. The reason I disliked him so much."

Rose leaned back in the plastic chair. "Does your lawyer know you're talking to me?"

"No. But he will." She sent a silent apology to Marsh.

"Will he know before or after he reads it in the *Sentinel?*"

"Does that matter?"

"Not to me. Either you know what you're doing, or else you're a damn fool. I can't say I care too much, whichever it is."

Astrid took a deep breath. "One day I discovered, by accident, that Granger had a box of souvenirs. Things that had belonged to other people. I believe they were *memento mori*. Souvenirs of the dead."

"So what's wrong with that?"

She was stopped by the simplicity of the question and the complexity of the answer. For it was the souvenirs that had made her realize Granger was something more, and more dangerous, than a man who tried to brainwash impressionable kids into following him and working for him. He wanted people *not* to work, a special kind of people; and she had not fully known why until the night he died—had thought at first that the souvenirs were some kind of private research program. Or simply an exercise of his power.

"Come on," Rose said, "what's wrong with keeping souvenirs?"

"They belonged to a certain kind of person," she said carefully—remembering what he once had told her when she asked him if men like Michelangelo should have given up their work: "I'm afraid that the truth sometimes leads in painful directions. Charles Darwin, you know, was excited by his discovery of evolution but was also made quite ill, since evolution takes place by murder."

She leaned across the table. "The souvenirs were from talented, very bright people, who were, or were becoming, Granger's victims. He had . . . prevented the survival of some of the fittest."

"What the hell do you mean? That he killed them?"

"Yes, in a way. Killed their spirit."

"Jesus," said Rose tonelessly. "I guess this was worth coming for."

Chapter Nine

Jake Waldo put down the *Sentinel* with enough force to rattle the breakfast china and swore softly for nearly a minute, while his son stared. "Did you read this story?" he asked finally.

"No," said young Jake. "I have the art pages."

"Well, read it now." Waldo stabbed a finger at the headline: CAIN SAYS GRANGER HAD SECRET "VICTIM" FILE. "Look at it!"

Jake's gray eyes darted to the paper and back. "Why would she say a thing like that?"

"God knows. She found some crazy box of souvenirs and claims that it proves Granger was looking for people to destroy. That woman ought to be in a mental home instead of on Rikers Island. Are you reading the story? What's the matter with you?"

"I'm just . . . why don't you tell me what it says?"

"Because I'm leaving. And don't expect me home till late. This will be a very full day. If they know what's good for them, certain representatives of the press and the law are going to find time to see me."

"You mean because of the story?"

"Did you think I'd just sit here and let Martin Granger's name be pulled into the mud?"

"No, of course not."

Jake looked at his father's face, from which all signs of its normal affability were gone; determination had settled like concrete in the eyes and heavy jowls. He hated seeing his father in this mood; anticipating it had been one of the chronic fears of his childhood. Equal in force to what he felt as he picked up the paper when his father had gone.

The words seemed to jump in rhythm with his pulse:

> . . . a tooled leather box that Granger accidentally left open one day. . . . Astrid Cain says the items it contained were souvenirs of people who had worked for Granger and whom he had induced, or was trying to induce, to abandon the careers they loved. . . .

His eyes moved convulsively down the paragraphs, stopping each time they found a name:

> . . . a high school chemistry medal inscribed to "Harry Pine." According to Cain, Pine was an Institute fellow who committed suicide while under pressure to give up bioengineering. The *Sentinel* has learned that such a man did work for the Institute and did commit suicide, five years ago. . . .
>
> . . . also a ring with an Excalibur symbol and the initials "EK." Cain found personnel records for an Ezra Kerr, but he had moved from New York and left no forwarding address. . . .
>
> . . . a letter signed "Lee" from someone who wrote that he was giving up his career and thanked Granger for helping him to do it. . . .

Near the end of the article Jake's eyes froze on a sentence:

> . . . a wooden figure of a bird that Cain claims was carved by someone she will not name but knows to have given up the career he wanted, under Granger's influence. . . .

He closed his eyes and put his head in his hands. It was that day, he thought, when he had been waiting for his weekly session with Dr. Granger, desperate because his charges at the Home had spat on the prints of the *David* he was showing them and had taunted him till he ran from the room. She had been so sympathetic that he had told her about having wanted to study sculpture instead of taking the degree in psychology; but the agitation had remained, and Dr. Granger had had to spend an extra hour with him, calming him with those perceptive eyes and reminding him of the value of the work he was doing, to himself as well as to others. After that she began to seek him out, wanting to know more about his fieldwork at the Home; and there had been that day in the park, when she had come up behind him unexpectedly; she probably had seen it, before he could get it out of sight. . . .

His eyes flew open with a sudden hope, and he read the passage again. It was true: She hadn't used his name, so there was no way his father could know. And clearly he had not known; his anger had been directed solely at Astrid Cain.

Jake reached for his coffee, took a long sip, and read the end of the article:

> In this story of the accused who turns accuser, where is the truth? Perhaps we will learn it in court. But in the meantime, where are "Lee"? And "EK"? And the carver of the bird? If they came forward, they might tell us whether Astrid Cain was a reporter who was on to a genuine story—or a woman who turned everything she saw into a motive for murder.

Jake put his head back in his hands.

* * *

"Sandy, what is all this in the *Sentinel?*" said the light, crisp voice of Louis Chapin.

"More evidence that your daughter-in-law is headstrong and unpredictable." Marsh was in the solarium of his town house, surrounded by roses and morning sunshine.

"You mean you didn't know she was going to do it? Hadn't you told her not to talk to the press?"

"To answer the second question, of course I had told her. Not strongly enough, apparently, but she certainly understands now."

"And the first question?"

Marsh curled two fingers under the soft yellow bud of a King's Ransom, to help keep emotion out of his voice. "She told me after she had done it but before the column appeared."

"But why? I don't understand."

"Let's say she wanted to make sure I would do my job the way she wants it done." A thorn snagged Marsh's finger, and he felt a prick of the anger he had been unable to control with Astrid. "You want me to go into court and try the victim, don't you?" he had said, almost shouting in the tiny room at the prison, knowing she was forcing him closer to a trial tactic he had always regarded as cheap. And then he had heard himself lecturing her, telling her that the law was an honorable thing, a creation of and for men's rationality, not a parade of games and tricks. And that had had the oddest effect: Her eyes had filled with tears, and she had said, "I'm glad you're my lawyer, Sandy. Forgive me, please, for everything I'm doing to you?"

Chapin was asking a question, repeating it. "I said, will this hamper what you're doing?"

"No." Marsh sighed, aware that it would make things both easier and harder.

"Does Astrid really believe what she told Rose Custer? That Granger destroyed people?"

"Yes, she does."

"But that's absurd. Martin Granger did more for the poor and the retarded than half the welfare agencies in New York State. Do you know that he sent three full-time volunteers up to Lilac Hill, where Rosalie is? And that's just a small private place."

"No, I didn't know that."

"David idolized the man, you know." There was the kind of pause that substitutes for a sigh.

Marsh thought of the Custer piece and its mention of "an award from a prominent scientific organization" that was part of the "souvenir collection." No, he thought, he would not tell Louis Chapin the identity of "a brilliant young scientist whom Cain declined to name." At least, not until he had to.

"Governor Collins," said one of the reporters, thrusting a microphone at him, "may we have your reaction to the piece in the New York *Sentinel*?"

Hart Collins moved toward his waiting limousine in majestic silence, but reporters blocked his passage.

"How do you feel about the fact that the man who provided part of the intellectual foundation for your campaign has been called a spiritual killer?"

Collins stopped. "For the record," he said slowly, "I have held the ideas on which my campaign rests since I was a freshman in the House of Representatives. But as to the charge, I call it incredible and irresponsible. It appears that Martin Granger has been victimized by that woman in more ways than one." He turned and moved down the walk, leaving microphones thrust after him like a small forest of spikes.

When he reached his suite in the hotel in downtown

Indianapolis, he called a meeting of his top lieutenants and speechwriters.

"I want two things," he said, "and I want them right away. First, no more references to Martin Granger. None. When the press asks why, the reason is that we don't want to give undue publicity to the impending trial. From now on, the New Equality has no founding father but me."

"And the second thing?" asked his chief aide.

"See if there's anything more that can be done to get that damn trial over with soon—and the right way."

Lauren stood in a basement storage room at the Martin Granger Institute, surrounded by cardboard cartons. There were dust marks on her taupe cashmere dress and a smudge on her matching boots. For the tenth time in the past two days she cursed herself for having had the things from Martin's study sent over here when he died. She had spent a whole day searching the house, with no success, and finally she had come to the Institute, allegedly to discuss the effects of the *Sentinel* piece with the new director but in reality to look for the tooled black leather box.

Once more she went through the last of the cartons, but it definitely was not there. She sank tiredly against a large case. Perhaps, she thought, Martin had destroyed it himself; but that did not seem likely.

She herself had discovered it by accident, four years earlier, and the sight of the letter had frozen her, calling up the feelings she had always told herself she did not really feel. The knowledge of the letter had stayed with her for weeks, festering, and then had come boiling to the surface in the midst of a battle when Martin was threatening to divorce her.

"People are beginning to talk, and I can't have that," he had said, adding bitingly, "Of course I personally don't care how widely you dispense your favors. But to be indiscreet—that's simply brainless."

"What else do you expect?" she had cried. "That's what you're always telling me I am!"

"I'd love some evidence to the contrary. However slight."

"You bastard! Why don't you tell me, for once in your life, why in the name of God you wanted to marry me?"

"Well, since you demand an answer, nobody is perfect, my dear. Once I too succumbed to the lure of the flesh and its second-rate pleasures."

"But you haven't wanted that for years!"

"Very true. Which, for any normal woman, would constitute grounds for divorce. But you seem to want to stay with me. Why is that, I wonder? Are you afraid I'll keep the house and the cook? Or could it be that you know you'll get exactly nowhere on your own?"

She had screamed at him, denying it.

"Don't yell," he said mockingly. "It's bad for the voice."

She had been too furious to speak, memories of their years together rising up in a red mist; then she had grasped at the thought of the collection. "I don't think you have any right to criticize me. Not with the trophies you keep in that little black box."

"What do you mean?"

"I found it, that's what I mean. A medal with some man's name on it and a ring with initials. And a letter that I certainly know about, don't I? Better than anyone else! And I'm not so stupid that I can't make a guess about what the other things mean. Would you like me to go into a divorce court and talk about my guess?"

He had not shouted back. Instead he had looked at her appraisingly. Almost admiringly. The fight had ended with a truce, in which he had promised not to criticize or interfere with her so long as she was discreet. And as he left the room, he had turned back and said, without mockery for once, "You're very beautiful, Lauren. Truly you are. A golden girl."

She grimaced at the memory, feeling the packing case dig into her back. Maybe he had meant it, she thought. Maybe he really had married her for her beauty. Maybe, if he hadn't been a worse lover than some virgin farmboy, they could have gotten along better. But if he did admire her beauty, then why had he kept sneering at it, making her feel it was the lowest and cheapest of all things, calling her his fancy scholar's equivalent of a stupid broad? Why had he—

She stood up suddenly, her violet eyes widening. Could it be that simple? she thought. That he really *had* wanted her for her beauty, and when he realized what a failure he was between the sheets, he had fought back by trying to make her feel as cheap as he could?

But that was so . . . ordinary, she thought. Like something from a confession magazine. And if it was true, then she really was as stupid as he claimed, not to have seen it all those years.

I'm not stupid! she thought angrily. Maybe what she had just realized was part of the explanation, but it couldn't be the whole thing. Surely Martin had wanted her for other reasons.

And the proof, she thought, was that after the fight about the divorce and the truce which the souvenir collection had brought about, life with him had been easier. Not that he was any less mocking, any less able to make her feel awkward and fumbling; but sometimes, for fleeting moments, she would feel again that he needed her in some way, that the kind of awed closeness she had felt for him in the beginning was still there.

But now, she thought, the Cain bitch had made public property of the souvenirs, and conceivably they could lay bare the whole story of her marriage—and more. Much more. So they would have to be found and burned. She forced herself to make one last search.

"Mrs. Granger," said the secretary, peering in at her with concern, "the director sent me down to ask whether you're all right. Have you found that photo album you wanted?"

"No." Lauren straightened and reached for her handbag. "I'm just sorry I took so long. I guess I got lost in memories."

"Ah," said the secretary sympathetically. She considered telling Mrs. Granger that some men had been down in the storage room a week ago, with a subpoena. But they hadn't taken a photo album, so why bother the poor woman, who already looked so distressed?

"I don't know what the hell we're coming back here for," said Hugh Riley, as the elevator doors closed and he and Damon were swept up into the *Blade* building.

"I want to see if Hal Ruby has anything more to say now, after the Custer piece."

"But why us? Last time he was about as friendly as if we'd had open sores. We should let somebody else talk to him. Maybe some of the DA's squad."

"You don't think they've been here already?"

"Then why not let them follow through?"

"Because I want to touch every base myself."

Riley looked at the set of his partner's face; the two lines bracketing the mouth seemed even deeper, he thought, and whatever was rimming the dark eyes had been there for weeks. "I think this case is getting to you," he said.

"No way."

"Yeah? I remember when you didn't even want to believe Cain had done it. Of course that was before she paid you her little midnight visit. And don't tell me *that* didn't get to you, because I know it did."

"I don't like bribes."

"Yeah. But don't you kind of wish you had taken that one? Not even a little bit?"

Damon squared his shoulders. "What the hell does that matter? It's what she did that matters."

"Well, you'll get your revenge in court. Hey, if you were running the prosecution, would you do it the way Lowell did? I mean, not give it to the grand jury and hold it as a bombshell for the trial?"

"Dammit, will you shut up and concentrate on Hal Ruby? I want to make that sonofabitch talk."

"Listen, sourass, don't take your troubles out on me."

They were quiet until the elevator slid to a stop at their floor.

"Sorry, Hugh," Damon said.

"Yeah. OK."

Hal Ruby opened his office door to them. "When the secretary said you were on your way up, I had a feeling of inevitability."

"That's good," Damon said. "Even better would be a feeling of gregariousness."

Ruby took his suit jacket from the back of his desk chair and put it on. "What would you want me to talk about?" he said carefully.

"For openers, the piece your competition ran last week on your ex-reporter."

"Ah, yes, that." Ruby sat down and laid a hand to his face, depressing the flesh of his cheek. "I wasn't surprised, of course. It's all of a piece with the attitude to Granger that Cain had all along."

Damon sat across from him. "How would you describe that attitude?"

"Hostile."

"And vindictive?"

"Yes, if you like."

"It's not a question of what *I* like. But it's been obvious from the start that you knew more about Astrid Cain's motives and actions than you were admitting."

"I suppose it has. But I'm telling you now."

"So you are. And why is that, I wonder?"

"Perhaps I've decided to be a good citizen and cooperate with the police."

Riley gave a sarcastic grunt, which he covered by sitting in the chair next to Damon's and asking quickly, "Was Cain hostile to Granger from the beginning?"

"No," said Ruby. He paused. "At first she was simply interested in getting a story. But a couple of months into her leave of absence, she came to see me, and by then she was hostile. In fact, she was like a woman with a vendetta. I tried to reason with her, but she wouldn't listen. I can only assume she had found that collection of souvenirs and had developed her ridiculous theory about them."

"She didn't mention them to you?" Riley asked.

"Not exactly."

Damon leaned forward. "Did she write about them, though?" There was no answer. "We'd like to see the story on Granger that she handed in to you."

Ruby swiveled around in his chair, facing a corkboard filled with clippings and cartoons and a printed sign reading, "Comment is free, but facts are sacred." After a moment he said, "I give my reporters every kind of leeway, and I give them hell sometimes, too. But I try to make them feel they can count on me. Ask them. Ask anyone out there in the newsroom. They know they can depend on me."

"I don't have time to question a lot of reporters," Damon said.

Ruby's back stiffened. "I'm simply trying to explain that there are ethics in the newspaper business, if not in yours. One doesn't violate them easily."

"Ego te absolvo."

Ruby turned around slowly; his upper lip had a mustache of

perspiration. He pulled something from a lower drawer of the desk and tossed it up. "There's the piece on Granger she turned in last spring. It's not objective reporting, as you'll see. It's not even acceptable as personal journalism."

Damon took the sheaf of papers. "What is it, then?"

Ruby dabbed at his upper lip. "The work of a woman who couldn't distinguish facts from her own projections."

"Who was out of control?"

"Yes."

"Who was angry enough to commit murder if she got the chance?"

"How could I know that?"

"You could have an opinion."

"I . . . yes, I suppose she was that angry."

Damon sat back. "Then as a good citizen, you'll want to testify to all of that in court."

Ruby stood up. "That's all the time I can give you today. I have a paper to get out."

Damon studied him for a moment. "You know, I think it really does hurt you to hand over this article."

"Haven't I just told you that it does?"

"Yes. But I'm not sure what's causing the hurt."

"That is none of your goddamn business," Ruby said. Then his voice grew loud. "Go do your police-academy psychologizing someplace else. I'm a busy man."

But was he also a truthful one? Damon wondered as they left. He and Riley debated it all the way uptown, certain that Ruby's sudden cooperation had been motivated by pressure but unable to decide who might have applied it.

The article Ruby had given them was a long one, describing life at the Institute. "Granger claims to believe in rational, objective principles of behavior," Astrid had written, "but it is impossible to know what will please him or outrage him on any given day. His staff may have great professional autonomy, but it lives under a kind of psychological dictatorship." The charge was backed up with firsthand examples and a few quotes from others. She did not mention the souvenir collection as such, but she told the story of Harry Pine, and she wrote of "another brilliant young scientist now planning to abandon his career because of Granger's influence."

It was in the final paragraphs that Damon found what he was looking for, evidence that she had been out of control. "Dictators always have their admirers," she wrote. "Mussolini, after all, made the trains run on time. Granger runs his Institute like clockwork, but his real goal seems to be the manipulation of human beings, perhaps even their destruction." She concluded by saying, "Shakespeare put this bitter reflection into the mouth of Gloucester in *King Lear:* 'As flies to wanton boys, are we to the gods;/They kill us for their sport.' He might have been describing Martin Granger."

Damon sat back, his eyes tight with satisfaction.

When he got home, the apartment door swung open before he could unlock it. Marie stood there, smiling and holding Sancho. "It's a surprise," she said. "For two weeks I don't see you, so I thought I would surprise you. Do you mind?"

"No, it's all right. I don't care."

She hesitated. "You are working too hard, I think. You should relax, go to a movie or something."

"I'm too tired."

"Sancho, you are getting my sweater full of hair," she said crossly, putting the dog down. "I bought a record today, Paul. Callas in *Anna Bolena*. Should we listen to it?"

He hung his suede jacket in the hall closet. "Maybe later. Right now I just want to change and get rid of this gun and collapse." But it was not exhaustion, he thought; it was a kind of tension of concentration that he could no more slip out of than he could his skin.

She followed him down the hall to the bedroom. "Maybe we could just talk, then."

"Fine." He put the gun on the night table. "What do you want to talk about?"

"Oh, anything," she said, with a sarcasm that he rarely heard from her. "The weather. The big orders of makeup I sold today. The election, The new *Butterfly* at the Met. The way that I—"

"The election," he interrupted, taking off his shirt. "Talk to me about that."

Her eyes widened. "But why?"

"You're old enough to vote in this one. You must read about it, hear about it."

She sat on the bed, frowning and arranging the pleats in her skirt. "Well, some people say that the man in the White House should stay there because he is good for business. But other people say that all he does is play tennis and veto everything. They say that Collins would do a lot more for the poor and the minorities. I guess that's me, isn't it?"

He smiled, hanging his shirt in the closet.

"I hear people say that Collins would bring—what do you call it? new blood?—to things because he has a better way of helping the poor, of making them feel not ashamed to be poor."

"And what do you say?"

"I am not ashamed to be poor. But that is because I am working not to be. But then I read in the paper that there is some trouble for Collins, because the man he got his ideas from was murdered this summer, and the woman who killed him is saying—" She stopped abruptly. "Now I see why you wanted to talk about the election."

"Oh?" He rummaged in the dresser for a sweater.

"Yes. You are working on the case of the woman who killed this man, aren't you?"

"Yes. I told you that before."

She hesitated. "One night this summer, when you were sleeping, you said her name. I didn't even know it was a name, but I remembered it. I remember everything about you. Then I start to see this name in the newspapers, and you are working on the case. And you start to get colder and farther away. And I start to wonder . . ."

"Wonder what?"

"If you know this woman, if she means something to you."

He pulled an old green sweater out of the dresser. "Not anymore."

"And you think she has killed this man?"

"Without a doubt. She killed him."

"You say that so . . . funny. Like a priest talking about mortal sin."

"Isn't that what murder is?"

"Yes, of course."

"And she's not going to get away with it. Not with any of it."

"Paul, I'm so sorry. To see that somebody you loved is not the person you thought—"

"I never said I loved her. Jesus!"

"Then why are you upset?"

"I'm not. It's just part of my job. And it doesn't concern you."

"Oh no?" Her dark eyes were blazing in her small cat-face. "For weeks now, for months, you are like one of those robots in the movies. 'Hello, Marie. Good-bye, Marie. I don't care if you want to stay, Marie. I don't care if you want to go, Marie.' Do you care about anything, anything at all?"

"I told you in the beginning what I was like. But you've got some different picture of me in your mind. You don't see what I am."

"No! You are changed, that's what it is!"

"No. You just want more from me." He stood looking down at her, holding the sweater. "The best thing you could do for yourself would be to walk out of here for good."

She looked up at him; the white T-shirt he wore made his shoulders seem massive. She put up one hand to touch his chest. "But how could I do that? I want to be with you."

"Jesus, I don't know why. I don't give you anything you deserve." He took her wrist. "Why don't you go?"

"I will if you say, 'Marie, go and don't come back.' Hah! You can't say it, can you?"

"Yes, I can." He paused. "Marie, go and don't come back."

"No!" She pulled violently with the wrist he still held. He was caught off-balance and fell on the bed beside her. "I will make you want me," she said.

She began to kiss him, his eyes and cheeks and throat, trying to force from him the signs that his body wanted hers. She was reaching to take off her sweater when he put a rough hand on her arm.

"Dammit, Marie, this isn't what you really want."

"Yes, yes, it is."

"Marie, listen to me. I've hurt you already, and I'm going to hurt you even more. There's no way I can keep it from happening."

"I don't care. From now on, I am going to be like you. I will not care. That way, you can't hurt me."

He closed his eyes. But even when she came to him, the tension that was now part of his life did not fully dissolve.

Chapter Ten

Judge Kenneth Cox surveyed his courtroom.

For the second day it had gathered in an overflow load of press and spectators, their coats still damp from the snow that was falling delicately but turning into a muddy gruel as soon as it touched the streets of Foley Square.

The jury—seven men and five women, their occupations ranging from cleaning woman to retired insurance executive—wore intent, slightly self-conscious expressions, aware that Ben Lowell and Sanford Marsh had fought over their selection for nearly a week. Needlessly, in the judge's opinion. He had long ago concluded that the first twelve people willing to serve would do as well as any other twelve. But Lowell had seemed bent on social conscience, whereas Marsh had looked for hardworking family types. The attorneys were suffering, Cox thought, from a case of spotlight fever.

He shifted in the chair, aware that a spotlight was on him, too. From the moment the trial had been put on his calendar, word had come down through the party's channels that Hart Collins was "interested" in the proceedings. When Collins had won the election, Cox had expected the interest to diminish, but the president-elect, busily polishing the New

Equality programs for which a bare majority of the electorate had chosen him, was now described as "concerned."

In a second-row seat, where Cox was certain Ben Lowell had planted her, sat Martin Granger's widow, her face grave and lovely beneath a black fur hat. She gave the judge a melancholy smile, as if to suggest that she trusted him to rectify her grief.

Mentally, Cox frowned, but outwardly there was little change in his bland expression. There rarely was.

He had been cursed with a round, cherubic face that had stubbornly refused to age, even when his hair had grayed and disappeared around it. As a young man, in order to convince others that his face was animated by an adult sensibility, he had had to work harder and louder than any of his friends in the radical movement. Then, as he grew older and ceased being active in the cause, concluding that communism was not the only or even the best answer to social injustice, he had had to bear the patronizing censure of those who claimed he never had taken the issues seriously. Now, when he wore the robes that were his reward for years of service to the political establishment, there still was little clue on his face to the intensity of his interest in the ideological questions that had fired his youth, or to the cynicism that had made him reject most of the standard answers.

The works of Martin Granger had intrigued him, precisely because they offered something more than standard answers. Often in this courtroom he had thought of Granger's focus on the psychological, rather than economic, needs of the masses: If the cultural ghettos were the root cause of many of the crimes that came before him, was money really the cure? He had seen so many billions poured into those ghettos, with little reduction in their size or, seemingly, in their effects. He was too disillusioned to believe that Granger's ideas could make a real difference; but his interest in the trial and in

Martin Granger went well beyond the question of whether Astrid Cain had killed him.

He leaned forward in the chair that had been built up to compensate for his lack of height and turned his attention to Ben Lowell.

In a manner as precise as the press of his three-piece charcoal brown suit, Lowell called Dr. Fontana of the medical examiner's office.

Fontana's language was technical, but that did not prevent a vivid mental picture from forming in the listeners' minds as he described the spike that jutted upward from one of the heavy abstract steel sculptures at the edge of the Granger terrace and then detailed the effects on Granger's internal organs of being penetrated by that spike, driven in by the force of his 170-pound body, which had reached a velocity of 35 miles per hour at the moment of impact. The neck had also been broken when the head snapped down on the flagstone terrace. Either injury alone, the doctor stated, would have caused death.

In her second-row seat, Lauren Granger put her head in her hands. Lowell directed a long look at her, which pulled the eyes of the jury with it.

"Now, Doctor," he said, "could you infer anything about the nature of the fall from the position of the body?"

"Since the body was impaled at the abdomen, I infer that the deceased was facing outward when he fell."

"Standing on the balcony and looking out?"

"Yes."

"A position that provided a perfect opportunity for someone to come up from behind, across the thick carpet of the study—"

"Objection!" Marsh said.

"Sustained," said Cox automatically. "Suppose we remember the rudiments, Counselor."

"Of course, Your Honor," said Lowell. He seemed about to dismiss the witness and then turned back. "Doctor, was there anything in your autopsy findings to indicate whether the deceased's fall could have been caused by some natural condition?"

"No. However, we do know that the deceased did suffer from a condition that would not show up on autopsy."

"Oh? What condition was that?"

"He had a cardiac arrhythmia known as Stokes-Adams attacks, or drop attacks."

"Please describe the nature and effects of this condition."

"Stokes-Adams attacks are caused either by an irregularity of the heartbeat or by a temporary actual stopping or pausing of the heartbeat, such that circulation to the brain is no longer adequate, which results in a fainting episode or a drop to the ground. Usually these attacks are only temporary, and circulation is restored enough for the person to regain consciousness."

Cox watched Sanford Marsh, whose nostrils had flared for a moment when the cardiac condition was mentioned. No doubt, Cox thought, Marsh had hoped to introduce it himself, as his explanation of the fall; but surely he was realistic enough to expect the state to bring it up first in order to defuse it.

When Marsh rose to cross-examine, his suit, which seemed perfectly to match the pewter gray of his hair, was so quietly elegant that it had the effect of turning Lowell's sleek tailoring into a shout.

Marsh got the doctor to acknowledge that, by itself, a fall from a third story would not usually be fatal. "In your nine years with the medical examiner's office, have you ever come across a homicide committed in this manner?"

"No," said the doctor. "But I have observed that human beings can find many ingenious ways to kill one another."

"The jury," Cox said, before Marsh had fully turned to him, "will disregard the witness's last remark, which is gratuitous."

Marsh smiled. "Doctor, let's turn to something that the jury may properly need to hear more about." He began to ask about the arrhythmia, getting the doctor to repeat that it would not show up on autopsy and to once again describe the condition in detail; and he underscored the fact that it was aggravated by emotional stress.

"And so," he concluded, "the autopsy does not show that Martin Granger suffered a cardiac arrhythmic seizure, a Stokes-Adams attack, on the night of June 23?"

"No. By the nature of the condition, it couldn't show that."

"But equally, then, it could not show that he did *not* suffer such a seizure?"

"That is also true," said the doctor equably.

On balance, Cox thought as Marsh sat down, it would seem to be a draw.

Lowell stood up briskly, to introduce a mock-up of the Granger balcony and terrace and to call another witness, an investigator who had conducted a number of tests, using sandbags of the same weight as the deceased. They showed that a body falling from the balcony would strike the sculpture in the majority of instances.

"So the fatal impalement was not a fluke, then, but was a likely result, which anyone could reasonably expect if a man were pushed from that balcony?"

Cox sustained Marsh's objection and gave the jury the futile instruction to disregard the question. Lowell smiled.

The first witness after the noon recess was Detective Hugh Riley, Shield Number 5279. The man, Cox thought, must spend his working life in plainclothes, but his manner suggested that his tweed jacket and dark slacks were an uncomfortable substitute for a uniform.

Riley stated that he had arrived at the Granger brownstone at ten forty-seven P.M. on June 23 and had been let in by the defendant, who identified herself as the deceased's secretary and the party who had called the police.

"She took us through the house," he said, "to the terrace in back and the body on the sculpture. She said it was Dr. Martin Granger and he had fallen from a balcony on the third floor. She said it was an accident, that they had been talking up in his study and he had been on the balcony."

"She used that exact word, 'talking'?"

Riley consulted his notebook. "Yes, sir. She said that while they were talking, the deceased had slumped over the railing suddenly, those were her words, and then he fell before she took in what was happening."

"Please describe the manner in which she gave you her information."

"She was pretty cool and businesslike. Like a good secretary, I guess you could say."

Lowell smiled. Then he switched to questions about the location of the terrace in relation to the buildings that adjoined and overlooked it, establishing that there were at least several dozen windows from which the terrace was visible.

"Is it accurate, then, to state that here was a body in full view, almost on display, which could have been seen by a lot of people if they had looked out their windows and which therefore could have been discovered at any time?"

Judge Cox automatically ruled, "Sustained," but the implication could not be erased: that Astrid Cain had called the police only because she had no real alternative.

Lowell concluded with a series of rapid-fire questions about the information the defendant had given the police: Did she tell you that she was a reporter? that she had quarreled with

Martin Granger? that her husband had worked for him? that she was trying to get other public figures to discredit him? that her husband was planning to give much of his money to the deceased?

To all but the first Riley answered, "No."

Although Lowell was leading his own witness, the judge was pleased to note that Marsh accepted that the content of the answers was true and did not waste the court's time by objecting.

"Would you say, then," Lowell asked, "that Astrid Cain Chapin was a woman who tried to cooperate with the police, tried to help in your investigation?"

"No, sir. No way. I'd say she held back on just about everything."

Sanford Marsh rose and paused a moment before cross-examining. "Detective Riley, how many homicides have you investigated in your years on the squad?"

"Oh, I guess over a hundred."

"Have all the people you questioned been cooperative?"

"Well . . . no, sir."

"Do you find that often there are other reasons for their lack of cooperation? Other than guilt, I mean?"

Riley sighed. "Yes, sir."

"Thank you. No further questions."

"But a lot of times they *are* guilty, you know."

There was a sputter of laughter in the courtroom, which made Riley flush.

Cox turned to the jury. "Ladies and gentlemen, this is another gratuitous remark, which I see you have heard and which is out of order. I remind you that it is you, and only you, who will establish the guilt or innocence of the defendant."

But the defendant herself, Cox noted, had joined in the laughter. She seemed to exercise no control over the emotions that played freely across her face. Or perhaps, he thought, she really was a woman who had no concept of control, as Lowell had worked to establish the day before in his opening statement.

While Lowell had described a woman driven by hatred and by the fear of losing her husband's money, Astrid Cain had sat quietly enough, wearing a plain, black dress; but her face had been all burning eyes, framed by the conflagration of her hair. It had taken little effort to imagine her as a woman who, in Lowell's words, "could not conceal her hatred even after she was arrested and who went on trying, from prison, to use the weapon of publicity against the man she had already sent to a gruesome death."

In the defense opening, Sanford Marsh had countered, in his stately and resonant voice, with another explanation: The defendant's actions, he said, were motivated by a very deep love for her husband, whose mysterious absence was a source of great pain to her. Months ago, she had seen her husband begin to change and to suffer a paralysis of the spirit, which coincided with his going to work for Martin Granger and led her to want to investigate. Marsh admitted that she had deceived Granger but said it was not uncommon for newspaper people to work undercover; and in any case, the defendant had come to feel that she had a story which the public, as well as her husband, should know. "You will learn," Marsh had told the jury, "that her suspicions of Martin Granger were not unreasonable ones, even if they cannot be proved to be true."

At that point the defendant had half-risen in her seat, a quick, defiant movement that had flagged every eye in the courtroom, and Marsh had smoothly acknowledged that his client was "a woman who feels things strongly." But, he had concluded, "far from committing murder, she has only been following a course of action dictated by her duty as a newspaperwoman and, above all, by her love and concern for her husband."

The battle lines, Cox thought, had been clearly drawn by those opening statements: vengeance versus wifely devotion.

He turned back to the witness chair, which Hugh Riley had left. The next witness was being sworn in: Detective Paul Damon, Shield Number 5480.

The defendant's face changed again, noted the judge, but this time it was as if a shutter had dropped, leaving an unnatural stillness as the only motion. She had control after all, he thought, and wondered why this witness should be the first to call it into play. In fact the man looked as motionless as she. As he answered questions, his back and wide shoulders were held mathematically straight under the navy jacket and pale blue shirt; and his eyes were fixed on Ben Lowell as if by a tight, invisible cord.

"When you questioned the defendant at the stationhouse on August 15, what did she tell you about her feeling toward Martin Granger?"

"She said, quote, I hated him."

There was a murmuring in the courtroom. Lowell paused for it, but the witness gave no sign of hearing it.

"Did she explain why she hated him?"

"No. She refused to explain."

In a seat halfway back in the courtroom, Marie Lazare leaned forward, certain that it was crucial to hear Paul's testimony but unable to attach any significance to the sentences he was uttering. She had told him she was going to attend the trial, and he had said, "All right," in the same flat voice he was using now. And then added, "It's probably a good idea."

She could feel the loud, fast bumping of her heart; that frightened her, because nothing had been said to cause it. She gripped the back of the bench in front of her.

"According to what Astrid Cain told you," Ben Lowell was saying, "why did she wait until the night of June 23, the night he died, to tell Martin Granger that she was married to one of his associates?"

"She said she couldn't have gotten her story if he had known."

"Did the defendant characterize her marriage to you?"

"Yes. She said it was a happy one."

"Despite the fact that she hadn't heard from her husband in months?"

"That is what she said."

"During this interview, did you make it plain to her that her situation was a serious one?"

"She realized it."

Lowell paused and took a long look at the defendant. She, Judge Cox noted, was staring at the witness, but he had not once glanced in her direction.

"Now, will you tell us what happened on the night of August 17—that is, two nights after you had questioned the defendant, when she realized that her situation was a serious one?"

"Yes. She came to see me at my apartment, a little after midnight."

"What reason did she give for this midnight visit?"

"She wanted . . . We had known each other some years ago. She said she wanted to talk to me as a friend."

"And did she?"

"She asked me to help her."

"How?"

"She asked if I would tell my colleagues that she was innocent and get them to call off the investigation."

"Did you refuse?"

"Yes."

"What did she do then?"

"She offered me a bribe."

There was a soft sound, as if a collective breath had been drawn in the audience.

Marsh leaped to his feet, ungainly for once. "Your Honor, I object! This is irrelevant!"

"Overruled," said Cox.

Marsh sank down, his eyes jumping from his client back to the witness stand.

"She offered you a bribe," Lowell repeated. "And what was the nature of this bribe? What did this woman, who had told you she was happily married and who is described by my colleague as a devoted wife, what did she offer in exchange for calling off the investigation?"

Judge Cox finally leaned over. "The court is waiting, Officer."

"Yes. She offered to sleep with me."

"Thank you," said Lowell into the hubbub. "No further questions."

Sanford Marsh looked urgently at his client; only a few minutes were left of the recess Cox had granted him. "Don't send me up there to walk into any more surprises. Is there anything else, anything at all?"

She nodded a mute No, waiting for a wave of nausea to pass. Her mind was going in a futile, sick circle: How could she think Damon would have to testify about that night, because she had not dreamed there would be a trial, but there was a trial, and she had convinced him all too well. . . .

Marsh ran his hand across his eyes. "All right. God knows what else he might say if I don't stop him. I'll have to get him to acknowledge your past relationship."

"Do you have to do that? Can't you let it go?"

Red suffused the fine leathering of Marsh's face. "I was under the impression you were interested in being acquitted. I have to salvage your credibility. And my only hope is to destroy that detective. If I don't, his testimony is going to destroy you."

His purposeful manner dropped for a moment, and he looked at her helplessly. "I still can't believe it. Why on earth did you do it?"

"I told you. I thought he could help me. I was afraid. And he was . . . I've just explained what he was."

She bit her lip against the desire to tell Marsh the truth, to be free of its awful weight. But if I told you that, she thought, you *would* resign the case.

Damon watched Sanford Marsh rise and move toward him.

It was, he thought, as if the past four months had been just a preparation for this day in court—no, the past eight years had been. To have forged, out of the cheap metal of passions and errors and defeats, an impartial instrument of steel—that was what he had undertaken when he had joined the force. And finally he had achieved it. In a courtroom, which was appropriate.

He looked impassively at Marsh and waited for the first question, feeling nothing but the tensed readiness of his mind and the light pressure of his hands resting on his thighs.

"Detective Damon," said Marsh, as courteously as if they had just met at some official dinner, "you look very stiff and rigid in that chair. Are you sure you are quite comfortable?"

You can't throw me with that cheap trick, Damon thought. He squared his shoulders. "I'm fine, thank you."

"You're sure? Good. Now, you stated that you knew the defendant some years ago. Did you know her well?"

"Yes."

"You were more than friends?"

"Yes." It was all as expected, he thought: Astrid had told

Marsh a great deal—perhaps everything. But he was ready, even for that.

"In fact, were you not, for a period of nearly three years, in love with Astrid Cain?"

"Yes." He was aware of a movement from Ben Lowell, a startled cocking of the head, and of a rustle in the audience.

"Tell us, please, how you separated. Was it you who broke it off?"

"No." He looked back at the memory, and felt nothing.

"Then Astrid Cain was the one who left you?"

"Yes." He thought of the man who had gone to the door a dozen times that night, wanting to bring her back, and felt nothing.

"Why did she leave you?"

"I had made a decision she did not approve of."

"What decision was that?"

"To join the police force."

Marsh's blue eyes were two innocent questions. "Wasn't there more to it than that?"

"Yes. I had decided to join the force instead of practicing law."

"And you had completed law school and passed the bar exam, had you not?"

"Yes." He thought of what he once had planned for his life, and felt nothing.

"And the defendant objected to your abandoning the law?"

"Yes."

"So she rejected you, criticizing a major life decision you had made. That rankled you, perhaps?"

"No."

"You are so different from the rest of us, then, that it does not hurt your pride and make you angry if the woman you love criticizes you and walks out on you?"

"That was eight years ago."

"Please answer the question."

"I mean that it does not affect me today."

"I see. So you had no particular feeling when Astrid Cain came back into your life as the suspect in a murder investigation?"

"No. It was just another investigation."

"But you used your past association, did you not? You kept her from knowing that you were working on the case, and then walked in to question her on August 15 in the hope that your presence would throw her off-balance. Isn't that true?"

"It's a common technique."

"And perhaps we had better not discuss the ethics of it. Now, during that interrogation, didn't you offer to help Astrid Cain?"

"I believe I said that I could help her if she would explain her actions. Which she refused to do."

"Did you tell her specifically what you meant by 'help'?"

"No." But I would have helped her, he thought, if she had admitted killing Granger.

"When Astrid Cain came to your apartment on the night of August 17, what was your professional assessment, as a trained detective, of her state?"

"I thought she was tense. Nervous."

Marsh turned to the jury. "So, when Astrid Cain goes to see a former . . . an old friend, who has offered her some kind of unspecified help, she is tense and nervous." He swung back to Damon. "Isn't it true that when you saw the state she was in, you knew you could get her to do almost anything?"

"No, that is not true."

"Isn't it true that you felt a desire, a perfectly understandable desire, to get back at this woman who had criticized and rejected you?"

"No, that is not true."

"You felt no desire to humiliate her?"

"None."

"It didn't occur to you that if you could get her to say or do something injudicious, you could use that against her and discredit her?"

"No." It occurred to me, he thought, that she was guilty.

Marsh took his glasses from his breast pocket and appeared to study them. "So you claim that Astrid Cain, out of the blue, offered to sleep with you if you would call off the investigation. What exact words did she use?"

"It was her behavior that made clear what she meant."

Marsh put the glasses on and leaned forward as if in amazement. "She never made the offer in so many words?"

"No."

"Then how can you be sure you weren't reading things into her behavior that she did not intend? That the idea was in *her* mind and not simply in yours?"

It was time to put an end to this, Damon thought. "I can be sure because of the way she behaved. It's not difficult to tell, you know. There are women on 42nd Street who make their meaning quite clear without saying a word."

Marsh's voice was suddenly tight. "Is that the comparison you wish to offer this court?"

Yes, he thought. "I'll leave that to the court," he said.

"I think you had better. Now, will you—"

"For example, the defendant came over to me and kissed me. Then she—"

"I'll ask the questions, please."

"Then I asked her outright if she was offering to pay me, and she said Yes."

"I said that I would ask the questions!"

"Then ask the right ones."

"Your Honor—" Marsh began, but Cox was already speaking.

"Please conduct yourself as if you had received courtroom training at the Police Academy, Mr. Damon."

Marsh looked at Damon without expression for a moment.

"You claim that the defendant was offering you sex as a payment?"

"Yes."

"You couldn't have been mistaken?"

"No."

"You wanted me to ask the right questions. Let me try this one."

There was a pause, and Damon knew suddenly that Astrid had told Marsh everything and that he was going to gamble on using it. I'm ready for you, he thought. She's not going to get away with it. With any of it.

"Did you refuse the bribe you claim you were offered?"

Damon glanced at the prosecution table, where Ben Lowell was waiting to hear what he had every right to expect; for when Lowell had asked, on the day he first told them, "You turned her down, I hope?", hadn't the answer been merely a contemptuous "Would I be telling you about a bribe if I had accepted it?"

"I'll repeat the question," said Sanford Marsh. "Did you refuse the bribe you claim you were offered?"

"Of course I refused. I treated her like any other whore."

After a moment he realized that Ben Lowell was still looking at him expectantly, that the words had been said only in his mind, not to the court. He felt a series of pressure points on his thighs and saw that his fingers were digging in tightly, like a string of leeches. He put his hands on the arms of the chair.

Of course I refused; that was the response he had determined to give, if it came to this. He had to say it, to do whatever was necessary, because he had to make certain—

Before he could stop it, the rest of the thought formed in his mind, like the call of someone leaping from a cliff, whom he could not reach.

To make certain of her guilt. Those were the words that

had come into his mind. Because that was what he had meant. He suddenly saw the past four months, since the night she had come to him, not as a cool, dispassionate search for the truth but as a journey of justification for what he wanted to believe. For what he needed to believe so badly that he had gone right to the edge of perjury for it.

He became aware that Marsh's lips were moving, which must mean that he was speaking again. After a moment the words penetrated: "I am asking you what your response was to this alleged bribe."

He looked at the defense table. Astrid's face was crooked and white, like badly painted china. To make certain you were guilty, he thought. So I could maintain my indifference.

The knowledge washed over him, each wave reaching farther than the one before. To deny what I felt that night, he said to her silently. Because to admit it would be to know how much . . . things still could matter to me. So you had to become as low as I could make you. Your guilt was the necessary ingredient, the price I made you pay. For my indifference.

He saw her struggle to move, and fail. He turned back to Marsh. "I slept with her."

There was an eruption of noise and a loud gaveling from Cox.

Damon's eyes went out to the crowd till they found Marie. The man who could not be reached, he thought . . . and then could not finish the thought. He did not know how it would, or should, end.

"Let me understand this," Marsh was saying. "You claim that Astrid Cain offered to sleep with you as a bribe and that you accepted?"

He felt suddenly more tired than he could bear, and he leaned forward with an effort, his hands hanging loosely over the chair arms. "Yes. I mean, no. I don't think one can say that a bribe was accepted, since I made no attempt to stop the investigation."

Marsh's pewter eyebrows rose disdainfully. "So the offer you claim she made was a bribe and was reprehensible, but your acceptance was blameless?"

"No. I don't mean that. I only mean that she did not get the result she wanted."

"But you did, didn't you? You succeeded in getting your revenge for the way Astrid Cain had left you eight years ago."

"No. No. We had been . . . We once had . . . It's difficult to explain what happened that night."

"Then let me help you. I suggest that you tricked the defendant into coming to see you, by your clever and ambiguous offer of help. I suggest that you then forced yourself on her. I suggest that afterwards you felt guilt over what you had done. But you could not accept that guilt, so you rearranged things in your own mind in order to make *her* seem like the guilty party."

He cradled his hands, seeing that the last part of it was true, though not in the way Marsh meant—that what he had done was to turn his own response, his very capacity still to respond, into an indictment of her. "I have just admitted my own responsibility," he said. "I wanted to sleep with her, and I did."

"I see." Marsh removed his glasses and pointed them at the jury in time with his next words. "I see very clearly. In fact, I think we all do. No further questions."

Ben Lowell rose, his anger as visible and as startling on him as a soiled shirt would have been. Without leaving the prosecution table, he said, "On August 18, did you or did you not tell myself and several of your colleagues that Astrid Cain had offered you a bribe?"

"Yes, I did."

"Are you now saying that statement was not true?"

"No. It was true. She did offer."

"And did you force yourself on her?"

"I . . . No."

"So she was a willing and eager partner?"

"Objection! The witness cannot know what was in her mind!"

"I'll rephrase," Lowell said quickly. "Did she offer any resistance to you, verbal or physical?"

"She . . . No."

Lowell turned to the jury. "No further questions," he said contemptuously.

The jury shifted in their seats.

After a while Damon felt the bailiff shake his arm. "Please step down, sir. You're excused."

But I'm not, he thought. There is no excuse.

He left the stand.

Marsh was telling her to rise because the judge was leaving the courtroom.

She stood. It took all her effort. She did not know for which reason: because of the boomerang that was now encircling her own neck even more tightly, or because of the man through whom it had sliced in its passage.

Chapter Eleven

Outside the windows of the cabin loomed the peaks of the Wasatch Mountains, white and distant. On the primitive kitchen table the remnants of soup and sandwiches had congealed and dried. On the portable cassette recorder beside the narrow bed a tape of the Brandenburg Concerti was playing for the fourth consecutive time.

Dr. David Chapin stretched and brought his hand to his face to check the date on his watch. As nearly as he could remember, he had been in this place for three and a half weeks. And out of New York—and the world—for nearly six months. He wondered if he should consider moving on; but motion, he had learned, could be just a substitute for true progress, which had to be internal.

Sometimes he wished he could turn himself into the subject of one of his own experiments: section a block of spiritual tissue, slip it into the electron microscope, and make a definitive finding. Would it show a change in the structure of the cells—less predatory, less engorged—or would they have stubbornly resisted the modifications of new knowledge?

He thought of the actual experiments he had conducted for so long, and so often fruitlessly, submitting those poor creatures of the sea to the artificial life of a laboratory tank and the artificial death that began with anesthesia and exposure of their brains to the probing of microelectrodes. . . . "Isn't it strange," Martin had once observed, "that one is drawn to biology because of his interest in life and yet winds up destroying life? But I suppose that's not the only paradox that confronts you."

David turned his head to the framed photograph, taken on his wedding day, that he had propped on the crate beside the bed. She was not really beautiful, he thought, but there was something inside her, something luminous, that he finally had been able to see and to appreciate. And when she looked at him, so much like a child, as she was doing in the picture, he could accept that what she had to teach him was the right lesson to learn.

His eyes moved from the face of his sister Rosalie to that of his wife. Divine strength, he thought, for that was what the name Astrid meant; he had looked it up soon after they met. And she did have a kind of strength. The kind born more of simplicity than divinity, perhaps. He had basked in it for a long time, taking pleasure in her ability to reduce everything to a simple question of what would make one happy. She would never know, he thought, how many times he had sat in the study, clutching the arms of his chair to hold himself back from going out to her and drowning all sense of conflict in the soothing flow of her words and the lovely motions of her body. . . .

He got up quickly and went to rummage in the single wooden cupboard for something to eat. The bread was stale, the number of cans had shrunk to two, and the coffee was gone. He pulled on some warm clothes and boots and went out to start the old Ford he had bought in Denver; it was the fourth of the progressively more battered vehicles for which he had traded in on his random passage to the West, putting a distance of comfort as well as miles between himself and the wealth to which he had grown so accustomed.

The road down to the store was treacherous with snow. He drove cautiously along the hairpin turns that had been carved into the skin of the mountain. It was impossible to travel across the country, he had learned, and be unaware of Nature's overwhelming presence and power. No matter how much man thought he had conquered her, she dominated his physical landscape just as surely as she mandated his role in society. "We must fight Nature's tyranny," he thought, the sentence from Martin's book coming into his mind as smoothly as if it were his own thought, "by reminding her favorites that their 'natural gifts' are arbitrarily bestowed and must therefore be used as a trust that benefits all men."

And what had been Nature's gift to him? David thought. The mind of a scientist, created in mocking reversal of Rosalie's; and he had used it blindly, pushing aside all doubts that he was worthy of its rewards, ignoring the chasm that yawned between the world of living human problems and the esoteric challenge of the biophysics of one synapse. Then Martin had put the terrible question to him: "What have you done with your ability, David, except to indulge yourself in the pleasure of using it?"—and had peeled away the layers of sham in his answers.

The wheel of the Ford suddenly refused to obey his hands, and he skidded through a terrifying moment. When it was over he laughed, thinking that if he were not careful, he would kill himself in the process of trying to resolve the question of his life. He wondered if that necessarily would be a bad thing, but he made himself concentrate on the road until it widened in front of him and he saw the white rectangle of the store.

He bought enough things for two weeks and paid another month's rent on the cabin, which the storekeeper owned.

There was a newspaper on the counter; he deliberately had not read one since he had left the world, nor had he listened to radio or television.

It occurred to him that the country must have elected a president weeks ago and that he had completely forgotten to vote for Hart Collins, as he once had promised Martin to do. One more failing, he thought, hesitating for a moment and then picking up the paper. Within moments he saw a story that referred to "President-elect Collins."

An announcement bordered with holly caught his eye: *Only 16 Days Till Christmas.*

Then he saw the story next to it.

The storekeeper was shouting at him before he heard the man's voice and looked up to say that he was all right. Still, the cup of coffee was welcome, and he sat on a stack of food cartons, sipping it and holding its warmth against an onslaught of guilt and anger.

It could not matter that he had not yet fully grappled with the decision he had escaped to make; if she was on trial for killing Martin, he would have to go back.

Astrid, Astrid, he thought. The coffee cup shivered in his hands.

"My differences with Martin Granger are well known," Professor Llewellyn Jones told the court.

His manner combined the authority of years in the classroom with the bland impartiality of the openmindedness on which he prided himself.

"For example," he said, "last year I published an article in the *Journal of Social Sciences,* in which I pointed out Granger's failure to take sufficient account of the effects of social conditioning."

"Then will you tell us," Ben Lowell said, "why you were

not willing to be quoted by Astrid Cain in the article she told you she was preparing?"

"Certainly. Ideological differences within the profession are one thing. Biased attacks in the public press are quite another. And it was clear to me that she intended the latter."

"Sustained," said Judge Cox to Marsh's objection. He ordered the jury to disregard the answer and turned to Lowell. "Just ask him what she said."

Before answering, Jones folded his thin hands in his lap. "She asked if I had knowledge of any persons who had been harmed by their association with Granger. And she wanted to know if I objected to his method of requiring people to do extended periods of fieldwork in areas unrelated to their interests—if I did not think that was unnecessary and harmful."

"And did you have any such thoughts?"

"Certainly not. I consider Martin Granger to be one of our most important thinkers." He smiled. "I cannot accept every aspect of his theories, but that does not mean he was harmful."

"Thank you," said Lowell. "Now, will you tell us about a phone call you received on July 30 of this year?"

"With pleasure. Miss Cain telephoned me. She said that the police had been questioning her in regard to Granger's death, and she asked me—begged me, really—not to tell them about her visit to me. Of course I refused, and she became very angry."

"What did she say?"

"She called my humanitarianism into question. She said I could not be truly concerned about people if I were unwilling to help an individual in trouble."

The crowd waited for Marsh to cross-examine, expecting a strong challenge, but he was very brief.

"When Astrid Cain interviewed you, did she give you any

reason for wanting to do a negative article on Martin Granger?"

"Oh, she made a speech that I suppose was her rationale, but I—"

"Yes or no, Professor?"

"If you insist on a simplistic answer, then, yes. However, she had no real—"

"Thank you, Professor."

As he left the stand, Jones's manner conveyed exasperation with the black-and-white procedures of the courtroom.

Senator Roscoe Harding managed to suggest the same thing even before he was sworn in.

As Lowell took him through an account of the visit Astrid Cain had paid to him the previous March, he continually strayed from the path of the questions, his raddled face shining with perspiration and his hands moving in expansive gestures.

"No, I was not really a supporter of Martin Granger's. Of course, he was involved in something that concerns all of us—how to help our citizens live in greater equality. In that sense, Granger and I were brothers. But I fail to see how anyone can work for the betterment of society without looking to our Lord for guidance. And I pray that our new president will look for it and get it, even though I did not work for his election."

Frequently Judge Cox interrupted and ordered him to simply answer the question. Each time Harding responded with a heavily polite "Of course, Your Honor," which suggested disbelief that the short, pink-cheeked man on the bench was actually a judge.

Ben Lowell grew even more crisp, so that the questions began to sound like pencils snapping in half. Finally he got from Harding that Astrid Cain explicitly had told him she wanted to attack Granger in print and had requested his help.

"Well, of course I didn't agree. Turn the other cheek, that's my motto. And then I told her a story she didn't much like to hear, about a woman from my own constituency. This fine woman has two children with brain damage, and when she ran out of doctors and money and hope, somebody told her about Martin Granger and the Grants of Last Resort that his Institute gives out. And sure enough, she got the money to take her children to a specialist in Switzerland, and they were helped."

Marsh, who had made repeated objections and could have challenged this last testimony because it was irrelevant, said nothing, and he declined to cross-examine.

When a tall, big-boned, graying woman took the stand, the crowd did not know at first what she had to do with the proceedings. But as soon as Lowell established that she was the mother of Harry Pine, there was an anticipatory rustle, for she was the first witness whose testimony might pertain to the "souvenir collection" that was to many the most tantalizing feature of the trial.

Mrs. Pine had large hands that kept playing with the buttons of her purple wool suit as she told how Astrid Cain, claiming to be doing research on former Institute personnel, had come to see her in April and had questioned her extensively about her son, his work in bioengineering, and his acceptance by Granger as an Institute fellow when he was only twenty-two. The defendant, she stated, had asked her why a chemistry medal that Harry had won in high school should be in Dr. Granger's possession, but she had been able to offer no explanation. To the crowd's disappointment, Lowell moved on quickly, eliciting that the defendant had asked repeatedly if Harry Pine ever expressed dissatisfaction with Dr. Granger; she particularly had wanted to know if there were any signs that he doubted his work or himself.

The witness had saved all her son's letters, which she had

shown to Astrid Cain, and at Lowell's request she read a passage from one of them to the jury, her pleasant voice low-pitched and steady: "This was written when he had been at the Institute for three months. He says, 'Martin—I am now on a first-name basis with him—is incredibly generous with his time. One day last week he spent four hours with me, discussing the experiments I hope to do when I've finished my fieldwork at the Home for the Aging. He has the most stimulating mind and is always asking questions that keep me thinking for weeks." Sanford Marsh rose to object that the testimony was irrelevant, but Judge Cox smiled amiably at the witness and said he would allow it.

"Did your son ever write to you that he was thinking of changing his career?"

"Yes. After a few more months he wrote that he was getting more and more involved in his work with elderly people. Here, he says, 'I am beginning to think that I have a real obligation to help these people. What if the bioengineer turned into a social worker?' And a month after that he wrote, 'I'm trying to decide what is the best course for my future, and Martin is giving me a lot of help.'"

The letters had slowed, she said, and finally stopped, until the one that arrived the day after he committed suicide. She read that, too: "'Dear Mother. I've been given the gift of a brain, so I should be able to straighten myself out, but I can't. I only know that I can't live this way any longer. So I have decided not to live. Please don't hurt too much for me. After today I won't be hurting at all.'"

"And what was Astrid Cain's reaction when you showed her this letter?"

"Well, she was sympathetic, but she asked if I didn't think it could mean that Dr. Granger had put pressure on Harry in some way, had made him feel guilty or something, and had, well . . ."

"Driven him to suicide, is that what she suggested?"

"Yes."

"And what did you tell her?"

"I said I didn't see how that was possible, because Harry had admired the doctor so much, and anyway, I'd had such a nice letter from him after Harry died. And besides . . ." She hesitated, her hands now lying still in her lap.

"Did you think there was a possible explanation for your son's death, having nothing to do with his career or with Dr. Granger?"

"Yes," she whispered.

"I know this must be painful for you, but in the interest of truth, can you bring yourself to tell us?"

"Yes. Harry was . . . He had always fought . . . I knew he couldn't help it . . ." She gave Lowell a look of mute appeal.

"Was your son a homosexual, is that it?"

She nodded.

Lowell waited for the crowd's sympathetic murmur to subside.

At the defense table Sanford Marsh sighed, knowing that much of the woman's testimony was legally irrelevant but knowing also that objections would be futile. Cox had made it plain they would be overruled, and in any case they carried the double risk of antagonizing the jury and underscoring the testimony itself. He felt a moment's irritation with his client, who looked perfectly calm, no doubt counting on him to undo everything later by using the souvenir collection.

He looked back at Lowell, who was saying to Mrs. Pine, "Did you give this explanation of your son's death to Astrid Cain?"

"Yes. I did."

"Did she seem to accept it?

"Well, she never said she didn't, but she asked a lot more

questions, like whether it . . . the problem, I mean . . . had upset Harry very much before, and why it suddenly should be enough to make him . . ." She looked at Lowell helplessly.

"Did you see an article in the New York *Sentinel* on October 14 of this year, an interview the defendant gave to Rose Custer?"

"Yes."

"Let me read one sentence from it. Quote, According to Cain, Pine was an Institute fellow who committed suicide while under pressure to give up bioengineering. Close quote. Do you agree with that?"

"No." She smiled sadly. "I almost wish I could."

"Well, Mrs. Pine, I think that you have shown great courage in coming here to say what you have, and I for one will not trouble you with more questions."

The time was four-thirty, and the air in the courtroom was thick with sympathy.

Sanford Marsh bent his head to the defendant's for a long moment. Then he looked up and said, "I have no questions for this witness at this time."

On the early television news there was an artist's sketch of Mrs. Pine testifying while the gray and dark red heads of Marsh and the defendant huddled together. "At the end of the fourth day of the trial," the reporter concluded, "the prosecution had added telling details to its portrait of Astrid Cain as a woman blind to everything but her vendetta against the dead man."

Marie Lazare watched it at the end of her voice lesson, on her teacher's set, staring past the images to the memory of the way Paul had turned from her when she ran to him after his testimony, and the shameful way she had reacted, until that Mr. Lowell had come to her and calmed her down. "You know," said her teacher, "I wish they'd tell us what happened to that detective she slept with."

Jake Waldo watched at the home of the publisher of the *Blade*, where he and thirty others were attending a fund-raising dinner for the ballet. "Well, I think that woman is crazy," said one of the guests. "Never trust a redhead, I always say." Jake smiled.

His son watched on the flickering black-and-white set in the common room of the juvenile home, his mind leaping once again to the subpoena that lay hidden in his dresser drawer at home. He turned off the set with a jerk and sat staring at the blank screen.

Damon watched in a bar on Seventh Avenue, where he had gone not so much to drink as to escape the silence of his apartment.

"I don't think that broad killed him, do you?" said the man on the stool next to his.

Damon smiled without mirth.

"Looks like you don't much care, either."

He looked at the man sharply and said, "No. That's not true."

He saw that his manner seemed strange to the man, who grunted and turned away. Like Riley, he thought, who had been unable to accept his explanations. Perhaps they were unacceptable.

"Are you still in love with her, then, is that it?" Riley had asked.

"No. It's just that I was too determined to believe she was guilty."

"Yeah? I don't think that's going to go over too good when they bring you up on charges."

"For 'conduct unbecoming'? But they won't. Hugh, I'm resigning from the force."

Then Riley had exploded, his face growing so red that it turned his sandy eyebrows to snow; one minute calling him an ass and the next, a hell of a good detective; pleading with him to take whatever he had to, demotion or even suspension, but not to quit.

"And what the hell are you going to live on? Have you thought about that?"

"Yes. I have enough to get by for a while. An aunt of mine who never did a decent thing in her life finally did one when she died. She left me some money."

"So what? Money isn't the reason. I know it. Why do you have to resign? Why?"

He had wanted to explain that it was because his conduct had been truly "unbecoming"; that he had betrayed the department code, which required objectivity of an officer, and his own private code, which demanded that emotion never run his life.

But that had proved impossible to say, so he had given only the other part of the reason: "I'm resigning because there is something else I have to do, and I can't do it on the force."

"Yeah? What?

And when he told him, that was when Riley had turned away, disbelief and disgust and affection waging an open war on his face.

Damon finished the beer he had been nursing for the last half hour. Better to get on with it, he thought; why waste time when a decision had been made?

He went out, exchanging the yeasty warmth of the bar for the cold fluorescence of the streets, and caught a cab. The driver was young. On the seat beside him was a book that looked like a textbook. Halfway uptown Damon said, "It's hard, working your way through school, isn't it?" He relapsed into silence after he heard the Yes.

The address was a town house in the East Fifties, on a street sliding downward from chic. Damon could see into a foyer with a marble floor and an antique brass coat stand.

After a long time Sanford Marsh came to the door. When he opened it, his patrician features retracted slightly, as if a delivery boy had come to the wrong entrance. "I can't imagine what you want," he said.

"May I come in and tell you?"

They went into a small, formal room off the foyer. Marsh sat on what looked like a genuine Chippendale chair and said, "I have work to do in my study. What is it you want?"

Damon remained standing. "I'm offering you my services. As an investigator. I've resigned from the force, so there is nothing to prevent my working for you, and I think my years of experience could be useful. Of course I don't know how many investigators you already have." Marsh did not answer, merely lifted his gold-rimmed glasses from his nose and then replaced them, so he went on. "You're entitled to know why, of course. The damage I did to Astrid Cain in court was not done for good reasons, even though I was telling the truth. I don't think those reasons need concern anyone except me, but the results do, and by my own code of justice, I owe it to the defense to try to make up for the damage." Marsh still said nothing. "For instance, I have reason to believe Granger's cook knows something she hasn't told. She's very difficult, but I've established a kind of rapport with her, and I could keep working on her. I think it's possible that she might even be the anonymous caller the poice were looking for."

"And that would help us? Do I take it that you have now decided Mrs. Chapin is innocent? I'm afraid I can't follow your *volte face*."

There was no way, he thought, to make Marsh understand that all he wanted now was to search for the truth, wherever it led. "If there was an eyewitness," he said, "I'd like to help find her." Marsh did not answer. "Of course, I'd work on anything you thought best. If you're doing anything with the souvenir collection, trying to locate some of those people, I could help with that."

"No, I don't think that would be necessary." Marsh got up and moved closer to Damon; they were of a height. "I don't think we need your help at all. Among other things, it would only buttress the charge that she bribed you, by looking as if it had worked."

"I realize that, but no one would need—"

"That's not the only reason. I think you are simply feeling a need to assuage your guilty conscience. And I won't let you do it at my client's expense."

After a moment Damon said, "I can't blame you for thinking that."

"Thanks, but I don't need exoneration from you. Or anything else."

"Yes. Well, good night."

But before he went out, he turned back. "Will you at least tell her I made the offer?"

"That's up to me to decide, isn't it?"

It was eight-thirty when he rang the bell at the Granger brownstone.

He rang it five times; at the sixth, he thought, he would give up. For tonight only, because he was not taking Marsh's No for an answer. He would just have to work on his own; then if he turned up anything, Marsh wouldn't, couldn't, refuse. And this was the most promising place to start.

He was halfway down the short brick walk when he heard the door open and turned to see the bulk of Helen Jones, draped in a shapeless brown robe.

"Hello," he said. "I thought nobody was home."

"She's not."

"I came to see you, not her."

She seemed to consider, staring at the walk as if his statement and the bricks were of equal significance; then she opened the door fully and let him in. He realized that he had never seen her standing and that she was short: only five-four, he guessed, but the horizontal spread of her flesh could be distorting his estimate.

They went into the kitchen. On the table was half a baba au rhum, a plate with a partially eaten piece, and a glass of milk.

"I see you've been cooking for another dinner party."

"No," she said; and he realized that it was just a bedtime snack for herself. She offered him some, but he refused.

"Helen, do you know where Mrs. Granger has been going every day for the past week?"

"I never ask her."

"She's attending the trial of Astrid Cain for killing Dr. Granger."

"Oh, yes. That's right."

"Have you been reading about it in the paper?"

"No."

"Or hearing about it on the radio? The radio always seems to be on in here. And all over the house."

"I never pay any attention to it."

"So you don't realize that Astrid Cain stands a good chance of being convicted?"

"Isn't that what it means to be on trial?" Her voice was dryly amused.

His training kept him from looking surprised; he had become used to treating her as if she were slow. "Then you must realize how important it is for anyone who knows anything to come forward."

"I realize."

Without pausing, he asked, "Would Mrs. Granger be angry if you told what you know?"

For a moment he thought she was going to answer; instead

she picked up a fork and finished the piece of cake on the plate. She wasn't slow, he thought; she was malicious, playing a game with him for reasons he could not imagine.

She drank the milk. "I haven't said I know anything."

"Then why do I have the strong feeling that you *want* me to keep coming back and asking you these questions?"

That had been a mistake, he saw. He watched her cut another piece of cake and resigned himself to the only approach that she ever seemed to tolerate. "Where did you learn to cook and bake the way you do?"

She paused. "I studied."

"In a school?"

"No. By myself."

"Do you plan all the menus?"

"Yes."

"Mrs. Granger never makes suggestions? The doctor never did?"

"He didn't care what he ate. And she knows I do a better job than she could."

"How do you go about deciding what to serve?"

She turned her head to the counter. "My files."

"Those black cases? What kind of files?"

"One for recipes. One for every meal I've served. And one for people who come here a lot, telling what they like and what I've given them already."

Was there no moment of her life, he thought, that did not revolve around food? "Do you have cards on some of the doctor's associates, then? Some of them must have come a number of times. How about a Harry Pine, for instance?"

She seemed to frown, her raisin eyes nearly disappearing. "Oh, yes. He came a lot, years ago. Very polite. But anything with liver he couldn't touch."

"May I see?"

She nodded and told him to take out the bottom case,

which he brought to the table. He flipped to the Ps and found a card for Harry Pine.

"I thought so," she said. "I wrote, 'No liver.' But he loved veal. He was here a lot."

At least fifteen times, Damon saw. "Was Mrs. Granger at these dinners with the doctor's associates?"

"No. She had her own friends."

Damon flipped back to the Ks. "Here's an Ezra Kerr. Do you remember him?" Over twenty times.

She peered at the card. "That was a long time ago."

"What about him?"

"He was tall. Part Indian. He gave me a recipe for Indian pudding."

"Do you know what happened to him?"

"No. He went to work someplace out West, I think. I don't know."

"Do you recall anyone who was named Lee?" She looked away for a moment. "Do you?"

"Yes."

"What was his full name?"

"Leonora."

"It was a woman?"

"Yes."

"Do you know her last name?"

"Jonas."

"How long ago was this?"

"A long time."

"More than ten years?"

"Yes."

"Fifteen?"

"About that."

"Why isn't there a card on her?"

"She never ate here."

"Then how do you know about her?"

"She was . . . The doctor knew her."

"Did she work for him?"

"No."

"Then what did she do?"

"She was a singer."

"What kind? Nightclubs?"

"No. Classical."

Her answers were coming mechanically now, almost as if she were hypnotized by the even pace of the questions. Without changing that pace, he asked, "Were you asleep on the night Dr. Granger was killed?"

"No."

"Were you in your bedroom?"

"No."

"Did you see and hear the quarrel?"

He saw her mind register the sequence, and before she could pull away entirely, he showed her a card he had located. "How about this one, David Chapin?"

"Yes?"

"It looks as if he hasn't been here since April. Do you know why?"

"No."

"Did you know that he is Astrid Cain's husband?"

"I heard it."

"Was there any other Lee, one who did work for the doctor?"

"What in hell are you doing here?" said Lauren Granger.

She wore a silver fox coat and gray boots, and her voice was as cold as the aura of outside that still clung to her. "This is the third time I've found you in my kitchen, badgering my cook. I had to put up with the first two. But not this one. Get out or I'll call some of your *ex*-colleagues."

He rose. "The more you don't want me to talk to her, the more certain you make me that she wasn't asleep when your husband died. Maybe you should think that over."

She blew out a long breath, distorting her perfect mouth. "Jones, I don't want you to speak to this man again. Ever. That is an order."

As Damon walked past her, out to the hall, he said, "Hasn't anyone told you that the slaves were freed in 1863?"

Lauren stood for several moments, clenching her hands in the deep pockets of the silver fox. Stop overreacting, she told herself; but there was no denying the spasm of panic that had seized her when she discovered Damon. It was as if she had been standing for weeks on ice that was thin but holding and had suddenly heard a crack; he was a new, unpredictable factor, and her nerves were as thin as the ice.

On balance, Ben Lowell had assured her, Damon's testimony had worked to their advantage, despite the double-cross it contained; but it had also given the press a day of sensational headlines, and sensation was just what should be avoided. The point of the trial, she thought angrily, was not to hear about Cain's sex life but to restore the good name of Martin Granger. And the prestige of his widow.

When Hart and Honeybud Collins had begun gently but firmly to push her to the outer edges—sitting her below the salt at banquets, leaving her out of their private dinners, failing to return her calls and then apologizing with overdone Southern charm when she next saw them—she had taken it all with public good grace and had gone for three weeks to join one of the "Hart Campaign Trains" in the Southwest, trapping Collins on her return into a public expression of gratitude and a private acknowledgment of appreciation for her sensitivity to "an awkward situation."

But she still was being held at more than arm's length, and where—or if—she stood on Inauguration Day rested on the outcome of the trial. And now, she thought, that goddamn unpredictable detective had come around getting Jones to talk. . . .

She looked around the spotless kitchen, at the copper pots that glowed on a wall rack and the knives that hung with their sharp tongues out. It would be so easy, she thought, to take out one of those tongues and plunge Jones into permanent silence with it.

She actually made a move toward the rack before she realized it and stopped herself. She smiled and sat down next to the woman. "I didn't mean to shout at you."

"It's all right."

"But I really would rather not have that man around here. What was he asking you about?"

"My menus. Things like that."

"Now, listen," Lauren said, in a voice like sugar-coated steel, "I want the whole story. What did you tell him about Lee?"

Chapter Twelve

"Sentinel Finds One of Granger 'Souvenir' People," said the box on the front page. "See Rose Custer's 'Diary of a Trial' on Page 3."

Damon tossed his coat on the couch, along with the rest of the papers he had bought on the way home, and tore the *Sentinel* open to the article:

> Today in court there was new evidence of Astrid Cain's obsessive belief that Martin Granger was evil. And out of court, there was evidence to dispute her. A man who says he is the "EK" the *Sentinel* has been searching for made his existence known and gave an account of himself that contradicts Cain's interpretation.

Damon sat at the table and mechanically reached down to pet Sancho, who was barking furiously after being left alone all day.

> In court, spectators were treated—if that is the word—to the unusual sight of an editor's testifying against one of his own reporters. Hal Ruby, metropolitan editor of the New York *Blade,* visibly uncomfortable in his courtroom role, stated that Cain had told him

she "wouldn't care if she wrote another word as long as she ruined Granger."

Ruby described the article on Granger that Cain had submitted to him as "unusable" and "irresponsible." After a scuffle between Defense Attorney Marsh and Prosecutor Lowell, the article itself was accepted in evidence, and Ruby read from its final paragraphs, in which Cain wrote of Granger's desire to destroy people and cited, in comparison, Shakespeare's description of "flies to wanton boys . . . who kill . . . for sport." Cain created a brief scene in court by shouting out that she had not written those words. Yet they contain a view very similar to the one that she expressed to me in the (in?) famous Rikers Island interview, printed in this paper six weeks ago.

Is there any truth to that view?

Not according to "EK"—whom Cain identified to me as one of the people Granger had destroyed by getting them to abandon their careers.

"EK" is Ezra Kerr, a 40-year-old former fellow of the Granger Institute, who has been working for the past eight years with the Chippewa Indians in northern Minnesota. Word of the *Sentinel*'s search for "EK," as well as for "Lee" and the unnamed "birdcarver" mentioned by Cain, finally trickled into the isolated hamlet where Kerr works.

"Yes, I did have an Excalibur ring," he said, referring to one of the objects Cain says she found in what she called Granger's "souvenir collection." "The ring was from a society I was elected to in college, for students with unusual achievements in the arts or sciences."

Kerr states that he left the ring with Martin Granger when he switched out of his field, physics, and went into the work he does now, which he describes as "counseling, teaching, and manning a First Aid station for the Chippewa tribe." One of his grandparents was a tribe member.

"The suggestion that Martin Granger ruined me is absurd," he said. "In fact, he helped me to reach a decision that is the best I've ever made. Thanks to Martin, I was able to reject the whole technology-money-materialism treadmill and turn a self-indulgent life into one of service."

First there was Harry Pine, whose mother testified that his tragic suicide was caused by guilt over his sexual proclivities. Was it?

Now there is Ezra Kerr. Was he brainwashed and destroyed, as Cain says? Or was he guided to a better life?

Is the trial going to resolve these questions?

Damon closed the paper. On the rug in front of the couch were the shredded remains of one of the other dailies and a dog that looked pleased with itself. "You're as bad as Rose Custer," he said, picking up the mess and taking it into the kitchen. "She just ruined a lot of my paperwork, too."

He had spent much of the last three days trying to follow the leads from Helen Jones. They were all he had, unless he could think of a way to get Jones herself out of the Granger house and ask her more questions. He had been back three times; twice there had been no answer, and the last time the maid had hissed that she had orders to call the police if he returned. So he had gone after information on Kerr and Leonora Jonas.

He could not, and would not, use the Police Department's sources—even if the word on him hadn't yet gotten everywhere, he wouldn't pretend to anyone that he was still Detective Paul Damon—so he had gone to the masses of public records that existed on every citizen and were available to anyone, provided one knew where to look. And now all the work he had done on Ezra Kerr—looking through old voter registration lists at the Board of Elections, consulting the City Register and the Record Room, contacting two private firms that did record searches—was turned into a waste of time by Rose Custer's column.

He got out a beer and walked back to the living room. The wind off the river was snarling and beating on the windowpanes as if they were a cell door. A cell on Rikers Island. He shook his head sharply and turned away from the windows. For the moment, he thought, there was nothing to do but hope that the phone would ring. And that if he could find Leonora Jonas, she wouldn't say the same things Ezra Kerr had.

None of the public records had yielded anything on her; it was as if she had never existed, at least not in the city of New York. On the chance that she was indeed a singer and had been enough of one to make the newspapers, he had gone to the reference room at the Public Library, where he had pored through indexes, working backward from fifteen years ago.

He had found her name with ridiculous ease, mentioned in several reviews of the Manhattan Lyric Opera Company. Then he had called the American Guild of Musical Artists, which listed her as inactive, having ceased to pay dues nearly thirteen years ago. Her manager had been a Conrad Erlanger, who was retired but still had a phone listed in Queens, and Damon had left a message for him to call.

He finished the beer and was walking over to put on a record when the locks clicked on the front door. It swung inward, and Marie stood there, keys hanging from her hand and her mouth hanging too, in surprise. Sancho danced around her, but she ignored him.

"I called fifteen minutes ago," she said. "There was no answer. I was sure you were out."

"I just got home."

"I wanted to pick up my things." She wore a red wool cap that covered her hair tightly. Her face was tight, too. "But I didn't want to see you."

"I'm sorry." He thought that he couldn't be less ready to see her, either, but that he owed it to her not to let it matter. "It sounds as if you've decided we're through."

"Isn't that what you told me a dozen times to decide?"

"Yes, it is."

"Well, then?"

"Then come in and do it. But I hope you'll at least talk to me about it." He took her coat and led her to the couch.

She sat staring down at the red boots that peeked from below her plaid slacks, and did not speak until Sancho jumped up and settled between the two of them. "You had a dog before, didn't you?"

"Yes, I did."

"And Astrid Cain gave him to you?"

"No. But he was important to both of us."

"You still love her," she said, as if she wished it were a question.

"If I tell you I do," he said carefully, "you will think that's the reason for the way I've treated you. But it isn't. And if I tell you I don't love her, then everything will seem unintelligible to you."

"Just tell me, Paul," she said tightly.

He tried. "She was part of the reason I decided to . . . well, to cut myself off from things. And people. I never really gave you a chance, Marie. But it had nothing to do with you, or with her, really—" He broke off, sounding fatuous to himself, like a Sunday school teacher.

"I see," she said. "You don't know what you feel. You are

out of practice." He laughed sourly, and she turned on him. "I am not making jokes."

"Nor am I. But if I say I don't know what I feel, you'll think I am holding the door open."

"And you wouldn't be?"

The phone rang. Sancho barked wildly, and she quieted him.

The polite voice on the line identified itself as that of Conrad Erlanger. "Oh, you must have wanted my father. I'm afraid he died last year. Is there anything I could help you with?" But to all his questions the man could only answer in the negative. "I'm sorry," he said finally, "but I knew very little about Dad's business. And we're selling the house and moving, so we've thrown out all his files."

Damon hung up and was staring into the distance when Marie came over to him. "Are you trying to find some opera singer? Why?"

"It really doesn't concern you," he said without thinking.

"That's right," she cried. "Nothing about you concerns me. That's what you always say."

How simply a truth could be stated, he thought. She had just named the means he used to hold her, and everyone, away: a kind of verbal fence, with phrases that turned on as automatically as electricity whenever anyone approached too closely.

"It's not supposed to concern me that you've resigned, either. I have to find out by calling the stationhouse and asking for you."

"I'm sorry," he said, aware of its inadequacy.

"So who are you working for, then? Why are you trying to find this person? Is it for her?"

"Yes."

She said nothing.

"Look, Marie, I'll try to—"

"No, don't explain. You see, for once I don't want you to. Because I understand. Maybe more than you do. Just tell me about what you're doing. Why is this singer important?"

He looked at her determined little face, sharp as a triangle under the red cap, and told her, concluding with the only lead that he now had left.

His last act of the day had been to pay a visit to the Manhattan Lyric Opera, which was reduced from its former prominence to seedy quarters on Great Jones Street, near the Bowery. A harassed young woman who seemed to be a general factotum had looked incredulous when he inquired about old personnel and payroll records, and he had wandered into the large ex-manufacturing loft that seemed to smell and taste of dust and served as a rehearsal hall, where a small chorus was being drilled in *Cavalleria Rusticana.*

"Leonora Jonas?" said the leader during a break, "Never heard of her. But I only work here when I have to. Ask the chorus. There are a couple old faithfuls who still think the good old days are coming back." And one of them had finally recalled her: "Very pretty, with a gorgeous high E flat. My God, I haven't thought of her in years. I suppose she just gave up and went back home—someplace in the Midwest, it seems to me. She hung around with . . . now, who the hell was it she was friendly with? I just can't think of the name. Yes, sure, if it comes to me, I'll give you a call."

Marie was frowning when he finished. "And if you don't hear from this woman, you are stopped?"

"Until I think of some other angle."

"I could help you. Some of my friends are singers, you know. They work all over town, in choruses and churches and wherever they can. I could tell them to ask around for anyone who knew this woman or heard of her." He started to speak, but she cut in. "And I wouldn't do it because I was trying to make you need me or feel grateful to me. No, don't touch me, and don't look sorry for me. When I hear you in the court, and when I learn you have resigned, I realize there is this . . . this business that still hangs over you from years ago and I have to get out of the way while you settle it. So I make up my mind to come here when you are out and take my things and pet Sancho a little and then go away until it is all over for you. But as soon as I see you, I am like always, trying to find out if you love me or not!" She pounded her fists on her thighs and made an angry sound that brought the dog off the couch with a growl. "No, no, Sancho, I am not mad at you or at him. Just at me!"

She put her face in her hands for a moment and then looked up. "I *am* taking my things and going away from you, Paul, while you finish . . . all this. No, please don't say anything. Don't tell me it doesn't matter or you don't care. Just let me get my things and leave."

"All right," he said. "And I won't say it. That it doesn't matter."

"Hey, Cain, you gonna take the stand pretty soon?"

The three girls at her table in the dining hall looked at her expectantly. News of the trial's developments had reached every cell, via the omnipresent intercom radio, and her fellow inmates had refused to allow her to remain aloof any longer. She was, at the moment, the celebrity of Rikers Island, awaited eagerly when the green van brought her back from court each day. She found her status alternately amusing and pathetic.

"Yes, I'll be taking the stand next week," she said.

"What about all that stuff they said in court yesterday?" asked another of the girls, a prostitute. "Was your husband really going to give all his money to that Granger dude?"

"Yes, he was." On the final day of prosecution testimony, Harvey Baxter had reported his conversation with David about the money and her own call to him; David's lawyer and the Institute's treasurer had testified; and Ben Lowell had been able to conclude his case by showing that the formal transfer of David's stock to Martin Granger was to have taken place on June 24—the day after Granger died.

"You know something?" said the third girl at the table, who was awaiting trial for aiding in an armed robbery. *"I'd* kill somebody to keep that kind of money. Of course," she added thoughtfully, "they say he was real concerned about the poor."

"I think you should have killed him, Cain," said the prostitute. "You sure you didn't?"

She smiled faintly. "I'm sure." It was hard to make real that admitting to murder would give her added stature in their eyes. But, she thought, it was no harder to accept than the news Marsh had given her yesterday: that David was back but did not want to see her yet.

After lunch she and the rest of the inmates were herded back to their floors. She re-entered her cell, trying once more to lock her ears against the maddening intrusion of the radio music and her mind against the prospect of the weekend: almost forty-eight hours before the court reconvened.

"Why hasn't he come to see me?" she had asked Marsh repeatedly.

"My dear, I don't fully know. He's very agitated by all that has happened."

"Did you give him the tape? Has he heard the tape?"

"Not yet."

"Make him listen to it, Sandy!"

"I'll try."

"He knows everything that's happened in court?"

"I'm afraid so."

"I have to see him!"

"I'll try, my dear. He sends you his love."

She sank on the hard, narrow bed, staring out her window at the inner court of the Women's House, which was caked with muddy snow. There were books on the windowsill—the plays she had been reading in French, whose poetry and exuberant life had kept her sane in the months before the trial. She reached for one of them, but her hand fell back, and her eyes returned unseeingly to the courtyard. David sends his love, she thought, repeating the sentence over and over, to convince herself that he meant it. And that she wanted it.

The officer had to say it several times before she took it in: "Cain, there's a visitor for you." Then she leaped up so quickly that it made her dizzy. "Is it my husband?"

"The name is Paul Damon. Now, come on, Cain, I haven't got all day. You want a pass to go down or not?"

There were pairs of people at nearly all the white tables. He was at one by the window.

She walked over, too conscious of her ugly jumpsuit, and sat down, putting her hands on the table as required, like his. He was wearing a pale blue turtleneck sweater that made his hair seem even blacker. She searched his face for a clue of some kind, but his eyes were as impersonal as those of the officer monitoring the visiting room from behind the plastic bubble.

"I think it will be easiest," he said, "if I make this short and to the point. You know that I've resigned from the force?"

"Yes."

"Has Sanford Marsh told you that I offered my services to the defense?"

She was able to match his tone and hide her astonishment. "No."

"I didn't think so. He turned my offer down. But I'm doing some investigating for you on my own. That's why I'm here—to give you some information and to get some. Since I damaged you in court, I owe you something in return."

"But you told the truth."

"Did I?"

"Yes. I did try to bribe you."

She saw something in his eyes, as painful as the flick of a whip and as quickly gone, but it seemed to have touched her own temples, which began to throb.

"Never mind," he said. "The point is that I've followed up some leads on the people you claimed were Granger's victims, the souvenir people. By the way, has Marsh sent anyone to get a deposition from this Ezra Kerr that Custer located?"

"Yes."

"Has he had any luck in locating 'Lee'?"

"No."

"Well, I have, and I want you to let him know."

As he told her what he had found, she felt the pressure at her temples increasing. "You can't be doing this," she said.

"But I am. Only I'm stymied for the moment. So I need you to tell me everything you remember about the letter from Lee that you saw in Granger's collection."

She was going to refuse, but the first hint of feeling had touched his face, and it was excitement, so she told him.

"You're sure?" he said. "She was writing this letter from a school for deaf children?"

"Yes, I'm sure."

"So Granger got an opera singer to give up and go teach the deaf. My God! That backs up your interpretation of him, all right."

"Of course I didn't know she was a singer, or even a woman. I did try to contact some of the deaf schools in this area, but I was asking about a man named Lee, so I didn't get anywhere."

"I'll start on that right away."

"No, Damon, you can't." She wanted very badly to lift her fingers from the table and press them against her head.

"Yes, I can. Do you know where I got this lead? From Granger's cook. And that's the other part of the reason I'm here. We—the police, I mean—suspected from the first that she might be the anonymous caller. She swears she was asleep that night, but I've kept working on her, only now I'm *persona non grata* at the Granger house and can't get to her anymore. So you've got to tell this to Marsh: that I got her to admit she wasn't asleep the night Granger died. He's got to talk to her and see if he can get anything more out of her. Astrid? What's the matter?"

She saw her own expression reflected in the sudden concern of his. "Go away," she managed to say. "I can't let you help me."

"Why not?"

"Because of what I've done to you."

"I know what you're thinking."

"No, you don't."

"You think that if you hadn't come to see me that night, I wouldn't have resigned from the force."

But that's only part of it, she thought. She looked down and saw her hands turn over on the table and curl up, like animals in pain.

"I don't think you were right to do what you did, but I've come to understand it. You were . . . I suppose you were desperate. You weren't thinking straight. Something I know a little about myself."

I have to tell him, she thought; I have to. She looked up at him. His face had never seemed so ugly, or so beautiful. "Damon, there's something you have to know."

"All right. But first I have something to tell you. Years ago, when you left, you said that what I was going to do would be like committing suicide. I thought you were wrong.

Last week in court I learned you were right. I realized that I was willing to do anything—my God, even to commit perjury—in order to help convict you. I needed you to be guilty, so there wouldn't be anything to threaten me. Because that's what you were—a threat to the detachment I thought I finally had achieved, toward everything in my life. But I didn't see that at the time. I couldn't. No—wouldn't. What's that saying? 'None so blind as those who will not see?' Wait, let me finish. You've done something important for me, even though you didn't intend it. I learned that one can't live . . . underground. What one tries to bury comes back to the surface, stronger than ever. But twisted. And ready to make one turn against the things one had loved. When I realized that living in the way I've tried to live had made me want to destroy *you* . . . Well, I don't care what it cost me to learn that. But it also hurt you. So now I want to do what I can to repay you."

Her head had dropped forward, so that he could see only the smoky red hair and the fine white line that parted it. He sat back in the narrow chair and let himself experience fully the sensation of relief, admitting finally that this was the real reason he had come: not to get or pass on information, important as that was, but to say these things to her. To do what he could to soften her existence in this place, which seemed to him even more stultifying than he remembered. It might be the nicest "home" some of its inmates had ever known, but for her it could be nothing but a daily crushing of the spirit. Yet, incredibly, she was not crushed. Only thinner and paler. Her hand was close to his on the table; he wanted to touch it, but he told himself that was not allowed. "Do you still want me to go away and not try to help you?"

She lifted her head. "Your anonymous caller, the one you think might be the cook?"

"Yes?"

"She isn't. There isn't any eyewitness. Don't waste your time looking for one. I'm the one who made that anonymous call to the police, to your Detective Riley. I'm the one who gave him the snatches of conversation from the quarrel. That's why they're accurate. I made other calls, too. I called Professor Llewellyn Jones and begged him not to tell the police I'd been to see him, so he'd do just the opposite. And when you didn't find out about the stock transfer, I called Harvey Baxter, for the same reason."

"I don't understand," he said carefully.

"Don't you? I was using the police—using you—doing everything I could to get myself arrested for murder."

"I still don't understand." He said it because he was beginning to.

She leaned back, her hair falling in two little scythes on her shoulders. "The *Blade* wouldn't use my piece on Granger. Maybe it was irresponsible—I don't know anymore. I tried to approach other papers, but the word had gotten around that I was wild, not to be trusted, and they weren't interested. Besides, I wasn't just offering some scandal about his personal life—they might have accepted that. I was saying that he was dangerous. And that, no one was willing to consider. How could someone who cared about the poor and was fighting for equality be dangerous and evil? It was like trying to tell people that God isn't good. They couldn't take it in. Then Granger died, and all the eulogies started, and the testimonials and the election hype. People were talking as if Granger's theories applied to just the poor and the disadvantaged. No one was saying a word about the other side of it, what it meant for the people who were talented and successful. And I *knew* what it meant—I'd heard Granger say it the night he died. Don't you see? People had to know about him. Especially my husband. Because he was one of Granger's victims. But my husband was gone." She took a deep breath.

"Get on with it," he said.

She told him about the robbery. "I still don't know who did it, but I think it must have come from Jake Waldo. He and the *Blade* publisher are friendly. I also think they put pressure on Ruby to turn my article over to you. And to change the last paragraphs. Change them cleverly, using my style and picking up what I'd told Rose Custer in that interview. Damon, I never wrote what they read in court! But how could I prove it, since all my copies had been stolen?"

"I see," he said slowly. "But what they read in court doesn't exactly distort your view, does it?"

"No."

"Let's get back to why you wanted to be arrested."

"I thought that if I could get myself suspected of Granger's murder and even arrested for it, I'd be safe from Granger's political friends. And when I turned over the tape and was released, then I wouldn't be just some crazy, unknown reporter. Every paper in the country would want the story of the tape, because it would be the 'stunning new evidence' that had suddenly gotten me released. And finally, people would know the truth about Granger and what he was doing."

He knew there were other things to feel, but for the moment incredulity outweighed them. "I knew you were impulsive," he said. "I kept telling myself you could be crazy enough to kill him. I never dreamed you were just . . . crazy."

"I thought I was safe, you see. With the tape. But it boomeranged. Everything did."

"Jesus," he said. "Jesus. Does Sanford Marsh know all this?"

"No. Would anyone who knew it still want to help me?"

He felt a cold prickle at the back of his neck. "You said you were using the Department? And me?"

"Yes."

"Then tell me why you came to see me that night."

He thought she looked as he must have looked on the stand, in the courtroom.

"To bribe you," she said. "But not in the way you think." She lifted her hands at the wrists and let them fall back on the table again. Her wedding band made a tiny clink. "When I walked into the stationhouse that day and learned you were on the case, when we talked . . . You'll never know how badly I wanted to tell you everything. But I couldn't. I knew you would stop me. And then I saw that you were actually a threat. You were struggling to believe I was innocent. And working to get me off. I couldn't let you. So I had to make you think I was guilty. And the only way I could think of was to . . ."

"To?"

"To make you believe I had become the kind of person who would offer that kind of bribe."

"You deliberately tried to make me believe the worst of you?"

"I . . . Yes."

"Did it occur to you that you might be the one person in the world I might still want to believe in?"

"Yes. That was the worst of it."

"Well, then," he said flatly, "it worked out just the way you planned."

"No, it didn't! You have to believe that, Damon. I never planned for you to have to testify about it in court. How could I? I never thought there would *be* a trial. And God knows I didn't plan to . . . I thought I could just . . . do it. As if it were a role in a play. Not something that would—" She stopped as if she had touched hot metal. "I thought I had to do it, that's all. But there's no point in talking about it now."

"That's right." The lines around his mouth tightened before he went on. "Do you remember certain conversations we had years ago? About the law?"

"Yes," she said hesitantly.

"Then maybe you remember defending it to me as a noble profession, in spite of those who abused it. You said I shouldn't let myself be stopped by those who played games with it and used it to further their own ends."

"Yes?"

He leaned toward her, his voice a sword. "Who's using it now? You are. Playing games with the police, tricking your own lawyer into defending a liar without even knowing she's lying—"

"I haven't told any lies! From the beginning I've told the truth about Granger's death—to you, to the rest of the detectives, to Sandy Marsh. I've lied to no one."

"But you never told the whole truth. If you had told Ben Lowell what you've just told me, you could have prevented the trial."

"Do you really think so? Don't forget that I gave him *proof* of my innocence—which he ignored. Just the way you did."

"Because you had used me!"

"Yes! Yes! There's nothing you can say to me that I haven't already said to myself."

"No? How about this? You've got the lowest of all rationalizations—that the end justifies the means. Since your intentions were good, that makes it all right to use people. And incidentally to waste the taxpayers' money on police investigations and a trial."

"And what else is being done with taxpayers' money—yours and mine and everyone's? It's being used to support Granger and his Institute. Aren't *we* being used for what other people claim to be good intentions? I had no say in the fact that my own money went to support the man who was destroying my husband!"

"All right," he said after a moment. "I'll grant you that. But I don't believe you had no other way to get your story out."

"Then don't believe it! Maybe there was some other way to do it, but I wasn't smart enough to figure it out. So what should I have done? Just sat back while my husband was destroyed? While other people were destroyed?" She was too angry to stop herself from going on. "I know what your advice would have been: Quit caring. Step aside and just watch. Give up." She saw a tremor run through his hands, as if they wanted to lift and strike. "But I'm not like that. So I did the only thing I could think of!"

"Oh, no. You didn't *think*. You jumped in without any thought of the consequences, the way you always have. If you'd been thinking, you'd have realized that the tape could be interpreted against you as well as for you. If you'd been thinking, you'd have considered the position you were putting me in. And I wouldn't have resigned from the force."

"Yes," she said. "I'll grant you that." The anger left her so suddenly that she felt weak without it. "Isn't it ironic, Damon? That *I* should cause you to give something up?"

She looked at him, but his eyes were locked against her. "I wanted to keep Granger from ruining any more lives," she said. "I still do. And if they convict me, let it be because I succeeded, because I got people to know the truth about him. That's all I can allow myself to think about now. Or to feel. But I couldn't let you help me without knowing everything. Now that you know it, I don't expect your help."

"No? Aren't you going to offer to go to bed with me again if I keep on looking for Leonora Jonas?"

Her lips opened, but no words came out, only the sounds of her breath, leaving by ragged steps.

He stood up abruptly, looking away. It seemed hours before an officer came to rescue her and take her back to her cell.

III

SIGHT

Chapter Thirteen

In the sunless morning light a small group of demonstrators was starting to gather in Foley Square. One of them adjusted a sandwich board reading, "Granger Believed in Equality—Do You?" Another hefted a sign that said, "Stop Cain and Her Smear Campaign."

David Chapin walked doggedly past them, following his parents and Sanford Marsh into the grimy lobby of the Criminal Courts Building, and then into one of the elevators. There was a strong smell of disinfectant, struggling to mask the odors of vomit and urine; David felt a moment of yearning for the clear, sharp air of the Wasatch Mountains and for their distance from this place in both miles and spirit. But then the guilt descended again.

As soon as he had returned from Utah and learned all that had happened, his own terrible role had become clear. None of it would have occurred if he had stopped Astrid from going to work for Martin in the first place. Or if he had been able to make her see the truth about Martin. Or if he had not gone away when Martin died and left her to attack him publicly in such ugly, unforgivable ways . . . The hardest word in the language, he thought, was "if." No, it was "how"; for how was he to save both of them, Astrid *and* Martin?

"I hope this won't be too hard for you, David," his mother whispered, touching his cheek as the elevator stopped. "But I think it's the best thing."

He nodded and followed Marsh down the hall. At nine o'clock last night he finally had capitulated to Marsh's arguments: "You must be in court tomorrow, David. It's a critical part of her defense that she was a loving wife, doing what she did in order to help you. The press has broadcast the fact that you're back, and if you don't make a strong show of support, it will look very bad. But I refuse to let Astrid take the stand with you in the audience unless she's had a chance to see you first. I can't put her through that, and I won't. You must see her yourself and tell her what you feel." And so he had agreed, because there was no way to explain his reluctance.

"All right," Marsh said, "she's in that room. I pulled a few strings, and you should have at least half an hour before the session starts."

He pushed the plain wooden door that seemed to weigh like stone. She was sitting at a table; she stood up quickly and then froze, waiting for him to move. She was very lovely, he thought.

He went to her, took both her hands, and kissed them. She sat down again, her eyes fixed on his with the hazel intensity he remembered so well. He took a chair opposite hers. "Has it been terrible for you?" he said.

"Yes. And how has it been for you?"

"Difficult."

There was a long silence, which she finally broke. "This shouldn't be awkward, should it? But it is."

"It's my fault. I don't know what to say to you."

"Oh . . . that you missed me. Or that you don't think I killed him."

"Both," he said.

"Do you mean that?"

"I don't lie to you, do I?"

"Not about us. But you hide from me."

"I had to go away, Astrid."

"From me?"

"Yes, in part. You have a way of making everything seem too simple."

"Ah." She reached up to touch the chain that was visible in the neck of the white blouse she wore, underneath the jacket of a gold suit. "Do you remember when you gave me this chain? On our first anniversary?"

"Yes," he said, recalling it all too vividly: the card on which he'd written, "For Astrid, because life with her is a charmed circle"; the smile with which she had read it; the small ceremony she had made of his fastening the golden circle around her neck.

She looked at him, paler now than she had been then, and unsmiling. "Once, when the police were questioning me," she said, "I was so tense that I broke the chain. But I had it fixed. I didn't want anything from you to be . . . broken." She waited, but he said nothing. "You didn't want to see me, did you?"

"No."

"Why not? Was it because of Paul Damon?"

He knew that he owed her honesty, at least. "Not really. I thought you would want to talk about Martin."

"Yes. Shouldn't I?"

"I don't think you can be objective about him."

She looked away for a moment. "Sandy says you won't listen to the tape. Why not?"

He clenched his hands and then relaxed them. "If it's not going to be used in the trial, it can't be that important."

"It's important for you. You're the whole reason I made the tape."

"To turn me against Martin. I know that. When I was away, I could see it so clearly—how you had worked to make me reject him. And I remember the state you were in when you went to see him that last night. So I don't think I want to hear the way you must have talked to him."

"How about the way he talked to me?"

"What do you mean?"

She reached out to touch his arm. "David, he said some things that are important for you to hear. Some things about you."

"I know very well what Martin thought of me."

"No, you don't."

"You're wrong."

"Then why don't you listen to the tape and prove that I'm wrong?" He didn't answer. "You're afraid to listen to it, aren't you?"

"No! No. I simply don't want to hear you attacking him, insulting him, turning the last moments of his life into ugly ones."

She snatched her hand away. "What in God's name did that man do to you? What kind of power does he have over you, that you're willing to put out your eyes for him?"

"Don't make me angry, Astrid. I swore not to get angry, because I want to help you. It's my fault you're in this terrible mess."

She smiled sadly. "Does that mean you realize that everything I did was done for you?"

"I realize you thought you were helping me. But you can't help me by trying to destroy Martin! If you keep on doing that, I'll never forgive you, Astrid. Never."

She put her face in her hands. After a while, her voice muffled, she said, "Have you decided to give up your work?"

He didn't answer her; he couldn't.

Her head lifted slowly, and her eyes locked on his as if they wanted to reach into his brain. "David," she whispered, "tell me what I can do to make you listen to that tape. At least give me that much."

She was lovely, he thought. So lovely. "All right," he said. "You can stop trying to destroy Martin."

"Mrs. Chapin," said Marsh, rising to continue the questioning after the noon recess, "you have explained how you went to work for Martin Granger as his secretary on January 15, in order to try to understand what was happening to your husband. Will you tell us what you learned?"

His voice was gentle. As her own had been all morning and would continue to be. Must be. A rational, believable voice, as Marsh had been advising her all along; and now there was a reason neither of them had anticipated to mute it still more. She directed her gaze to the jury. "The first thing I noticed was that Dr. Granger asked me several times about my career ambitions and seemed disappointed when I said I was content to remain a secretary. I questioned some of the other Institute personnel. I learned that he had had those conversations with many people and that the more talented and dedicated a person was, the more Dr. Granger was . . . the more Dr. Granger pursued him. I found six people who, under his guidance, were considering giving up their present careers, which they loved."

As Ben Lowell made another of his many objections, she glanced again at David. He was in the fourth row, watching her; his look was both blank and intense, as it had been so often when they were fighting. But at least he was not locked inside himself; he was listening.

"What else did you observe that seemed relevant to your concern about your husband?"

"The Field Studies part of the program at the Institute. Before David took his leave of absence, he had had to do fieldwork, as almost everybody did, and his had consisted of working with mentally retarded persons. I thought that was an odd assignment for a neurophysiologist. It seemed like a crue— Well, I wondered about it."

"You mean because your husband had a mentally retarded sister?"

"Yes. So I tried to find out if David's assignment had been an unusual one. I learned that it wasn't. For example, a chemist who had a mongoloid child was sent to do research with gifted children. And a psychologist whose specialty had been the creative personality was sent for six months to study and work with migrant farm workers. I began to wonder if there was a deliberate pattern, an attempt to break desire apart from—"

"Your Honor," said Ben Lowell, on his feet again, "I must protest once more. It is not Martin Granger's methods and procedures that are on trial here."

Judge Cox looked up blandly from some notes he was making. "Since it is your contention that the defendant's perceptions of Martin Granger were so distorted that they constitute a motive for murder, I fail to see how you can object to letting us hear those perceptions."

"Go on, Mrs. Chapin," said Marsh; he was smiling slightly.

She moved to rest one hand on the arm of the chair. "Another thing that interested me was why Dr. Granger would praise some people and criticize others. I couldn't see the connection to their performances. When I finally asked him about it, he said that it was sometimes necessary to dramatize Nature's arbitrary system of rewards and punishments. He seemed indifferent to the demoralizing effect this had on his staff." Ben Lowell snorted audibly. "And I thought that it was perhaps partly responsible for my husband's . . . growing lack of motivation for his work."

Marsh nodded. "So you had all these thoughts and observations in your mind by March 1 of this year. What happened that afternoon?"

"I was working in Dr. Granger's home, in a little room off his study, typing notes for his new book. His study phone had been acting up all day, and suddenly he rushed out, saying he had an important call from Hart Collins that he would finish in his bedroom and I should go in and hang up the study phone. When I went in to do it, the bottom desk drawer was open. I banged into it, and as I stood there, bending over and holding my leg, I saw a black leather box in the drawer. It was unlocked, open. There were some objects in it." She took a deep breath. "One of them was a scroll signifying election to the American Science Foundation. It belonged to my husband."

The whole courtroom seemed to lean forward as Marsh produced something from the defense table. "Is this the box you saw?"

"Yes."

There was a sharp sound from the second row, from Lauren Granger, which seemed to catapult Ben Lowell to his feet. He advanced on the judge, followed by Marsh.

Thank God for Sandy, she thought. Even if she had pushed him into it, by talking to Rose Custer, he had seen that the collection itself must be subpoenaed, before Rose's article appeared and let the whole world—and Ben Lowell—know that the collection existed.

As the two attorneys argued before the judge, she looked at David again. He was talking to his parents. She wondered what explanation he was giving them; he could not lie to them, as he had to her, and say he had lost the scroll. After a while he looked up at her. Are you starting to understand? she cried silently to him. His eyes were indecipherable, but at least they were not hostile.

After the sidebar conference Lowell sat down with his jaw tight, and the box and its contents were introduced in evidence. The voice of reason, she reminded herself again, making her careful way through Marsh's questions: Yes, she had feared the scroll was a symbol of career renunciation, particularly since the collection also contained a letter from a "Lee" who had given up a career; Yes, she had tried to locate the owners of the other objects; No, she could not accept Mrs. Pine's explanation of her son's suicide, because of the presence of his chemistry award in the collection; Yes, she had felt she had grounds for an article outlining her suspicions.

"Will you tell us what happened on the night of June 23?"

David was watching her, his face as still as a carving. "That was the night my husband told me he had decided to turn over his stock shares to Dr. Granger and was thinking seriously of giving up neurophysiology. We had a . . . we argued about it. I told him he should leave the Institute and use the money to finance his own researches." She raised her hands to push her hair behind her ears. Only the facts, she thought; nothing of the choking sense of frustration and the useless pleading. "David said that I had never understood Martin Granger. That it was time for Granger to know I had been spying on him and that he, David, was going to tell him. I said, 'Never mind, I'll tell him myself. I'll go right now.' I got my . . . I took my purse and ran down and got a cab over to Granger's. He was upstairs in his study. It was a hot night, so the doors to the balcony were open."

"What did you say to him?"

"I told him that I was a reporter and that I was Mrs. David Chapin."

"What was his response?"

"He got very red in the face and began to pace around the room." She looked at David. "He called me . . . several names, for which I suppose I can't blame him. He said he would expose me for what I was. And then I told him what I thought *he* was."

"What did you say?"

"What I've told the court. Most of all, that I was afraid he was trying to destroy my husband." The muscles around David's mouth knotted. "To . . . to influence my husband to leave a career that I knew made him happy."

"Did Dr. Granger deny your accusations? Did he deny that he tried to influence people in the way you have just described?"

"Yes. At first." She was speaking directly to David now, not caring if everyone knew it, commanding him not to look away. "Dr. Granger said that people often came to him for career guidance, that he tried to help them. He . . . talked a great deal about his theories. I told him that was an evasion. I got more and more angry. So did he. Then I said to him, 'But David is brilliant. Doesn't it matter to you that he's *brilliant?*'"

She felt the anger pushing up inside her, and she clutched the gold chain at her neck, holding her fist over it and over the words she did not dare say now, so long as David was still looking, still listening. "And Dr. Granger indicated that . . . it did not matter. His attitude . . . made me realize . . . that I had not been foolish . . . to be concerned for my husband." She sat back slowly in the chair.

After that it was easy—simply to say that they had continued to shout at each other and then to state how he had died and how she finally had run to look over the balcony and then gone back in to call the police.

"Did you kill Martin Granger?"

"No. I did not."

Marsh took a long pause. "Just one thing more, Mrs.

Chapin. "The court is aware that your husband has been away for a long time, since Dr. Granger's death. Has he now returned to stand by you?"

"Yes, he has."

"And is he now in this courtroom?"

"Yes." And has he heard? she thought.

"Thank you, Mrs. Chapin."

Ben Lowell came toward her, tapping the legal pad in his hand and smiling; it was, she thought, like hearing the warning rattle of a snake.

"Mrs. Chapin," he said amiably, "you wrote an article for the *Blade* on your views of Martin Granger, did you not?"

"Yes."

"Did you call him a dictator and charge that he was searching for men and women to destroy?"

She took a moment to frame her answer. "Those were the words that have been read to this court."

"Are you suggesting that was not your view of Martin Granger?"

She hesitated. Dictator, she thought, had been the wrong word to use, for dictators wanted slaves and power; and those were not the essence of Granger's goal, which, she finally had learned, was both more personal and harder to accept. "The article," she said carefully, "reflects the view I held at the time."

"Why has your language suddenly become so much more moderate?"

"Perhaps because I am in a courtroom, not a newsroom."

"You mean you do not want the jury to see your true feelings?"

"I would have to let the jury do its own interpreting."

"As I'm sure they will." He was still smiling. "Do you deny that you hated Martin Granger?"

"I . . . No."

"And you wanted to see his reputation destroyed?"

"I thought his influence should be re-examined."

"Answer the question. Did you want to see his reputation destroyed?"

She turned her head, to look for David, and instead her glance caught on a face several rows behind him: a young woman from the Institute, to whom she had talked a month after Granger's death, only to learn that his influence was as potent as ever. "If I had the courage of my convictions," the woman had said, "I wouldn't be here, collecting a fat salary for working in the kind of lab I've always wanted. I'd be . . . oh, I don't know. Maybe with those miners' families in West Virginia, where I did my field studies."

"Did you want to see Martin Granger's reputation destroyed?" Lowell said again.

"If it deserved to be, yes."

He raised a scornful eyebrow and switched to a new subject. That was to be his tactic, she saw: to try to force her into displaying emotion by throwing her off guard with a scattershot approach. She took a firm grip on the arms of the chair and answered as monosyllabically as she could—to questions about the price of her gold suit and the rest of her clothes and everything else in her life-style: "And yet you expect the jury to believe that you weren't desperate at the thought of losing your husband's money?"

"Yes. I'm sure people can understand that if one loves a person—"

"Just answer the question, please."

In the middle of something else, he would suddenly ask her again if she denied hating Martin Granger, but she managed to respond as if she did not mind the repetition and to go on: How many people work for the Institute? Over a hundred, but you talked to only twenty-five of them? And based a conclusion on only six? That is hardly the scientific method, is it?

Then it was a switch back to the article: What was its purpose? Wasn't it to destroy Martin Granger's reputation? Do you deny that you hated him?—and then suddenly to the night of Granger's death: "You claim that he 'just fell' from the balcony?"

"Yes."

"Did you try to stop him?"

"Well . . . no."

"Why not?"

"It was so unexpected. It was over before I realized."

"You claim you saw a man falling to his death, and yet you made no attempt to stop him?"

"I believe I've just explained why."

"Do you deny that you hated Martin Granger?"

"Your Honor," Marsh said, "the witness has already answered this question several times. Why is counsel repeating it?"

"Mr. Lowell?" said Cox.

"With the court's permission, the witness has tried on direct to obliterate the fact of her hatred from the jury's mind."

Cox smiled. "Well, I think we can take it that you have now refreshed them sufficiently."

"As Your Honor pleases."

Then it was a switch back to the money and then once more to the renunciation of careers: Are you better qualified than Harry Pine's mother to understand a young man you never met? Don't hundreds of people change their careers every day? Didn't you change your own career? So it isn't necessarily evil to change? Oh, it isn't? Only for people who worked for Martin Granger? But you haven't even talked to all of them, have you? Why is it wrong for your husband to consider some other field?

She permitted herself to look at David and to smile. "Because he was good at his work. And because it made him happy."

"Ah, yes. And you loved him so much that you couldn't bear to see him change that career. Is that what you said?"

"Yes." She thought David wanted to smile back, but he looked as tired as she.

"You didn't love your husband enough, though, did you, to keep from sleeping with a former lover?"

She felt the smile congealing on her face like a smear of mud. It took moments, precious, damning moments, before she could move the muscles of her mouth and master herself to speak. "When one is under investigation for a murder one did not commit, the pressure can make one do regrettable things."

"Is that so?" Lowell smiled. "I have no more questions at this time."

Damon stood in the hall as the crowd jostled out of the courtroom.

He saw Rose Custer, and then Lauren Granger came out with a man he knew to be Jake Waldo, her arms agitating her white cape as she talked. She looked up and saw him, then jerked her eyes away.

He had thought he would wait till the Chapins came out, to get a better look at the man for whom she was undertaking all this. Then he asked himself why; did he really expect to learn from the man's face whether he was worth it? And what difference did it make whether he was or wasn't?

He headed for an elevator, past two women screeching at each other outside another courtroom. This building, he thought, this Temple of Justice—where winos and addicts camped in the lobby, where thieves robbed even the judges' chambers, where lawyers made deals in the halls and abandoned their mandate for truth inside the courtrooms—this was where her future would be decided.

The anger he had felt on Rikers Island had stayed with him all weekend, like a predator in chronic search of food. It was easy to feed; all he had to do was to think of how she had used him, to say that it was poetic justice for her to be caught in her own trap. But then he would visualize the Women's House, carving her existence down to the size of a five-by-eight cell, and he would pick up the phone to track down a list of schools for deaf children, until the predator returned and asked him why he, of all people, should try to help her. This morning he had decided to feed the creature again: to come and sit far back in the court and hear Astrid testify. And to prove, once and for all, that he would be a fool to help her.

But he had not seen what he expected. On direct examination she had said much less than she could have, speaking as carefully as if she were walking on knives. Like the character in the children's story, he thought, the little mermaid who had her tongue cut out in order to acquire human legs and then had endured a swordlike pain with each step she took. And all for the love of a man who— His eyes slowly widened. Had Astrid, too, sacrificed her tongue for the man she loved?

It would explain a lot, he thought. Including the way she had held herself in check with Ben Lowell, who had advanced on her with a face like those of the hecklers of long ago, trying to shout her off the platform, to use all their skills to destroy her, not because she was guilty but because she had tried to say something they did not want to hear. And he himself had been in the audience then, too, about to stand up and defend her, not because of the way she looked up there on the platform, with her body taut and her cinnamon hair whipping in the wind, but because, if one believed that something was right, one had to stand up in its name. . . .

He stood outside, at the south entrance to the Criminal Courts Building, buttoning his coat against the wind, staring up at the inscriptions cut into the granite portals, at which he had not really looked for years. One of them read, "Only the just man enjoys peace of mind."

He squared his shoulders and headed off.

"What is your name?" asked Sanford Marsh.

"Jake Waldo, Junior."

"And your address?"

"Forty-six Sutton Place South."

"Where do you work?"

"At ISCEV. I mean, at the Martin Granger Institute."

"How long have you been there?"

"A year and a half."

"Would you explain something of your work to the jury?"

"Well, I'm in psychology. Behavioral psychology. That's what my degree is in. So what I . . . I mean, I'm involved in doing research on the conditioning effects of certain cultural institutions. Like prejudice, for instance. I mean, how a black person adjusts his behavior to conform to certain attitudes about blacks. It's important work. Very important. That's what I do. Part of the time, I mean."

As he talked, he kept his eyes averted, and his hands made constant aimless journeys to his face and clothes.

"And what do you do the rest of the time?"

"Well, I'm still with . . . I'm keeping on with my field studies, too. Several days a week I teach art appreciation to some of the . . . of the boys at the Houston Street Home for Juveniles."

"Are you qualified to do that?"

"Sort of. Yes. I mean, I studied art myself for a while." His hands scrabbled at the knees of his trousers.

As the questions went on, the spectators began to exhibit an empathic tension, as if they too were dreading the approach of some crucial question, whatever it might be.

When it came, they all knew it at once. Marsh took the carved figure of a bird from the defense exhibits, and Jake Waldo, pulling back in the chair as if the bird were alive and were aimed at his eyes, admitted that he had done the carving.

"But it was nothing," he said. "Really nothing. I just used to like . . . I carved things in my spare time, and Dr. Granger wanted one of them, so I gave it to him."

To Marsh's subsequent questions—Weren't you seriously interested in art? Didn't you want to study to be a sculptor? Did you discuss this with the defendant?—he kept repeating, "But it was nothing," as if that were a magic formula which would get him safely through the questioning.

Finally Marsh held up a sheaf of papers. "Mr. Waldo, you made a number of statements to me on the tenth of last month. You told me that you gave this carving to Martin Granger as a pledge that you would cease to care about art. Those were your exact words. Do you now deny them?"

"Yes. I mean, no. But what I said isn't what I meant. You got me confused, I guess."

"You are a Phi Beta Kappa, *summa cum laude* graduate of Columbia University, and yet you confuse so easily?"

"I guess so." Jake twisted in the chair for a moment; then he sat erect and for the first time spoke like the scholar Marsh had described. "That carving was only a symbol of the fact that I wasn't going to waste my time anymore. I don't have any talent for art, just a facile knack. There was a time when I wanted to indulge it, but that would have been a terrible waste of my life."

Marsh's long pause seemed weighted with defeat. Then he turned to questions about Astrid. He managed to elicit that her conversations with Jake had been couched in terms of concern for the boy's happiness, not of hatred for Granger. Then he sat down wearily.

For the first time the boy looked out at the crowd—at someone in particular, it seemed—with a kind of supplicating eagerness.

Damon was sitting halfway back; he followed the boy's glance and thought that its target must be the father. Waldo, Senior, was several rows ahead of him; he thought he saw the grizzled head nod slightly.

"You see?" a woman behind Damon whispered to her neighbor. "There's nothing so terrible about those souvenirs, the way she was trying to claim."

"I guess not," came the rejoinder. "I wish I'd had Granger to talk to *my* son. Then maybe he wouldn't have gone off with that rock band."

There it was, Damon thought. Unless Marsh had something better than the testimony of this pathetically nervous boy, Astrid's contention—and everything it had led her to do—was going to seem like a hallucination. Or a vendetta. Unless something began to pay off. Something like the grotesque idea he finally had allowed himself to take seriously.

He had gone home the day before and attacked his list of schools for deaf children. All except one had had no record of a teacher by the name of Leonora Jonas—or the other name he had given them. The remaining school, in Connecticut, had said its files were in bad shape and he had better call back the next day or, better yet, come up and look for himself. He had decided to go and had even arranged to rent a car.

But this morning the whole idea had seemed impossible. Although he had gone to pick up the rental car, he hadn't gotten on the West Side Highway to head for New England;

instead he had driven down to Foley Square, admitting finally that he wanted to hear the day's testimony, that it might somehow affect the search for Leonora Jonas.

But that wasn't the full reason, he had thought, heading into the courtroom; what he really wanted was to talk to Astrid. To be certain that she still would want his help. That her husband's return hadn't changed anything.

There had been no way to get to her as yet; she sat at the defense table without once turning her head. Perhaps, Damon thought, that was because the Chapins were not in the fourth row today, or anywhere else in the courtroom, as far as he could tell.

Ben Lowell was rising to cross-examine. The Waldo boy waited, motionless now, as if he were too tired for tension. Or else had nothing more to fear.

"Mr. Waldo," Lowell began, "would you say that the defendant had misinterpreted what you told her about yourself?"

"Yes. Yes, I would. Completely."

"Why do you think she would do that?"

"Objection," Marsh said.

Someone plucked at Damon's sleeve, and looking down the row, he saw that the message had been passed on by his neighbors from a figure kneeling in the aisle. It was Marie, and she was making urgent motions for him to come out. He eased past his neighbors carefully, but there still was enough disturbance to make heads turn and whispers of recognition start up again.

As soon as they were out in the hall, Marie pushed her hands into the pockets of her coat and looked up at him. "Paul, I got my friends to ask around about that woman you are trying to find, the friend of that opera singer. They found her, and I went to see her. She is with me now, waiting in a coffee shop just up the street."

He spoke carefully, over the jolt of excitement in his chest. "Marie, that's incredible. I don't know what to say."

She took his caution for criticism. "I did it to help you," she said defiantly. "When people who matter to you are in trouble, you have to help them."

"Yes. You're right, Marie. Right about a lot of things. But I didn't mean for you—"

"And I didn't do it to make a debt for you! I did it to be part of what is happening to you. To *do* something, not to just sit and wait. And now, after we see this woman, I can go back to waiting and know that I helped. I ask only this one thing. When it is all over, you have to come to me and tell me, straight out. You have to say: Marie, good-bye, I decided I don't want you, or else— Well, you know what else."

He touched her cheek. "Yes, I do. And I will tell you straight out. That's a promise, Marie."

"Well, good," she said. "Then let's go."

Her name, said the woman in the coffee shop, was Naomi Rostov, and she was sorry but it had to be said up front that she wanted money for talking. "I wish I didn't have to, but my last two jobs paid carfare and zilch."

Damon took out his wallet and put two ten-dollar bills next to her coffee cup.

She tucked them swiftly into her purse. "For that I can give you a synopsis of the plot. The complete libretto will come a little higher."

"Let's hear the synopsis."

She leaned back in the booth. She had black hair and a Slavic face that must have been exotic once, before bitterness became a permanent resident. How many like her were there in New York, Damon wondered—musicians who never made it and whose love of their art slowly curdled into a fight for survival? "Lee and I met at Manhattan Lyric," she said. "She was fresh from Minneapolis or some place like that, and I guess she brought out my mother instinct, because I kind of took her under my wing. Before long they were giving her leads, but she was real insecure about it, always saying she didn't know if she was good enough."

"Was she?" Damon asked.

Naomi Rostov sighed. "She needed more technique, but she had a hell of a voice. Not that that means anything in this town. But sometimes she could make you think of Galli-Curci."

"What happened to her?"

"Well, I was away for a while. I got a job with the road company of a musical—not what I wanted, of course, but the money was good. When I got back, Lee was all tied up with some guy, some doctor she met. I forget exactly, but he might have been a shrink. Anyway, she treated him like a guru, and he was always talking to her about her voice. I never could get it straight what he was saying, and besides, I wasn't seeing too much of her anymore. Then one day she tells me she's giving it all up for a while and goes off to work in a school somewhere. And I never heard from her again." She opened her purse. "In here I've got an old picture of her that I dug out. Would it be worth anything to you?"

The grotesque idea returned to Damon as a prickling across the back of his neck. He put out another ten and took the photo. It showed a woman in costume for a role, something like *Lucia,* with long dark hair cascading around a face that looked familiar. He peered more closely. "Was her hair really dark?"

"No, that's a wig. She was blond."

Then, with a jolt that exploded all his prior thoughts, Damon realized why the face was familiar: It was younger, and it bore an expression that was not characteristic of her, but it was a good deal like Lauren Granger's.

"All right," he said finally. "The synopsis was good. Let's talk about the whole libretto."

Chapter Fourteen

The wind off the river gusted down the street, whistling its icy way into the rented car, from which Damon was watching the Granger brownstone.

At six-thirty he finished the coffee congealing in a paper cup. At seven he ran the engine again, just enough to warm his fingers. At seven-thirty he began to wonder if he would have to wait till tomorrow to talk to Helen Jones. Even so, it would be the quickest way to corroborate Naomi Rostov's story and to learn its ending. He shook his head, still unable to accept it. He had been right, after all, he thought, to suspect that the names were the clue. But not Jonas-Jones. That was, after all, the commonest name in the world; even in the trial there had been a Jones, the professor from Columbia. The relevant similar names were Leonora-Lauren.

He had gone, in his memory, over and over the police reports on Lauren. But they had never really investigated her, since they hadn't suspected her of any complicity in Granger's death or of being the anonymous caller—any more than they had suspected Astrid of making the call. He had gone to the Marriage License Bureau and learned that thirteen years earlier a twenty-five-year-old named Lauren Frazer had married

Martin Granger. But none of the schools for deaf children—including the one in Connecticut, which finally was able to answer his questions by telephone—had records of a teacher by either name, Frazer or Granger. Dead ends everywhere, he thought, unless he got to Helen Jones. And could get her to stop playing her malicious little games.

At eight-twelve a cab pulled up in front of the house, and Lauren came out, wearing her silver fox. The cab drove off and turned north on Riverside Drive.

Damon waited for five minutes, then got out, stamping his feet. When he rang the Grangers' bell, the door opened almost immediately. "Yeah?" said a burly young man. His voice had an all too familiar quality: the smug hostility of those who carry their confidence in a holster.

"Is Father Lawrence here?" Damon improvised.

"Who?"

"Is this 415 West 85th Street?"

"This is 84th, fella."

"Oh. Stupid of me. Sorry." He got away quickly, to give the man as brief a look at him as possible, because he knew already that he was going to have to come back. If Lauren was worried enough to have a bodyguard on Helen Jones, then Jones must know a great deal. She would have to be gotten out.

Forty-five minutes later he was back. A cheap yellow cap, purchased in a discount store on Broadway, covered his hair, and he wore dark glasses from which the lenses had been knocked out. He had a delivery cart, coaxed from the manager of a supermarket by means of a deposit and a story about an undercover job; from the cart he took two boxes, filled mostly with bags of potato chips but with a layer of other items on top. In the corner of one was tucked the billy club he had had in the car. He rang the bell.

"Nobody told me about groceries," said the young hood.

"Yeah?" he said in a light, high voice. "Well, I don't know you, either, buddy. Ask the fat lady. The cook."

The man hollered, "Hey, you! In the kitchen! You order some grub?"

Damon prayed for a long moment. Then Jones came waddling out. "Hi," he said quickly. "It's me, Damon from Gristede's. Sorry I'm late tonight."

She blinked. "Hello."

"OK," said the man. "Leave the stuff right here."

"What the hell? You trying to screw me out of a tip and a cup of coffee? I always take the order to the kitchen, don't I, Miss Jones? I hope you've still got some coffee left." He prayed again.

"Yes," she said after a moment.

He took the boxes to the kitchen, the young hood right behind him. And then he got a better idea than the billy club. "You know what?" he said to Jones when she came in. "You oughtta be on one of those coffee commercials." He picked up the coffeepot and lifted the lid. "You put eggshells in the grounds?"

"No," Jones said.

He took out the basket and saw that the pot was nearly full. The man was standing uncertainly by the groceries. Damon moved toward him. "You ever smell coffee like that?"

"What are you, some kind of coffee freak? Hey, take it—" The man howled and grabbed his crotch, where the stream of hot coffee had landed.

Damon got him from behind, found the shoulder holster, took the gun, and slammed him into a chair. "Helen, is there anybody else in the house?"

"No."

He told her to get some towels, quickly, and when she did not move, he said, hating it, "I've got the gun now, so you'll have to do it." She did. He put the gun on the counter while he tied the man's feet and arms. Then he cut off the sobbing and cursing by stuffing a dishcloth in the man's mouth and securing it with another towel.

"Helen," he said, panting, "I want you to come with me."

She stared, her whole body seeming to ripple with fear. "Leave? Go out? I . . . I can't."

"Then why didn't you tell this man not to let me in? Because some part of you wanted to see me, wanted to be rescued. Isn't that true?" She didn't answer. "The gun is still on the counter, Helen. Take it if you want to, and give it back to your bodyguard here. Or else come with me. That's your only choice."

"Leave?" she said again. "Where?"

Where indeed? he thought. Then he had an inspiration. "I'll get my father to take us up to visit a friend of his. A wonderful cook, who's got a kitchen almost as nice as yours. You can't stay here, Helen."

She looked at him as if she had no will of her own. He lifted the man to his feet and with his other hand took Jones's arm. "Let's go to your room and get some of your things." He moved down the hall with his double burden, to a room that was as bare as a nun's, without even a crucifix. He threw the man on the bed. Jones had no suitcase, so he was helping her roll some clothes inside her brown robe when they heard someone come into the front hall.

Damon shut the bedroom door and waited, hearing a voice call, "Helen?" several times. Footsteps came down to the door. "Helen, are you in there?"

He held his breath. "Yes," said Jones.

"Where the hell is Max?"

The man on the bed thrashed. Jones ran her tongue over her lips. "He went out."

"Out? That sonofabitch. Wait till I talk to— All right, Helen, I'm going up to bed now. You're sure you're all right?"

"Yes."

The footsteps went away.

They waited in silence for twenty minutes, during which Jones sat on the room's one chair, like an inmate in a cell who had forgotten how to leave it. Finally Damon eased her out, carrying her bundle in one hand. She moved with perilous slowness, and he was sweating by the time they reached the front hall.

A whirring noise came from behind the door of the small elevator. "She's coming back down," Jones said. Her eyes glazed with fear, and she would not move.

"Helen!" he said urgently. Then he put his hands on her back and pushed, pushed the bulk that was both unyielding and soft, until finally he got her out the door.

David Chapin heard a click, signifying the end of the recording. He switched off the tape in the portable cassette player.

But the room still was not silent. There was a loud sound, like the thumping of blood, which could be felt as well as heard because it came from within him. "No," he whispered. But he barely could hear his own voice. He said it again, loudly. "No!"

It was Astrid's fault, he thought, for hounding Martin, screaming at him like one of the Furies, goading him, accusing him of being a killer. One couldn't blame Martin for having lost his temper. She had admitted that herself, in court. Then afterward she had insisted that he had made her a promise and would now have to keep it. Would have to listen to the tape. He should never have given in to her, he thought. What did he owe her, after she had slept with another man? Why should she be trusted, ever again?

He got up quickly and walked across the room, the bedroom in which he had grown up, with the white dresser and desk and the cool white spread on the bed. Outside, the lawns of the Chapin estate were gray and frozen, a wasteland lit by the moon.

Martin could not have said those things, he thought, could not have spoken of him in that way. Yet Martin had said them.

The thumping blood noise increased.

If Martin had meant it, he thought—had really felt such contempt for him—then Martin could not be what he had seemed: a man dedicated to good. A man who had spent hours listening to him, who had not flinched from naming the truth but had tried to show him a way to make peace with himself . . . No, he thought, it clearly was not possible that Martin had meant what he said. Therefore, Martin must have had some other reason for saying it.

He squinted out at the gray lawns. Actually, he thought, what Martin had said about him on the tape boiled down to one thing: the fact that David Chapin was useless. And there, as always, Martin was right; for hadn't he still failed, after six more months, to come to the right decision?

The blood noise was receding somewhat. Martin, he thought, would certainly have suspected that Astrid was planning to run home and report everything he said . . . Was it perhaps a test? Martin must have grown tired of him and his indecision, must have wished he could do something to help speed up the process. Perhaps Martin had concluded that shock treatment was in order . . . that if he made a seeming rejection, a devastating one, which was reported back, it would serve to jolt away the lethargy and indecision . . . to establish, once and for all, whether David Chapin was worthy or not . . .

He stood for a long time, watching the moon move slowly into the clutches of the dead branches of an elm.

Once he had gotten Jones out of the Granger house, Damon

stopped by the luncheonette on Broadway to pick up his father, and by ten-thirty the three of them were in Sarah Meier's apartment on West 114th Street.

Sarah had worked for his father, helping out with the baking until her arthritis got too bad. She was a childless widow, whose apartment seemed cluttered as an antidote to the emptiness of her life; she was delighted at the thought of a visitor but puzzled by the reality, for Jones was silent and disoriented, her eyes dull, her face sleek with perspiration. They took her into the kitchen and gave her some coffee and strudel, which she took as if they were a lifeline. On Damon's instructions, Sarah and his father ignored her and talked about business at the luncheonette.

After a while Jones's eyes began to scan the items in the kitchen, and Damon began to work slowly toward his goal. "Helen, you've been with the Grangers for about twelve years?" She nodded. "Was Mrs. Granger there when you started?" She nodded again. "You've known her a long time, then. What was she like at the beginning?"

He watched the words penetrate slowly. She winced and then said, "I don't know what you mean."

"Well, Mrs. Granger is a very attractive but very hard woman. Was she like that when you first came?"

"No. She was . . . more quiet."

"Do you know what she did before she was married?" She nodded. "Was she a singer?"

Her eyes jerked to his and then dove back for cover. "Why do you ask me that?"

"I'll tell you if you'll answer my question. Was she a singer?"

She wiped her lips. "Yes."

"She sang opera?"

"Why is it important?"

"She might know something that could have a bearing on

the trial of Astrid Cain. Was she a singer with the Manhattan Lyric Opera?"

"Ask her."

"Would she tell me?" Jones did not answer. "Did she teach for a while at a school for deaf children?" Still no answer. "Were they happy when they first got married, she and the doctor? Did you think they were a loving couple?"

"He said they were."

"He talked to you about her?"

"Sometimes."

"Did he . . ." Damon hesitated. "Did he tell you why she gave up her singing career?"

"I want to go," she said. Her face was shiny again.

"Go where? Back to a woman who keeps a guard on you? Back to Lee?"

Her mouth made small sipping noises, but not because she was drinking her coffee. Christ, he thought, what was he doing to this pathetic creature? If he forced her to speak, what would happen to her when she finally went back to Lauren? And what would she do if she couldn't go back?

Sarah Meier took the decision out of his hands temporarily. "Miss Jones looks exhausted to me. She'd better get some sleep, and you can go on with this in the morning."

She bustled off to make up a bed in one of her spare rooms. Jones followed her docilely, like a giant lamb anticipating slaughter.

Damon's father sighed. "She has such dead eyes, did you notice? I never saw eyes like that, except on one other person."

"Who was that?"

After a while his father answered. "Sam. What kills the eyes that way, Paul? Did you ever figure that out, in all the years you've been investigating people?"

"No. I never did."

"At least I still see a son when I look at your eyes. In fact," the old man added, reaching for more coffee, "tonight you kind of look like you did when you were still in school. Excited, kind of."

He was back at eight o'clock the next morning. Sarah Meier opened the door and whispered, "She's been up since six-thirty. We're in the kitchen. She's fine as long as we talk recipes."

"I know," Damon said.

In the kitchen he took a cup of coffee and watched Jones, who was kneading dough. She seemed quite willing to answer Sarah's questions about yeasts and whole-grain flours and the best method for croissants. To get any other kind of answers, he thought, would obviously require the long way around.

After a while he interrupted the culinary conversation. "Helen keeps a file of all her menus, going back for years. And I'll bet she remembers most of them even without the file." Jones nodded, pressing the dough. "When's the last time you made . . . oh, Yorkshire Pudding, Helen?"

"In October. She had a big luncheon."

"How about Chicken Kiev?"

She thought for a moment. "February."

"That's right, you told me. How about . . . let's see, how about June 23?"

"I'd have to know who was there."

"I think it was just Dr. Granger."

"Then I don't remember. He never wanted much."

"But June 23 was the night he died. Surely you remember the last meal you made for him?"

She folded the dough over and pressed it with her hands. "Just a salad. But the next day he was supposed to have a big party."

"So you were preparing for that?"

"Just one thing. I usually do meringue shells the night before."

"Do you turn the heat off and let them dry for a while in the oven?" Sarah asked.

"Yes. About an hour."

"Once I went to bed and forgot all about them."

"I've never forgotten," Jones said.

Without moving a muscle, Damon asked, "So they were fine when you went back to the kitchen to check them out?"

"Oh, yes."

"That was about ten o'clock?"

"Something like that."

"And the terrace doors were open, so you heard voices?"

"Why, Helen, what's the matter?" Sarah asked. Jones was staring at her hands in the dough, as if they were caught in glue.

"You heard the quarrel, didn't you, Helen?"

Her hands moved and then sank back.

"You went into the living room and stood by the terrace doors and watched, didn't you? You saw Dr. Granger die."

"Yes," she said helplessly.

"You saw him slip and fall? It was an accident?"

"He was shouting . . . saying . . ."

"Saying what?"

She wrenched her hands from the dough and sat down heavily.

So, he thought, his instinct had been right, after all; for a moment he forgot he was no longer on the force, and wanted to tell Riley. And to tell Astrid that life had imitated art and made her fake eyewitness real.

He leaned over the woman. "Helen, you have to tell what you saw. You have to go into court and tell what you know. *Everything* you know."

"I can't. I can't."

But she had to, he thought, no matter what it cost her. There had to be a way to make her agree to testify—for a subpoena without her agreement would be meaningless. For the rest of the morning he and Sarah tried to find that way, begging, cajoling, and arguing.

Finally, wearily, he said, "Helen, you came with me last night because you trusted me, didn't you?"

"Yes."

"Then will you trust me again? If you go into court, nothing will happen to you, I promise." He told himself that it was not a lie, that he would somehow make sure it was true.

She blinked and wiped her lips. "All right," she said. "If you go with me." She put her head in her hands, on which the dough had caked and dried. "Oh, I'm so tired. So tired. So tired."

"I don't know," Astrid said, "whether I can take any more, Sandy."

"My dear, I'm so sorry." Marsh's eyes were threaded with red wires of exhaustion. He pushed aside the remnants of his lunch; they were eating in the same small room off the court where she had talked to David two days before. Was it only two days? she thought.

"I don't understand it, Sandy. How could he simply . . . not accept what was on the tape?"

Marsh rubbed his eyes. "I once knew a very devout man," he said slowly, "who believed he had witnessed a miracle. When it was demonstrated to him that there was a perfectly rational explanation for everything he had seen, he said that the explanation had only been sent to test his faith."

"But David is a scientist!"

"So were a lot of intellectuals who went to Russia in the thirties and convinced themselves that purges and slave labor camps did not exist."

"None so blind . . ." she said, hearing Damon's voice in her mind.

"Exactly."

She turned away. Had she been blind, too, she wondered—imagining David to be something he was not? No, she thought; in the first year of their marriage, the year of smiles, he had been a sensitive and charming man, buoyed up by his work, absorbed in it. But even then, she knew, there had been another element in him—something that had needed reassurance, which she had seemed able to give.

There was weakness in him, always, she thought, using those words for the first time, expecting a surge of self-reproach but feeling only the hollowness of acceptance. Did you think you could make him strong? she asked herself. The answer was both worse and better than a Yes would have been; suddenly the events of the past year swirled into a new perspective, and she saw that part of her desperation to save David from Martin Granger had come from a kind of guilt. An awareness that she felt less and less for him each day, which she had tried to deny by doing more and more.

She asked herself whether she would have muted her testimony for David's sake if she had not been so conscious of the change in her feeling for him. Whatever the answer, she thought, it did not matter anymore.

She looked back at Marsh. "So David has decided to go to Lilac Hill and Rosalie? To spend the rest of his life working with retarded people?"

"He says that is what he wants."

Granger had won, she thought; and she still did not really know how he had done it. Why, but not how.

She closed her eyes on another painful realization: Until now she had half-consciously been feeling that what she had done to Damon would somehow be justified if she were able to save David.

Damon had been right, she thought, when he accused her of using the ends to rationalize the means.

She shook her head and reached for her paper container of coffee. The contents were cold and bitter. "Tell me, now that he's heard the tape, does David still think I didn't kill Granger?"

Marsh hesitated. "I believe he thinks you wanted to."

"Well, then," she said tightly, "you were quite right. The tape is dangerous."

"At least David has agreed not to make his career decision public until after the trial. I told him that could do you too much damage. Lowell would find some way to work it in on rebuttal. He already has a string of witnesses waiting in the wings to testify to Granger's virtues and brilliance, if Cox will allow them."

"Oh, let him talk about David," she said. "Let them put it in the headlines that David is doing exactly what Martin Granger wanted. That his wife was a fool."

"That," said Marsh, "would be a very reckless thing to do."

They sat in silence. She nursed her coffee and her bitterness, almost enjoying the sensation of being, for once in her life, beyond caring.

Damon got down to Foley Square just after one o'clock and found the room they were in. Marsh looked up at him with weary disdain. "What do you want now?"

When he told them, Astrid said, "But Damon, that can't be. I told you there wasn't . . . I mean . . ." Her voice faded away like smoke.

Marsh rubbed his eyes as if to wipe the dislike from them and took out his gold pen. "Sit down. Tell me everything this Jones woman said to you."

After ten minutes Marsh studied his notes and then leaned back to stare at the paneled wall. "Let me be sure I understand this. Helen Jones, whom you apparently have abducted, tells you that she saw Granger die. But she has not actually stated what she saw, whether it was murder or an accident." Astrid started to say something, then stopped. "At the same time, you suggest that this woman, who you admit is unpredictable and unstable, could testify that her own employer, the wife of the deceased, is the Lee of the letter. But Helen Jones has not confirmed this bizarre hypothesis of yours in so many words. So I do not yet know what she actually would say if I put her on the stand."

"That's true," Damon admitted, "but—"

"Nonetheless, I am to subpoena this unpredictable woman, work with her, and hope for the best. With the knowledge that what Ben Lowell might do with her on cross is even more unpredictable." He sat erect, his patrician features hard. "No."

"Sandy, you can't mean—"

"Look, Marsh," Damon cut in. "I know she's difficult, but I do have her confidence, at least to some extent. Suppose that I were the one who worked with her and then questioned her."

"On the stand, you mean?"

"Yes."

"As a temporary member of the defense?"

"If it came to that, and it might, I would be willing."

Astrid was staring at him. "Damon, do you know what you're saying?"

"Yes. I do."

"And so do I," said Marsh stiffly. "Astrid, this man has no trial experience, if I recall your description of his past. I do not think that the combination of an unstable witness and a novice attorney is what we need just now."

Astrid put her hand on Marsh's arm. "Don't you realize what Damon has done for us?"

"I remember only too well what he did for us just a short time ago, when he testified for the prosecution."

She took her hand away slowly. "Sandy, I don't believe this. Are you going to refuse—"

"I told you when you brought me word of what this man was doing—doing against my wishes, remember—that I had already talked to Helen Jones, months ago. Just as I talked to everyone else, however unlikely, who might know anything that could help you. I am satisfied that Helen Jones was asleep when Granger died. I am satisfied that she is a pathetic and vulnerable creature. And if this man has kidnapped her and browbeaten or bribed her into telling wild stories that he imagines would help you—well, I do not intend to allow it."

"You mean you think he is feeding her stories he invented? But how could he? And why on earth would he?"

"Perhaps he wishes to recapture your affections. As to how he could do it . . . well, he is one of the few who have heard your tape. He could easily feed this Jones woman just enough key phrases to make her sound half-convincing to us."

Astrid's mouth was a shocked and angry circle. Then she turned to Damon. "Nothing that I know about you, today or in the past, would make that explanation possible. But if I'm wrong, you must tell me so."

"You're not wrong. But Marsh is correct about one thing. I have heard the tape."

"I know that. You know the whole story? That it's not going to be played in court?"

"Yes. Lowell told me."

Marsh spoke into the silence. "Remember that this man was able to hear the tape and still believe you were guilty. Doesn't that tell you something about the value of his help?"

"There are things you don't understand, Sandy. And what are we going to do instead of taking his help?"

"What I had planned. Those three ex-employees of the

Institute. Character witnesses. Granger's doctor, who will confirm the arrhythmia—"

"Will that be any better than recalling Mrs. Pine, the way you did this morning, and getting nothing from her?"

Marsh placed the tips of his fingers against one another. "I am giving you my best advice."

"I know," she said softly. "And I've taken it. But perhaps you are too tired to think straight about this."

Marsh struggled to keep his fingers braced, to hold back the feelings that were clotting together and rising inside him in a ball: resentment of the detective, whose testimony had done such damage to the case and who now presumed to judge and advise him; of Astrid, who had pushed him into a trial strategy that was alien to his nature and had backfired constantly; of Jake Waldo, Junior; and of everything else that had seemed to slip out of his control. He told himself it was irrational to feel these things, and braced his fingers still more tightly, so that the veins stood out like knotted blue ropes.

"Damon," Astrid was saying, "tell me why you're doing this. Is it because you've forgiven me? Or is it still to pay a debt?"

"Let's just say it's . . . *quand même.*"

She smiled crookedly. "Do you know that when you came in just now, I was ready to give up, for the first time?"

"And it would be the first time, wouldn't it?"

"I guess it can sometimes seem as if there are good reasons."

"Once I wanted very much to make you admit that. But I find I'm not glad to hear it, after all."

Astrid smiled again, but this time it was not crooked. The two of them, Marsh thought, had forgotten his existence.

She leaned across the table. "Do you really believe you can get the truth from Helen Jones?"

"I think so. But it's a gamble."

"Then it's one I want to take. Sandy, we have to go along with Damon, do what he is suggesting."

"No," Marsh said.

"Sandy, please. I know I've put you in some very difficult positions, but this is something you have to do."

"No." Marsh put his hands on the table; they were shaking slightly. "I've been pushed to go against my judgment too many times in this case. I won't do it again. If you ask me to, I'll resign."

Astrid closed her eyes. The lids seemed almost translucent, and they trembled. "All right," she said finally. She looked at Marsh. "Sandy, I'm so grateful for everything you've done. You've been wonderful."

Then she turned back to Damon. "I never expected to ask you this question again. Will you . . . practice the law?"

"I've already said I would question Jones, if there's no other way."

"I don't mean that. I mean to do everything. To take over my defense."

It was Marsh who finally spoke. "I always said you were reckless, Astrid. Foolhardy."

But neither of them was looking at him.

Chapter Fifteen

Sancho grabbed the plastic bone in his teeth and made a series of dashes toward the kitchen. Then he ran back, dropped the bone into the old piece of blanket that was full of chew-holes, and worked at it furiously.

The dog, Damon thought, was only reacting to his own tension. Both the couch and the rosewood table were covered with books and papers: law books, transcripts of the trial, reports from Marsh's investigators. Judge Cox reluctantly had granted a recess for Thursday and Friday, and now only Saturday night and Sunday remained, in which to resurrect what he once had learned in law school.

Under that pressure his mind had already reduced the scene in Cox's chambers to a few vivid details: the sag of Marsh's shoulders—and voice—as he announced that he would turn over the case; the deepening pink in the judge's absurdly round face as he listened; the tiny pulse in the base of Astrid's throat, when she told Cox that she did indeed understand what she was asking and that she believed Paul Damon was essential to her defense; and the drumfire of Lowell's fingers as he snapped out objections in which the word "unorthodox" figured prominently.

Reporters had besieged Damon as he was leaving the court; one of them had asked, "Why do you think Judge Cox agreed to this?" Underneath his noncommittal answer he had been thinking that a judge might very well grant such an irregular request if he were out to get a defendant; and that thought had triggered the memory of Judge Garrick Evans. He had pushed it aside, swearing he would approach this task *tabula rasa,* with nothing from the past in his way.

But of course that was not possible. A dozen times already, as he worked, he had stopped to look off into the distance and the years at the law student, and the man, that he had been—remembering the way his life had closed, like a fist, against the possibility of more betrayals, in and out of the legal profession. And if he now had learned that such a closing was self-defeating, did it mean he was to go back to the law? Not in the harried, impossible way that he was now functioning but as a consciously planned lifetime commitment?

He shook his head and admitted that he did not know. All he could feel was the tension of preparing for Monday; all he could commit himself to was the single, looming task of trying to save Astrid.

Sancho attacked the plastic bone again. Damon stretched his legs under the table and got up. "Hey, boy," he said, "you want to go out for a while? Up to visit a couple of cooks?"

Sancho's quizzical look seemed to ask whether that was a good idea, and Damon grinned. "You're right," he said. "It's not." The dog probably would be just something else that would frighten Helen Jones. His grin faded. He had gone up to talk with her two more times, and although she was now less disoriented, she still answered less than half his questions. He finally had coaxed from her enough information to be sure that she really did know how Granger had died—if he could keep her from disintegrating on the stand before she told it to the court—but he had gotten little more from her about Lauren Granger. Except the name of the school for the deaf where "Lee" had taught; and that was a chilling piece of news because the school was one he already had called, which had no record of a teacher named Jonas. Or Granger. Or Frazer.

It was possible, he thought, that he would have to abandon the whole issue of "Lee." But then there would be no chance at all to substantiate Astrid's version of what Granger had done to people. Marsh's investigators had turned up nothing helpful. Even their deposition from Ezra Kerr in Minnesota had indicated that he would be more useful to the prosecution than to the defense—a fact that Ben Lowell undoubtedly knew.

Damon bent back to the legal pad on which he was outlining alternate strategies. One column said "Jones." The other was headed "Without Jones"—what to do in case she failed him. Lauren's name was there, crossed out and reinstated half a dozen times; did he dare subpoena her and then confront her with the picture and the Lee letter? But it was one of the rudiments never to put on a witness unless one knew what to expect from him or her, so that left only Marsh's original plan. He went over it once again.

The phone rang. Sancho barked, and Damon leaped up, afraid that it was Sarah Meier and that something had happened to Jones.

But it was Marie.

"Paul?" Her voice was high and strained. He knew why, in the pit of his stomach, even before she told him. "Paul, I have a message for you. From some . . . some men who have taken me someplace. They say to tell you . . . to tell you that you cannot put the cook on the stand. Because if you do, they will . . ." Her voice rose to a crack. "They will take out my tongue. I told them it wouldn't matter to you, because we are not together anymore, but they don't believe me. They say, Why were you helping him, then? Because I told them I was, they made me tell them—"

He cut in urgently. "Do you know where it is they've got you?"

"No. They came to my place and asked me a lot of questions and then they took me out and shoved me into a car and drove—"

The phone clicked and went dead.

Sancho whimpered and jumped into his lap.

He patted the silky white head, staring into the distance. "I know, boy, I know. As soon as you decide to try to fight for something . . ." He looked down and saw that the dog was not Cyrano.

He shook his head, to clear his vision. "I never should have taken you in," he said. "Or her. If I hadn't let her in . . ." He thought of the gentle, laughing presence in his life that Marie had been, that she was; and he knew that despite all his efforts, some part of her had crept past the barricade he had erected; that if he had been as indifferent to her as he claimed, he would have broken with her long ago. She had given him, he thought, the sensation of watching his own youth, as it might have been. And he had taken it, while declaring that it did not matter.

He reached for the phone to call Sanford Marsh and ask him to take back the case.

Sancho looked up at him, one ear twisted sideways, as if to ask whether that was a good idea.

Was it? he thought. If he backed away now, what would that mean to the rest of his life?

To care, he thought—to hold any person or any thing as a value—was to accept the risk of pain and loss. And not to let the risk keep one from fighting to hold the value. Marie had known that. And had acted on it.

He took his hand away from the phone. It still might be, he thought, that he would have to abandon Jones—with all that would mean for Astrid. And for Granger's victims. But it would not be without a fight.

He thought of calling the squad, of asking Riley and the others for help. But what use could sheer manpower be by Monday morning, especially without any leads? He put Sancho down from his lap and pulled his chair closer to the table. Use your goddamn brain, he thought.

Lauren Granger pulled the white sweater off over her head, not caring that her lipstick smeared it, and stepped quickly out of her slacks. Her bra and pantyhose came off in jerky movements, and she slipped into the tub. The water was scalding, just as she wanted it, and after a while her protesting body armored itself in numbness.

She had already showered at Karl's place, as soon as he let her out of the round bed under the ceiling of mirrors, but that was not enough to wash away the memory of what had happened in the bed.

She told herself that she had had no choice, that Karl was the only one to whom she could have turned to provide a means of keeping Jones safe. And then, when Jones had been taken in spite of Karl's man—by that detective, obviously—and when Ben Lowell said that the detective was replacing Marsh for the defense, there had been no choice but to go back to Karl once more.

Listening to his taunting, she thought, was the price that had to be paid: "Well, Lauren, you dropped me like a pair of dirty shorts when your old man died. You were too busy with your political crowd to give me the time of day. So I don't see why I should get my boys to help you out now. Unless you'd like to climb on the bed like a good girl. Then I might help you out, because I ain't had a good piece of high-class ass lately."

She groaned, sinking deeper in the tub. He was just a common gangster, she thought, despising herself for having gotten mixed up with him in the first place and for needing his help now. And for having a body that responded to him, clawing at his hairy back, guiding him with her hands, taking him in convulsive, greedy jerks.

"I couldn't help it!" she said aloud. It was all Martin's fault, she thought, for hitting back at her because of his own failure, making her feel so useless and cheap . . . telling her she could never be anything on her own . . .

She began to soap her body, soaping and soothing herself with the thought of the Lauren Granger to whom some of the most important people in the country had paid deferential attention, and would again, when the trial was over . . . the Lauren Granger who might not have had the singing career she deserved but who had turned out to be better known than "Leonora Jonas" ever could have. . . .

The doorbell rang, sending the soap skidding from her hands. She stood up in the tub, panicked and indecisive. There was no one else in the house; she thought she simply would not answer. But the bell kept ringing and ringing, driving in the thought that it might be some message from Karl's men, some trouble. She got out of the tub, toweled, pulled on a silk robe, and took the elevator down to the front hall.

It was indeed trouble. "What do you want?" she said, shivering under the silk.

Paul Damon stepped inside and closed the door. He looked huge, and the lines of his face were as sharp and cold as the wind off the river. "I've come to see Helen Jones," he said.

She stared at him, clutching the robe around her as if the action could gather her thoughts as well, fumbling for an answer, knowing it was stupid as soon as it was out. "Jones is not here right now."

"Then I'll just wait till she gets back." He sat in one of the small chairs opposite the elevator door.

She made an effort to think clearly. Was it possible that he didn't have Jones after all? She had told Karl he did, that he must have hidden her with his girlfriend, the one who had made a scene after his testimony and had called him out of court on the very day Jones disappeared. But when they took the girl, Jones wasn't there, Karl said; she admitted she had been helping Damon, though, so they kept her to use as a lever. . . . Of course he had Jones, she thought. Someone had had to tie up the guard; who else could it have been? "Get up!" she said to him. "Get out of here."

"I'm waiting for Helen."

"She's not here! You know damn well where she is. You came in here and took her yourself." He looked past her as if she were not there, any more than Jones was. "Get out of here, or I'll call the police!"

"Why don't you?" he said.

"You bastard!" His expression did not change. "You can sit there till your butt rots off, but it's not going to help your little brown girlfriend."

He stood up so quickly that she took a step backward. "Good," he said. "That's an admission that you've taken Marie. Now we can get to business." He reached inside his coat; she tensed, expecting a gun, but it was only a piece of paper, and she bit her lip against a nervous laugh.

"I'm serving you with a subpoena," he said. "If Marie Lazare isn't in my apartment, unharmed, by noon tomorrow, this subpoena will be in effect as of Monday morning. Go ahead. Open it."

She did. Her eyes widened, and her left lid began to twitch. "But this is for Leonora Jonas."

"That's the idea," he said.

The sound she made was halfway between a gasp and a laugh.

"See you in court," he said. "Unless I see Marie Lazare first."

By five o'clock Sunday she had not appeared, nor had the phone rung.

Damon had gone over it a hundred times, looking for the explanation. He had gambled that the possibility of being exposed as a victim of her own husband's, with all that meant about both of them, would be an even greater threat than having Jones take the stand. If it wasn't, what did that mean? Either, he thought, it meant she was prepared to risk testifying and planned to lie her way out of his questions. In which case she was shrewd, for he had very little to pin her down with. Or else it meant she was not shrewd at all—was simply too far gone in panic to think or to care. In which case his visit probably had aggravated the panic and had been a mistake. In either case, he thought, was he really prepared to call her to the stand?

He reached for the legal pad on the table, covered with notes that added up to nothing, and tried again.

At six-thirty he went into the kitchen, realizing he hadn't eaten in twenty-four hours. The phone rang. He reached it in the middle of the third ring.

"Paul? They say to tell you the same thing, not to put that woman on the stand."

"Are you all right?"

"They haven't . . . done anything yet. But I am very afraid. Paul, I think these men are—"

The phone went dead.

There was a silver Christmas tree in the lobby of the Sutton Place co-op, decorated with gold balls, and the security guard had a gold reindeer tucked into his cap. Damon gave the man his name, and after a pause Jake Waldo's voice, distorted by the intercom, said to send him up.

The apartment was all chrome and glass and black leather; the only color came from Waldo's florid face. "Ah, yes," he said, "the prosecution witness who turned his coat inside out. Sit down."

"No, thanks."

"What can I do for you?"

"I came to find out if you are one of those who really believe that politics justifies anything, even kidnapping and torture."

Waldo's color deepened. "I'll assume you're going to explain that."

"Do I need to?"

"Yes, if you want to have any kind of conversation with me."

"Very well." He told it to Waldo in terse sentences. "I've already made what I believe you would call a counteroffer to Mrs. Granger, and she has declined. I know that you and she are, shall we say, friendly? I don't know whether she is doing all this with or without your knowledge and consent. If it's the former, I'm wasting my time. If it's the latter, I want you to know and to do something about it."

Waldo looked at him for a moment, his mouth clamping around the prominent teeth, and then walked over to the table on which he rearranged several pieces of decorative quartz. "You know," he said softly, "when I learned you were going to take over the defense, I made a few inquiries about you, among my friends in the legal profession. Only one of them knew anything—Garrick Evans. You recall him?"

"Oh, yes." Damon squared his shoulders. "What did he tell you?"

"That you are fond of leaping to conclusions."

"Did he also tell you how much he loves animals? Never

mind. I'm sure you got the laundered version of what happened. The bloodless version. If you're a friend of his, I suppose there's no point in talking to you."

"Mr. Damon." Waldo picked up one of the quartz pieces, which suddenly looked like a weapon. "Your insinuation that I am involved in a kidnapping is offensive. And your suggestion that if I am not involved, I have the power to stop it, seems unrealistic. Surely it's the police you want? But of course they may no longer consider you worthy of their help."

At the door Damon turned back. "Tell Evans he used to have a better class of friends years ago."

When Damon had gone, Waldo hefted the quartz from one hand to the other, weighing what to do. If the man was right and Lauren really had done something so insane, then, he thought, it would be fatal to get involved, even to the extent of trying to stop her. For if news of the kidnapping was made public, then she could implicate him, and probably would. His angry color rose again at the thought of her; although she had adjusted to the political realities imposed by the trial, lately she had been exhibiting some of the early warning signs of panic. And panic was like righteousness—people in its grip were dangerous.

No, he thought, much better to stay out of it altogether. And if, God forbid, it all did come out and the detective claimed he had been told about it and hadn't done anything to stop it, then he would say that he had tried frantically and unsuccessfully to reach Mrs. Granger. And that he was more shocked than anyone at the way the strain of widowhood and the trial had obviously unhinged her.

His decision made, Waldo put down the quartz and went back to the den to watch the rest of the fund-raising drive on the public television station. He was just in time to hear his name cited as the giver of the evening's largest pledge.

"That was a pretty long walk," he said when young Jake came in, still wearing his coat.

"Yes." Jake sat down, stared at the screen for a while, got up, folded his coat, put it on the couch, and sat down again. "Dad," he said abruptly, talking over the TV sound, "I met that man in the hall. Paul Damon." Waldo snapped the remote control switch. The silence was loud. "He told me why he came to see you."

"If he told you some wild, crazy story, I'm sure you knew what to make of it."

"Well . . . no, Dad. I didn't. Not really. But I guess you've called Mrs. Granger and found out it's not true?"

It was because his father—who never hesitated—hesitated for a moment that Jake felt the fear run in liquid spurts to his hands and knees.

"Everything is fine," Waldo said firmly. "Take my word for it."

"Nobody has kidnapped a girl? And threatened to cut her tongue out? She's studying to be a singer, did you know that?"

"There's no need for you to worry."

"Yes, there is, Dad. Because if you're involved in something like that, then . . . well, I feel as if I'm part of it, too."

"Did that detective bastard put that crazy idea in your head?"

Don't look that way, Jake prayed silently, knowing what the face of stony anger had the power to do to him. Somewhere inside him, in the churning of his fear, was a small hard spot of determination; he felt suddenly that if he did not cling to it tonight, he would drown for the rest of his life. "If Mrs. Granger *had* had that girl kidnapped," he said slowly, "you would do everything you could to stop her. Wouldn't you?"

"How can you even ask such a question?"

"That's what people say when they don't want to answer. That's what you said when you told me what I had to say in court and I asked if you wanted me to become a liar."

"No, Jake, no. Not a liar. Just someone who wouldn't help to attack a dead man's reputation."

"Because of the political realities?"

His father sighed heavily. "Listen, Jake, things happen in the political arena that one would never condone if they happened anywhere else. Politics requires one to sacrifice . . . certain niceties in order to get things done. That's why I'm glad you're not involved. You're too good for politics, Jake. Too fine a boy."

"I'm twenty-two."

"Yes, of course. Too fine a young man. You have to live a better life than I have. You have to spend your life doing good, making good things possible for other people."

A thought struck Jake so forcefully that he almost cried out. "You mean," he said, "that I'm supposed to atone for you?"

"No, no. Of course not."

But the thoughts kept coming, like bubbles bursting out of the fear. "That's why you said it would have been a waste of my life to go on with sculpture. That's why you said it would have killed you if I did."

"No!"

"And that's why you wanted me to go with Dr. Granger—so he could make me accept it!"

"I never asked Martin to do anything but help you. Jake! I love you! Don't you believe that?"

The two of them stared at each other; their eyes were the same pale gray, but the father's were tinged with red.

"I did believe you," young Jake said finally. "That's why I did what you wanted. No," he added conscientiously, "that wasn't the only reason. I was afraid of you. I guess I still am."

"Don't say that, Jake. Please."

"But it's true." He stood up. "I don't even have the guts to threaten you now. I wish I could say to you, Dad, if there's a kidnapping and you don't do anything to stop it, then I'll go into court tomorrow and tell the whole story about Granger and me. But I don't know if I could, because I'm afraid of what you might do to me afterwards."

His father turned away, as if he had something to hide.

"So I'll just say that it will be hard to believe you love me, if there's something you could do for that girl and you don't do it."

Waldo did not move, except for one tremor of his shoulders.

After a moment Jake said, "Good night, Dad," and went out.

"This is a very unusual proceeding," Judge Cox said to the jury. "It is not of course unusual for additional persons to join the defense during the course of a trial. Or even for the defense to change counsel altogether. But as of this morning Mr. Paul Damon, whom you have already heard testify for the prosecution, will appear as defense counsel. And that, of course, is highly unusual."

The jury, as one body, swung to look at Damon; their expressions of shock were mingled variously with pleasure, suspicion, and disapproval.

"The court has permitted this," Cox went on, "at the urgent request of the defendant, who is fully aware of the nature and meaning of her request. You are entitled to know that Mr. Damon has resigned from the New York Police Department, in which capacity he testified earlier, and that he is a member of the New York bar, which qualifies him to practice before this court. I further advise you that this change does not mean you are to disregard his earlier testimony."

Some frowns on the faces of the jury disappeared. Cox paused. "Mr. Damon, in view of the unusual circumstances, I will grant your request to make a short statement at this time."

Damon rose. "May it please the court," he said, feeling the words as strange on his tongue as a foreign language. "Ladies and gentlemen of the jury, Judge Cox very rightly cautions you that the testimony I gave as to my investigation of the defendant is still part of the record you must consider. I stand by that testimony. But I am here because there is evidence that was unknown to me at the time, which the defendant wishes to have presented to you and which I am in a unique position to provide. I intend to show you, beyond any reasonable doubt, that Astrid Cain Chapin did not kill Martin Granger. That is all I wish to say before proceeding, Your Honor."

"Very well. Call your next . . . er, your first witness."

"I call Leonora Jonas," Damon said.

There was a rustling and shifting in the packed courtroom—packed but still empty, Damon thought, for the crucial people were not there. He had hoped until the very last moment—had gone up at seven-thirty to get Jones, who was now sitting in the witness room with Sarah Meier, mammoth and trembling in her green uniform-dress. But there had been no sign of Marie. And no word from Jake Waldo, who was not in the courtroom either; but that, he thought, was only to be expected.

"Leonora Jonas!" the bailiff called. "Leonora Jonas!"

Lauren Granger was not in her second-row seat nor anywhere else in the courtroom; that, he had been afraid of. But not until he talked to Astrid had he been sure of what to do without her.

"Let the record show," he said, "that the witness Leonora Jonas, who has testimony pertaining to defense exhibit C, has failed to respond to a subpoena."

As the courtroom rustled again, he looked at Astrid. Her eyes seemed too large for her face, but when he called for her to take the stand, she nodded. She wore a soft, pale gray dress with a high collar and a full skirt; it seemed to Damon that she moved to the stand in a cloud of smoke.

If this was a mistake, he thought, at least they were both making it with full knowledge of the consequences—for everyone. Before the court opened, he had told her about Marie and all he had tried to do to get her released. "So you see," he had said, when the shock and the anger, and the fleeting moment of regret, had all played across her face, "you're on trial because you wanted to save your husband. And now, because of a girl who has the bad luck to think she loves me, I don't dare call the witness you need."

"Of course not. No, you mustn't risk it." She had looked away. "It's Cyrano all over again, isn't it? Including the fact that it's my fault."

"I'm not blaming you. And this time I'm not giving up."

Then he had told her what he saw as the only alternatives, if Lauren did not show—either to go ahead with what Marsh had planned, or else to take a big gamble.

That was when her eyes had become too large for her face. "I can't see that I have anything more to lose. It seems you've been luckier than I, Damon. Your Marie is worth saving." And then she had told him about her husband.

He walked toward her; she was sitting calmly in the witness chair, hands folded in her lap. "Mrs. Chapin, I'd like you to go back once more to the night of June 23."

"All right."

"Is there something about your conversation and quarrel with Martin Granger on that night that you have not told the court?"

"Yes."

Out of the corner of his eye he saw Ben Lowell freeze, like

an animal scenting danger. "Will you tell us now, please?"

"Yes. I use a tape recorder in my work as a reporter. I carried it in my purse that night. I made a recording of the entire conversation with Martin Granger, up to and including—"

The courtroom exploded with sound. Judge Cox gaveled furiously. When Damon could be heard again, he said, "Is this a copy of that recording?"

"Yes."

"Your Honor, I offer this in evidence—"

The sound exploded again, and Ben Lowell advanced toward the judge.

"All right, Mr. Lowell, all right," Cox said. "I will see you two gentlemen in my chambers before making a ruling."

As Damon moved toward the chambers, Ben Lowell caught him by the arm. "You sonofabitch."

"I told you Wednesday I wouldn't be bound by any deal Marsh had made. *Tabula rasa,* remember?"

"And I told you to remember how much ammunition I can throw at that tape, if Cox allows it. And I'll throw it all."

"Fine. That's your job." He looked at Lowell's face, in which each separate muscle was registering anger. "Look, Ben, can't we put aside the personal animosity?"

"After the kind of witness you were for me? No way."

"But it wound up working to your advantage, didn't it? Not that that's an excuse. Someday I'd like to tell you how it happened, though. It wasn't as cut and dried as it might seem."

"Save the rationalizations for your client."

"You're entitled to that attitude. I don't suppose you'd consider just going in and telling Cox you agree to the tape?" Lowell gave him a contemptuous look. "OK," Damon said. "But I'm curious about one thing. Do you want to keep it out for practical political reasons? Or because you really admire what Martin Granger stands for?"

"What the hell has that got to do with anything?"

"It doesn't. I just wondered." Whether you are one of the pragmatists or the idealists, he thought.

"Listen, I don't have to tell you anything. But nobody's got a better record on social issues than I have."

"And where does that get you?"

Lowell looked at him for a moment. Then he said softly, "High places. Higher than you'll ever get, you sonofabitch. Even if you win this trial. Now let's get in and see Cox."

Perhaps, Damon thought as they went inside, there was a category he hadn't yet considered: the man who was idealistic only because it seemed pragmatic.

In his chambers, at his desk, the judge listened quietly. The blandness of his manner seemed to act on Lowell like a goad. "We don't even know that this tape is the real thing!" he cried.

"That's easily fixed," Damon said. "Your office has had the real thing since August, when the defendant turned it over to you."

Cox leaned forward, but Lowell cut in. "And I'll tell you something else I had—a stipulation. Your Honor, we had a stipulation, Sanford Marsh and I, that this tape was not to be introduced in evidence."

"Ah," said Cox. "You are familiar with the tape, then."

"Yes. And I consider it to be— We had a stipulation!"

"You don't have one with me," Damon said.

"Your Honor, I could have used that tape on direct examination. But I gave up my right to do so because of the stipulation. I could have tried my whole case differently!"

"That's a valid point," Cox said.

"Thank you, sir." Lowell began to relax a bit. And why not? Damon thought. If Cox was looking for a solid, pragmatic way to rule against the tape, Lowell had just given it to him.

"I'll want time," Cox said, "to think over the whole question of the stipulation."

If only they would do it, Marie thought. If only it would happen. And be over with.

She drew a short, ragged breath and looked again, for the thousandth time, around the small room with the blue stucco walls and the one window that gave on a frozen field. From behind the door came the muted sounds of a television, which went on nearly all the time, broken occasionally by a laugh or a shout from the two men who were out there, beyond the door, drinking, and who looked in on her periodically or dragged her out to make those useless calls to Paul. The men wore masks with faces that had been designed to make children laugh. Somehow that made it more horrible: that she saw only the faces of a cat and a mouse, in grinning contradiction of the bodies beneath them.

Before they cut out her tongue, they were going to rape her; she had been sure of that since last night, when one of them had brought in a bowl of soup and had thought she was sleeping. He had called softly to his partner, and then the two of them had stood above her, their liquor breath mingling with the tomato smell of the soup in a sick-sweet way that made her want to gag. But she had not dared to move, so long as they stood there and looked at the thigh she knew was exposed beneath the edge of the blanket and whispered to each other about "eating chocolate." When they finally went out, she had been drenched in perspiration; and it seemed hours before she could drag her mind away from the memory of the cellar on Fox Street, five years ago, and the six Barracudas who had thrown her on the floor and stood above her.

Paul would not come to save her this time, she thought;

and so there would be no escape from the hands that would hold her legs apart and the swollen, red organs that would . . .

She cried out and then waited in panic for fear they had heard her and would come in, with their knife and their cat and mouse grins and their faceless bodies. But the sounds from the next room went on undisturbed.

It was all her own fault, she thought. She had been so proud of herself: proud that she was not like so many of the girls with whom she had grown up, who were content to stay within the city's Haitian community and to be the passive object of some man's desires and commands. She had broken out of all that and had been just like any American woman, going after anything she wanted, thinking she could be a singer and could have a man who didn't even want her. But God, she thought, had known that it was not right to try to force a man to be in love. It was only a man who could force himself on a woman . . .

The lump of nausea rose again. If only they would do it, she thought. So it would be over with.

Chapter Sixteen

The face of a young female reporter moved into medium close-up on the television screen.

"This new development in the Cain trial raises a number of questions. Why was the tape recording never mentioned before today? Is it the reason, as he seemed to be suggesting in his remarks to the jury, that Paul Damon made his startling switch from prosecution witness to defense attorney? And the most important question of all: What ruling will Judge Kenneth Cox hand down tomorrow on the tape?"

"Turn it off," Lauren Granger whispered. Then she shouted, "Turn it off!"

But there was no one else in the room with the mirrored ceiling, to which she had run on Sunday to hide. Karl was out, on some business involving his operations in Newark, so she had to crawl across the bed and find the remote control switch herself.

She lay in a huddle, feeling that the mirrors and the walls were about to close in on her. If Cain had a tape, she thought, it must show that she hadn't killed him. And if it did, then everyone would believe what she had been saying . . . and then if Helen took the stand and talked . . . If only Martin were here, she thought. He would understand. And he would be able to figure out some way to deal with the creature and her damning knowledge—

Her mind veered away from the thoughts she knew would come next. She rolled over quickly and lay looking up at the ceiling, at her image in the mirror. "You're a smart girl," she said to it. "A nice, smart girl. Get up and do something."

She sat up. Then she walked around the bed to the telephone and dialed the number of Madison Guaranty Trust.

He came on the line almost immediately. "Lauren, where in the name of Christ are you? I've been calling all over Manhattan."

"I'm not in Manhattan. Jake, I just heard about the tape on TV. You have to keep it out. You can stop it, can't you? You can get to the judge and stop it?"

Even through her tension she could sense that his silence was an unusual one. "Jake? Will you do it?"

"Lauren," he said, and now it was not the silence that was different; it was the metal harshness of his voice. "I've been trying to reach you because I have an ultimatum for you. Either you see that that girl is released, now, tonight, and that she is unharmed, or else I'm going to call Hart Collins and tell him what you've done, that you had her kidnapped. And when I've finished telling him, believe me, he will be finished with you. And so will everybody else. Do I make myself clear?"

She hung up the phone slowly.

"You know," said the man, in the tone of an idle observation, "it seems to me that things are gettin' just a little too excitin' in that courtroom of yours."

Judge Cox looked at the visitor who had arrived unannounced at his bachelor apartment near the UN. Everything about the man seemed idle and careless. He had settled his lanky frame into an easy chair, flinging one leg over the side; he gestured aimlessly as he talked; and his voice was as lazy as a Southern summer. "I reckon you know who I am," he had said when he appeared at the door; and of course Cox did. He was one of the inner circle of Collins aides whom the press had begun to call "the Kentucky Colonels."

"I don't see," Cox said slowly, "that what happens in my courtroom is your affair."

"Don't you?" said the man. He lifted his right hand and drew slow circles in the air. "Well, maybe they misinformed me. They said, you know, that you were a pretty loyal kind of fellow."

"Loyal to what?"

The visitor sighed. "Well, to the president, of course. And to the country."

"Are you saying that Hart Collins is asking me to go into court tomorrow morning and rule that tape inadmissible?"

The visitor sat up abruptly. "Now, look here, Judge, don't you be sayin' a thing like that about a fine man like Hart Collins. That's way out of line."

"Then why don't you tell me where the line is?"

"Oh, now, now." The man relaxed again. "This is just a little chat about the future, Your Honor. For instance, I thought maybe you'd like a little sneak preview of the Inaugural address. Mr. Collins is goin' to call for an overhaul of the welfare system, did you know that? I mean a *real* overhaul. He wants it to incorporate psychological help and counseling. He figures we should try to educate all of them—the people who administer the programs *and* the people who get the aid—to the fact that there's no stigma attached to bein' needy. That it's not a man's fault if he needs help, because it's just kind of an accident of nature. Mr. Collins figures that if we do that, we might have a hope of makin' those programs really work. Because we can't just keep throwin' money at the problem, can we?"

"No."

"Of course we can't. The taxpayers won't stand for it. And so it would be just a doggone shame if somethin' happened to keep John Q. Public from seein' the worth of Mr. Collins's plan. Don't you think?"

"Tell me," said Cox, "do you know what is actually on that tape?"

"Now, who's talkin' about a tape? I'm not. And I know Hart Collins isn't. He's just talkin' about the good of the country. Let's just all remember that."

Like a child, Cox thought; they saw his ridiculous face and size and thought they could treat him accordingly—like a child, to whom one simply gave orders, without even the dignity of consultation.

The visitor stood up to leave. "Of course," he added offhandedly as he stood in the foyer, putting on his sheepskin jacket over his sweater and dungarees, "it just might cross Mr. Collins's mind, when he's thinkin' about the good of the country, to wonder where the best place would be for Kenneth Cox to serve it. I mean, maybe the federal bench needs a man like Kenneth Cox, needs him just as bad as he wants that bench. Or maybe he's gettin' too old and tired for that."

"It's hard to believe," Cox said slowly, "that this conversation is taking place."

"But it isn't," said the man pleasantly, looking down at Cox. It was a long way down; he was very tall. "I surely don't recall talkin' to you about anything except the future of this great country."

"Are you all right, Helen?" Damon asked.

Her eyes blinked rapidly, and she clutched even more tightly the large, scuffed leather purse in her lap.

She was worse today, Damon thought. After sitting much of yesterday in the witness room, she had resisted coming to court again this morning. When he went up to get her and

Sarah, she had sat stubbornly in the kitchen, saying she did not want to go out, and it had taken all his and Sarah's powers of persuasion to finally get her into her huge brown coat and out to the elevator. And now he would have to prepare her again.

"Look, Helen," he said carefully, "I don't know if I'll be able to call you to the stand today, either, for the same reason as yesterday. But I need very much to have you here, in case."

"Why are you doing this to me?" she said petulantly. "Why can't you leave me alone?"

"Please, Helen," he said, casting a look of appeal at Sarah.

Sarah nodded and took out the thermos of coffee she had brought and the bag of croissants. "Are you hungry, Helen?"

Damon closed his mind to the contemptibility of the bribery and hurried back to the courtroom. They had just brought Astrid in. "Any news?" she said.

He shook his head.

"I'm sorry. So terribly sorry." She touched his arm, and for a moment they both looked at her hand, the long fingers very pale against the black wool of his jacket. She took her hand away. "Cox is ready to rule this morning, then?"

"Yes."

She sat silently for a few moments, as he spread out his papers on the table. The courtroom doors were opened, and the noise from the hall swelled in as the crowd began to enter. Suddenly Astrid stiffened.

"What's the matter?" he said.

"Didn't you hear it?"

"What?"

"Someone went by with a radio. Playing rock music." She shivered. "It's on the intercom at Rikers Island, all the time. Do you have any idea what torture it is to listen to that day and night? To want to hear something by Mozart or Beethoven so badly you could scream? But you can't get those other sounds out of your ears." She turned to him, her voice suddenly jagged. "They're going to convict me, Damon. The jury doesn't like me, I can tell. They're going to send me to stay in a place like that for years, and I won't be able to stand it!"

"You won't go," he said, as if she were a child. "I won't let you go. It'll be all right, Astrid. It'll be all right."

She caught her breath. After a moment she whispered, "Sorry. I'm OK now."

He went back to his papers, as the room began to fill up. "Hello," she said in a strange voice, and he looked up to see Jake Waldo, Junior, standing in front of them.

"Mr. Damon," said the boy. He kept his eyes averted from Astrid's. "I have a message for you. From my father." He was slightly breathless.

"Yes?"

"The girl is free. My father has her."

Damon felt an overwhelming urge to feel relief but held it back. "Where is she? Why does he have her?"

"She just . . . well, someone called this morning and told him where she would be, on a certain corner, and he went right away to get her. Then he arranged to have her taken to the hospital, and they're on the way there right now."

"Hospital? What did they do to her?"

"She's all right, my father said. But she's in a state of shock. He said to tell you he would see that she got the very best care."

"Did you see her yourself?"

"No. I stayed home till he called me back and said he had her, and then he told me to get right down here and let you know."

"What hospital was she going to?"

Jake's pale face went a shade paler. "Oh, my God, I never asked. And he didn't say."

"I don't know," said Damon tightly, "whether I should believe your father."

"But you have to believe him."

"Why?"

"What is it?" Astrid said. "Why can't you believe him?"

"Because he's a man who deals with Garrick Evans."

The doors from the judge's chambers opened, and the bailiff called for the court to rise.

"Mr. Damon," Jake whispered, "please believe my father. Please give him this chance to . . . to make up for both of us."

"Find a seat, Jake."

The boy looked at him, his gray eyes wide with intensity. "You can call me back to the stand, if that will help. I'll tell the truth this time." He turned to Astrid. "I want to help you. I always did. But I wasn't . . . well, never mind. I want to help you." Before she could answer, he moved away.

"What are you going to do?" Astrid whispered. "Call Jones or not?"

"I don't know." But an idea had come into his mind, risky but tantalizing, a way of using Jones to forestall Lowell's challenges to the tape.

Judge Cox was arranging some papers in front of him; he stacked them in a neat pile, moved it to his left and then to his right. He seemed oblivious of the eyes watching him expectantly. Two minutes went by before he looked up and out; his round face was flushed.

"Fifteen years ago next month," he said, "I was sworn in as a member of the judicial system that upholds the Constitution of this land. The judge who was administering the oath to me had to bend down to do it, because I am a very short man." He paused. "My lack of stature may have led some people to believe that I am also a small man in spirit. A man who cannot reach as high as justice and does not always try."

While the entire room watched in astonishment, he slipped

out of his chair and stood up, as if to flaunt the way he was diminished by the massive desk before him. "I shall always reach for justice," he said slowly. "No matter what. *No matter what*. Let that be part of the record." He stood for a moment, flushed and erect. Then he sat down again.

"What was that about?" Astrid whispered.

Damon shook his head, but she saw that his eyes were narrowed against some inner sight.

Cox moved the stack of papers back in front of him. "The tape recording," he said, "is admitted in evidence."

The audience rustled, heads turning to look at Damon. He did not move.

"Mr. Damon," Cox said, "you may proceed."

He looked down at his notes, then over at the prosecution table, where Ben Lowell's fingers were drumming on a legal pad, like an overture to the attack he would mount against the tape.

Damon stood up slowly, weighing his idea. If only he could be certain that Marie was all right, he thought; if only he could trust them.

"Your Honor," he began. Then he stopped, looking at the man to whom those words were addressed. If there were Garrick Evanses in the world, he thought, there were also other kinds of men, who did hold justice sacred. Yet he had been ready to believe the worst of Cox, to assume the judge's decisions would be slanted against Astrid. Just as, he thought, he had been prepared to believe the worst of her. He heard the words she had said to him years ago: "It's not just Evans. It's Sam and Roy Vance and all the people in your life whom you ever let yourself love. You're going to let them have that kind of power over you?" The nature of that power, he saw suddenly, was that it altered his perceptions. It made him, of necessity, look for the worst. Made him almost need to find it, in order to justify the course he had chosen.

He looked outward again, at Cox, then squared his

shoulders and decided that this time he would take the side of trust. "Your Honor," he said, giving the two words a grave emphasis, "I will now call a witness who I didn't know would be available until just a few moments ago."

"I thought we were going to hear the tape recording. After all I— Well, never mind. You can try your case any way you like, of course."

"Thank you, Your Honor. This witness is in a position to testify to some of the material on the tape." He looked at Astrid. "I call Helen Jones."

The witness chair had arms, and she could not wedge her bulk between them. She stood waiting, stolidly, until the bailiff brought up a straight chair. She wore her green uniform-dress and clutched her purse. Her colorless hair was pulled into a knot, accentuating the shiny expanse of her face.

She raised her arm to take the oath, her sleeve falling back to reveal a crepey wing of flesh. When the clerk had finished asking whether she swore to tell the truth, she looked back at him blankly.

"Do you understand the oath?" Judge Cox said. "If so, you must say, 'I do.'"

"I do." For the first time she looked out at the courtroom. Her eyes were like sunken camera lenses, registering but not responding.

"What is your name?" Damon asked.

"Helen Jones."

"And your address?"

"I'm not sure anymore."

Damon felt the tension rising in him; would she fail him with the second question? "Miss Jones, don't you live and work in the home of the late Martin Granger?" Her head moved slightly. "Let the record show that the witness signified Yes. Miss Jones, in what capacity did you work for the Grangers, and do you now work for Mrs. Granger alone?"

"I'm the cook."

"How long have you held that job?"

She blinked. "Twelve years."

"Would you say that you have a good memory, Miss Jones?" She looked uncertain. "For instance, are you capable of recalling the exact menus you have prepared, months and even years ago?"

"Yes."

"Fine. Now, would you please describe the physical arrangements of the rooms in which you live and work? Tell us where they are located in the house."

"My kitchen is across from the dining room. I sleep right behind the kitchen." Her voice was breathy with effort.

Damon drew a quick sketch on the blackboard he had had brought in. "And both rooms open on the hall, which in turn leads to the living room and the terrace?"

"Yes."

"Were you in the Granger home all day and night on June 23?"

"Yes. I was always there."

Damon pointed to the sketch. "Were the terrace doors open that night?" She didn't answer, so he repeated the question.

"I don't remember."

He felt the perspiration start to bead his face, and pushed back the shock of black hair that hung over his forehead. "Please try to remember. Were the terrace doors open?"

She was not looking at him now; her eyes were focused somewhere in the courtroom.

"Did you come out from your bedroom around ten o'clock on the night of June 23, in order to check something in the kitchen?"

"I . . . yes."

"What did you see and hear?"

"I don't remember."

He looked at Astrid, whose face mirrored his own tension. He saw that at the prosecution table, Ben Lowell was smiling. Then he looked out at the audience, where Jones was staring, and saw that Lauren Granger had come in.

He thought for a moment that he would kill the woman, but he squared his shoulders and went on. "Miss Jones, you have told me that when you got up on the night of June 23, you heard the voices of Dr. Granger and the defendant, coming through the open terrace doors. Do you now deny it?"

She made a movement he could not identify; it was dissipated by the sheer size of her body.

"Your Honor," Lowell said, "I must object to this. Counsel seems to be cross-examining his own witness, instead of examining her."

Cox looked at him for a moment. "Overruled. I understand your objection, but it seems readily apparent that this is an unusual situation."

"Thank you, Your Honor," Damon said. He pushed the hair from his eyes again and turned back to Jones. "Did you witness Dr. Granger's death?"

Waves of noise from the spectators washed over her like water over stone. Judge Cox called for silence and then said, "Answer the question, please."

She did not respond. Cox leaned toward her. "If you have information bearing on the death of Dr. Granger, you must tell this court. Do you understand?" She nodded. "Very well, then. Did you see Dr. Granger die?"

One hand went up to her lips and then sank down again.

"Aren't you interested in helping us determine whether your own employer was or was not murdered?" She did not answer. "Miss Jones," said Cox in exasperation, "I remind you that you have taken an oath to tell the truth. A woman is on trial here for murder. Are you aware that your testimony could be crucial to her freedom or to its loss?"

"Yes."

Cox looked nonplussed, and Damon was about to cut in. But the judge went on. "Well, for heaven's sake, doesn't that matter to you? Don't you care whether a human being is found guilty or not? Whether she is free or not?"

"Not really," Jones said.

Cox's chair creaked in anger. "Are you telling this court you are indifferent to justice?"

"Helen," Damon said urgently, "please assure the court that you do care to see justice done."

"But he wants the truth. And I don't care. About anything."

"Mr. Damon!" Cox said.

He could not answer. He could only think of the words she had just said. She was a creature who truly cared for nothing, except for a single gross pleasure that would kill her before her time. But that did not matter to her, either. She was dead to every value, even her own life.

She had actually achieved, he realized, the goal to which he had aspired for so long. She had succeeded in removing herself from the act of living. In becoming only a watcher.

He looked at the mountain of flesh in which she had buried herself, from which she responded only to food and to threats; what, he thought, could have driven her to such a state? What could she have given up?

He heard the self-confession implicit in those words, but he had no time to consider it, for his mind was racing again along the track he had abandoned earlier; he was looking at Astrid and hearing again what she had said about music, how it could become a kind of torture. . . .

He heard Cox saying, "Mr. Damon, I am going to hold your witness in contempt of court."

His mind was still racing far ahead; he tried to pull it back, but instead it slammed into a wall. The picture, he thought despairingly, the picture of Lee. How could it make sense if the woman in the picture looked like Lauren? Then he saw the answer, and he said aloud, forgetting where he was, "My God!"

"Mr. Damon! I'll hold you in contempt as well!"

"I beg Your Honor's pardon," he said. "For reasons that do not concern the court, I have not until this moment been fully aware of the nature of my own witness. If Your Honor will please indulge me once more, if you will give me just a minute, I think I will be able to show you that this witness deserves not the contempt of this court but its understanding."

At the rear of the court, in the row into which she had wedged herself despite the occupants' protests, Lauren Granger pushed back violently against the pressure of a shoulder.

She had had to come, to find some way to keep Jones from talking; but she couldn't think clearly. Spurts of rage kept smearing her vision—rage at Jake Waldo, at Paul Damon, and at Jones herself, who had been momentarily frozen by spotting her but who was going to go on. . . . If only she could think of something, could keep the anger from clouding her vision. . . .

She brushed a hand in front of her eyes, pulled her silver fox more tightly about her shoulders, and watched Paul Damon as he bent to whisper something to Jones and then stepped back to face the court once more.

"Miss Jones," Damon said, "are you familiar with the name Leonora Jonas?"

She blinked. "Yes."

"You once told me she was an opera singer whom Dr. Granger had known years ago. Is that true?"

"Yes," she said, after a moment.

Forgive me, Helen, he thought, knowing that what he was going to try to do was cruel. But it would be even more cruel to Astrid not to try. "I believe that Leonora Jonas is now in the courtroom," he said. "Am I right?"

"Your Honor," Lowell said, "what kind of games is counsel playing about this Jonas woman?"

"Mr. Damon?" Cox said.

"She is in the courtroom, Your Honor. But there is a confusion as to her identity. I am hoping this witness will clear it up."

"I am beginning to lose track of what it is you want of this witness. Please get to the point, some point."

"Yes, Your Honor." He moved closer to Jones. "Leonora Jonas called herself 'Lee,' is that right?"

"Yes."

"And at Dr. Granger's urging, she gave up her operatic career?"

"Objection, hearsay," Lowell said.

"Sustained."

Damon cursed his own stupidity. But how else to do it, hemmed in on one side by the rules of procedure and on the other by Jones's blank eyes? She had answered only one question in their brief whispered interchange a moment earlier—and answered it only because he had caught her completely by surprise; still, that answer had assured him he was on the right track. But how to get her to follow it with him? All right, he thought; it would have to be a frontal attack.

"Miss Jones, did you once go by the name of Leonora Jonas?"

There was a pause, and then a voice said, "No."

Damon whirled around.

"She's not Leonora Jonas. *I* am. Don't let her tell you she is, because it'll be a lie. If you want to know about Leonora Jonas, ask *me*."

Judge Cox gaveled angrily. "There will be order in this court! Madam—the lady in the rear—either take your seat and be silent, or else you will be barred from this court."

"Isn't this the place where you want the truth?" she shouted. "Helen Jones will lie! About everything!"

"Who is that woman?" Cox said.

"It's Mrs. Martin Granger," Damon said. "She has come into this courtroom for the explicit purpose of intimidating and slandering my witness, and I ask that she be removed."

"Your Honor," Lowell cried, "she is the wife of the deceased!"

"I am aware of that," Cox said. He looked to the back of the court. "Mrs. Granger, your presence here rests on your ability to remain silent. Bailiff, if she disrupts the proceedings again, remove her."

Lauren sat down slowly.

But she had achieved something, Damon saw when he turned back to Jones, who sat in a kind of trembling rigidity, her face glassy with perspiration. *"Do* you lie?" he asked gently.

"No."

"Then I ask you again. Are you Leonora Jonas?" She opened the clasp of her purse. "Are you?"

"Mr. Damon," Cox said, "what is the purpose of this line of questioning?"

"May it please the court, I wish to establish the true identity of this witness. And to show that her prior existence as Leonora Jonas accounts for her indifference to testifying to this court."

"And once you have established that, she will then testify to what, if anything, she knows about the death of Martin Granger?"

"Yes," he said, and prayed that it would be true.

Cox looked at the witness; as Damon talked about her, she

had not reacted. But one of her hands had disappeared inside her purse. "All right," Cox said. "Proceed."

Damon went to the defense table, where Astrid's eyes once more seemed too large for her face, and picked up a small piece of paper. "Miss Jones," he said, "I want to read you part of a review from the New York *Sentinel* of fourteen years ago. It pertains to a production of *Rigoletto* by the Manhattan Lyric Opera. It says, quote: Leonora Jonas, making her debut in the role of Gilda, was wonderfully effective. It was not merely her voice, which is of a remarkable purity, putting one in mind of the young Lily Pons, but also the freshness of her manner. She is slim and young, and in her hands the 'Caro Nome' truly seemed like the ecstatic virginal confession of love that Verdi intended. Close quote."

The courtroom was still, looking in disbelief at the woman whose flesh oozed over the chair in which she sat.

"Miss Jones," Damon said, "was that reviewer describing you?"

Her hand came out of her purse and went to her mouth, carrying a piece of croissant.

Still at the defense table, Damon reached into his briefcase, took the cassette he had made from a private recording of Naomi Rostov's, and slipped it into his portable recorder. "This is the voice of Leonora Jonas," he said. "Was it your voice?"

It was the mad scene from *Lucia*. Jones sat stolidly, chewing on the pastry, as the voice began its caressing duet with the flute; then—as the voice continued, sometimes languorous, sometimes darting and soaring above the instrument in silvery defiance, the trills and runs perfectly executed, seeming to come from a throat that had never known effort—she began to shake, her obscene body rocking and undulating in the chair; and when the voice made its final, lovely stratospheric leap and then was silent, she gave a terrible, muffled, croaking sound; and no one could be certain on what she was choking: the half-eaten food that fell from her mouth, or the knowledge of what she once had been.

The entire courtroom seemed frozen; it was as if no one could move while she still moved, still rocked and made her choking sounds.

When she finally was silent and motionless, there was what seemed to be a collective sigh.

"That is your singing, isn't it?" Damon asked.

"It . . . was." Her voice was flat, a terrible antithesis of the living, silvery sounds.

"Your legal name is Helen Jones, but you once used Leonora Jonas as your professional name?"

She nodded.

"Why did you take that name?"

"Because of . . . Beethoven."

It took him a second to understand. "Because Leonora is the name of the heroine in Beethoven's opera?"

She nodded again.

"And why did you give it up? The name, and your career in opera?"

"Because I didn't . . . deserve it."

Another tremor shook her body, and from the small, dead wells of her eyes ran the single track of a tear.

Chapter Seventeen

"Mr. Damon," Cox said, "does your witness perhaps need a short recess?"

"No, Your Honor. I prefer to go on." Before she can recover, he thought, and once more he silently asked her forgiveness—for ever having believed that only malice or mental deficiency could explain her behavior.

He walked to the exhibits and then back to her. "This letter was found among Dr. Granger's effects, dated July 10, thirteen years ago. Did you write it?"

She looked at it and whispered, "Yes."

"You wrote it from the Taylor School in Rhode Island, a school for deaf children?"

"Yes."

"Why did you go there?"

"He said I should."

"Dr. Granger?"

"Yes."

"Why?"

"I should be with people . . . who couldn't hear any voice at all."

"Why?"

"To learn . . . not to care."

The two lines bracketing Damon's mouth deepened. "But what qualifications did you have to teach deaf children?"

"I didn't teach. I worked in the kitchen."

And that, Damon thought, explained why his questions to the schools had had no results; he had been asking only about teachers. He held up the paper in his hand. "Would you please read this letter to the court?"

He put it into her hand, and she began to speak, "'Dear Martin.'" She paused. "'It is five in the morning, and I can't sleep. It is quiet now, different from the day, when you do hear the children's voices sometimes. But those voices are so strange and sad. The children do learn to communicate, and their progress is rewarding, but knowing that they cannot hear, can never hear, makes it very hard, you see.'"

"Just a moment," Damon said. Despite what he was feeling for her, there was also an exhilarating tension, as if his mind were inordinately clear and purposeful. "You are not reading this letter, are you? Are you reciting it from memory, even though you wrote it over thirteen years ago?"

"I have a good memory. I learned *Lucia* in three days."

He took the letter from her gently. "Then go on."

After a moment she did. "Next it said, I've made my decision. Thanks to you, because I couldn't have done it without your help. I've accepted that there will never be peace for me in the career I thought I wanted. One must be worthy of one's work—isn't that what you always said? But for now, that doesn't matter." She paused again. "Then it says, Good night, Martin. Lee."

"Let the record show," Damon said, "that the witness has completed this letter almost word for word, from memory." A memory, he thought, that had turned, or had escaped, to tasks far beneath its capacity. "I think we may accept that this witness is indeed Leonora Jonas." Judge Cox nodded almost imperceptibly. "Miss Jones, how did you meet Martin Granger?"

For a moment he thought she was not going to answer. But she did.

"He came backstage one night. It was after a *Lucia*. He was with some friends. They asked me to go to dinner with them." Her eyes seemed to be looking into the distance, which was within herself, and her voice had a dull, heavy sound, as if the chains of years of silence were still clutching at each word.

"Did you go to dinner with them?"

"Yes. I said I shouldn't, because I was watching my weight, you see. I always had to. And my costume seemed a little tight that night. But I had done a good Lucia, so I said maybe I deserved a good dinner after all. He said it was interesting, the question of what people deserved."

"Your Honor," Lowell said, "surely this is irrelevant and immaterial. This kind of ancient history—"

"I want to tell it," Jones said. "Let me tell it."

Judge Cox had not ceased to watch her face. "Subject to connection," he said softly, "the witness may continue."

"You saw Dr. Granger again, then?"

"Oh, yes. He would come to performances by himself, and afterwards we would go out and talk. I could talk to him, you see. About my voice. I could tell him how terrible it felt every time, before I went on, because I could never be sure that my voice would be all right. That it wouldn't suddenly desert me. Because I really didn't know how I did it, you see. It just seemed to come."

"Did Dr. Granger help you to understand your fear?"

"Oh, yes. He made me see that it was a symbol. Of the fact that I hadn't done anything to deserve my voice. It was just something I had been born with, the way some people are born beautiful, or ugly, or tall, or without one of their fingers."

"But Helen," he said, unable to hold back the question, "hadn't you worked very hard to train your voice? Hadn't you studied?"

"Oh, yes."

"Then how could you regard your talent as just a . . . well, as an accident of Nature?"

She blinked. "Because of what I felt, you see. If I had deserved to have a voice like that, I wouldn't have been frightened to sing, would I?"

At the defense table Astrid made a sharp sound, quickly stifled. That was the answer, she thought; that was how Granger had done it. The quality of vulnerability she had seen in David and in the others—the quality that, along with talent, was a precondition of Granger's interest—its nature was now being confessed by Helen Jones: a kind of chronic, underlying doubt of one's own worth. Granger must have claimed that the very presence of the feeling proved its truth.

A line from *Hamlet* came into her mind: "As if increase of appetite had grown by what it fed on." Except that here, that which fed on its own satisfaction was not desire; it was self-doubt. No wonder, she thought, that all David's intelligence, and all her own arguments, had not been able to break the vicious circle.

She looked outward again, at the man who was now her attorney, his dark eyes almost black with concentration on his task. Whatever else he once had given up, she thought, he had never felt what David had. From the first moment she had seen him, she had felt the existence in him of something inviolable—experienced almost by direct perception, as if it were part of the very lines of his body—something with darker, harsher colors than her own, which had made her feel the difference between them as not only a contrast but also a challenge. And a bond. She would stake her life that its essence had been not doubt but certainty.

And the proof, she thought, was how splendidly he had failed to wall it off and repress it.

She looked up at his craggy face, intent with purpose, and his taut bearing; and she almost smiled. But she did not, because there was also the sight of the woman in the witness chair.

"I needed Dr. Granger, you see," she was saying in her dead, halting voice, "because the attacks, the way I felt before I sang, got worse and worse. And he would always talk to me afterwards, for hours, as long as I needed. He was always there when I needed him."

"You saw a good deal of him, then?"

"Oh, yes."

"Did you—" Damon stopped, caught by a sudden suspicion that there was something here Naomi Rostov had not known. "Are you saying that you and Dr. Granger were more than friends?"

"Oh, yes."

"Were you lovers?"

She blinked. "Yes. Yes, we were." She stayed immobile, while the noise swelled and Judge Cox called for order.

Damon's mind raced to incorporate the information with the question she had answered when he had whispered to her earlier, when he had realized what the picture could mean. It was time, he thought, to make that answer public and to find out what else lay behind it.

"Miss Jones," he said when the room was quiet again, "do you have a sister? Or rather, a half-sister whose maiden name was therefore different from yours?"

"I . . . yes."

"Is she a woman," he said harshly, "who calls you 'Jones'

and treats you as a servant? Is she Mrs. Martin Granger?"

"Yes."

This time there was little noise; it was, instead, as if everyone's eyes had widened. At the prosecution table, Ben Lowell's face was frozen in astonishment. At the back of the court, Lauren Granger rose and then sank back in her seat, her hands clutching her coat tightly, like knots.

"Did your sister," Damon said, feeling his way, "tell you that you must never let anyone know you were Leonora Jonas?"

"Yes."

"Did she— What did she say would happen if you ever told?"

"I would have to go."

"Where?"

"I . . . don't know. Anywhere."

He understood then. "She would turn you out, and the very thought frightened you?" He paused. "Let the record show that the witness signified Yes. Miss Jones," he said gently, "before you came with me to court, when was the last time you had been out of the Granger house?"

She hesitated. "Ten years ago."

"What!" said one of the jurors, and instantly turned red.

"Would you tell us," Damon said, still feeling his way, "how you came to work as a cook for your own sister and brother-in-law?"

"They let me," she said simply.

He could not make sense of it. "Let's go back a bit. When you were singing with Manhattan Lyric and . . . having an affair with Dr. Granger, where was your sister?"

"She came here, after a while. From Minneapolis. We lived there, you see, in a big house near Lake Nokomis."

A connection fell into place. "And was she going to be a singer, too?"

"Oh, yes. We had the same teacher. Mr. Petersen. He told me that I should come to New York, that I was good enough. So I did."

It was so simple, Damon thought; she had not lied to him about Lauren. He just had not asked the right questions. But now he could see them opening up before him. "So your sister came to follow in your footsteps. Did she try to sing with Manhattan Lyric, too?"

"They said her voice wasn't right, you see. But she did get a job for a while. She sang in a piano bar in the Village."

Shut up, shut up! The words rang in Lauren Granger's mind like a furious bell. Shut up, Helen—Helen, whose voice had finally come back. Who was once again taking the limelight. Just as she had done years ago, when the shy child who was the product of their mother's first marriage had begun to sing in the church choir. Then the whole family had begun to dote on her. And all they could say about *her* was "Oh, but Lauren is the *beauty* of the family. That's all we expect of *her.*" But when she came home with her dates and her Prom Queen title and her beauty pageant awards, it still was not as good as Helen. "Oh, Helen has such a wonderful *voice.* And Helen is so *bright.*" She wasn't even ugly—she had just enough of their mother's features so people would say, "Oh yes, I see the resemblance." And now she had found her voice again. Paul Damon had coaxed it out. . . .

"How did your sister meet Dr. Granger?" he asked.

"I introduced them. At a party after a concert one night. She had been asking to meet him, you see. And they . . . they liked each other." She paused. "When I came back, they were married."

"Back from the Taylor School, you mean?"

"Yes. Well, after I left the school, I went home for a bit. To Minneapolis. But I had a kind of breakdown. And afterwards, I didn't know what to do. So I came here again, to see Martin. Because I needed him, you see. I wanted to be with him." She blinked. "They were married then, but he said I could live with them and do the cooking."

For a moment Damon was stopped—by the thought of the attractive girl in Lucia's gown, going back helplessly to the man who had stripped her of it, pretending his motive was love, and who then put her to work in his kitchen. He tightened his jaw, but then the path of the questions opened up again, pulling him on. "Did Dr. Granger have speakers for his sound system installed in your kitchen?"

"Oh, yes."

"Why?"

"He said that I should listen to music all the time."

"Why?"

"To . . . hear without hearing or caring."

"Do you mean that you were to go through—"

"Your Honor," Lowell said, "counsel is leading his witness. He's been doing it for the last half hour."

"I am allowing it in the circumstances," Cox said tersely.

Damon went on gently. "Were you supposed to go through the constant torture of hearing the kind of music you loved but had given up?"

She nodded. "Yes. When it doesn't mean anything to you anymore, then you can be at peace."

In the twelfth row of the court, young Jake Waldo put his head in his hands, hearing the words that had been said to him, too.

"And would it be the case," Damon asked, "that as you listened to the music, struggling not to care for it, you would find that food eased the pain? And that Dr. Granger—the man who was *helping* you so much—would do nothing to keep you from eating?"

"He didn't mind. He told me to spend whatever I liked on food, you see."

The woman next to Lauren Granger made a sound of outrage.

Self-righteous cow, Lauren thought. She swung her honey-colored hair. Martin should be here to tell the cow. He had known how to explain, to say, when Helen first came, that they were just helping her, doing their best for her. And that had been good, because then one did not have to worry about the feeling one got from the sight of her . . . the sweet, secret, dark-red feeling. . . .

Martin had felt it, too. She was suddenly sure of that. The night they had had the fight and she had thrown her knowledge of the souvenirs in his face . . . He hadn't minded her knowing. It had even made them get along better, in that odd way. And what else could that mean, except that he had felt the feeling, too? Even though they had never talked about it, had never said anything but "Poor Helen" . . .

"And your own sister," Damon was saying, "saw what was happening to you and made no attempt to intervene?"

In the rows around Lauren, heads turned to her and eyes stared, with an emotion too strong for politeness to mask.

No! she cried to them. No! Her mind began to hunt for a way around them, like fingers going blindly through a crowded drawer. It wasn't my fault, she thought . . . Martin did it all . . . He wanted victims, that's what Cain had said, that Martin was a monster . . . The fingers found something and clutched. I was a victim, too! she thought. Martin never wanted *me* to be anything, either! That's why he married me!

She looked up and out, wanting all the faces and eyes to know what she had found and to pity her, the way they were pitying Helen; but her glance caught instead on the witness stand, and the sweet, secret, dark-red feeling shot up inside her with the intensity of orgasm. You bitch, you bitch, Helen-you-bitch. With your voice and your fancy Harvard scholar . . . but *I* got the scholar . . . and he knew what to do with you, oh, Christ, he knew. Knew how to bury your voice inside a ton of blubber . . . Martin knew, yes, he knew . . . knew how much I hated you, because he did, too . . .

She jerked back in her seat. "No," she whispered. But it was too late. She had seen, in that moment, why it was that Martin wanted her: for a reason deeper than her beauty, or than any pleasure he got from demeaning her. Martin had wanted her because she was . . . like him.

"I'm not," she said aloud, oblivious of the stirring around her. The fingers of her mind began to claw for some new hold, struggling to avoid naming what it was that she was not. I'm not . . . I'm not . . . not stupid! she thought eagerly. That was it. Not stupid. Smart! Hadn't she done everything possible to keep the secret of Helen? For Martin, as well as herself? Hadn't she outfoxed that goddamn detective until almost the end? Until he hauled Helen-you-bitch to the stand and started coaxing the story out of her, making all the faces turn soft. . . . The dark-red feeling swelled once more.

She swung her hair and stood up. "Paul Damon!" she shouted. "You think you're so smart! But you're not! I am, but you're not!" Two bailiffs were rushing toward her. "Wait till you see the girl! Just wait!" The men's arms reached for her. "They raped her before they let her go! Raped her!" she cried over her shoulder, as they took her out.

He was unable to think. Even after order had been restored and Cox was waiting for him to go on, he could not pull his thoughts together, away from the picture of Marie on the floor of some cellar. . . .

"Mr. Damon," Cox said, "will you proceed?"

"Yes," he said mechanically, and could not get beyond that word. He looked out at the crowd and saw Jake Waldo, Junior; that finally freed his mind, for the boy looked as stricken as he himself felt. Young Jake had acted in good faith, he thought. And so had he. Perhaps even Waldo, Senior, had done so. And now he would have to go on acting. Somehow.

With an effort that made his hair feel damp against his skin, he forced his mind back to where it had been before Lauren had called out. He had had an idea, that was it—an idea that would be an extension of the plan he had when he first called Jones to the stand and that would, if it worked, clear Astrid definitively . . . an idea that had been making him feel a new surge of excitement, of the thing he had been feeling for days, co-existing with his anxiety for Marie. . . . Think of her later, not now, he ordered himself; and his mind began to function again, telling him that his idea was worth the risk it entailed.

"Your Honor," he said, "I will now play the tape recording."

Lowell rose quickly. "I have the right to cross-examine this witness, Your Honor."

"But I am going to ask the witness to testify to the events that are recorded on the tape," Damon said. "I intend to use the tape to demonstrate her memory. I will ask her to tell us what she saw and heard, moment by moment, and then I will play the section of the tape to which she has just testified. The witness and the tape, side by side. To show that her memory is reliable."

Cox's look managed to be both admiring and skeptical.

"Your Honor," Lowell said, "it sounds like a stunt of some kind."

"Are you making an objection?"

"Well . . . no. Just a comment."

"Very well. Proceed, Mr. Damon."

Despite everything, he felt the excitement rise again. He picked up the tape. "Miss Jones, this is a recording, made by the defendant, of her conversation with Dr. Granger on the night he died. Have you ever listened to it? Or even seen it?"

"She recorded it? It's all there?"

"Yes."

She sat back in her chair, as if to move away from the information.

"Have you ever listened to or seen this tape?"

"No."

"I am going to play the tape. When you hear the words that were the first ones you heard on June 23, please stop me. Do you understand?"

Her head moved slightly. He put in the tape and depressed the "play" button.

After a moment Granger's voice, from a distance, said, "How mysterious and urgent of you. But I'm quite alone. Lauren is out for the night, as usual, so no one will bother us. Sit down."

"I'd rather stand." Astrid's voice was tight.

"Suit yourself. I seem to be unable to get up, myself. Spring fever, I think. Although it's actually summer, isn't it? Two days ago."

"Yes."

"All right, all right." There was a tolerant smile in Granger's voice. "Obviously you're determined to get on with it, so let's hear it. What's bothering you? I'm always glad to help, if I can."

A pause. "I've come to tell you that I've been working for you under false pretenses."

"Oh, dear. Don't tell me you've been married all along and now you're pregnant and are going to leave me?"

"Yes to everything but being pregnant. You sometimes read the *Blade*. Have you ever noticed the by-line 'Anne Cain'?"

"I can't say that I recall it. A relative of yours?"

"No. I'm Anne Cain."

A pause. "Say that again."

"I'm Anne Cain. I write for the *Blade,* but I'm on a leave of absence."

A hearty, somewhat strained laugh. "So the demure little creature is not what she seems? You've been lying to me?"

"'Creature.' That's the way you think of people, isn't it?"

"Suppose you get to the point. Why did you come to work for me? To write about me?"

"To see if I could find out what kind of man you are."

"Who sent you here? Was it Fred Walters?"

"To my knowledge, the publisher of the *Blade* doesn't know what I've been doing. Only Hal Ruby."

"Ruby? I don't know him."

"The metropolitan editor."

"Well, Astrid, I don't see why you had to do it secretly. If you wanted to do a story on me and the Institute, why didn't you just tell me? I'm always happy to accommodate the press, you know that." The voice was still hearty.

"I didn't want the press treatment. I wanted the truth."

"And what the hell is that supposed to mean?" The voice was closer and harsher. "Just what are you suggesting? Wait a minute, wait a minute. Anne? Your name is Anne? You write for the *Blade?* I know something about an Anne . . ."

"Yes. I just said I was married. My husband is David Chapin."

"What!" A pause. Then, more softly: "I always suspected that David had trouble at home. He said so little about his wife, never brought her to meet me. And now I know why. What kind of woman are you, to come spying on me behind David's back?"

"The kind who doesn't want to see her husband destroyed. And it wasn't behind David's back. He knew I was coming here."

"He sent you?"

"No. He had nothing to do with my coming. But I did tell him."

"And he let you? That devious sonofabitch. After all I've done for him . . ."

"All the help, you mean?" Anger spilled into Astrid's voice. "The help that is trying to make him give up his work? Listen, *Doctor* Granger, I know what you've been doing to him. I did find out what kind of man you are. And I think you're despicable."

"That's enough." It cracked like a whip. "You will now shut up."

In the witness chair Helen Jones raised one hand, like a child at school. Damon switched off the tape. "Is that where you first heard them?"

"Yes. Where he told her to shut up."

"What did you hear next?"

She had been staring at the tape, leaning slowly forward like someone sighting a dangerous animal. She spoke to it as if her voice could calm it. "Dr. Granger said he could understand why she might be upset. That it might seem he was trying to influence her husband, but he was only trying to help. He said a lot of people came to him for advice and he always tried to help them see what was best for them to do. He talked about one of his books. She said that wasn't the point, that he was evading. She said, do you keep souvenirs if you've really been able to help people? He got angry. He wanted to know what she meant. She said, I mean Harry Pine. And David. And Lee." The last word was faint.

"Stop there, Miss Jones." It was working, Damon thought exultantly; it was going to work. He turned on the tape again, and the dialogue she had summarized with remarkable accuracy crackled through the courtroom, Astrid's voice high and angry, Granger's at first patient, almost professorial, the resonant public voice that was familiar to many in the audience; but it began to change, breaking with little explosive cracks as the tape went on, past the passage Jones had described.

"You little bitch. You liar. You come here to be my secretary, pretending to be loyal to me, and all the time you're spying, rooting around in my personal possessions to manufacture garbage for your paper. You're not a journalist. You're a cheap, devious opportunist. Fred Walters is going to hear about this. The whole goddamn world is going to hear. By the time I'm finished with you, there won't be a paper in the country that will hire you!"

"That's the kind of thing you enjoy, isn't it? Destroying a career?"

"Yours—yes, indeed."

"And what about David's? And the others'? That's what I want to talk about. I don't care what you do to me. But David— Why did you want that scroll of his? And don't tell me it was to help him, because I know it wasn't."

"Ask him, then. Ask David. He'll tell you it's because I'm helping him. He'll tell you about the hours I've spent with him, talking about his sister and the guilt he feels over his brains and his honors and his life as a golden boy."

"Why don't you help him get over that guilt, then?"

"My dear woman, none of us can ever do that."

The sound of a deep breath—Astrid's. "You say you're a compassionate man. You tell us all to have more concern for the people Nature has cheated. And you work for them yourself. I've seen you get money for them, spend hours of your life on them. So why can't you have some compassion for people like David? David works hard, you know. He's *using* the ability he has. He's not some kind of useless playboy. He could be, but he isn't. Doesn't that mean anything to you?"

"David knows very well what his sins are."

"His . . . sins?"

"Would you prefer a euphemism? 'Merits,' perhaps? No, the better word is 'sins.' Of omission. For all the things he hasn't suffered or gone without. People like David have to learn that in the infinite scheme of things, they are nothing."

"David is . . . nothing?"

"Of course. We all are. David must learn to accept it."

"But David is brilliant! Doesn't it mean anything to you that David is *brilliant?*"

"Why, yes. It means I have to cure him of deriving any comfort or credit from that fact. To make him see that his work and his honors and his achievements do not make him one millimeter better than his sister who drools and plays with dolls."

A pause. "I'll kill you for that," said Astrid's voice, icy with purpose. "I'll pray to God to send me the chance someday to kill you for that."

There was a sharp intake of breath, of many breaths, and Damon switched off the tape. Several of the jurors, he saw, were frowning at Astrid. She was sitting absolutely still, open to their glances and to all the others that were directed at her, the wings of dark red hair pushed back, making her face even more naked and vulnerable.

He looked at Jones, whose stare was unmoving, as if the dangerous animal were ready to leap and she could not get out of the way. "What did you hear next?" he asked.

"He . . . Martin . . . the doctor said . . . I can't . . . I . . ."

Suddenly he understood. This must be the deepest reason for her long refusal to admit she had witnessed Granger's death—something deeper than her fear of Lauren or even than her painfully acquired indifference: the fact that she could not bear to recall the dialogue that was coming next. Could neither forget it—nor live with it. Helen, he thought, when this is over, I am going to see whether there is any way in the world to help you. He spoke gently. "We'll continue without you for the moment, Miss Jones." He started the tape again.

There was a short laugh—Granger's.

Then Astrid's voice went on. "There are clean ways to kill, shall I tell you about them? Because you wouldn't know. Don't walk away from me! There are nice, clean ways, like using guns or knives. But you'd rather tear people in two, tear them away from the things that give them pride and pleasure and self-respect, and then watch them turn into zombies."

"I've had just about enough of your sophomore-year analyses."

"Have you ever felt a decent emotion in your life? Have you ever loved what *you* do? No, God, what am I saying?"

"What could you know about my work or my methods?"

"Because if you loved what you do, that would mean you loved destroying people like David."

"I don't love it!"

"You do! I can see it in your face. You're like those people David told me about—those scientists who get some kind of pleasure out of killing their laboratory animals. You actually *enjoy* it!"

"I don't! I don't. It has to be done, that's all."

"Why? Why does it have to be done?"

"They can't be allowed to think they own the earth. And they do think it, all those golden boys and girls with their brains and their talent and their beauty!"

"Are you saying . . . that you hate them?"

"Yes. Yes! What did they do to deserve what they have? Nothing!" The voice was erratic now, as if he were pacing out of control, as if he knew he should halt the words but could not stop the relief of speaking. How long, Damon wondered, had the hatred been festering in him? From what childhood seeds of envy and resentment had it sprung, to find its secret relief in causing the suffering of others? "They collect smiles and praise from the rest of the world like some kind of goddamn tax we all owe them from birth."

"But . . . but they work, they—"

"I don't give a royal goddamn what they do! They don't deserve it! It should be taken away from them, all of it, till they're nothing, till they—"

"Shut up! Please! David is—"

"David is just where he should be, where they all should be, with everything beaten out of them. I learned how to deal with them years ago. *That* was the great Granger experiment, and it worked. My God, how it worked! The golden creature who turned into a nothing. A *big* nothing!" He laughed, a sound as rich and obscene as mockery at a funeral. "When you can do that to them, then you can stand to let them live!"

"Shut up! I'll find a way to shut you up, I swear I will!"

"No, you won't. Because I'll ruin you, too."

"I'll find a way! People have to know what you are!"

"How would you get them to believe you?" The laugh came again.

"Shut up! I'll kill you if you don't shut up! I'll kill you!"

There was a sudden, total silence. Damon had switched off the tape. He saw the reactions that were playing on the faces of the jurors, even the most stolid of them: They believed that they would next hear Astrid kill the man. But they did not blame her.

In the silence, Helen Jones began to whisper. "He said I was . . . a great experiment . . . that would help other people. . . . He said that to me . . . when I . . ." Slowly she looked down at herself, at the flesh that spread out in rolls and pillows.

"Helen," Damon said gently, "you *can* help someone, help her very much, if you'll just tell us what happened next, what you saw and heard next."

"He said . . . I was . . . a great experiment . . ."

"Helen, please tell them." It was Astrid. She was crying, but not for herself.

Judge Cox's eyes came slowly away from Jones's face; he looked as if he thought he should say something to Astrid but could not think what it was. Ben Lowell did not move. He had not moved for ten minutes.

"Helen," Damon said again, "will you tell us what happened next?"

She gave a tiny, desolate sound, and then she told it.

"There wasn't anything, for a while. Neither one of them spoke. He was standing by the railing. I could see him so clearly, his shoes and his red shirt. And the chains he always wore. They were moving up and down, because he was breathing hard. After a while I heard her voice again. She said, I think that's the most vicious thing I've ever heard. He said he didn't care what she thought, that the conversation was finished, and so was she. She called him . . . a monster. She started to say something else. Then it was quiet again, for a bit. Then he kind of grabbed at his chest and grunted. And after a minute he slipped down on the railing. She called out. Then he just . . . rolled over the railing and fell down. And landed. I was right inside the doors. Close to the sculpture. I saw him die, you see." A tremor shook her body. "I watched him die. And I . . . didn't care." She put her swollen fingers to her face, in an agony of relief and shame. "I didn't care!"

Could there be, Damon wondered, a more fitting epitaph for the man who had taught her to live by those words? If only she could see that, for once, those words were the right ones.

He waited, saying nothing, till she finally took her hands from her face and looked out. She blinked, as if she had just come out from the dark. "What happened next?" he said quietly.

"I just looked at him for a while. Then I looked up and saw her. Staring down at him. She didn't see me. So I went away. Back to bed."

"At any time before Dr. Granger's fall, could you *see* the defendant?"

"No. Just her voice."

"She never came out on the balcony until *after* he had fallen?"

"No."

"And you were looking up all the time?"

"Yes."

Then Damon pressed the recorder switch again, and the courtroom listened to what she had just described.

It was accurate.

When it was finished, there was no sound or movement.

Damon turned to Lowell. "Your witness."

Lowell rose slowly. "I don't . . . I have no questions." He seemed to listen in surprise to his own words. Then he sat down.

"In that case, Your Honor," Damon said, "the defense rests."

He sat down, too, drained of everything but the thought that he had done it. *Quand même.*

Astrid touched his hand. He looked at her, at the pity and gratitude—and more—that were in her hazel eyes. And gradually the things that were inside him began to return to life: the surge of relief and of anxiety for Marie. Together, in equal force. And also the realization that, incongruously, despite all the unhappiness the trial had both caused and revealed, he had known a sense of excitement and pleasure in his own functioning. That he had been a man fully committed to what he was doing. Caring about it. And, yes, even loving it.

Chapter Eighteen

Snow from the blizzard that January had unleashed on the city was piled in banks, like giant meringues. They glistened when the sun shone, and even though they were already glazing with soot, people were still feeling the cheerful goodwill that always seemed to grip New York when it had once again survived one of Nature's onslaughts.

"Your dog—he like snow?" said the superintendent of the building, who was shoveling a path to a lopsided snowman.

"It looks like it," Damon said, pulling Sancho out of one of the meringues. "Do you know if Miss Lazare is home—4G?"

The man put down his shovel. "She been sick, I think. Not go anywhere. Too bad. Nice girl."

"The nicest. Look, I want to surprise her. Will you let me in the front door, so I don't have to ring the bell and let her know it's me?"

The man looked at him speculatively. "You family? Uncle?"

Damon suppressed a wince. "No. A good friend."

The man studied him a moment longer. "OK. Is all right, I think."

Damon knocked at the apartment door and quickly called

out, "It's Paul," so she wouldn't be afraid. There was no answer. Then Sancho barked a couple of times, and her voice came from behind the door. "Please go away."

"You can't keep on hanging up the phone and refusing to let me in the building."

"I told you I didn't want to see you."

"And Sancho? How about him?" She didn't answer. "Marie, we're going to stand here until you open that door. All night, if we have to. Or all week."

Slowly the door opened a couple of inches, and her face appeared behind the chain.

She was a strange case, that's what Joan O'Neill of the area Sex Crimes Squad had told him. "She wasn't actually raped, you know. But in her state of shock, she talked as if she had been. And I gather that just before they let her go, the two men told their boss on the phone that they had done it. Wanted him to think they were really macho, I suppose. Anyway, she seems to have spent most of those three days and nights expecting it to happen, and in certain respects, it's as if it did. She has the nightmares and the fear. And a case of guilt, I think, but she wouldn't talk much about that."

If Lauren Granger were ever found, Damon thought, she would pay for what she had put Marie through, pay in court and on Rikers Island. But at least, wherever she was, she must be paying in some measure already, stripped of everything by a press that had made good copy out of her treatment of Jones.

"Marie," he said to the face behind the chain, "you made me promise to come and tell you what I decided. Don't you want to hear it?"

"No."

He maneuvered Sancho closer to the door's opening, gave the furry white rump a gentle nudge, and let go the leash. "Oh!" she cried, as the dog went in and began to bark and leap up on her.

When she finally undid the chain, she was laughing and crying at the same time, hugging Sancho, finally sinking onto the floor with him.

Damon stood looking down at them. Suddenly Marie scrambled to her feet, sending the dog off to prowl the corners of the room. She pulled her robe tighter; it was a cheerful red, in contrast to her grave little face. "You won the trial," she said. "I read about it."

"Yes. And I couldn't have done it without you. If you hadn't found Naomi Rostov, I wouldn't have known enough. Or have had the recording. That's what finally made Jones talk, you know. And after she did, after the tape was played, it didn't take much longer. The jury was out for only two hours."

"That's good, Paul. I'm glad you won."

But she didn't sound as if she felt glad. Or anything else. She sounded the way he always had with her—present but unreachable. He said, "I've come with an offer. Jake Waldo—the man who took you to the hospital? His son has asked me to find out if there's anything they can do for you. I thought maybe you'd like the chance to study voice full-time, without having to work. They certainly have the money. I'm not too sure about the father's motives, but I know young Jake is sincere. It would give him a lot of pleasure to help. Will you talk to him about it?"

"Oh . . . I don't think so, Paul."

"Is there anything else you would rather do?"

"Not really."

He watched her move aimlessly around the small room. "Do you want to hear what I've decided?" She didn't answer. "Well, I'll tell you anyway. I never gave you the chance you deserved, Marie. But in spite of myself I felt—and I still feel—something very strong for you. For your spirit and determination, and the way you always looked at the world through a smile. And kept me from setting up permanent camp behind the wall I was trying to build. For all of that—I guess what I feel for you is a kind of love. All I know is that it won't let me leave you like this."

"I think," she said slowly, "that that is just a long speech to say you love me like a sister."

"Then why did I want to sleep with you?" She shivered, involuntarily. "No, Marie, you're not going to build a wall around sex. Or anything else. I won't let you."

She made a funny little sound, like a moan. "It's not right."

"What isn't?"

"For you to be here."

"Why not?"

"Because . . ." Tears suddenly flooded her voice. "I wouldn't leave you alone. I kept after you and after you, when you didn't want me. That's why God had to punish me. That's why I had to promise Him I'd never see you again."

He went to her and picked up the small, shaking body, settling with her on the sofa, holding her tightly till she finally was quiet. Then he raised her face with one hand and waited till she dried her eyes. "Marie, listen to me. You're not going to take on a guilt you haven't earned. Over my dead body. I've seen what guilt can do. I'm going to do whatever it takes to get you back on your feet. Spend every night with you, if that's what you want, take you to see young Jake Waldo, get your life set up properly, so you can smile again and want to study singing again. And not shiver when you think of sleeping with somebody. Is that clear?"

"You just feel sorry for me. You feel you *have* to be with me, like some kind of duty."

"No, Marie. God knows it's true that I owe you a lot, including the kind of treatment you deserve. So my duty would be to come and tell you I've decided to spend the rest of my life with you, if you'll have me. But what I *want* to do — and I'm going to do it—is to make sure you can spend the rest of your life the way you should."

She stared at him. He saw the gold flecks in her eyes begin to reappear, like hints of sun after a rain.

And she saw the strong, square face that had been a symbol of everything she wanted since the first night she had seen it. But she saw it suddenly as a face she had never truly known— not only because Paul had held himself aloof from her but also because she had placed her own symbol over him, like a mask, never quite looking at the man underneath. He had told her that—that she never saw him clearly.

She had never asked herself what that man wanted, she thought. Only what she wanted of him.

"Oh, Paul," she said softly, "it was good that you came, after all. I was afraid to see you, I guess. But now, when you are truly honest and show yourself to me, it is not so hard."

He kissed her gently. "Listen, I've brought Sancho's things with me. He wants to come and live with you." She smiled. "And I've got two tickets to the Met tonight. *The Magic Flute.* Will you come?"

•

"I've read most of what you submitted," said the managing editor of the *Sentinel.* "I liked the off-Broadway series you did for the *Blade.* That was a nice idea, to do a diary of one show from backers' auditions to opening night."

"Thank you," Astrid said. She was determined not to let him see how much she wanted to be hired as one of the reporters out there in his newsroom, punching out stories on the computer terminals.

"Some of your things were pushing too hard, though. I like the idea of trying to relate the arts to other issues, but it doesn't always work. When you drag politics or economics in by the heels, that's what it reads like—something you just dragged in."

"Maybe I needed a better editor," she said carefully.

A grin flashed a crooked path across his face, which looked as if it had been hastily assembled around his very brilliant blue eyes. He had got his start, she had heard, by filing dispatches from Korea, and was said to regard working under fire as good training for a newsman. "I'll level with you," he said. "You were a good arts reporter before the business with Granger. But some people here feel that the trial made you too much of a public figure. The wrong kind."

"Notorious and irresponsible, you mean?" She leaned forward. "I'll level with you, too, Mr. Zacharias. I *was* irresponsible over Granger, in a way. Even if I was right about him. I leaped into some of the things I did without really thinking through the consequences. I hoped I've learned the danger of doing that."

She saw on his face the chain of thought that led him to say, "What's happened to that detective who defended you, by the way? He seems to have dropped out of sight."

"I don't know. I haven't seen him since the trial ended."

Zacharias raised one graying eyebrow. "Well, I'll give you this much. Your trial sold a lot of papers for us."

"And I liked your coverage of it. That's one of the reasons I'd like to work here."

"What are the rest?"

"Well, I need a job." He laughed. "And I think . . ." She hesitated, then decided that if she could not really talk to him, there would be no point in working for him. "I think you're following up the story in Washington the best of any paper in town."

"Do you? Why?"

"Because you're covering it as if it's a war of ideas, not just of money. As if it's more than the loyal opposition trying to hold down spending by the new man in the White House."

He eyed her speculatively. "And you think your trial had something to do with that?"

"I think it's hard not to ask questions about Collins's new programs in the light of what Granger said on my tape."

"For some people, maybe. But a lot of them just denounced Granger as a sick man and let it go at that."

"I know," she said and then imitated a Southern accent. "'A tragic case of psychological problems destroyin' a man and turnin' him against his own ideas.'"

"You don't agree?"

"If you really want to know, I think he was only taking his theories to their logical extreme."

This time both his eyebrows shot up. "Meaning that anyone who goes along with his views would wind up pulling people apart like flies?"

"No, of course not. The fact that he got pleasure out of ruining people was his personal sickness. And I certainly don't think that anyone who is concerned about the unfortunates of this world is a monster."

"I'm glad to hear it," Zacharias said sardonically. "But then what are you saying?"

She remembered the long hours of thinking it all through, after the trial, and the issue that had seemed the hardest, until she had realized that it contained the answer. "Do you remember 'EK'?" she said. "Ezra Kerr?"

"Sure. The physicist who went back to his grandmother's Indian tribe. What about him?"

"He seemed like a contradiction to me. Since he wasn't suffering, why did Granger keep a souvenir of him? If the real goal was to make people suffer?"

"I'll bite. Why did he?"

"I think it was because Kerr did fit, though in a different way. After all, he was a very talented man whose talent had been destroyed, if you like, even if the man himself hadn't."

"Meaning?"

"Meaning that that's what Granger's ideas are really all about—taking anybody who is exceptional in any way and getting rid of the exceptional part. Making him give it up. Because, look, if you say that all people should be equal—I don't mean politically, but equal the way Granger preached, as if nobody deserves anything more out of life than anybody else—then I don't see where else that idea *can* lead. It *has* to mean dragging us all down to the lowest level of ability. Turning a singer into a cook, taking a physicist out of the lab and sending him back to a tribal camp. It's all very well to talk about lifting up the unfortunates, but at what price? By making the Helen Joneses think they don't deserve to be any more talented or happy than anybody else, and so they should give it up?"

"Hey, take it easy," Zacharias said.

She saw that she was leaning way over the desk, clenching her hands to make the points. "I'm sorry." She sat back. "I'm afraid I get fired up about it."

"Don't apologize. I like fire. So long as the *Sentinel* doesn't get burned."

She lit a cigarette, held up the match, and blew it out very carefully.

He laughed again. Then he studied her for a moment. "Suppose I told you that I basically agree with you?"

"You do?"

"Don't look so amazed. You're not the only one who ever questioned the Granger school of thought, you know."

"I realize that but it surely seemed as if I was, for a long time. I guess I should have brought my original piece on him to you, then."

"I wasn't in this job last year. And if I had been, I don't know whether I'd have taken the piece. I'm not sure you had enough evidence at the time." She winced. "When you write for me, I'm going to grill you like hell. Make you back up everything in quadruplicate. They say I'm worse than the legal department, sometimes."

"What exactly does that mean, Mr. Zacharias?"

"The name is Zack. It means you've got the job. Arts and general cultural. And not because of your sociopolitical theories, either."

"Why then?"

The crooked grin flashed again. "Because you go after what you want."

She let herself into her apartment, on Riverside Drive in the Seventies, and turned on the radio; it was playing one of the Brahms violin sonatas. She stood for a moment, looking down twelve stories at the river and the park. Green was beginning to soften the lines of the trees, which were lit by the white moonlight of the arc lamps on the Drive. A wind had risen and had set the green in motion, a slow and sensuous dance against the flanks of the buildings.

She took off her coat and went into the small bedroom to change her dress. The closet was small, too, and overflowing. Too many Chapin clothes, she thought; but they were all she had taken, or would take.

She would have liked to have the good wishes of the senior Chapins, but she could understand their polite, tight-lipped farewells, testimony to her refusal to help David, or even to see him, after the trial, when the final revelations had plunged him into a profound depression. "Whatever I owe David," she had told his parents, "has been paid in full," almost wishing she could tell them the whole story of what she had done. But no one would ever know that. Except Damon.

She pushed the thought of him aside and reached into the back of the closet for an old pair of rust slacks and a matching shirt she had had since her first days in New York. She got a cup of coffee and went back to the living room, sinking into a low tweed chair, letting the music move over her as the wind outside was moving over the trees.

She was very far away, in some green and gentle place, when the doorbell rang. It took her a moment to come back, to put her coffee aside and go to the intercom. "Yes?"

"Damon."

She stared so long that his voice came again. "Will you let me in?"

"Of course." But after she had pressed the buzzer, she did not move.

The moment she saw his face, and the wide shoulders under the suede jacket, she felt her body tighten against the power of a response she had known she would feel. But not so strongly, like something that had shaken free in the silence of the past months and was now demanding restitution.

He did not move either, just stood inside the door looking at her. "It's been four months and three weeks," he said finally. "Since the trial ended."

"Yes."

His eyes left her face then, and he came into the room. "When did you move in here?"

"About two months ago." She sat back on the tweed chair, on the edge of the cushion. "How is . . ." She pushed her hair behind her ears. "How is Helen Jones?"

He took off his jacket and put it over a dining room chair.. He was wearing tan cords and a brown sweater. "You wouldn't believe how many people have wanted to help her. Offers of jobs and places to live, from all over the country. Somebody even started a 'Help Helen' fund. It's been really heartwarming. And the Granger Institute—or I should say ISCEV, the *ex*-Granger Institute—has given her all kinds of psychiatric counseling."

"Has it helped?"

"In some respects, yes. At least she seems to be shaking free of some of the guilt. And the weight—she's lost forty pounds. She's moved into the same building as Sarah Meier, and they've developed some kind of relationship. She seems to like to talk to Sarah, to go over and over everything with her, and the doctors say the ventilation is the best thing for her. Dad—would you believe this?—my dad wants the three of them to open a restaurant together."

"Is that possible?"

"I gather it's not impossible. And I guess it would be a big step forward—for her to live in the world again." He paused and looked directly at her. "A wasted life is the saddest thing there is."

"Yes," she said faintly.

He began to move around the room, pausing at a sideboard on which stood a crystal vase in the shape of a leaping fish.

"Sandy Marsh sent me that," she said, "filled with roses from his solarium. The card said he was glad to see that my judgment had been better than his. He wished me all the best. Now that I was free to live my life again."

Damon ran one hand slowly along the curve of the vase; she felt the movement on her throat. "Are you getting a divorce?" he asked abruptly.

"Yes."

He came to stand in front of her, looking down. The shock of black hair was slanting across his forehead. "I want you to know," he said, "that I'm applying to rejoin the force." She put one hand up to her throat. "I want to face being brought up on charges. No, don't say anything. It was my action as well as yours, and I have to take all the consequences, just as you did. I've got a year from the date of my resignation to reapply—that's until December—but I'm going to start next week."

"And what about the law?"

"Well, if you care about it, if you think the law is all that stands between civilization and barbarism, then the police force is the front line, isn't it? That's another reason I want to go back and square myself with them and serve them as well as I can, even if they bust me back to patrolman." He began to move around the room, touching objects, running his hands along the back of the couch. "I learned something because of your trial. Not only in the courtroom but when I first started looking for Leonora Jonas. I learned how it feels to not just do a conscientious job but to give a damn, personally, about the process and the outcome. Let's say I've decided that's the only way to live." He stopped and smiled at her, but his look went inward, as if he were smiling at his own capacity to do so. "And so, for a while, I'm going to be that kind of cop. A man who knows the difference between emotional calluses as a professional requirement and . . . and life behind a wall."

He sat on the edge of the couch, one long leg close to hers. "But there's another reason I have to square myself with the force and clear my record. The place I want to go eventually, when they'll have me, is the DA's office. I think being an ex-cop is a hell of a good background for that. I think they can use more men who know firsthand the problems a cop faces. And men who won't use the office as just a training ground and a springboard. Who will take the prosecutor's oath very seriously—'not to prosecute, but to see that justice is done.'" He smiled again. "So maybe I'll have the privilege of trying another case before Kenneth Cox someday. I'd like that."

"Damon," she said wonderingly, "I haven't seen you like this for a long time. Maybe ever."

He looked at her, his eyes very black. After a moment he said, "What I really came for was to tell you about Marie."

She tried to keep her voice neutral. "How is she?"

"Well, tonight she's having dinner with young Jake Waldo, who seems rather smitten with her. I don't know that it's mutual, but . . . who knows? You may not have saved your husband," he said softly, "but you did liberate young Jake. He's back at art school, you know."

"Yes."

"And yesterday, at the Waldos' expense, Marie enrolled at the Juilliard School. She's all right, Astrid."

She closed her eyes against the enormity of the relief.

"If she weren't," he added slowly, "I couldn't be here. I told you that four months and three weeks ago."

"I think I could have stood it, however long she needed you. But I don't exactly know how."

"I would never let Marie spend the rest of her life with a man who loves many things about her but who is . . ." She opened her eyes. ". . . who is part of someone else."

He lifted his hand and touched his fingers to her mouth. "I should have known that the night you came to see me. But I didn't want to know it." Her lips moved beneath his fingers. "I told you on Rikers Island that I'd realized the perils of trying to drive oneself underground. But I didn't name the worst peril of all. Depriving oneself of joy. You can't wall off pain without shutting out happiness, too. So I had to tell myself that what I felt for you was . . . nothing."

She moved back to look at him. "So did I, Damon. It frightened me that after all the years we'd been apart, when I thought I loved another man, I could still feel what I did. As if I'd never left you."

"As if I'd never made you leave." He stood up, pulling her with him, and put his hands around her throat. "I did it then because you were too much a part of me. And now that's the reason I want you back. So nothing more of our lives will be wasted. Not another moment."

She smiled, moving through the space between them.

Excerpts from
A wartime novel of romance and courage
HEART OF THE STORM
by
Patricia Wright

Coming from ACE in March

Rupert came into the room on a blast of cold air and delight. "My God, what a day I've had!" He kissed her hungrily. "Come and talk to me while I change." He began ripping off tie and jacket.

She followed him into his dressing room, laughing. "Tell me what you've done. Were you able to talk the bank into a loan?"

"Not exactly. What did you think of the slip? Did you meet Sisley?"

She nodded. "He seems a very strange man."

"But one of the best designers on the south coast. I was lucky to get him." The words were mechanical, as if he had been saying them all day. "We start building next month."

"So he told me. Were you really so sure of Castellan that you ordered timber and engaged two extra men before you had the money?"

He dragged on a clean shirt. "Sure I would get it somewhere, and I have." His face was taut and frowning again. "Let it be, Faye. I know what I'm doing."

"Do you?" She knew she should have kept silent, that this was a moment for enthusiasm and the worst possible time for a quarrel, but the words slipped out and could not be recalled.

"What the devil do you mean by that?"

"I'm sorry, I—" She broke off, remembering her resolution

on the road. She kissed him. "I've been a fool, darling, to bring it up now. Let's talk about it later, we'll hold up the supper if we don't go soon."

There was a short silence, then Rupert turned and straddled a chair, arms across the back. "Tell me now." His eyes flicked over her as if criticism at once disqualified her from intimacy.

"Very well," said Faye levelly. "I distrust your Mr. Sisley and I couldn't begin to add up how much that slipway will cost to repair. He is designing a damned great motor cruiser he's been in love with for years and no one has allowed him to build before. Until he's built it, he is not interested in knock-down dinghies for holidaymakers."

Rupert crossed the space between them in a single stride and gripped her arms. "I will give you this one warning, Faye. Keep your hands out of my affairs! Others have faith in me even if you haven't; by the end of the week I'll have raised the money I need."

"I have faith in you, my darling. Faith and so much love." She kissed his stiff, angry lips and put her arms around his neck, dragging at his grip. "You asked me what I thought and I told you; it makes no difference to anything else between us."

His eyes were a bright, sharp blue, his face utterly still. "I never thought you a woman for cheap tricks, Faye."

She felt her blood chill. "Cheap tricks?"

"There is a name amongst men for women who try to win every argument by offering their bodies when it goes against them. I never thought to use it for you. You would do well to remember that you have not stone under your chisel any more, you have me, and I will never be tidily chipped out to your satisfaction."

"I wasn't—"

"Oh yes, you were. If women can't win by one means they will try another, except when I ask you to win for me of course. God knows what you said to that fellow Castellan last night to put his back up, perhaps you should have tried putting your arms round his neck, too."

Faye's heart lifted, for behind the hurtful words one thing was unmistakable. Jealousy. With time to think, Rupert had realized that in two hours Castellan had tapped something in his wife which he had never seen, and animosity had flared so sharply between them because of it. And a man of Rupert's temperament was jealous only where the full strength of his love was committed. He did not yet know it, but perhaps she ranked with Reydenham after all.

"It isn't true," she said at last. "None of it is true. I wanted to hold you and so I did. Never anyone else, my love."

"Ah well, perhaps we're going to be late for the harvest supper after all, and I'll take your way of settling our differences." Something in his voice startled her, but his expression had eased, his eyes were clear again. His hands slid from her arms to her back, to the fastenings of her dress; where his mouth had been cold against hers, now her protests were silenced. Rupert had been a passionate, demanding, and exultant lover, never before an inconsiderate one. She was completely unprepared for being taken in fury, for the agony of love when it was turned into retribution.

It seemed absurd to worry about money when everyone had expected a holocaust within hours of the outbreak of war, but as the strange winter of 1939 dragged on this became Faye's overriding worry. It started quietly enough, with a bill from the solicitors for drawing up her power of attorney, a small amount, but she decided to wait to pay it until she received a balance sheet from the bank: when she did, she could not believe the figures she saw. She knew, of course, that Rupert had overspent on Beauty but assumed that most of this was covered by lower expenditure at Reydenham and by backing he had received from elsewhere. Now she saw precise columns of red-inked figures amounting to nearly four thousand pounds overdrawn: the manager would be grateful to have the matter adjusted without delay.

She wrote to Rupert at his army address of mysterious figures, and his reply contained no reference to money. She wrote again, more urgently, and then again in panic, for bills were flooding in. Installments were due on Beauty's engine, the builders who always carried out repairs on the estate had not been paid for a year; then the War Agricultural Committee wrote, laying down plans for increased production at Reydenham, offering grants and subsidies to speed the work, but veiled threats also if it was not done.

Rupert wrote again, at last. His course was cut short and he was under orders for France; Faye's hopes rose and she turned the pages of his letter hastily, but there was no mention of leave before he went. Surely soldiers always had leave before they went abroad? She wrote again and on Christmas Eve, at last, he rang up.

She was overjoyed to hear his voice and for a moment could not scramble her thoughts together, the four months he had been gone a gulf of loneliness and anxiety she could not cross. He sounded cheerful, delighted to be going to France. "I was thankful to be in the group pulled out of the course, you never saw such stuff as we were meant to be learning! In France at least it will be the real thing."

"Not fighting? You aren't going to the front?"

"I don't know. I have to report at Abbeville, I've sent you a temporary address."

"Have you any leave first? Can I meet you in London? Will you be coming through Dover?"

He laughed. "Steady on. I don't know whether I'll come through Dover or not. I'm still you-know-where at the moment."

"Surely you must have embarkation leave?"

"I don't know," he repeated. It seemed strange to Faye that he should know so little when he was off within days, and she suggested again that she should meet him in London.

"For heaven's sake, Faye," he said impatiently. "I can't just go off to London now! How is Christopher?"

"Oh, Rupert, do you know, he's beginning to speak? He follows me everywhere and hardly falls over at all."

He demanded to hear more, and they forgot time until the operator interrupted. "Rupert," said Faye desperately. "Could you ring again? I must talk to you about all the money we owe. What should I do about all the bills coming in?"

"I can't ring again today, I'll try tomorrow. You'll manage, love. Tell the bank I'm in France, and then they'll have to leave the overdraft until I'm back."

"Sorry, your time is up, caller," the operator interrupted.

"I love you Faye. God bless." His voice was relieved, delighted to have got off so lightly; crisis no longer existed when he was not connected with it.

Faye replaced the receiver carefully, hands clammy. He would not ring again tomorrow. She remembered all those months when he had concentrated everything on Beauty and ignored the coming of war: now he was immersed in war and the ruin threatening Reydenham had no meaning for him. No, that was not true; love of Reydenham was the force which had driven him into greater and greater risk, and finally to disaster. Hold what you can for Christopher, he had said. He knew, she thought, he knew what he had done and said his farewell to the valley those last few days before he left. Certainly, he must have leave but would not come, unable to bear the reality of his inheritance packaged for the auctioneer's hammer. She stopped on her way upstairs, and stared at the Ludlow portraits. How could she hold anything at all for Christopher in the storm now building over Reydenham?

Faye leaned out as far as she could, craning to see the bow. They had been ferrying troops from the beach to a destroyer most of the morning, and although the sea was still calm, there was enough surf on the beach to crunch Beauty's delicate bow each time. She could see splinter marks and Alf was baling below; they were headed empty back to the beach and she felt overwhelming relief in the certainty that this must be their last trip.

She heard a shout and turned to see a fighter low over the water, guns firing, torn water racing toward them, bullets slamming through Beauty's fragile planking, an enormous roar, and it was gone again. It happened so fast she was still lying sprawled over the bow as Beauty shuddered once and water gulped through great splintered tears, its weight wrenching split timbers further apart. Before her eyes the stern broke away, throwing Henry into the sea, Alf trapped and screaming as they rolled, then she was swirling dizzily downward into cold darkness.

She touched something once and kicked herself away in panic, terrified of being trapped in wreckage. Chained by the wrist in the mud of the Scheldt until I am dead; tilting senses flung confused images together in her mind, so she had scarcely consciousness enough to retch her lungs free of water when she surfaced.

She felt hands, an edge of wood against her ribs, light swinging across her sight. She was fearfully sick.

She had been picked up by a whaler from the destroyer they had been filling all morning; as they went alongside she opened her eyes and saw Henry sprawled beside her on the planks, sodden and gasping as she was, but alive. Not Alf, she remembered. Not Beauty any more.

Willing hands helped her to scramble up the side of the destroyer. The need to move, not to get in the way, to remember that every foot of space belowdecks was filled with wounded, was itself a restorative. She stayed on deck and they left her thankfully, for they had fifteen hundred on board already, lifted from the beach, saved from the water, sick, wounded, and starving; the remnants of a gallant rear guard, half of them French. She was not even the only woman; there were three nurses and a Belgian nun, no one could summon up the energy to ask how she had come to the beaches.

"Here, miss." One of the soldiers stripped off his tunic. "Put this on, it's dry. Not clean, though," he added with a grin.

She was trembling and could not undo the buttons of her ambulance tunic, so the men around her did it for her, offering French Army greatcoats, British battle dress, anything dry they still possessed. One of the Frenchmen had brandy in a flask. Vive la France, she thought hazily, the British would have weak, sweet tea. The spirit nearly made her sick again, then formed a puffball of warmth in her stomach, feet and fingers seeming a great distance from her eyes.

Faye looked up and saw the Frenchmen silent, one or two in tears. She held the hand of the nearest, without thought of strangeness. "You'll come back." She felt tears on her own face, too. She pushed to the rail and looked where Beauty had been, but there was nothing to mark it any more. The Frenchman took a long swig at his flask and passed it to her again. "Finish."

"No!" Her grip on his hand tightened urgently. "Not finish. We'll all be back."

His teeth showed white against stubble and dirt. "Finish cognac, not war. Now is time for cognac, later war again."

She drank deeply. It was a time for cognac. You'll see, Henry had said long ago, one day she'll go right nobly, and she had.

On an empty stomach and an endless stretch of time without rest, Faye Ludlow came home drunk to Dover.

Rupert whirled round. "Just how often do I have to tell you to keep your interfering paws out of my affairs? You may have looked after it awhile, but Reydenham is mine! I'll not mortgage it to any damned bank, and I'll not have you perpetually asking why we don't do this or that!"

"I wanted to help," said Faye quietly. She detested his overbearing manner which worsened with every setback he suffered, yet was too well aware of the humiliation in which it was rooted not to feel sympathy for him. He needed to succeed in all he did, if only to compensate for her success during the war; only she knew that she would have failed too, but for Castellan money.

She was relieved to hear him laughing later, and surprised enough to come up from stacking firewood in the cellar to find its cause. He did not often laugh nowadays. The cellar steps were stone and her soft shoes made no sound: from the entry she saw Rupert with Susan in his arms. His back was turned to her, but Susan saw her at once, and smiled, and drew his face down to hers again.

Faye was so astonished she could not move. If anger had broken first she would have torn them apart with all the force of her own unslaked longing, but it did not. She stood transfixed and then Susan's deliberate defiance drove through consciousness with a single stroke, cleaving thought from mind, will from intent. The sensation was as physical as snapped bone, and wiped out everything except the urge to hide in the dark.

But short of death, life has no ends.

She did not know long she sat on the cellar steps, head on her knees. She heard Christopher calling in the end, and went up and cooked the lunch. He was making a model airplane, so she admired it; Rupert had lost his coat, and she found it for him.

Somehow she ate, and sat, and spoke and stood: they did not seem to find her manner strange. Perhaps no one really looked at her any more.

She stood at the window afterwards and saw Rupert striding down the valley road. Dickson's farm lay that way, and Susan, gone before Faye came up from the cellar. Watching him, she was not sure. When he returned, she knew.

He was relaxed and smiling, teasing Christopher instead of finding fault, and when he kissed her the dregs of a different passion rested in his touch. She muttered some excuse and fled to the kitchen, and stood leaning against the wall, forehead on cold tiles. She ought to be angry, she would feel better if thought was stripped clear by rage, instead there was little left but weariness.

She went over to the stove and her hands did all the things they had to do. She heard a voice speaking, and listened, surprised. In silence again, she realized it was her own: she thought back laboriously to discover what she had said, the first fresh stir of will dredging through recollection. She had spoken aloud the reassurance she had used so often: don't make a great drama of it, you know it has happened before. It happens to millions of women every day, if not always before their eyes.

It happens to men, too.

She stared out at the slope of the valley she loved so well, brilliantly green with the heat of another year. She had not been unfaithful with her body, but she had wanted to be; and was unfaithful still with all the strength of mind and heart.

HEART OF THE STORM
Patricia Wright
Ace Books
31977-7 $2.95